About the author

I'd describe myself as happy go lucky unless it comes to Manchester United... (sometimes), but life is about living, experiences and fun, and writing this book was a heck of an experience. Writing has always been my secret lover, muse, however you want to frame it. I just love writing and creating and to be able to share it with the world is amazing.

A Witch's Echo has been an amazing journey from late nights to writer's block but to see it coming to life is wonderful. So, I say to any writer, young and old, to keep going. Every story deserves to be heard. Finally, my parents taught me humility so thank you to everyone reading this. You've made it a dream could true for a kid from south London.

A WITCH'S ECHO

Rauf Balogun

A WITCH'S ECHO

Vanguard Press

VANGUARD PAPERBACK

© Copyright 2024
Rauf Balogun

The right of Rauf Balogun to be identified as author of
this work has been asserted by him in accordance with the
Copyright, Designs and Patents Act 1988.

A CIP catalogue record for this title is
available from the British Library.

ISBN 978-1-80016-543-4

This is a work of fiction. Names, characters, businesses, places, events and in-
cidents are either the products of the author's imagination or used in a fictitious
manner. Any resemblance to actual persons, living or dead, or actual events is
purely coincidental.

*Vanguard Press is an imprint of
Pegasus Elliot Mackenzie Publishers Ltd.*
www.pegasuspublishers.com

First Published in 2024

**Vanguard Press
Sheraton House Castle Park
Cambridge England**

Printed & Bound in Great Britain

Dedication

Dedicated to my grandparents. I hope I've done you all
proud. I miss you all.

Acknowledgements

I'd like to thank all of the Pegasus team for helping in bringing my story to life, my loved ones for everything. They have been my rock throughout it all and finally to God because without Him I'm nothing.

CHAPTER ONE

A FRIEND FROM THE DARKNESS

Ravensborough was a proud town as it had always stood on its own two feet. But unlike any other town it was special. It had been the last of its kind, a place totally inhabited by magical folk and creatures alike but just like any other town it had its secrets. Our story begins at the noisy town hall.

"Order! Order!" boomed a voice.

The chatter came to halt. The grand council of Ravensborough consisting of three witches and wizards had finished deliberating. They had come to a unanimous decision that the wall at Kenbury Forest would remain. Head wizard Mortimer Gravethorpe asked for hush again as the council got ready to hear the testimony of Conor Blackstone, a young boy who had come before the council to convince them that he was ready to attend the town's secondary school, Ravensborough High. The grand council had previously suggested that it would be best for Conor not to attend public schooling until after his thirteenth birthday as they deemed that to be the appropriate age for the fellow children of Ravensborough to integrate the young man without being judgemental. Conor was no ordinary boy; there was a uniqueness to him as he was a witch, the only one of his kind. The room was silent as Conor walked to the front.

"Thank you, f---"

"Time is of the essence, Master Blackstone," interjected Mr Gravethorpe visibly becoming impatient.

This had thrown Conor but it hadn't surprised him; if there was anyone in Ravensborough that hadn't liked him it was Mr Gravethorpe. He had often wondered why as he hadn't done anything too excited to care. Conor continued, "I'm here today to provide you with irrefutable evidence on why I should be allowed to attend Ravensborough High."

The council collectively slumped back in their seats as they looked on highly unimpressed. Conor was no fool. He had quickly noticed this and, thinking on his feet, he spoke again. "Could I be excused? I'm not feeling too well."

Mr Gravethorpe reluctantly nodded his talon-like fingers gesturing towards the doors. Thankful, Conor slipped out of the room to where his grandmother Amelia Blackstone, head witch of Ravensborough and regular member of the grand council, had been waiting. She had been unable to participate in the council's decision as ruling on family matters was forbidden.

"What do I do, gran? What do I say?" squawked a beleaguered Conor as he crashed onto the seat beside her. "I know they are waiting for me to trip up. I'm lost without you in there."

"Look at me, Conor," smiled Amelia her mahogany like ski lighting up as she did so. "I heard what you said in there and that's not you. Don't try to be something you're not. Just be yourself and show them why you deserve a place at Ravensborough High and why they would be lucky to have you. You're special, don't forget that."

Now more determined than ever, Conor stood up and strutted back into the main room. For the next ten minutes, the room was silent as all eyes were transfixed on the young witch who began to articulate his feelings. He spoke carefully not wanting to mince his words.

"Thank you, Master Blackstone," said Mr Gravethorpe inspiringly. "The council and I will now take into account everything you have said and call you back in when a decision has been made." Conor struggled to conceal his smile as he exited the main room. Surely, he had done enough.

But Conor's smile soon vanished. Twenty minutes went by and nothing had happened. Amelia was a little worried which was evident by her constant pacing around the corridor. This had been in complete contrast to the emotions Conor had been displaying though as he was surprisingly calm remaining perfectly still in his seat almost as if he had accepted that the outcome would not be the desired one. The main room doors then opened and both Conor and his grandmother were then summoned before the council who had reached its decision.

Mr Gravethorpe rose to speak.

"As you are aware, Master Blackstone when a matter is brought before the council for it to be passed it must be accepted unanimously by all members. The council has taken into consideration the testimony you provided and whilst you were very articulate and you spoke with real emotion which showed how deeply you care we feel it best that we reject your proposal as we feel that your introduction into Ravensborough High would completely destabilise its structure and could in turn lead to utter bedlam."

It was over, Conor thought to himself. He had remained in the main room for a brief moment hoping he had been the victim of a cruel joke but the look in Mr Gravethorpe's eyes was telling him he hadn't. Conor then rose to leave not uttering a word. Once out of the room the harsh reality of the situation became apparent as the young witch slumped into his seat which seemed colder than before. Amelia looked on as her fellow council members began packing their things away. She hadn't bought the council's excuse; she was sure something sinister was at work.

"I demand to see the ballot paper," she said authoritatively.

"While I understand you're upset Amelia you know that's against the rules," choked Mr Willows.

"Oh, just give her the sheet, Archibald. It's her grandson," said Miss Joyce.

"Mortimer won't like this," bemoaned Mr Willows as he handed over the paper.

Amelia merely glanced at the emerald sheet for a moment and her tuts became boisterous as her suspicions had been confirmed. She knew who had voted against her grandson. "You're despicable, Mortimer. I know we have past but we agreed when we created this council, we wouldn't allow it to affect our decisions... our professionalism."

"I have no idea what you mean," replied Mr Gravethorpe swiftly getting to his feet. "Our past had nothing to do with my decision. The stability of my school was and is the only thing I thought of before giving my decision."

But Mr Gravethorpe's words had fallen on deaf ears as Amelia had turned her attention to the remaining council members. "Are you going to let him do this? I understand Conor is a very complex case, we have never had to encounter something like this before but he has lived his whole life being excluded from school and playing with others. I've had to lie to him hundreds of times on why he couldn't play with the other children. I'm begging you, please allow him the chance to be a regular child before it is too late."

Amelia's words had seemed to work as the forlorn look on the council members' faces had brought them into a huddle. Amelia looked on anxiously as the sound of heated whispering grew louder and louder before a serene quiet filled the town hall. The rest of the council minus Mr Gravethorpe all glanced at each other before nodding.

They had decided to overrule the previous decision, much to Mr Gravethorpe's annoyance. The main room door was slightly ajar enough for Conor to hear the change in decision and he rose from his seat. He then ran into the room and wrapped his arms around his grandmother.

"Thanks for not giving up on me, gran," he whispered

They made their way out of the town hall still unable to stop themselves from smiling. It had been one of the best days they had had in a while but as they made their way to their car, they were surprised to see somebody had been waiting for them.

"Congratulations, Master Blackstone," said Mr Gravethorpe.

"Thank you."

"No thanks are required...but just remember, you'll still have to pass your inspection before you can come to my school," he said staring at the young witch.

Mr Gravethorpe's stare was more menacing than earlier but nothing was going to dampen Conor's mood as he merely walked past him still smiling. But it hadn't been as beaming as before. Two months had passed since the meeting at the town hall and Conor, still in an excitable mood, could not contain himself as his inspection was just over the horizon.

"Gran, gran..."

"Yes," quivered Amelia. "What's the matter? Are you okay? What's happened?"

"I'm fine, I just wanted to know when we were going to begin practising some spells."

"What's the rush? Your assessment is not for a few more weeks, we have plenty of time. I thought we could spend the day having fun. We could bake or you could follow me to get my broom fixed as I've being having problems with it braking and turning." Those ideas hadn't really sounded fun considering they had baked three cakes that week but Conor hadn't been surprised as this was one of the ideas his grandmother would bring up whenever he'd talk about his inspection. It was almost as if she didn't want him to do it. "I can't," Conor said quickly.

"Why not?"

"I'm going to meet Mr Bell. He said he was going to go over some potions with me as that is one of the parts of the inspection."

"I know you're excited Conor but you mustn't get ahead of yourself---"

"STOP!" shouted Conor suddenly. This had been the final straw. He couldn't take it anymore , the comments, the putdowns. "Just stop!"

"Stop, what?" asked a stunned Amelia.

"Ever since the meeting you've pushed away any talk of my inspection and I want to know why... Is it because you're afraid to be alone, afraid you won't have anyone to talk with when I'm gone?"

"Conor, I understand you're anxious about your inspection but that does not give you the right to speak to me like that."

"Then stop trying to hold me back," murmured the young witch.

Becoming increasingly blue in the face Amelia looked on stunned by her grandson's behaviour and demeanour. "Conor, I've had enough of your attitude, apologise and go to your room."

"No."

A look of almost instantaneous regret was sprawled across the young witch's face that he had just said that. He remained still, his breathing becoming more and more frantic. What was his grandmother going to do? The silence was torture. Why had she not said anything yet?

"What was that? I'm not going to tell you again. Apologise and go to your room."

The room remained devoid of noise. The tension was palpable; the constant ticking of the clock was all that could be heard. A single bead of sweat dripped off Conor's head and his eyes darted across the room. His mind was awash with contemplation of what to do or say next; he was in uncharted territory as he had never argued with his grandmother before.

"Well," said Amelia sharply. "Aren't you going to apologise?"

"NO, BECAUSE I'VE DONE NOTHING WRONG," shouted Conor.

"GET OUT!"

"FINE, I HATE YOU."

The door rattled shut. As the dust settled both Amelia and Conor realised the magnitude of the argument that had just taken place. Both instantly regretted their actions and respective parts but were proud and stubborn people who weren't about to back down. Conor then spent the best part of twenty minutes roaming around Ravensborough before deciding that he would go to the Harrowood Café to get something to eat as he was unsure whether there would be dinner for him when he returned home.

"What a pleasant surprise... what can I get you?" beamed Mr Harrowood as Conor entered.

"Could I get the usual, please?"

"One portion of fish and chips coming right up." The café then fell silent much to Mr Harrowood's surprise as Conor had never failed to make the same joke after asking for his order. Worried, Mr Harrowood sat beside his customer. "Conor, are you all right?" he asked. "You seem a bit down."

"No, not really. I had an argument with my gran and she kicked me out," responded Conor despondently.

"Oh... how about I rustle up your order and we can talk about it after you've finished?"

Conor nodded while showing a hint of a smile. The meal had gone down a treat as Conor found himself hunched back but this had been for a brief moment as Mr

Harrowood came and sat beside him. "All right son, now you've eaten what happened between you and your gran?"

"She was mad at me for not helping her fix her broom."

"Her broom," replied a slightly puzzled Mr Harrowood.

"It's the name of her car. She refuses to call it anything else and is still upset that they outlawed them."

"Come on now. I may be old but I am not foolish and I know your gran loves the bones off ya. She wouldn't tell you to leave for that. Now what really happened?" said Mr Harrowood chuckling to himself.

"We were having an argument about my inspection and I said something really bad."

"When you say bad what do you mean exactly? Did you say her food was awful or something?"

"I said I hated her."

"Wow!" said a stunned Mr Harrowood. "I'm not going to lie to you but what you said was really bad. I've known your grandmother a long time and I never thought that I would see her happy again especially after your mum died but she is and it's because she loves you and I know you love her and when we love someone so much we argue because we care about that person enough to only want the best for them and that's all she wants for you, the best."

Conor remained still as Mr Harrowood's words had resonated with him; maybe he had overreacted.

"Do you want me to call your gran?"

Conor again responded with a nod. As Mr Harrowood went into the back to make the call the door to his café had creaked open and a young wizard by the name of Ryan Willows had entered looking as devious as ever. He began considering in which way he was going to gain revenge on Mr Harrowood for casting a freezing spell on him earlier that day but on spotting Conor he soon abandoned his plans for revenge as his mind had shifted to something much more cunning.

"Well, well if it isn't little Conor Blackstone. Where's your gran?" said Ryan cynically. "I thought you guys were joined at the hip."

"What do you want, Ryan?" said Conor through gritted teeth.

"You seemed down in the dumps so I thought I'd come and cheer you up."

"Go away! My gran said you're bad news." "Mr Harrowood, have you finished in there?" Conor was becoming increasingly agitated.

"You have an inspection with Gravethorpe. Right, here's word of advice: if you're going to come to Ravensborough High you're going to need one thing."

Conor knew he should have ignored Ryan as his reputation around town was rather bad but he couldn't help himself. "And what's that?" he asked.

"A friend and I'm your guy."

The door to the kitchen then burst open. "Get away from him! You'll poison his mind with your wicked ways," said Mr Harrowood snarling at Ryan.

"Buzz off, you old geezer. Me and my new mate are chatting and don't think I've forgotten about what you've done. I'm going to get you for that."

Mr Harrowood soon resembled a tomato as he began huffing and puffing.

"When you've finishing hanging around this fossil I'll be outside to finish our little chat."

"GET OUT!" barked Mr Harrowood. "Stay away from that boy, he's trouble."

"I plan to ... did you speak to my gran?"

"I did. She said you're allowed back home but she won't be picking you up so I guess it's walking for you."

Conor sighed. He had half expected it. He then began walking towards the door but before he left he turned to face Mr Harrowood one final time. "Thanks for the chat, it really helped."

"Anytime," smiled Mr Harrowood.

As Conor left the café he began thinking about how he was going to apologise to his grandmother. His mind was again awash with thousands of thoughts on what to say or do or if he should even say anything at all and just go to his room and let everything blow over till the morning. Just then his train of thought was disturbed by a sudden jolt on his neck

"Who's there?" said Conor turning sharply. But to his surprise the pavement was empty.

Despite that peculiar occurrence, Conor decided to refocus and put into action his plan of how to apologise but as he continued his sense of unease still lingered. He was sure he was being watched. Again, he turned quickly but again no one was there. "I'm losing it," he said chuckling to himself. But as he turned to head home something had caught his eye. It was a piece of paper. Normally he would have ignored it but there was something different about this piece of paper; it gleamed like the moon's reflection on a river. He picked it up and stuffed it in his pocket before continuing on.

Durfold Street was a far cry from Harrowood's café as it was perfectly quiet. Conor was glad to be home but as he approached the front door he halted as though he could hear his grandmother speaking to someone. But that was preposterous. Who could she be talking to? He went to reach for his key but again stopped as he heard more whispers. He tiptoed towards the window to see what was going on and as he peeked in his eyes widened with shock: his grandmother had been speaking to someone, his mother or rather a photo of her.

"I wish I could hear what she is saying," he whispered. Aha, he would be able to hear what they were saying because when he was younger his mother had taught him an eavesdropping spell. He began skipping with glee as he readied himself to perform the spell but there had been a problem; his old rotten wand had been upstairs. Conor was stumped. How was he going to cast a spell without his wand but as he crashed onto the welcome mat his gaze met something that had been a wand. Of course, his grandmother always kept one in the garden in case of emergencies. He crept towards it slowly but as he reached for it the front door rattled.

"Hello, who's there? I'm Amelia Blackstone, head witch of Ravensborough so whoever's out there better leave now." Conor's heavy breathing stopped as he crept up to the window and with a twirl of his wrist, he began to recite the eavesdropping spell.

"Ears hear me now widen your mind
Render the world motionless
Allow me to hear the information I seek
make the speaker's words echo for me"

And with that, Conor could hear everything in the house from leaky dripping tap to the slight patter of Queenie, his grandma's pet bearded dragon.

"Darling, I'm so sorry I've let you down. I've tried my hardest but I don't think I can be the rock that Conor needs. You were great at these things. He's growing up so fast and I feel that with each passing day I'm losing touch with him. I don't know what to do or what to say anymore I've just..." Amelia paused fighting back the tears. She took a moment to compose herself before continuing. "Look at me, I'm a mess. Conor has his inspection in a few days and I've been busy. I know you would have been so proud of him going off to school with others for the first time and I wish you were here but I promise you that I will not let you down and I will make you proud just like you made me so proud."

Conor was rendered motionless. What was he doing out here? He should be in there with his gran but as he began inching towards his door his pocket began to shake and glow. He looked down, stunned. What was happening, he thought, but before he could say anything he was floating in mid-air speeding across Ravensborough. He then landed with a thud. He had been transported to Kenbury Forest by the wall and as he was taking in his surroundings, he heard footsteps in the distance.

"Hello, who's there? My gran is head witch so if you try anything I'll get her to turn you into stone," he exclaimed tightly holding his wand.

"Relax, grandma's boy. It's me, Ryan."

"Ryan, what have you done?" said Conor angrily. "Why am I here?"

"I was here because of you," replied Ryan, smirking.

"Because of me," spluttered Conor in disgust. "I barely met you two hours ago, and now you're telling me that you were in this forest at the dead of night and it's because of me," Conor added, more confused than ever.

"It's not my fault you picked up the note I chucked at you."

Of course, the piece of paper. He knew there had been something odd about it but that still hadn't explained why he was in the forest with Ryan.

"Well, did you read the note because if you had you would have known that it was a wizard transportation note?"

"A what?"

"Doesn't your gran tell you anything? A wizard transportation note is when a wizard writes to another person a place to meet and if the note is still on that person at the time they are transported to the meeting place."

"Do you have any more?" asked Conor.

"No, why... did you wanna go somewhere else?"

Conor sighed as he collapsed next to a tree. He was stuck here.

The silence that the residents of Durfold Street had become accustomed to had vanished as Amelia, concerned by her grandson's absence, began going door to door hoping to find him. But each door was a disappointment. Now back home, Amelia decided to call Harrowood's café. As the phone rang a million thoughts passed through her mind ranging from completely rational to downright crazy.

"Hello, Harrowood's Café, Mr Harrowood speaking."

"Ben, it's me. Is Conor still there?"

"No, he left quite a while ago. Is he not home yet?"

"Well, if he were at home would I be calling you?" snapped Amelia. "I'm sorry. I'm just worried sick I haven't seen him since we had the huge row. Do you have any idea where he could have possibly gone after he left the café?"

"He said he was going to come straight home after he left... no wait, actually before he left he was chatting to that troublemaker Ryan Archibald's boy."

"Oh no, not him. Do you have Mr and Mrs Willows address or phone number? Maybe he has gone over to their house?" asked a more relaxed Amelia.

"Yeah, sure. They live over at Christwood Meadows. I'll give you Archibald's number. I hope you find Conor," said Mr Harrowood reassuringly.

"I hope I find him, too."

Amelia knew that time was of the essence if she was to find her grandson before it became pitch black. But as set out she came across the glowing note on the floor. As an experienced witch Amelia was fully aware of what was scrunched up before her and while she knew she should have ignored it as it was probably a prank from one of the young wizards, she had a nagging feeling that it was a potential clue. Her eyes began to bulge as she read the note. Had she read correctly? She then began to read the note aloud.

Hey, grandma's boy when you decide that you want to have some real fun and you want to ditch the old folks meet by the wall at Kenbury Forest at eight o'clock. Your friend, Ryan Willows.

As her eyes hit the last word on the note, she knew she had no time to waste as her grandson could be in grave danger that he was not even aware of. Kenbury Forest was filled with insistent chatter as Conor still demanded to know why Ryan had summoned him but Ryan, having had too much fun, resisted Conor's questioning. Getting nowhere, Conor decided to change his approach hoping this would yield the answers he required.

"Why are you out so late?" Conor asked. "Aren't your parents going to worry where you are?"

"Nah, me and my parents have an understanding. They know I'm like a cat. I come and go as I please but I always make it back for supper time," replied Ryan with a smug look on his face

"That must be so nice being able to go where you want when you want and knowing your parents are fine with it. I wish my gran was like that sometimes," said Conor enviously.

"I'm sure your gran is only looking out for you."

"What are you talking about? Do you know what it's like to feel like you are suffocating and not being given the space to breathe?"

"Hey, I'm just saying that some people would kill for that type of affection and protection."

"Yeah, I guess you're right... Ryan, are you all right?"

"I'm fine."

"Are you sure? I'm a good listener," said Conor softly

"You... a good listener?" said Ryan in a measly chuckle.

"I have to be being a grandma's boy."

Ryan smiled before sighing. "It's just when I see you talk about how protective your gran is of you it makes me kind of miss when my parents were like that with me if you get what I mean?"

"What do you mean? Do they not care about you anymore or something?"

"No, they do it's just not the same any more. Ever since my mum had the baby practically all her time is taken up and whenever she does have time, she is exhausted and my dad has become the lead dragon tamer so he's working all day and whatever free time he does have he spends it with me sister. Sometimes I just feel invisible."

"Is that why you act out so your parents notice you more?"

Ryan remained silent.

Conor had discovered a completely new side to Ryan. He wasn't those horrible things that Mr Harrowood, his grandmother and the rest of Ravensborough had said about him. He was nothing more than a boy worried that he wasn't loved anymore and here he was taking for granted the unconditional love that his grandma had showed him. Tonight's events had taught Conor a lot about himself and he now finally knew what he had to do to set things right with his grandmother. He stood up and walked over to Ryan.

"Come on, let's go home," he said.

But Conor's statement was easier said than done as Kenbury Forest was rather large and the two boys soon found themselves lost with the forest now shrouded in darkness. "What do you mean we've been here before I'm sure this puddle is smaller," bemoaned Conor

"Shhhh... what was that?" responded Ryan. The sound of twigs breaking had caused the boys to briefly stop. They then continued thinking nothing of it but again Conor stopped. He had seen something. It was a shadow but not something he recognised but it looked familiar both in its appearance and movement. He froze and looked in the shadow's direction. He could have sworn he saw the shadow stare back. Confused and frightened, he spoke. "Hello, who's there?"

The forest remained silent again as the young witch repeated, "Hello, who's there?" The shadow then began to creep closer and closer and it was approaching the boys at a frightening speed. It then stopped and stooped down as if it was picking up something before continuing its approach and had almost reached a puddle which was reflected by the moon. In a few moments Conor and Ryan would meet a third guest at Kenbury Forest. As the shadow was about to step out by the puddle a loud voice echoed throughout the forest. It was Conor's grandmother.

"Conor, Ryan, are you there?"

The boys turned to see if they could see someone approaching but they couldn't. They quickly turned their attention back to the shadow but to their disappointment it had vanished as had their sense of excitement.

"Boys, are you there?" repeated Amelia.

"We're over here," said Ryan.

"Oh, thank goodness, stay there. I'm coming to get you."

CRASH! The forest was deafeningly silent.

"GRAN WHAT HAPPENED? ARE YOU OKAY? WHERE ARE YOU?" yelled Conor.

"I'm over here by this rock," replied Amelia her voice becoming increasingly faint.

The forest didn't seem so big now as the boys travelled the short distance to the rock. "Are you okay, Gran?" .

"Yes, I'm fine. It's just my ankle"

"This is all my fault," blubbered Conor as he collapsed beside his grandmother. "I'm so sorry. You wouldn't be out here if I wasn't such a spoilt brat and look what that has caused. I'm sorry for taking you for granted. I promise from this moment on I will do everything to make your life a little easier."

Mustering all her strength Amelia stretched placing her hand on her grandson's wet but warm cheek. "No Sticky, you were right. I was being selfish. You are growing up. For so long it's been just you and me and since we lost your mum, I've been smothering you and for that I'm sorry. I guess I won't be able to smother you for a while," said a smiling Amelia.

"Ryan, do you have your phone with you?" asked Conor.

"Yea, why?"

"I need you to call your dad to come and get us. You need to tell them that my gran needs to go to the hospital right away. Okay?"

"Okay."

Ten minutes had passed since Ryan had called his father. The forest had remained silent since then but Conor and Ryan's minds were far away. Both had a look on their faces; they knew that they were moments away from encountering something they had never seen before. They looked at each other, then looked back in the direction of the puddle and finally at Amelia. Did they see the same thing? What was the shadow and should they tell Amelia? But before any of them could say something the sound of Mr Willows' horn sounded...

"Ryan, where are you?" said Mr Willows thunderously.

"We're over here, dad."

"Oh Ryan, how many times have me and your mum told you that you are not supposed to leave home after seven forty-five and who are you with? Another hoodlum."

"It's me Conor and I'm no hoodlum and neither is Ryan."

Mr Willows took a step back surprised at the way Conor had spoken to him. He then walked past the two boys to help his fellow council member but as he did so he turned to look at Conor again and the respect was apparent in his eyes. As Mr Willows helped an ailing Miss

Blackstone to his car Conor and Ryan trailed behind. Ryan looked over to Conor and nodded and with that nod both boys knew that a new friendship had been forged.

The awkwardness in the car on the drive to the hospital was growing by the minute as Mr Willows continued looking back at Conor through his rear-view mirror with visible disgust on his face. Conor was aware of this and knew that if he and Ryan were to remain friends he would have to swallow his pride and apologise.

"Excuse me, Mr Willows. I would like to say sorry for the way I spoke to you earlier."

"It's okay," replied Mr Willows.

"Archibald, could you stop by my house to drop Conor off, please?" asked Amelia speaking for the first time.

"No, Gran," interrupted Conor. "I'm not leaving you."

"I'm sure you remember what I said in the forest, Conor. We need to focus on your practice and you are going to need the rest so home now," said Amelia firmly.

"Fine," mumbled Conor.

"Oh, and Conor, you mustn't ever go back to that forest again. There is nothing there but mischief and trouble".

"Okay, Gran," replied Conor.

The clouds finally relented as the heavens opened. The rain was bitterly cold as Conor stepped out of the car. Once inside he raced up the stairs and got into bed, his mind uneasy. He managed to put aside his worry and fall asleep hoping he'd feel better in the morning but as he woke up suddenly, he had barely slept at all and his uneasiness had returned. He crept out of his bedroom before slithering down the stairs as he did not want to wake up his grandmother.

He began to pace up and down the living room. He couldn't take his mind off the forest and would have to disobey his grandmother as he had to know what was in the forest with him and Ryan. With his mind churning, Conor paused. He didn't want to upset his grandmother so he decided that he would tell her about what he saw in the hope that if he couldn't investigate what was there at least she would. He then crept back upstairs before slowly opening his grandmother's door. He was surprised she wasn't there and disappointedly retreated to his bedroom.

"Conor, Conor, wake up! You're going to be late for your first day of training."

"All right, I'm getting up," mumbled Conor.

"are you okay? I thought you'd be chomping at the bit to get started with your training."

"I am, it's just after last night … how's your leg, by the way?"

"Just a hairline fracture. Should be fine in a couple of weeks."

"Wait, if your ankle is fractured how did you get upstairs?" asked Conor.

"I told you, there was still use for my broom," smiled Amelia. "Are you sure you're okay?" she asked again.

"Just a bit nervous. I've never been to a school where if people don't like me…what if they treat me different because I'm the head witch's grandson?"

"Sticky, my Sticky," smirked Amelia...

"Gran," moaned Conor. "I'm not a baby any more. It's embarrassing. I've just turned thirteen."

Amelia's smile widened. "Conor, you might be thirteen but you will always be my Sticky whether you like it or not," she said as she floated towards the door.

"Actually, Gran there is something else I have to tell you."

Conor remembered what he had said to her last night. He knew he had to tell her about what he had seen but he didn't want her to rush her recovery. Quickly, he thought of something else to say. "I just wanted to know if you were going to follow me on my first day?"

"You just try and stop me," laughed Amelia.

"Oh!"

"What's the matter? Wait, don't tell me. You don't want me to come."

"Well, it won't help my reputation."

"I'm sorry you feel that way but I've told you thousands of times that no one's opinion should matter to you except your own. I know you're a teenager now and everyone else's opinion matters. I get it. I was young once but those other kids' opinions do not matter as one week they will love you and the next hate you."

"Times have changed. A hundred years was quite a while ago."

"Why you cheeky little sod! I'll have you know I was quite the athlete in my day."

"I bet." This brought smiles from them but as Amelia floated back towards the door another question popped into Conor's mind. "Wait, Gran! Who's going to help me train now?"

"Well, this morning I gave Mr Harrowood a call and he said he would be more than happy to help you with your training provided that you help him in the café at the weekends."

Conor slowly fell back onto the backboard of his bed seemingly uninspired by his grandmother's choice.

"What the matter? I thought you liked Mr Harrowood?" said Amelia.

"I do. He's just a bit boring."

"Conor, trust me. Mr Harrowood will get you in tip top shape before your inspection and I'm sure he'll spice things up to your liking. Now hurry along, he'll be waiting for you. Try to enjoy it," said Amelia.

"Fine, I will. Where does he want me to meet him?"

"He said he wants you to meet him at his café. Oh and Conor, be on your best behaviour. Please try to listen."

CHAPTER TWO

POTIONS, WANDS AND DRAGONS

With the summer drawing to a close Conor decided that bike ride to Mr Harrowood's café would be best as Ravensborough's famously cold and wet winter would soon render his bike useless. He thought it would be best to put last night's incident to the back of his mind so as not to distract him from his training but as he was doing so he rode past the Ravensborough High bus. He came to a halt and watched as the children boarded. He was in awe as that bus represented freedom; it represented normality.

It drove off leaving in its trail a ball of smoke and as the cloud settled in the air Conor closed his eyes and began to see himself attending Ravensborough High. It was wondrous as he saw himself running for that very bus. He saw himself among a large group of friends; he began to hear the sounds of Ravensborough High: the laughter of hundreds of children across the playground, their wrists rotating in unison as they practised spells in class. In that moment, any negative thoughts ebbed away but this was soon shattered as a booming voice beckoned him. Conor immediately knew who it was.

"Hey Blackstone, that's nice bike. Let's have a ride," said the voice.

"I would love to Marvin, but my gran said I'm not really allowed to let people ride it."

"I heard it's your inspection soon so I'm gonna take

31

this... wouldn't want you to have any distractions."

"B-B-but…"

"Problem?" hissed Marvin.

Lost for words, Conor slowly stepped aside. "That's a good lad," laughed Marvin patting Conor on the head before riding off. In that moment Conor's vision of school life had been altered. What was once rosy and full of ambition and hope was dark and full of despair. He knew that he was still an outsider and that was not going to change any time soon.

Several minutes had passed before Conor decided to continue with his journey to Mr Harrowood's café hoping training would liven up his mood. The streets of Ravensborough were eerily quiet that Monday morning. The silence had slightly surprised him because he knew the children being at school played a part but he couldn't understand where all the adults were. But this soon became an afterthought because when he went to turn the corner his gaze met that of Ryan's. They stopped and looked around frantically hoping someone would interrupt them but unfortunately for them no one appeared. They continued on with their impromptu staring contest, both waiting for the other one to speak.

"Why aren't you in school now getting your timetable?" asked Conor finally.

"After what happened last night my mum and dad said I could stay at home."

"So, why aren't you at home then?"

"I woke up this morning and my parents weren't there. I guess they went to get it for me."

"Oh, okay... it was great chatting but I've got to get to Mr Harrowood's. It's my first day of training," remarked Conor gazing at his wrist.

"Can I come? I'll be your personal guinea pig."

"Mmm, I'm not sure."

"Please!" whimpered Ryan.

"All right, on one condition. You have to apologise to Mr Harrowood and promise that you will never use one of those's notes on me again."

"Ahhhh.....Fine," bemoaned Ryan.

The two boys set off. The silence had returned as they continued towards Mr Harrowood's café but whilst the mouths weren't talking their faces were. Both boys' minds were on last night's events. Ryan had wanted to talk about it but he was mindful of being insensitive as Conor's grandmother had got hurt. Ten more minutes went by but Ryan's mind was still restless. He was going to explode if he did not speak but just as he was mustering up the courage to ask Conor about yesterday, he spotted a set of keys on the ground.

"Mate, I think you've dropped your keys. What type of keys are these? They look like bike lock keys." "Do you have a bike? Where is it?".

"Those aren't mine," replied Conor...

"Are you sure? I found them behind you and there isn't anyone else around?"

"ARE YOU DEAF OR JUST STUPID? I TOLD YOU THEY AREN'T MINE," barked Conor before snatching the keys and running off

Confused and stunned, Ryan looked on not sure what he had done wrong. He thought of what he should do. Of course he did not want to leave his new friend alone in his current state but he couldn't just chase after him. After all he had just bitten his head off. Ryan thought it best to leave Conor and then turned to leave but he had walked no fewer than ten steps before feeling uneasy and remembering something that his dad had told him "*A person too stubborn to talk is a person in the greatest need of help*". With these words swirling around in his head Ryan ran after Conor. The wind that late early September morning began to pick up leaving Mr Harrowood's café door whistling a disjointed tune. Ryan looked on as he

33

approaching cautiously not wanting another tirade aimed at him.

"You sure know how to make a guy work," he whilst regaining his breath. Conor remained silent.

"Look, I'm sorry about asking about the keys".

"No, I'm sorry for shouting. I get a new friend for one day and I've already scared him off," said Conor questioning himself.

Ryan smiled as he sat beside his friend. "It'll take a lot more to scare me off."

"Thanks."

"Now are you going to tell me what happened with those keys? I'm a good listener," smiled Ryan.

"Funny." "They were for my bike but Marvin took it."

"Marvin," said Ryan angrily "He does that to everyone. He took my wand the first day I met him. He always picks on the smaller kids."

"But you're not the head witch's grandson, you don't have to carry yourself in a certain way. "Besides my gran just got me that bike. What am I supposed to say to her when she asks where it's gone?"

"If you're willing to hear me out and listen to what I say next I will tell your gran I lost the bike."

Unsure about Ryan's motives Conor took a few moments to decide and then nodded. But as Ryan spoke Conor soon wished he hadn't said a word. "Aren't you gonna say something?" said Ryan.

"To be honest, I've purposely been trying to avoid talking about it. I just want to focus on my training and that what you're bringing up is what I want to completely avoid, forget even, however you want to describe it."

"I can't get that shadow out of my mind. What if it was, you know?"

"You know what?" asked Conor.

But Ryan didn't answer instead he gestured for quiet. Mr Harrowood's distinctive morning whistle could be heard as he walked towards his café. "Morning Mr Harrowood" said Conor sharply, but silence filled the air as the café door flew open

"Morning, Conor, it would have been a great one but the town's practical joker has decided to bless us with his presence this morning instead of doing what good children do and go to school," then tutted Mr Harrowood.

"Well, it's always a good morning when you're involved, isn't it Benny?" retorted Ryan.

"Why, you little brat! Get out of my café right now before I call headmaster Gravethorpe to come and collect you."

"Yeah right, you old troll," whispered Ryan.

"WHAT WAS THAT?" bellowed Mr Harrowood. His voice seemed to increase in decibels with each passing moment.

"ENOUGH, BOTH OF YOU BE. QUIET!" shouted Conor as he became increasingly tired of the constant bickering.

The room fell silent and momentarily Conor felt a sense of dominance that he hadn't before. All eyes in the room shifted towards him. The stage was his and he knew what he said next would shape the rest of the day.

"Ryan, wait outside, I need to talk to Mr Harrowood."

"Are you turfing me out?"

"Just wait outside," said Conor again winking as Ryan passed by him.

Ryan peered through the café window to see what was going on and he saw ferocious pacing by both followed by flailing arms. Just as the argument seemed to be getting more heated the pacing and arm flailing stopped and a visibly annoyed Mr Harrowood stormed into the back.

"Thanks," smiled Ryan as he re-entered the café.

"No problem."

The two boys went back to the table with the idea of continuing their previous conversation but the sound of strange noises from the kitchen quickly put paid to that. Conor decided to check it out but as he went to open the door the noises stopped.

BANG!

"What the heck was that?" said Ryan.

"I don't know but we'd better check if Mr Harrowood is all right."

The boys slowly edged towards the door but as they went to open it, it jarred halfway as if something was blocking it from the other side. They tried again, this time more forcefully. The door slowly opened and the sounds of pots and shattered glass could be heard scraping across the floor.

"Mr Harrowood, is your head all, right?" asked Conor.

"I'm fine. Give us a hand."

"What happened?" questioned Ryan.

"I was tired and thought the kitchen would be a great place to sleep. What do you think happened?"

Remembering what Conor had just done for him Ryan ignored Mr Harrowood's comments briefly leaving the kitchen before returning with a first aid kit and a broom. He then began clearing up while Conor cleaned and bandaged Mr Harrowood's head injury.

"What happened? How did you end up on the floor?" asked a puzzled Conor.

"I was trying to get my old wand from the top shelf as I wanted to give it to you so you could use it during the training but now it's broken," replied Mr Harrowood.

"Why wouldn't you just use your wand now to float down to you?" scoffed Ryan.

"Why don't you get back to sweeping and stop asking ridiculous questions?" ordered Mr Harrowood.

"Sorry, I asked."

"What are we going to do now with the wand being

broken? Are you sure you are going to be all right for us to begin training today?" asked Conor.

"Don't worry. We can go over to Witchhaven Valley to get it repaired. Shouldn't take more than an hour and then we will begin the training. Okay?"

"NO!" yelped Conor defiantly storming out of the kitchen. Mr Harrowood, taken aback by the staunch refusal, quickly followed his student. "Conor, what's the matter? Was it something I said?" asked Mr Harrowood.

Conor said nothing as he rummaged through his bag. "Those two pages state that Witchhaven Valley was where witches were forced to live as they were abused and mistreated throughout the rest of Ravensborough. How I can go there?" exclaimed Conor passionately.

"Oh," said Mr Harrowood softly. "I was a child when this happened and what those witches had to endure was terrible but we have progressed a long way since then and Witchhaven Valley is now a wondrous place full of witches, wizards, shops and houses."

"That's' not good enough," sneered Conor.

"Look, Conor. I cannot force you to go but it would hugely increase your chances of passing your assessment if you did."

Mr Harrowood stood up and returned to the kitchen. Conor sighed as knew that he needed to put aside his pride to give himself the best chance. Hastily, he ran into the kitchen and apologised to Mr Harrowood for being so rash and stubborn. Mr Harrowood pointed to the clock.

"What makes you so qualified to teach a witch?" asked Ryan as they left the shop.

"I'll have you know I studied witchology for three years at Crowsmith University," said Mr Harrowood proudly.

He continued to divulge more about his past as he, Conor and Ryan walked to Witchhaven Valley but after a while both boys became less and less interested and began to lag behind. Conor still had not forgotten what Ryan had mentioned earlier. What had Ryan meant by 'you know what'? Did he know what the shadow was or was he just as clueless as he was? Several minutes had passed since Conor began to question what Ryan knew about the shadow in the forest. He decided to quiz his new friend further but it would have to wait as something had attracted his attention, something magical.

"See, Conor, it has changed vastly different from those dark day exclaimed Mr Harrowood This is the cornerstone of Ravensborough. This valley is etched into our town's history, both good and bad,"

Conor stood there in awe of his surroundings and a sense of wonder took over his body. His head began to rattle furiously as he looked at the variety of shops on offer. Witchhaven Valley was distinctive by its colour which replicated the Ravensborough flag: green, black and white. The aroma of the valley tickled Conor's nose with the smell of olden days, from the purist potions being brewed to the fresh stench of wood being burned as new wands were produced.

"Come on boys, Basil's wand is here on the left."

"We will be there in a minute," said Conor "Hold on, Ryan. You are going to tell me what you meant by you know what and you are going to tell me now."

"All right. Hold your horses. I will tell you but not here... actually, I'd rather show you."

"Show me?" said a flummoxed Conor.

"Yeah, but we're going to have to ditch Harrowood."

Conor's smile began to shorten. For as much as he wanted to discover and find out more about what he and Ryan encountered in the forest last night, he couldn't just up and leave Mr Harrowood especially with his assessment around the corner. Conflicted, Conor began pacing before abruptly stopping and turning towards Ryan. "All right, let's do it," he roared.

"Do what?"

The burly figure of Mr Harrowood had rendered Conor still. "Well?"

"We were coming to join you," interjected Ryan quickly. "So, what's happening with the wand? Did Mr Basil fix it?"

"No, that piece of junk is so old it's gonna take at least two weeks to fix so he gave me this instead," said Mr Harrowood. "But it doesn't matter. Now come along, lads. I have to meet someone about the café so follow me and stay close. Where we're going is notorious for having gremlin pickpockets."

As they navigated their way through the remainder of Witchhaven Valley the sense of wonder that had taken over Conor had fully worn off as this part of the valley was dark and rundown. Only a few shops remained but one shop stood out to Conor. It was closed but it seemed that it once harboured something magical. He was about to ask Mr Harrowood what sort of shop had been there but before he could Mr Harrowood suddenly disappeared into an alleyway that resembled more of a black hole than anything else.

"I guess we aren't going to the forest today," sighed Conor.

"Oh yes, we will take this," said Ryan as he handled a shimmering piece of paper.

"Can't we just walk?"

"Nope."

The two boys then began to levitate. Conor braced himself as they were whisked away. Still rattled by his last experience, Conor had elected to close his eyes as he was definitely afraid of heights but before he could get them even halfway shut the boys had arrived at the entrance of Kenbury Forest.

"You idiot. I told you no more notes... but I'm kind of glad you did it."

"You can admire my genius later, let's get a move on."

They began to venture into the forest making sure to stay close together and not wanting a repeat of last night. Several dull minutes had passed since either of them had come across anything familiar. Conor had begun to venture a bit further than Ryan but with no luck. Seemingly hitting a dead end, Ryan's frustration had got the better of him as he began swinging his foot wildly kicking anything in his path.

"OWWWWWWWWWW MY BLOODY TOE!"

"Ryan, are you okay? What happened?"

"I stubbed my blooming big toe on that bloody rock."

Conor ran over to his friend but just as he bent down to help Ryan to his feet he saw the rock that had inflicted the wound. His eyes began to narrow. It was the same rock that his grandmother had injured herself on. He recomposed himself and helped Ryan back to his feet.

"Ah, Ryan, you really are a genius."

"Well, I try but if you don't mind me asking, how am I a genius?"

"Don't you see? It means that we must not be too far from the puddle. Come on!"

Conor could hardly contain his excitement. He began to gallop straight ahead leaving behind his ailing friend Ryan to limp after him. A hundred yards had evaporated underneath him, but as Conor then turned to see where Ryan was he suddenly felt the ground change...

SPLOSH! "I found the puddle."

"All right, see if you can spot any footprints. Maybe what we saw last night is still there and if it is we can capture it. Don't forget, take a photo."

Not a fan of swimming, Conor elected to walk around the puddle which had at least tripled in size since last night. With the puddle safely navigated Conor continued on looking for anything unusual but nothing stood out. He then approached the cave hoping something would present itself. Thankfully, it had as a trail of footprints led deep into the cave but the sound of hissing forced the young witch to the outside. He quickly took several photos before scuttling back not wanting a chance encounter with a snake.

"Ryan, I'm back. I got the photos."

"Let me have a look at 'em." As Ryan sorted through the pictures it was evident from the disappointment on his face that it had not been what he had hoped for or expected.

"So, was it the 'you know what' thing you mentioned earlier?" asked Conor.

"No, it's not."

"All right. Now will you tell me what you thought you saw last night?"

"I thought it was a--"

"Mr Harrowood!" blurted Conor.

Mr Harrowood looked at them, the disappointment clear in his eyes. Without having to say anything the boys got up and followed him out of the forest. They had prepared themselves for a verbal dressing down but no such treatment came as Mr Harrowood refused to speak.

"Don't blame Conor, it was my fault. I used a transportation note on him," pleaded Ryan.

"I think you should go home, Ryan," said Mr Harrowood.

"Okay."

Ryan's departure had done nothing to ease the tension as Mr Harrowood returned to his silence. Conor, thinking it would be best for him to go home, stood up and walked slowly towards the door but as he went to reach the handle Mr Harrowood darted in front of him. "Sit down! You're not going anywhere."

Conor sank back into his seat as Mr Harrowood slid over to the kitchen. He re-emerged a few minutes later grasping two cups in his hand. He then sat on the chair facing Conor and began to drink from his own.

"What is this?"

"Dragon Mucus, you looked like you were cold. That should warm you up."

"I always thought you were a good lad, Conor," said Mr Harrowood. "I've seen hundreds of children pass through my café but whenever you came by I thought now here comes a good apple. I guess I was wrong."

"I am good. It's just that last night me and Ryan saw a shadow in the forest so he thought it would be a good idea if we headed back to see if there was anything that could tell us anything about what we had seen."

"I didn't know that you were Ryan's sidekick because that's what he thinks of you; you can't keep giving into his demands. They are going to get more and more extreme and before you know it your life could be in real danger," said Mr Harrowood.

"Ryan's my friend. He would never ask me to do anything dangerous."

"A friend? Would a friend drag you away from your training when he knew this was vital to you passing your inspection? Would a friend suggest that you go back to a forest to investigate something that you may or may not have seen?" asked Mr Harrowood.

Conor remained wordless sure that anything he said wouldn't change Mr Harrowood's mind about Ryan. "I'm sorry for leaving earlier. Are you going to tell my gran about today?"

"I won't but you need to decide what you want to do about training for the opportunity that you've waited a long time or do you want to continue running around with your friend hoping to stay out of trouble? If you decide that you want to practise I'll be here at seven a.m. tomorrow."

As Conor walked home Mr Harrowood's words were still firmly in his mind. He wanted to pass his inspection and he knew that Mr Harrowood was his only hope of getting prepared but he didn't want to give up his only friend. He knew that Ryan would understand if he distanced himself for the reminder of the week. As Conor reached home he received a message. Seeing that it was from Ryan, Conor decided to ignore it.

"Hi, Sticky. How was your first day of training?"

"Gran, I'm really tired. Could we talk about it later?"

"Oh, all right then."

Conor wondered if going to Ravensborough High was worth all the fuss as being there at seven a.m. hadn't gone down well but as he neared the café he wondered how he would be received or what Mr Harrowood would have in store for him.

"Wow!" mumbled Conor. The café was completely unrecognisable. The tables and chairs had been removed and all that remained was a single table stockpiled with potions which were lithium zincoma, copper magnesia and mercury ionica. Also, on the table was a pen, action figure and a raven feather.

"Morning, Conor. I see you made your choice. Good decision."

"Can we just get on with the training, please?" said Conor not wanting to feel any more guilt.

"Right, as you know the assessment is split into three parts with the first requiring you to get a dragon and demonstrate control over it by getting it to complete simple tasks. The second task is a choice between brewing a growth potion, levitation or object manipulation. I will be teaching you all three and you pick what you feel you're best at and finally the final task is reanimation. Do you understand?"

Conor nodded before moving aside to allow Mr Harrowood to demonstrate. The café owner then began to mix the different potions. Conor circled the table slowly wanting to cover every angle. Mr Harrowood began to recite spells and with that the objects on the table came to life as a feather from a bird it was plucked from, levitated and floated.. The pen began to write furiously on the sheet of paper similar to Mr Harrowood's when taking an order.

As Conor marvelled at what he was witnessing he felt a gentle tug on his trousers. He looked down and was shocked to see the action figure moving as freely as Conor. It then began to ascend the table and when it had reached the summit it fell to the ground returning to its mummified state. .

"All right, Conor. I want you to try. Now wait here while I get more potions from the kitchen," he said placing the wand on the table.

Conor stared at the wand. As it was on the table he was in awe as he had been so close to wizards' wands before. He tried desperately to restrain himself from touching the wand but it was becoming increasingly difficult. He noticed an inscription and as he leant forward for a closer look he was disturbed by the noise of the door opening. Mr Harrowood then handed over the wand to him.

"Are you all right?" asked Mr Harrowood.

"Yeah, it's just that I've never used a wizard's wand before. What if I mess it up or break it?" replied Conor.

"Don't worry, I'm here. Take your time and I'm sure you'll get the hang of it," said Mr Harrowood encouragingly.

The day seemed to speed up as Conor practised the spell with varying levels of success as he struggled to grasp the power of the wand causing him to animate almost everything but the doll.

"Arrrh, this is pointless. I can't do it," moaned Conor throwing the wand to the ground before slumping into the only remaining lifeless chair.

Mr Harrowood quickly retrieved the wand before kneeling beside Conor. "You mustn't allow yourself to be discouraged. There is plenty of time to get the hang of it. At least you won't have any problem with the reanimation," he joked.

"It's not funny. How am I supposed to pass my inspection when I can't even reanimate the right thing? I'm hopeless," mumbled Conor sculking into a chair.

"I've had just about enough of this attitude…You're not hopeless and you will pass your inspection but you must start believing in yourself as magic can only truly work if you believe it, too. Now if you don't mind I'm going to need that chair, my knees are killing me."

With those words of encouragement Conor took the wand off Mr Harrowood but unlike before, he felt in control as he and the wand began to flow in tandem. Mr Harrowood looked on in disbelief as the objects began levitating in perfect unison. With the evening fast approaching and with Conor beginning to master the craft of levitation and reanimation Mr Harrowood abruptly halted the training session insisting on Conor going home as the following day's training session would test him physically. Mr Harrowood's decision left Conor frustrated but he respected him greatly and begrudgingly left.

The hail storm was particularly strong the following day as it pelted Conor who rushed to Harrowood's Café to begin his second day of his training but to his surprise the cafe was locked. Just as he turned around to retrieve his phone from his bag, he was disturbed by the honk of a car horn. It was Mr Harrowood.

"Today we are heading back to Witchhaven Valley. We need to get you a dragon,".

"Oh, I just thought were going to pick up where we left off yesterday," replied Conor.

"No, what you displayed yesterday showed me that you are ready to move onto the next phase of your training so if you're finished with your inquisition can we get a move on before you catch your death and your grandmother has me strung up?"

The drive to Witchhaven Valley seemed longer than the walk such was Conor's eagerness to get his first dragon. Looking for anything to distract himself Conor began to inspect Mr Harrowood's wand in the back beside him. Still intrigued by the inscription, he quickly looked up at the rear view mirror to check if Mr Harrowood was glancing back at him. He wasn't. He then leant in to read the inscription but he couldn't as it was in a language he couldn't understand. Conor's questions about the mysterious language would have to wait as they had arrived.

The aroma that filled the air was smoky and the clouds were dark and ashy as Conor and Mr Harrowood walked along. The scent became stronger and it dawned on Conor that Mr Harrowood had taken him to the Willows' dragon training facility which bore an uncanny resemblance to a dungeon. It was a sight to behold. While the outside was drab and dull the inside was anything but. It was vibrant and bursting with colour. There were various dragons in all shapes and sizes. Conor looked over the different dragons mulling over which one he should select before bumping into Mr Willows who had not seen since his grandmother's accident that night at Kenbury Forest.

"Hi, Mr Willows. How's Ryan?".

"How do you think he is doing when his new friend basically tells him that he wants nothing more to do with him?" barked Mr Willows.

Conor was shocked at what Mr Willows had told him. Granted it had been a few days since he had spoken to Ryan but still there hadn't seemed to be a problem. "I'm sorry, Ryan said he understood."

"What did you expect him to say?". "You were his friend and he didn't want to upset you but he also didn't expect you to act like he doesn't exist. That's despicable. You know what, I want you to leave my shop right now."

Feeling terrible, Conor began walking towards the door but again he was stopped by Mr Harrowood who ushered him to one side. "I understand that Ryan and Conor are having some issues at the moment but there is no need to mistreat Conor. I'm sure he and Ryan will sort it out and I know that Ryan wouldn't appreciate you fighting his battles," .

"Maybe you're right. I'm sorry, Conor," muttered Mr Willows.

"Apology accepted."

"Ben, if you're not busy could you help me take a look at something in the back that's giving me a bit of trouble?" asked Mr Willows.

"Sure, the car's acting up again,".

"I don't know why I persist with that piece of junk."

As Mr Harrowood and Mr Willows went into the back Conor began to look at dragons again. This had been a much harder task then he imagined as every dragon he'd look at would turn away. This was becoming hopeless as cage after cage remained closed and worse still only one cage remained. Conor approached slowly and to his present surprise the dragon did not run away.

He then opened the cage to inspect the dragon more closely but as he did, he noticed something. The dragon had a shorter damaged left wing and it was this imperfection that had made this dragon perfect for Conor as he knew better than anyone what it was like to be different. He then took the slivery blue beast in his arms and headed for the back.

"What are doing with that dragon, Conor?" asked Mr Willows irately.

"This is the dragon I've chosen."

"No, you can't have that dragon, it's defective. It can't even fly properly. Why would you want that one?" said Mr Willows.

"I agree with him, Conor". There are so many better

options out there. Are you sure that you want this dragon?"

"I don't want a different dragon. This one is special. I can feel it," said Conor defiantly stroking his friend.

"Well, you can't have him... I haven't fully tamed him so if you could put him back in his cage because the longer he's out the more unstable he could become," said Mr Willows.

"He seems fine with me so I'm going to take him."

"Archibald, if that's the dragon Conor wants let him have it. What harm could the little fella cause?" said Mr Harrowood.

"Fine, but if that dragon brings any trouble to Ravensborough or my door I'll be coming for you, Ben. Understood?" snarled Mr Willows.

As they left the dragon facility Conor couldn't help but feel that Mr Harrowood wasn't entirely happy with his choice of dragon but rather than challenge him, he decided to leave it as he had to focus all his energy on his new dragon. The journey back was filled with conversation as Mr Harrowood reminded Conor about what he had to do in the dragon part of the assessment.

The training with the dragon began but it was not without its troubles as Conor struggled to cope with its inconsistency as it was erratic in its movements and not entirely responsive. As the minutes turned to hours both Conor and Mr Harrowood found themselves becoming increasingly frustrated at the dragon's seeming lack of cooperation.

"Why don't we call it a day, eh Conor"

"Wait why, I think we're getting the hang of it" replied Conor defiantly

"I know but the both of you look shattered go home and get some rest…. Besides he still needs a name"

"Fine"

The walk home allowed Conor to evaluate how he had to approach his new companion. As he reached the front garden, he was met by his grandmother who suggested that he should rest as he had endured a long day but Conor was having none of it. He headed for the back garden where he spent his time trying various methods to coax the dragon out of its fragile state which might enable the creature to fly but alas without any success.

"What's up boy" huffed Conor as he sat on the wet grass beside his dragon. "I know what it's like to be looked down at I know your special let's show the world".

The largest but faintest roar filled the air as the dragon lifted by its owner's words began performing. Over the next two days Conor refused the help of both his grandmother and Mr Harrowood as he focused on getting himself and his dragon, who he'd still to name, in shape for the assessment that was now only a day away. Conor had become increasingly more confident of passing as the dragon began flying more freely and confidently.

Conor knew if he were to pass his assessment, he could not neglect the second part of the assessment so he headed upstairs to practise. As the hours passed Conor's room began to resemble a circus as various objects began levitating and flying in his room not to mention all the mess that had been made from potion making.

THUMP, the young witch trans-like state had been snapped

"Sticky it's me can we talk"

"Yh gran one sec" replied Conor as he waded through the empty bottles on the floor

"Conor, I just wanted to let you know that I am so proud of you and I know you're going to smash your assessment tomorrow."

"Thanks, gran."

"I want to give you something. I was going to give it to you on your first day but I feel you deserve it now". But before Amelia could finish Conor leapt to his feet and began to back away. "Gran I can't...... it was hers I'm not

49

worthy of it"

"Conor Blackstone get back here"

Begrudgingly the young witch obeyed his grandmothers' orders. "I know she'd be so proud of the young man you've become and I know she'd want you to have her first wand". Silence then filled the room as grandmother and grandson embraced.

"Thanks Gran"

"You're welcome, but now you have to give that dragon of yours a name," mumbled an emotional Amelia.

"I've got the perfect name, Sticky,"

Amelia smiled before handing Conor his new wand. As Conor held it, it dawned on him the importance of what his was about to face tomorrow. His nerves returned for a brief moment as a look to his smiling grandmother had reminded him why he had to pass the task in hand. He then gave her a hug again before heading for bed as tomorrow was the day he had been waiting for.

As the morning approached Conor lurked throughout the house his mood changing as the hours passed. He went from conveying supreme confidence to knee quaking nervousness highlighted by the fact he virtually had no nails left to help combat his nerves. He decided to go for a walk through Ravensborough in the early hours. He was amazed to see Ryan and as the two boys spotted each across the street, they glanced away quickly before coming to their senses and meeting in the middle of the street.

"What are you doing out at this time, grandma's boy?" asked Ryan jokingly.

"I couldn't sleep. My inspection is today," stuttered Conor.

"You need to relax. I know how hard you've been working. You'll be fine. You just need to believe in yourself. Do what you've got to do and you'll be going to Ravensborough High in no time."

"Thanks... I'm sorry for the way I treated you."

"Don't mention it."

"No, you were my first real friend and I shouldn't have tossed you aside. It was wrong. I hope you can forgive me,".

"I will on one condition. Stop with the soppiness otherwise you'll lose your focus and who would I have to boss around at school?" scoffed Ryan.

"Very funny but what are you doing out here this early?" Conor asked.

"I was coming to give you this." Ryan, after briefly rummaging through all his pockets, handed Conor a coin.

"Whoa, where did you get this? I thought they didn't make these anymore," said Conor marvelling at the three-headed coin.

"They don't, I found it when I had my assessment and had I was trialling for the football team. It's pretty lucky."

"Thanks…do you want to come with me to my assessment? I'm sure my gran won't mind."

"I can't. I promised my dad I'd help him at work today."

"Oh!" sighed a disappointed Conor. "I guess I'll see you at school then."

"I guess," said Ryan as he headed back up the street.

For the first time today Conor's mind was at ease as he walked home. His smile had also returned. He couldn't wait for his assessment but his smile dimmed as his grandmother greeted him at the door. "Where on earth have you been?"

"Sorry, I just needed some air."

"oh it's alright ….Are you ready?".

Conor nodded as he followed his grandmother inside. A full-scale argument was narrowly avoided in the Blackstone household as Conor reluctantly shovelled down the porridge his grandmother had made for him. It had been the first time he had eaten porridge in almost a year as the last time he did his face swelled up for a month.

"You see it wasn't that bad…don't forget to brush your hair. You want to make a good impression," shouted Amelia as Conor headed upstairs to get ready.

The drive to Ravensborough High felt endless as they seemed to pass thousands of trees. Conor sat perfectly still in the back seat grasping his new wand ever so tightly while glancing to his side at his dragon. They had arrived but as they pulled up to Ravensborough High Conor gulped as Mr Gravethorpe, dressed in an all-black suit,, stood at the gates.

"Lovely day, don't you think?" remarked Amelia.

"There is much to do Miss Blackstone so forgive me if there isn't time for me to gawk at the state of the weather."

As they walked through the hallway Conor couldn't help but notice the names of all the students that had graduated from Ravensborough High sprawled across the walls and ceiling hoping to spot his mum's name. Conor moved alongside Mr Gravethorpe who quickly stopped and began glaring. This caused the young witch to melt away. They had reached the field and Conor saw that everything had been set out. His palms began to sweat as his moment had arrived.

"Step forward, Master Blackstone," croaked Mr Gravethorpe in a booming voice. "Today you will demonstrate your skillset to me in a pair of assessments and then I and I alone will decide if you can attend my institution and my decision will be final. Understood?"

Mr Gravethorpe marched away and took his seat and leant forward waiting. Conor clutched the handle of the cage tightly as he moved over to the laid table and then commanded Sticky out of his cage. As he started the assessment three hoops were placed all across the sky.

"Come on Sticky, you can do it," he whispered as he knelt beside his dragon. This seemed to do the trick as the dragon began to fly although in an awkward motion, he still had managed to clear the hoops and safely land bringing the first part of the assessment to an end.

"Well done, boy. I knew you could do it." Conor then glanced at his grandmother whose smile was a welcome sight. He then glanced over at Mr Gravethorpe who was unmoved, his face emotionless.

The young witch composed himself as he geared up for the second part of the assessment. He had chosen the potion mixing. He placed the wand by his heart and went to the table and began to mix the potions before pouring them on the grass. He had made a growth potion but again there was no response from headmaster Gravethorpe.

Conor swiftly moved onto the final part of the assessment but to his surprise the doll that he had to animate was not the one that he had practised with at Harrowood's café. It was an ogre doll but undeterred and with headmaster Gravethorpe looking on, Conor set about his task reanimating the doll and commanding it around the field. For the first time he had begun to relax and have fun as he began to toy with the doll confident that he had done enough to pass. He flicked his wrist one final time to mummify the doll but to his shock the doll still moved around the field.

Even more shockingly it began to multiply. Confused and scared, Conor looked around for guidance but before his grandmother could pass on her wisdom hundreds of tiny ogres began to descend on the young witch dragging him to the floor. As he lay there he saw headmaster Gravethorpe get up and walk off. Sensing his dream walking off too, Conor managed to free one of his hands and grab his wand before enchanting all of the mini ogre's off him. He then cast a heating spell and with that the sky began to rain cotton.

Conor exhaled but the battle was far from over as the ground began to shake as a giant ogre stood before him. He began to cast every spell he knew but they were all ineffective. The ogre became more and more incensed and picked up his tormenter before hurling him across the field battered and bruised. Conor lay there defeated. What was the point of fighting, he thought. He had already failed but a shriek soon snapped him out of his sorry state and he slowly raised his head. The ogre had cornered his grandmother. Knowing that he had to act fast Conor noticed a slight tear in the seam of the ogre doll.

Mustering all his strength Conor got to his feet, steadied his wand and yelled "SEAMSEPRA". A flash of orange light sped toward the menacing ogre but the beast remained standing. Stunned, Conor lowered his head; he had failed again. But his head was soon raised in triumph as the ground shuddered and the ogre began to unravel. Conor now having fully regained his balance ran over to where his grandmother and dragon were.

"Gran, are you okay? Are you hurt?"

"We're fine," said Amelia mustering a smile.

Still exhausted, Conor stumbled towards the table as he was sure he had seen headmaster Gravethorpe writing before he left. He had as Conor picked up a note that simply read, IN MY OFFICE in block capitals. After cleaning himself up he and his grandmother made their way to Mr Gravethorpe's office. He was again standing as they entered the office and had been looking out of his window which overlooked the field.

"So, you saw what was happening out there and you did nothing?" barked Amelia.

"Yes, I was aware of what was transpiring Miss Blackstone and yes I did not intervene as I was watching to see how Master Blackstone would react," replied Mr Gravethorpe coldly.

"Are you serious? My grandson could have been killed out there and you did nothing because you wanted to see how he would react."

"Precisely, and as I suspected he lived up to

expectations. That's why I would like to inform both of you that I have granted Master Blackstone a place at Ravensborough High," he said.

Taken aback by what he had just heard Conor let out a tremendous cheer before recomposing himself and shaking Mr Gravethorpe's hand.

"Thank you, Mr Gravethorpe. I will try my best to become a productive member of Ravensborough High."

"See that you do. I will be keeping a very close eye on you Master Blackstone, a very close eye indeed."

As Conor and his grandmother walked through the hallway he began glancing at everything they passed. He wanted to enjoy this moment thoroughly but little did he know his life was about to change drastically forever.

CHAPTER THREE

RAVENSBOROUGH HIGH

Conor lay in bed staring at the ceiling his eyes darting all around the room. The day had arrived. He knew after today his life would drastically change and the home comforts, he was used to would no longer be there. This both excited and frightened him as he began to pace up and down his room, his mind swirling with thoughts of how he should approach his first day. But before he could think the sound of footsteps approaching his door sent him hurtling back towards his bed. The clock struck seven. Just two hours to go, Conor thought, as he lay awake still too nervous to sleep. The uneasiness of the day began to weigh heavily on his mind again as he had just remembered that he had a meeting with Mr Gravethorpe before the school day started. Becoming more and more anxious, Conor crept over to his desk and began to write. Writing over the years had become his secret thing as his thoughts were sometimes too heavy to bear.

Dear Mum,

The day has finally arrived. I'm going to school and I'm terrified. How is everyone going to be around me? To them I'm just the weird boy that hangs around with his gran. I know you would say to me to take this day in my stride and see it as a new wonderful adventure and go and show all those who doubt you what a Blackstone is capable of but I'm not like you, you were strong and brave. I miss you and I wish you were here but I'm going to try and enjoy it, not for me but for you.

Conor steadied himself, folded the note, gave it a kiss and closed his eyes.

BUZZ. The sound of the alarm stunned Conor as he stumbled to his feet. He glanced towards his dresser and began to stare at his uniform. It was wondrous from the navy-|blazer that any businessman would have been proud to wear to the grey jumper with the school's emblem perfectly stitched in and finally a long silky black and blue tie. he picked up his jumper and began running his hand over the emblem and for a brief moment any worries melted away. A firm knock on the door followed by a few words from his grandmother had brought Conor back to reality and he trudged out of his room. As he finished getting ready Conor went over to the note he had written and he placed it in his bag.

Amelia too had been busy that Monday morning. She was hard at work in the kitchen making a big breakfast for Conor but as she began whisking some eggs she began to worry. As she glanced at the time it wasn't like Conor to miss out on breakfast.

"Conor, come on! Breakfast is ready," she cried gleefully.

The house remained silent. Amelia's worries deepened as she headed upstairs to check on her grandson. Her face quickly scrunched at the sight of a slight opening in Conor's bedroom door. "Conor didn't you hear breakf—" Amelia stopped in her tracks, stunned nobody was there and a thousand thoughts passed through her mind. But they soon passed as she was sure she was being subjected to one of her grandson's pranks. Quietly, she crept towards the dresser giggling to herself before quickly opening the door but again she was left stunned as no one was there. But she thought nothing of it. She then headed towards the door thinking Conor would be in the bathroom but as she was leaving she couldn't help but notice that the bed was undone and as she lifted the duvet, she saw a note addressed to her but more importantly it was in Conor's handwriting. As she began to read the note her face changed, firstly to relief which quickly changed into anger. But as she reached the end of the note she understood exactly where Conor was.

The wind was particularly strong as Conor stood waiting for the bus. A buzz noise disturbed the silence. It had come from Conor's pocket and he looked at his phone. It was a message from his gran, a short *"Enjoy Yourself"*. Conor allowed himself a smile. He was glad that his grandmother had understood but the smile was soon wiped from his face as in the distance the ringing of a bell became disturbingly close. Conor recognised the sound; it was from his bike. Not wanting to make eye contact with Marvin, he quickly looked at the ground. "Welcome to the jungle, Blackpebble,". The wheels wailing as it screeched down the road

The bus finally arrived. The boisterous rambling of teenagers almost deafened Conor as the doors opened but as he climbed aboard the once vivacious lively bus became deafeningly silent until "Freak," mumbled a voice. Conor hoped the second deck would be more welcoming as he climbed the stairs. Thankfully it was as he spotted Ryan sitting at the back. Conor quickly hurried towards his friend as he could feel the eyes shifting in his direction once again. Seeing his friend in a foul mood, Ryan began telling jokes.

"I thought you loved my jokes. What's up?"

"Everyone was staring at me; didn't you notice how quiet the bus went when I got on?" replied Conor.

"Pay no attention to them. They're morons."

"Maybe. Their right. Maybe I am a freak."

"I've had about enough of this attitude. You've

worked so hard to get here and you are letting these lot ruin your first day… I'm not going to let that happen," exclaimed Ryan who then stood up and raced down the stairs. Confused and worried, Conor quickly followed intrigued by what Ryan was about to do.

"Oi, anyone giving Conor a hard time will have me to answer to. Do you understand?" he shouted as he stood at the front of the bus.

Conor stood there in disbelief as Ryan continued with his tirade. While he appreciated what his friend was doing he knew that Ryan's actions were going to do more bad then good. As Ryan finished his ramble the bus fell silent for a moment before erupting with laughter from both decks of the bus. Conor wishing the ground would swallow him up, quickly grabbed Ryan's arm dragging him back. Conor shook his head and glared at Ryan. The rest of the journey was highly uneventful. As the bus pulled up at the school it shuddered as everyone scrambled to get off. Conor remained back before skulking off. "Come on mate" smiled Ryan who had waited. The walk to reach the gates of Ravensborough High was brief Conor still a little unsure as to whether he belonged paused and took a sharp intake of breath before walking in. Ravensborough High was a school steeped in history with multiple awards and championships both in academics and athletics.

The main building was old and slightly beaten up but it had an aura of elegance about it. A long pathway led up to the front doors as the rest of the compound was covered with grass. The front doors too looked like they had been through the wars as the paint had started to chip away revealing the wood beneath. As Conor and Ryan walked in, they were greeted by a packed hallway. This had Conor taken aback. It was as if he had walked into a concrete jungle but he was also excited because you could lose yourself in this mess.

The struggle to navigate through the crescendo of

children began to overwhelm Conor and Ryan and they were being pushed from side to side. A sense of triumph was present as they finally managed to fight their way through the crowd but the triumph soon turned to despair as another wave students arrived.

BEEP!

"Would Master Blackstone join me in my office?" crowed headmaster Gravethorpe over the tannoy.

The once packed and disorganised hallway parted leaving a clear pathway to the headmaster's office and a huge uninviting black metal door which resembled that of a dungeon. Conor gulped as he entered.

"Did I give you permission to enter my office, Master Blackstone?" snarled Gravethorpe gesturing to Conor to leave.

"I'm sorry. I thought that you wanted to see me," replied Conor backing away.

"Indeed, I did. But in future it would be wise for you to knock as next time I might not be as understanding."

"My name is Conor just in case you had forgotten," proclaimed Conor.

"I am well aware of your first name Master Blackstone but in my school I will refer to you by your surname. It's much more formal."

"Okay, so what did you want to discuss, sir if you don't mind me asking?" .

"It was with regards to your class arrangements."

"Oh, good," replied Conor as he too had begun to wonder about what classes he was going to be in.

"I've been in discussion with the council as well as your grandmother and we've reached a decision... we feel that you would benefit being placed in a registration class with wizards as you may find the adjustment to school life easier. "Will that be a problem?"

"No, sir."

"Splendid,. "In that case here is your timetable. You will be in Professor Marigold's class which is in the Canterbury building on the fourth floor. Now hurry along, there is learning to be had," smiled Gravethorpe awkwardly.

A jubilant Conor entered the hallway, unable to conceal his excitement. He began skipping and prancing around, his arms raised in the air triumphantly as he held aloft his timetable. Finally composing himself, he headed for registration. The Canterbury building was vastly different to the main building as it was new and flashy resembling a tower.

Phew thought Conor as he put his hands on his knees. He had finally reached the fifth floor but it was rather odd as it consisted of only three rooms. Professor Marigold's classroom was located at the end the hallway. Conor began to allow the nerves to overwhelm him as he began to breathe heavily. He had reached the classroom but was unable to open the door . Thankfully, the door flew open and a large smiling figure stood there. "Hi, you must be Conor Blackstone. I'm Professor Marigold. We've been expecting you," he said jovially. Conor stood there unmoved, his lip quivering as he was unsure of what to say.

"Are you okay? You look like you've seen a ghost. Do you want to come inside?"

"Sorry, professor. I'm just a bit nervous. I didn't mean to ignore you," squeaked Conor.

"There is no need to be nervous in my classroom," said Professor Marigold reassuringly. "There won't be any judgement here... so let's go and meet your new classmates."

Professor Marigold walked back into the class with Conor following behind. The other children in the room instantaneously turned to the front and began to look at Conor with each face portraying a different reaction as

Professor Marigold began explaining and introducing Conor to them. The classroom which was awash with trophies, books and potions it was entrancing as the young witch looked for a place to sit.

"Over here mate" whispered Ryan, but trying not to endure further embarrassment Conor looked on for somewhere to sit before happening upon an empty desk.
Professor Marigold began to take the register and had barely checked three names when the classroom door flew open and a big, bruising presence entered.

"Sorry, professor I'm late is what people usually when they are late, Marvin,"

"Not now Goldilocks" retorted Marvin as he barrelled towards the back

"That's it. I've warned you about that. I'm going to get headmaster Gravethorpe. He'll deal with you." uttered Professor Marigold heading for the door

"Well, well, look who's in my seat," scoffed Marvin. "It seems like Blackpebble doesn't know that he is sitting in the king's seat. Move, now!"

"This your seat," whispered Conor.

"Yeah, it is, so move before I move you myself."

"I'll move... ogre," mumbled Conor.

"What was that?"

Conor stood up to move seats but he was stopped by Marvin who towered over him. As the two boys stood chest to face, Marvin began to grin as he stepped forward. Conor stumbled backwards and fell over. The class burst into laughter. After being embarrassed for the second time that day and with the children's laughter filling his ears, Conor, now enraged, stood up, drew for his wand and fired it. A puff of smoke filled the air and as it settled there was a collective gasp as Conor had given Marvin a large donkey's ears. "You'll pay for that," growled Marvin as he charged at Conor soon overpowering him. But just as Marvin was about to cast a spell, he felt a yank on his newly sprouted ears. It was Ryan. Marvin now turned his attention to him, grabbed the young wizard by his jumper and began to move him side to side violently.

"Get off him!" barked Conor as he got to his feet.

The three boys then became entangled knocking over chairs and tables as each had hold of the other. Professor Marigold and Mr Gravethorpe were deep in conversation as they reached the fifth floor but as they tried to enter the classroom they couldn't. Professor Marigold peered through the glass to see what had caused the blockage which had been a chair.

"I haven't got time for this," snarled Gravethorpe reaching for his wand.

The door blew open. The two men entered the room. They were greeted by overturned tables and a group of children bunched into a corner. Irate at what he had seen, Gravethorpe ordered an explanation. "WHAT IS GOING ON IN HERE? WHY ARE YOU NOT IN YOUR SEATS?" he croaked. The children all pointed to one corner of the class where Marvin had both Conor and Ryan by the scruff of their collars. "MARVIN," thundered Professor Marigold. The floor thudded as both Conor and Ryan came crashing down, but as they got to their feet the imposing figure of Gravethorpe greeted them. "The three of you to my office now," he said calmly.

Four chairs had been placed in the hallway besides headmaster Gravethorpe's office as the boys all took a seat with Professor Marigold also being present to avoid any more potential scuffles. One by one each boy was called in to give their version of what had happened in the classroom. Marvin was first.

Ten minutes had passed since Marvin had entered the office. The hallway was silent as the ticking of the school clock intensified. Ryan sat in his chair tilting back and forth, the worry on his face evident. Meanwhile at the other end of the hallway Professor Marigold began pacing, glancing at his watch and becoming increasingly agitated. Conor began to look for anything that would take his mind off his current predicament and then reached into his bag to inspect his wand. As he glanced over it, he noticed a slight chip towards the bottom.

The door to Gravethorpe's office opened. Marvin walked out followed by Gravethorpe who began patting Marvin on his back before pointing at Ryan summoning him in. As Marvin walked past Conor he began smirking devilishly and clenching his fist. For four straight minutes Professor Marigold continually looked in Conor's direction and then began to approach Conor before kneeling beside him. "What a first day, huh?"

"You could say that," said Conor brandishing a smile.

"I know how much of a hot head Marvin can be but I've never seen Ryan act this way. What happened back there?" asked Professor Marigold.

Before Conor could respond Gravethorpe's door opened and a visibly shaken Ryan walked out. Gravethorpe then summoned Conor. Ryan walked past Conor and the boys looked at each other. Ryan forced a smile before leaving the building; Conor then walked into Gravethorpe's office. Gravethorpe wasted no time in letting his feelings be known.

"I knew you were going to be trouble," he said shaking his head firmly "But this is incredible. One hour and you're already in my office."

"It wasn't my fault. Marvin tried..."

Headmaster Gravethorpe swiftly interrupted. "The question is not whether you were defending yourself. It is did you initiate the physical contact that includes using witchery?"

"Well, yes I did start it if you put it that way but he tried to..."

"Regardless of what, it does not give you the right to use witchery on your fellow peers. You have left me no choice Master Blackstone. You are excluded for the rest of the day and you shall serve a detention tomorrow after school."

"WHAT!" yelled Conor rising to his feet "You're excluding me when knowing Marvin started it… I'm starting to think you have a problem with me, sir."

"I know you are upset Master Blackstone but don't you dare question my professionalism. I have no problem… "Save your breath," hissed Conor as he headed for the door.

Still angered, Conor completely ignored Professor Marigold as he stormed out of the building. He could not understand why Gravethorpe had such a problem with him. Was it because he was a witch or maybe he was angry about still about being overruled by the grand council, something that was unheard of previously? A dark thought brewed in the young witch's mind but he quickly pushed it away. It was rather preposterous but as he continued walking the thought became less and less preposterous. After all, Gravethorpe did seem hell bent on stopping him from attending Ravensborough High. Maybe he had been the one that had sabotaged his assessment. It made perfect sense.

Another problem presented itself to Conor. Where was he supposed to go? Harrowood's café, he said. Yes, Mr Harrowood rarely asked questions and Conor was sure he would lend a sympathetic ear but as he neared the café Conor wondered if he had made the right decision. He went to turn but by this time it was too late as his name rang out.

"Conor, is that you?" asked Mr Harrowood holding some boxes.

"Hi, Mr Harrowood. Do you need a hand?"

"Yeah, that would be great but what are you doing here. Has school finished already?"

"Oh, headmaster Gravethorpe said that I only had to

stay a little while with it being my first day and all."

"Oh!"

Conor noticed the peculiar way that Mr Harrowood had reacted after he had answered his question almost as if he didn't believe him. Conor tried to avoid eye contact. This hadn't gone unnoticed as Mr Harrowood suspected Conor was lying. He knew that Gravethorpe was a prude and would never allow a student to have a half day no matter the circumstances but he also knew Conor well enough to know that he would never lie unless he was in trouble. "Take these and follow me," said Mr Harrowood.

"Where do you want me to put them?".

"Just set them aside by the counter. You must be hungry. You must have missed lunch. Right, let me give you a special treat as a little thank you for helping me today," replied Mr Harrowood.

"No, I'm fine thank you but I've got a sandwich in my bag plus my gran is expecting me home now as I promised I would help her with the gardening," chuckled Conor forcefully.

"That's odd I saw her this morning and she said she had a lot of work to do at the town hall. Maybe she finished early," said Mr Harrowood.

Conor stared blankly before quickly pulling out his phone. "I guess you're right," he chuckled hesitantly.

"That's settled then. Take a seat. I'll be back in a minute."

Conor's legs began to shake vigorously as he chewed on his nails. Mr Harrowood emerged from the kitchen with a plate in his hand. There was no need to stand up to see what it was. The aroma had said enough. It had been Conor's favourite chocolate cake with a sprinkle of pixie dust.

"Here you go lad… enjoy."

Conor glared at the cake before glancing at Mr Harrowood. Reluctantly, he began eating it but it had tasted bitter. He slammed his fork on the table and the plate was pushed to one side. He couldn't keep up the façade any longer and spent the next few minutes confiding in Mr Harrowood about what had happened at school as well as the concerns and suspicions about Mr Gravethorpe.

"I'm sorry to hear what happened but do you really think that Mr Gravethorpe would sabotage your assessment? I know he can come across as cold but he loves that school and I do not think he would risk losing his job just to stop you attending," said Mr Harrowood.

"I don't know. He seems like he cares about the school but you should see the way he acts towards me when no one is around. I think I should tell my gran."

"I think you should give Mr Gravethorpe the benefit of the doubt but if you still feel that he is picking on you then you should definitely tell your gran," said Mr Harrowood.

Conor remained defiant. He was going to tell his grandmother about Mr Gravethorpe's behaviour but Mr Harrowood was also defiant and spent the next few hours trying to change his young friend's mind.

"Fine, you win. I won't tell my gran," moaned Conor.

"Good, I think you're making the right decision." Mr Harrowood suddenly gasped. "Is that the time? You'd better be heading home. I'll drive you," said Mr Harrowood looking furiously at his watch. Conor couldn't understand why Mr Harrowood was so instant on getting him out the café or why he insisted on driving him home. It was only four p.m. but he wasn't about to argue.

"Are you going to tell my gran about what happened today... about Marvin?" asked Conor as they reached the Blackstone drive

"What thing... who's this Marvin you speak of?" smiled Mr Harrowood.

"Thanks," said Conor as he exited the car.

The lights being off surprised Conor as his

grandmother would usually have been at home but thinking nothing of it he opened the front door... "SURPRISE!" To Conor's horror, the house had been plastered with banners and balloons. His grandmother had organised a surprise party. The ladies began to approach Conor, but a flash from a camera had irked him.

"NO," yelped Conor as he burrowed his way through the women running upstairs to his room. The slam of the door echoed throughout the house.

Amelia chuckled forcefully. "Ah, bless him! First day of school probably tired him out. I'm sure he didn't mean anything by it," she said. "I think it best we leave it here, ladies."

The house emptied quickly as the other witches began murmuring disapprovingly as they headed home. Two hours had passed since Conor had gone to his room and with no sign of him emerging Amelia decided to check on him. Armed with a piece of cake, she headed upstairs. Knock, but there was no response. As Amelia began walking downstairs Conor's door slightly opened. Finally, a breakthrough, she thought, as she took the invitation and headed into the darkened room. As she entered she was surprised to see Conor was still in his uniform as he lay on his bed. She sat on the side.

"Are you mad that I ruined the party?" he mumbled.

"No, it's just a stupid party," replied Amelia.

"I heard your friends talking about you after they had left. They said some nasty things."

"They're a bunch of old bags. I don't care what they say about me."

Conor chuckled before sitting up.

"Was that a laugh I heard?"

"How do you do it, gran? How do you not let what people say get to you?" asked Conor.

"It's not like negative things don't annoy or hurt me but I promised your mother that I would take care of you so I don't have time to let what people say bother me. Besides if you choose to ignore what people say their words become nothing ... now I've got a piece of cake much too large for me to finish on my own and an extra fork here. Could you help me finish it?"

"Well, I guess I could help you. After all, if you tried to finish it yourself we'd be here all year."

"Why your cheeky little sod! Need I remind you I was quite the athlete in my day," she exclaimed .

"Yeah, like fifty years ago."

"Oi, one more jibe about my age and you'll be grounded for a week... you're just like your mother when she was your age."

"Gran, what was Mum like at my age?"

For the next hour Amelia began telling stories about what Conor's mother had been like when she was a child which ranged from sweet to absolutely bonkers. Conor also decided to tell his grandmother about some of the times they had remembered with his mother. While they were vague they brought a smile to Amelia's face.

"Heavens, you have school tomorrow. I'd best be off," remarked Amelia.

"Night, Gran."

The next morning saw Conor in a more upbeat mood. His grandmother's words had worked as he headed to the bus stop with a beaming smile but that smile would soon disappear as again he found himself an outcast as the bus went from blistering noise to quiet murmuring and pointing. He had figured word had got out about his fight with Marvin. Conor quickly darted off the bus to get some fresh air as he did not want to hear the rumours that were undoubtedly going to be spread about him.

"WAIT!" yelped Conor suddenly.

But it was too late. The school bus had driven off without him. Conor sighed as he began to walk. A faint ringing sound could be heard in the distance. It was the school bell; he was going to be late. He began to run frantically but as he reached the front gates he saw Marvin entering the building. He came to a dead halt and without thinking Conor pulled his wand out and uttered "*Espectral*". He was now invisible. If there had been one positive about missing the bus it was that Conor was sure that Marvin would be gone before the end of the school year as in the five minutes he had been following him, Marvin had managed to get five detentions. It must have been some sort of record, Conor thought, as he finally slipped past Marvin and headed for registration.

Conor began to wonder if he had reversed his invisibility as he certainly still felt it and his teachers didn't help either forcing Ryan to sit beside him for every lesson and handing out detentions to anyone who dared ask him a question. But during lunch something amazing happened. Conor's table was packed full of students wanting to hear about the fight. There hadn't been much to talk about but it was a start, he thought. For the first time that day Conor hadn't wanted the school bell to sound. He was having fun but it did and along with it came Ryan who had gone to inform Mr Allister he wouldn't be able to go to football training.

"You ready for DT?" asked Ryan.

"Can't wait," beamed Conor.

Design and Technology had been his second favourite lesson, the first being PE. He had got to know the teacher Miss Joyce at his council meeting. She was the only one who had been nice to him. Eager and in no mood to hang about, Conor and Ryan sped through the corridors and up the stairs but as entered the classroom they were stunned to see Marvin sitting at front of the classroom looking forward almost as if he was focused.

"Are you sure this is the right room?"

"I'm sure," muttered Ryan.

"So why is he in there?" said Conor through gritted

teeth.

Ryan shrugged, unsure of what to say. Conor then grunted as another class without Marvin would've been heaven but you can't have it all your own way, he smirked, as he re-entered the classroom. It hadn't been long before it was full as Miss Joyce was well renowned for being quirky and bringing much needed life to an otherwise drab subject. She started as she always did instructing the children to join her in reciting the school motto. A cry of *SATIS EST OPTIMUM* rang out. This had meant Your best is good enough...

Miss Joyce then explained what they were going to do this year but as she began go into greater detail, she was interrupted by constant chatting from Marvin with his twin brother Simon. Seeing Miss Joyce looking in their direction Marvin apologised and Miss Joyce continued for a few more minutes before again being interrupted by the pair again.

"That's it, Simon. Swap places with Conor now."

Conor instantly looked up. Had he heard correctly? Had Miss Joyce not heard that he and Marvin had just been in a fight?

"Why, Miss?" bemoaned Marvin.

"Yeah, Miss. I don't like him. Can't anyone else move?" said Conor.

"Quiet both of you. My word is final and before you say I am aware you had an altercation recently but this is a new day and I feel this will give you the chance to iron out your differences so enough of the whining and move, Conor," she ordered.

Annoyed, Conor contemplated whether to defy Miss Joyce's orders but quickly decided against it not wanting to get sent to Mr Gravethorpe's office for a second straight day. He then reluctantly got up and sat next to Marvin. Both boys tried their best to make one another uncomfortable with Conor leaning into Marvin whenever they had to write something. In return, Marvin, much taller than Conor, began to stretch forcing the young witch towards the edge of the table. As the tension between the two boys was about to reach boiling point Miss Joyce welcomed students to the front to collect some wood and tools as for the term they would be making their own dummy wands. Both boys leapt out of their seats and raced to the front with Conor just edging out Marvin.

The table shuddered as Conor returned to his seat and began to file down his wood. Happy with his progress he smiled but better still Marvin began to curse as he struggled. The young witch's smile design and technology was fast becoming his favourite subject. "He looks like he's gonna pop," whispered Conor.

"In need of something Conor?" asked Miss Joyce.

"No, Miss. I just wanted to tell Ryan... I'll just do it after class," said Conor as he moved away.

"Could I speak to you outside, Conor?" said Miss Joyce.

Conor gulped. What had he done now? Once outside he began apologising thinking Miss Joyce had seen him and Ryan teasing Marvin but to his surprise Miss Joyce began looking at him bewildered. But if hadn't been about teasing Marvin, why had she wanted to talk to him? "I won't do it," whispered Conor. He'd began wishing he had got caught teasing Marvin as Miss Joyce's request had been the worst thing imaginable. She had wanted him to help Marvin with his wand.

"I seem to remember during your council meeting you mentioning a willingness to work with all."

"Oh, all right but he won't let me," said Conor skulking back towards the classroom. After he had returned Conor remained quiet for a few seconds thinking what to say. He had it. "I---"

"Leave me alone," barked Marvin.

"Fine, enjoy your crooked wand," Conor sighed.

"You have to file your wood vertically so it's smooth."

"Thanks, Blackpepp ... Conor."

For the remainder of the lesson Conor and Marvin began chatting with the boys discovering that they had many shared interests. A happy Miss Joyce looked on with a smile on her face as the school day drew to a close. "All right everyone, tools down," she said.

KNOCK!

But before Miss Joyce couldn't even say "who is it?" the door opened and a small man stepped in. It was Mr Marto, the caretaker. He had to collect those who had detention that day. Miss Joyce stood aside as Mr Marto in his grizzly voice called out Conor, Marvin, Ryan and finally Simon and instructed them to follow him.

The bell had barely been sounding for a minute when the usually deserted hallway became full with hyperactive children from every angle. But this hadn't put Mr Marto off his task. He remained vigilant, his movements pincer-like. "You'd be wise to follow me. Last boy that tried to skip detention..." Mr Marto allowed himself a chuckle.

"What happened to him?" whimpered Ryan.

"Let's just say his mum had to keep a close eye on their cat,"

The hallway began to empty allowing Mr Marto and the boys to continue. To their surprise they had been led outside to the abandoned classroom.

"How can we have detention in here?" asked Marvin furiously

"Is it even safe?" asked Conor, sure he had seen the classroom move as the wind blew by.

"Stop your whingeing. The council including your grandmother said we could use it," croaked Mr Marto. "About bloody time too ... now get in," snapped the caretaker pulling the door open.

"Ahhh, look what you've done, you mug," wailed Simon as the dust from the door covered his waistcoat.

"Something funny," he barked, glaring at Conor and Ryan.

"No" said the boys in unison, trying their hardest not to snigger as they entered the classroom.

The room itself was dark and dingy. The stench of gone off newt eyes was present. The floors were creaky. There had been no seats, only four benches lined in a row facing a solitary blackboard and desk and as the boys went to sit down, Mr Marto swiftly left the room.

"You'd think they'd spruce the place up a bit after all we're not criminals," whispered Ryan brushing cobwebs off the bench.

But the conversation went no further as the door creaked open. Headmaster Gravethorpe had arrived. His hands were full, a bunch of papers in the right and a sand timer in the left. He placed them on the desk before walking towards the middle of the room stopping only once to glare at Conor. "Thirty minutes," he said robotically. "No noise otherwise you'll be joining me again tomorrow."

The sand dripped slowly. Each boy passed the time differently with Ryan following a fly. Conor too found himself in an unusual predicament. He had taken to watching Mr Gravethorpe seeing how many times he'd tug at his ear whilst marking fifty-seven in case you were wondering. But as the end approached Conor couldn't help but notice Simon and Marvin whispering while looking back at him. What were they talking about, he thought, but before his thought could go any further Mr Gravethorpe rose to speak. "You are free to go I—"

The floor suddenly trembled as Marvin and Simon bolted from the room. Mr Gravethorpe just stared before turning to face Conor and Ryan. "Tell those two they have detention again." Both boys nodded before leaving the room. Feeling guilty that Ryan had missed football practice Conor offered to buy him something from Harrowood's café.

"So how was it sitting next to Marvin?" asked Ryan ripping his tie off. "This thing doesn't half chafe."

"It actually wasn't that bad. He's quite nice when you get to know him. You could say we're friends now," said Conor smirking.

"Oh!" grunted Ryan, the jealousy in his voice apparent.

"Don't worry. I'm sure Marvin will still let me talk to you but then again, I probably won't have the time... be too busy with the cool people," chortled Conor.

But Ryan who had been further up the road hadn't found it funny quickly turning the corner as they neared Harrowood's café. "Oh, come on I was only joking," said Conor. "You should learn—". Conor stopped dead. He had now known why Ryan had said nothing as standing before them was Simon and Marvin. Both sets of boys remained silent, just staring, Conor was first to move stepping slightly in front of Ryan. He knew he would have to be clever to defuse this situation but he then went to speak and before his lips even moved Marvin pulled out his wand and bellowed "CONFUSIS".

Conor flew backwards and began to fade into darkness. Had it been a minute, maybe two, possibly ten? How long had he been out ? The sound of Ryan's pleas had brought him round. Conor's eyes flashed open. "Please don't," quivered Ryan again. "That's his mum's wand"

"Oh, really," said Marvin coldly. "How quickly do you think I'd be able to snap, Simon?"

"Not sure," giggled Simon. "Probably a minute."

Conor looked on hopelessly. He tried his hardest to get to his feet but his body failed him. The sound of the wand bending quickly became too much for him and he quickly shut his eyes thinking that hearing the snap would be less painful than seeing it. For a moment, everything was silent. Suddenly as large pops rang out Conor's eyes flashed open. There had been a hand in his face.

"Come on, we have to go," said Ryan frantically.

"What did you do?" asked Conor, gingerly getting to his feet.

"I froze them, it should last about three minutes if I did it right."

"Let's hope so," said Conor staring at his now frozen foes. "Let's split up. You go to your dad's shop and I will hide out in the forest."

"I'm not sure," murmured Ryan. "But if you think it best?"

"I do."

The two boys went their separate ways. Conor had been halfway across the road before he stopped and hurried back. He had forgotten his wand but as he prised it out of Marvin's hand, he was sure he felt Marvin tug back. Had the spell been wearing off already? Not wanting to find out, Conor scuttled away. Ten minutes had passed since Conor had entered the forest. He decided to text Ryan but as he reached for his phone the sound of ringing echoed with a voice quickly accompanying it.

"Marvin," whispered Conor, stunned. How had he known where he would be? But there was no time to think about that as Marvin was approaching and fast. Conor then thought of what do next but his thought was brief as he remembered that there was a cave located at the far end of the forest but to get there, he would need a distraction and fast. Suddenly something caught Conor's eye. It was rock. He quickly slithered over towards it and threw it.

THUMP!

The rock ricocheted off a tree before landing. Conor then peered over a rock; the sight of Marvin trudging off was wondrous. He then headed for the cave sure that Marvin would be returning. The cave was dark but a quick shake and flick of his wand soon changed that. He began slowly walking through. The sight of discarded crisp packets as well as a blanket was troubling but he'd rather be here than out there with Marvin. *Snap!* Conor turned swiftly but nobody was there as he continued on. The sound of twigs breaking hadn't stopped Conor who was sure Marvin had found him.

He then let out a huge breath before clutching his wand tightly. The footsteps from behind him grew louder and louder. Completely ravaged by fear, Conor, with his eyes firmly shut, began firing in every direction. The cave resembled that of a firework display as flashes of spells bounced around it.

"Wait!" squeaked a voice.

Stunned, Conor's eyes flashed open as he slowly began advancing through the cave not lowering his wand once. Suddenly a small hooded figure slowly began creeping from behind a rock. The figure stopped before slowly lowering its hood. Conor gasped then lowered his wand as what stood before him had not been a Marvin but a girl.

CHAPTER FOUR

NOT ENOUGH TEE FOR TWO

The two young children stared at each other, their hearts racing. Both were nervous as not a word had been uttered. Conor had completely forgotten about Simon and Marvin as he looked on in awe, fascinated by the girl who stood before him "My names C-C-Conor. What's yours?" he stuttered finally.

The girl remained unmoved.

"I haven't seen you in school. Are you new?" Again the girl said nothing then moved forward as did Conor but this seemed to discourage the girl who instantly reverted to her robot-like state. Disappointed and annoyed at himself, Conor decided to leave but as he was leaving the cave filled with laughter.

"I'm sorry, I couldn't do it anymore," said the girl, who continued to laugh.

"You couldn't do what?" said Conor stepping back into the cave.

"Act like a robot as you were about to leave."

"Oh!" laughed Conor awkwardly. "Do you have a name?"

"I do but my parents said I shouldn't talk to strangers let alone give them my name. But since you kindly spared my life, I guess I owe you. My name is Tee with two ees."

"Tee?" questioned Conor.

"It's not my real name," she said, "I just met you... but

it's a clue to my real name."

"A clue?"

"Yes, a clue. My name is similar to the name of a tea."

Conor began to rethink his approach to Tee. She seemed bubbly, energetic and full of life, everything he wasn't. He knew he had to show he was a bit more excitable as his normally conservative approach would surely bore her and then began think of ways to seem flashier. The ruffling of leaves had disturbed Conor's train of thought. He glanced downwards and saw it was the same snake he had previously encountered. He froze and his fidgety fingers went numb.

"Are you afraid of snakes?" asked Tee as she approached the snake.

"Are you crazy? Don't you know what those things can do to you?" blurted Conor. Still unfazed, Tee simply allowed the snake to slither through her fingers as she stroked it and it hissed its tongue in approval. She then stepped out of the cave allowing the snake to slide away.

"You said your parents said you shouldn't speak to strangers. Didn't they also tell never to touch a snake?" asked a perplexed Conor.

"I know how to handle snakes. There are a bunch of them where I used to live. They're a little scary but if you treat them right there's no trouble," replied Tee.

"What crazy town did you come from that would allow you to handle those deadly things? Don't you know that their venom is near fatal to us?" bemoaned Conor.

"Near fatal! What are you talking about? I know it can be dangerous but they have vaccinations for that."

"What are you talking about?" said a stunned Conor. "There aren't any cures for witches or wizards to pure snake venom."

"I'm not a wizard or a witch," laughed Tee.

"So, what are you?" A normal?" Conor said jokingly.

"What's a normal?"

Conor's stunned facial expression had caught Tee off guard but not wanting to agitate the situation she merely brushed it off. "A normal is a person without any magical essence," said Conor informatively.

"Very funny, you're trying to get back at me, aren't you?" said Tee.

But Conor's face remained unchanged. Bemused, Tee looked on and began to wonder why her new friend had been acting strangely. Briefly, it crossed her mind that maybe Conor in fact was not normal but that thought quickly passed as they looked similar. There were no glaring differences. Each had two eyes, four fingers and a thumb. Tee decided to ask some very vague questions to see if she could unearth where she was or who or what she had been speaking to.

"So, do you live in the forest?" she asked.

"No, I live in Ravensborough."

Odd, Tee thought. She had never seen a place called Ravensborough on any map in school. She had only known this place to be Kenbury Forest so decided to ask another question.

"Has Ravensborough always existed?"

"Of course, it's been around for hundreds of years. I know you're new to the area but didn't your parents tell you anything about the place you were moving to?"

These weren't the answers that Tee had been hoping for so she scrapped the vagueness and got straight to the point "Conor, if you don't mind me asking what are you?"

"You promise not to laugh."

"Promise."

"I'm a witch."

These words hit Tee like a speeding car. She stumbled back and began to smile and giggle unable to properly process what she had just heard.

"I knew I never should have told you," shouted Conor running out of the cave.

"Wait!" Feeling terrible, Tee quickly exited the cave and then sat on the far end of a log as Conor had been on the other side. "Why did you run out of the cave?" she asked.

"You're brand new to Ravensborough and you're already laughing at me...I'm the town freak," sighed Conor

Tee, feeling even more guilty, moved further around the log. "I wasn't laughing because you're a witch. I just laugh whenever I'm shocked or nervous. It's a lot easier than talking. I think you being the only boy witch is cool.... It makes you unique."

Conor smiled. He and Tee spent the next few hours chatting away about their lives. They discovered that while there were some big differences, they still shared many things such as a shared love for sports and both being thirteen. Tee raised the subject of family by showing Conor a picture of hers. Conor decided to be honest with her. Although they had only known each other a few hours he felt he could trust her.

"That must be tough living in a house with three brothers and a dad," said Conor.

"It can be... do you have any siblings?"

"No, it's just me and my gran. My mum died when I was young."

"I'm sorry to hear that. I guess if there's a silver lining you get whatever you want and don't have to share anything... no that's a stupid thing to say. Sorry."

"It's fine. Stop apologising, I don't want you feeling sorry for me," smiled Conor. "What's more worrying is how much you like ketchup. It's absolutely rank."

"I'll have you know ketchup counts as one of your five a day."

As nightfall set in Ravensborough Tee knew that she had to leave but was unsure of how without causing suspicion. She looked at her wrist as the moonlight shone on her bracelet. "I've got to go now but I want you to have this," she said.

"I can't," said Conor holding the bracelet in his hands

"Please…besides it's another clue to my name. It's my initials," chuckled Tee.

"But I don't have anything to give to you," said Conor regrettably. "I could walk you home instead."

"No," replied Tee suddenly. "My dad doesn't like it when I bring home people unannounced."

Tee stood up and began to walk off but before she disappeared into the shadows she turned around to wave to Conor.

"When am I going to see you again?" yelled Conor.

"I don't know. Maybe tomorrow, maybe never. I'll let you know."

"Aren't you going to tell me your name?"

"You're a witch. Figure it out."

Conor looked at the bracelet that Tee had given him and clutched it tightly. What a day, he thought. The evening breeze began to tickle his neck as he walked home. For the first time in a while his mind wasn't on Tee. He stopped, his eyes widened and he began to run. He had forgotten how he could have forgotten. He arrived in Durfold Street and ran towards his front door but as he began rifling through his blazer looking for his key the door opened.

"Conor Le…

"Don't say it," grunted Conor.

"Fine, but where on earth have you been?"

"I was at Ryan's house," lied a panting Conor.

"Don't lie to me. I spoke to Mrs Willows and she said you hadn't been there today so I'm going to ask again where you have been?"

Before Conor spoke, he contemplated what he should do. Whilst he hated lying to his grandmother he couldn't possibly tell her about Tee. He already had enough trouble trying to keeping his gran from inviting Ryan for sleepovers so he dreaded to think what she would say or do if she found out he had been with a girl.

"After last night, I couldn't stop thinking about Mum so I went to Mr Harrowood's café for a couple of hours to think and I lost track of the time…sorry for not calling."

"No," sighed Amelia. "I'm sorry for thinking you were doing something wrong and any time you're missing your mum let me know and we'll spend the whole day talking about her. Okay... now go and get ready for dinner."

"Okay," smiled Conor as he headed upstairs.

The rest of the school week seemed to breeze by as Conor found himself largely alone as Ryan had taken the rest of the week off ill. Conor suspected he had been trying to avoid Simon and Marvin, but that hadn't been the only reason why he had been unfocused as all Conor could think of was Tee. With the weekend fast approaching Conor decided he needed to keep busy so he arranged for himself and Ryan to visit his dragon who had been injured during the assessment.

The fog that Saturday morning was thick and heavy and the air was unforgivingly cold but Conor was determined to see his dragon. He was soon joined by Ryan but the walk to Witchhaven Valley was far from plain sailing as Conor's constant glancing at his phone followed by giggles soon began to annoy Ryan.

"Oi, give that back," said Conor chasing frantically after Ryan.

"Well, you've certainly been a busy boy haven't you" scoffed Ryan

"I have no idea what you're banging on about."

"Really, so you weren't laughing at these messages you were sending to somebody called Tee?" asked Ryan

"No."

"I don't know anyone in school called Tee. Is she new

or something?"

"Actually, she doesn't go to Ravensborough High. I think she goes to Christwood Academy."

"Oh, I thought you had no idea what I was talking about. Who is she and where did you meet?"

"Ah, she's amazing. I've never met anyone like her before. She's smart, funny and doesn't care about what people think about her and apart from you, my gran and Mr Harrowood she treats me like I'm normal and not a freak."

"So, is she your girlfriend or something?" asked Ryan grinning wildly.

"No, we're just friends. I don't even know her real name. She said it was similar to a flavour of tea," replied Conor

"It's probably Earl Grey. My mum drank gallons of the stuff before she had the baby."

"Earl Grey. That's a boy's name."

"No silly, that's the name of the tea. Her name is probably something like Emma."

"You think?" gushed Conor.

"I don't know and as much as I love discussing the potential name of a girl, I've never met my dad was expecting us like twenty minutes ago so can we make a move," said Ryan.

"Fine," sighed Conor.

As the two boys continued walking the once thick fog began to clear and the late September sun appeared, dull and uninspiring as ever. "Finally, my legs are killing me," sighed Ryan. But unlike before, Conor was not in awe. As they reached the valley the wondrous allure had vanished and had been replaced by frenzied panic as a stampede of people hurtled towards them. "Come on, I think we should go," said Conor, but Ryan remained unmoved as he began scanning the onrushing throng. "No," he whispered before disappearing into the crowd. Stunned, Conor looked on motionless. "Of course,, Mr Willows," he said and without giving it a second thought sped through the crowd. The once vivacious valley had become a shell. A smoky aroma filled the air and each building Conor passed had been damaged.

"What happened?" he murmured to himself, but the young witch wouldn't have to wait long for an answer as a familiar figure presented itself. "Stick---", but before Conor could even finish his sentence he dove frantically for cover as balls of fire hurtled towards him. This didn't make sense, thought Conor, his breathing finally returning to normal. What had happened to Sticky and where was Ryan and Mr Willows? In need of answers Conor re-emerged but he was met with an earth-shattering thud as his dragon charged towards him. Again, Conor found himself diving for cover.

SNAP!

Time seemed to stand still as Conor held his mother's shattered wand in his hand. His breathing became heavier. Seeing red, he then charged towards his dragon. The ground shuddered as the dragon tried to shake Conor off. A piercing screech reverberated through the valley as Conor drove the wand into Sticky's wing, and again the ground shuddered as the dragon collapsed. Conor stood over the dragon his eyes still full of fury ready to drive the wand into the wound one final time but as he was in mid motion he saw his reflection in his dragon's eyes. Disgusted by what he saw he threw his wand to the side. Just then the dragon returned to its original size and Conor picked it up.

Mr Willows and Ryan emerged to find an inconsolable Conor looking for help for his dragon. "Get over here, it's dangerous. I told you that dragon was going to be trouble," bellowed Mr Willows.

"I can't leave him, he needs help. Is there anything

you can do to save him?" pleaded Conor.

"Son, have a word with your mate. You know that dragon is dangerous. Just look what he did to my store and the rest of the valley. We have to look after our own," snarled Mr Willows.

"No, Ryan, tell your dad to help my dragon. Somebody must have done something to him. You know he's not capable of this."

Ryan was at a crossroads as he looked at both people asking for his help. As he looked at his father he saw someone who he respected immensely and who had just seen their livelihood destroyed before their very eyes and the culprit was a few feet away from them. He then looked at Conor. Who was he to take one of the few friends Conor had away from him? Both sides had valid points but ultimately Ryan had decided to side with Conor.

"Help the dragon, Dad. It needs your help," said Ryan.

"Are you having a laugh? You want me to help the dragon that has essentially put me out of business. Give me one good reason why I should?" Mr Willows asked.

"Because you once told me that I should help those in the greatest need."

"You're a good lad and one hell of a friend, Conor. Bring him over,"

"Here, please help him" wept Conor.

"His wing has been damaged and all my supplies were in the shop so I going to have to take him to the hospital to fix him up. Whilst I go there you boys head back into town."

The boys nodded and hastily departed. The walk back into Ravensborough was brutal as the fresh rain drenched them. Ryan wondered whether he had made the right decision as the seriousness of the situation dawned on him; he soon began to wonder if Conor would have made the same decision if the positions had been switched not to mention that Conor hadn't even spoken to him since they were at Witchhaven Valley which hurt him the most.

Similarly, Conor wondered if he had made the right decision. Maybe Mr Willows had been right all along that Sticky had been in trouble. A feeling of guilt began to come over him as the more he thought about his actions the more he regretted them; he had put his own selfish desires before everyone else's.

The slamming of the door had caught Conor by surprise. Had he done something wrong? But with nothing springing to mind he chalked it up to being the wind. A good night's sleep had allowed Conor to approach the day in a more positive light starting with him calling Ryan to thank him for his efforts yesterday. The conversation was brief as Ryan was still upset about yesterday but he accepted Conor's request; he wasn't going to pass up on a free lunch at Harrowood's.

A moment passed before Conor had realised what had truly transpired. OH NO he had just remembered he had agreed to meet Tee today panic was washed across the young witches face, his fingers began to twitch as he held his phone surely Ryan would understand; they were best friends after all they could meet another day but after yesterday he had pull through for his friend just then the same fingers that were twitching with nervousness began twitching with excitement as Conor had thought of the most brilliant plan and with that the young witch headed out.

The sounds of birds tweeting could be heard as he walked towards the entrance of Kenbury Forest. He then began waving as the person he'd chosen to meet had arrived.

"What did you want to show me, Conor? I'm absolutely starving," said Ryan.

"I think I spotted that thing we saw in the forest. It was near the cave. Follow me!" said Conor.

He began running towards the cave leaving Ryan lagging behind and as he reached it he softly began to call out for Tee not wanting to alert Ryan. Tee then emerged from the cave clutching a ball in her hands.

"I remember you bragging about how skilled you were so I thought you could show me or are you afraid to be shown up by a girl?" scoffed Tee.

"I'm offended that you have called into question my footballing ability."

But as Conor went to snatch the ball off Tee his name began to ring out. A panicked Conor quickly grabbed Tee before sprinting for the cave.

"What's going on?" asked Tee. "Are you in trouble?"

"It's those boys who were after me the day I met you," he lied. "We should stay in here. I'm sure they'll go away."

"No," squealed Tee. "You can't let them bully you," she added, stomping out of the cave.

"Wai----". But it was no use. Tee was gone. Conor's name rang out again. It sounded quite a distance away. This was good, Conor thought, as it would give him enough time to think of a way of getting Tee back into the cave.

Conor stepped out of the cave to see Ryan and Tee engaging in a shouting match. This was not what he wanted.

"Conor, are you not going to introduce me to your new friend?" asked Ryan.

"Of course, Tee this is my best friend, Ryan" said Conor.

"Hi, I'm sorry for giving you a hard time."

"No worries. I'm actually glad since he can't stop banging on about you," scoffed Ryan.

"Really," giggled Tee.

Conor glared at Ryan intensely.

"I'm starving. Do you guys want to grab a bite to eat?" asked Conor. "My treat."

"That would be great especially since you owe me lunch," remarked Ryan.

"What about you Tee? Do you want to come? You never know, if you're lucky I'll buy you some tea," laughed Conor.

Tee's belly grumbled. She had been hungry, desperately hungry.

"If I come I get to order anything I want but no tea. I hate the stuff," said Tee.

Tee began to become comfortable in her surroundings. It was nothing like she had read about and didn't seem to be any different to what she had been accustomed to. She then began to think why such slanderous and untruthful things had been written about Ravensborough.

Mr Harrowood had spotted Conor and Ryan through the window. He began waving indicating for them to enter the café. Ryan was so hungry. He marched to the counter to give his order as he and Mr Harrowood talked. Conor had invited Tee to choose a table and she had chosen the one towards the back.

"So, is there anything in particular that you want?" asked Conor.

"You're the local here, pick something and I'll get it. I trust your judgement."

"Okay, I will but I'm not going to tell you what I'm getting you," chuckled Conor.

"What, why?" asked Tee instantly regretting her decision.

"I thought you trusted my judgement," said Conor.

Conor stood up and joined Ryan at the front as he placed his order. Tee looked on as both Conor and Ryan began play fighting. "I'm not made of money," said Conor stunned by the amount Ryan had ordered. *Buzz*! Tee's phone began to ring. Not now, she thought, ignoring it but the buzzing was relentless as a barrage of text messages quickly followed. Left with no choice, Tee quickly checked her phone to make sure that it hadn't been important. As she peered at it another message arrived. As the name popped up Tee began to shake her head in annoyance as the messages had been from Edward Upton, a boy from her class.

The aroma of the food had become more potent. Tee looked up as Conor and Ryan approached. Tee's decision had been made and she hastily switched off her phone before sliding it into her pocket.

"Great, the food is here. I'm starving. Which is mine?" asked Tee, staring at the mountain of chips piled on Ryan's plate

Conor and Ryan looked at each other before bursting out laughing. Unsure about whether she had missed out on a joke, Tee began laughing as well. Feeling bad Conor explained that as she was a new customer her food was going to be brought to her personally by Mr Harrowood who wanted to get to know his new customers better.

"So, who is this young lady?" asked Mr Harrowood.

As Tee looked up to respond to Mr Harrowood she was taken aback as she was sure she had met him before, but was unsure where. She decided not to pursue her suspicion as asking questions would garner unwanted attention.

"Hi, I'm new to town and these two said I had to sample some of your food as it's the best in all of Ravensborough."

"While I don't like to blow my own horn, but I'd tend to agree with what the lads have told you," chortled Mr Harrowood.

Emily smiled. With the niceties over Mr Harrowood left them to finish their meal as the afternoon transitioned to the evening and with Harrowood's closing soon Conor looked at Ryan. The boys then began speaking with their eyes and hands. Conor wanted to know whether he should ask Tee about her real name. Ryan gestured that Conor should bite the bullet and ask.

"So, Tee I just wanted to know--- I just wanted to know if you enjoyed the meal?"

"Yes, it was lovely thanks. I'm glad I came after all," she said.

"Look, Tee, are you going to tell us your real name or what?" said Ryan forcefully.

Tee began smirking as she looked at them.

"You still haven't guessed yet."

"We think we've figured it out but we're not sure. I think your name is Emma Grey while Ryan thinks its Emily Grey," muttered Conor.

"Since you brought me a meal, I guess the least I can give you is my real name."

"Oh really... how kind of you," remarked Conor smirking as he did so.

"It's Emily Grey."

"I knew it," said Ryan triumphantly.

"Oh no," gasped Emily suddenly robbing the young wizard of a chance to gloat.

"What is it?" asked Conor sharply.

But silence was the only response heard. She had forgotten how she could have forgotten and without thinking she sped towards the door. The café remained silent for a brief moment but they soon screeched as Conor exited. The young witch's frantic search had to this point proved fruitless as he entered Kenbury Forest. "Tee, are you there?" he howled twice but much to his relief a familiar voice replied on the third attempt.

"What happened? Why did you leave? Was it something I did?" Emily remained quiet as she pondered what to do next. She couldn't reveal the truth but she didn't want Conor thinking she'd had a bad time, but a glint in the distance soon came to her aid as she knew what she had to do. "My ball!" I forgot my ball. My brother will kill me if I don't bring it home."

"Oh, ha-ha," spewed Conor not wanting to say

anything. "I'll help you find it." Very few words were spoken.

"I've found it, Conor," yelled Emily.

"That's great. Do you mind if I ask you a question?" enquired Conor nervously.

"Sure, what is it?"

"Why is that whenever I ask about your former town you shy away?" asked Conor.

"I'm not sure really. I don't have any bad memories, it's just when you constantly move from city to city, town to town you never really have a chance to get to know the place and create memories."

"I'm sorry... you don't have to continue if you don't want to," said Conor.

"Thanks," Emily smiled.

Feeling awful about making Emily reveal her past Conor thought he should ask if she wanted him to walk her home but before he could his back pocket began to glow as he began to ascend. Conor shook his head. "Ryan," he bellowed.

Once on the ground Conor began rifling through all his pockets before pulling out the wizard transportation note which simply read in block capitals *"NEVER KEEP A WILLOWS HUNGRY"*. Conor then began cursing as he made the short walk up Durfold Street.

CHAPTER FIVE

A FATEFUL WHISPER

The weekend's events had taken its toll on Conor. It had exhausted him so much to the extent that by the time Monday morning had arrived he was glad as it meant structure and normality for at least five days. He had decided against taking the bus as he wanted to avoid Ryan whom he still resented for his actions. As he arrived at Ravensborough High he was stunned to see every student lined up with their registration class. Professor Marigold gestured towards Conor who rushed to the back of the line where it was explained that Headmaster Gravethorpe had called an emergency assembly. The teachers began talking amongst themselves trying to figure out why leaving the children unattended. Whilst waiting in line Conor noticed Ryan had not yet arrived which was odd considering that he prided himself on his attendance and punctuality. But something else soon had the young witch's focus as the tannoy screeched.

It was Gravethorpe. "Would all year nine classes report to the assembly hall immediately" he cackled proudly. Sighs could be heard in the playground as the students got themselves into an orderly fashion.

Conor's class was last to be let in. "WAITTTTTTTTTTT!" yelped a despondent Ryan, his thumping and frantic footsteps lagging behind. But with his friend's word on the note still buzzing around his head Conor feebly shrugged before re-joining the line.

"Why would you do that?" whispered Ryan, still

trying to catch his breath

Conor remained unmoved.

"I know I promised I wouldn't use it again but you were taking an eternity and I got worried thinking something had happened to you."

"I'm not angry that you used the note. I'm angry that you thought I couldn't look after myself," moaned Conor breaking his vow of silence.

"I know, it's just I've never had a best mate before and I couldn't forgive myself if something happened to you."

Conor's stone like demeanour began to crumble as even though he hated to admit it he'd have done the same. But not wanting to give his friend the fullest satisfaction he meekly mustered a "we're good". Ryan smiled, glad to be back in his best mate's good books.

"I never thought I'd see the day that Ryan Willows was late for school. What happened?" chuckled Conor. This had brought a scowl from a teacher the class in front of theirs. "Don't get me started. Firstly, I woke up late then my dad begged me to help him move his supplies to the new shop and on the way there the car broke down and to top it off I forgot my school bag," sighed Ryan.

Conor began chuckling softly.

"What's going on? Why is there an assembly?"

"I'm not sure. I was going to ask you the same thing. Does he call many assemblies?"

"No, actually come to think of it last year was the only time he called a non-scheduled assembly. It was to issue a school-wide ban of using magic outside the classroom."

"Will you two zip it? We're about to go in," ordered a visibly nervous Professor Marigold.

The room they had entered was not the regular assembly hall. It was a small room barely big enough to fit every student. Being the last class in, Conor and his fellow classmates were forced to stand. The tension in the room was electric as every face mirrored one another. Even

Simon and Marvin were devoid of emotion. The overriding sense of fear was evident. It had even transmitted to the teachers who anxiously looked towards the door.

"Why aren't we in the normal hall, Marigold?" grunted Simon nudging his thicker shoulder brother.

"Shhh please, Simon," whispered an almost frantic Professor Marigold. "And for the millionth time, it's Professor Marigold."

"He's done this on purpose," whispered Ryan breaking his friend's malaise "What have we done?" But the young witch's question was met with a hushing gesture as Mr Gravethorpe entered the room. The floor creaked joyfully as he walked towards the front. "Looking very sharp, Ryan," remarked the head teacher, now in his element. "Wow! Maybe we aren't in trouble," chirped Ryan smugly but the young wizard was soon to be mistaken as the room filled with Gravethorpe's voice. Eyes around the room became that of ping-pong balls as they frantically followed his footsteps who had launched a scathing attack on the teachers berating them for displaying weakness in not enforcing the school rules to the fullest. The barrage lasted ten minutes as more and more of the room, seemingly getting smaller by the minute, filled with the dastardly headmaster's raspy voice but the best was yet to come as he began individually to summon pupils to the front. "And why did you feel the school rules didn't apply to you?" he asked several times over before ushering each one by one to a corner of the room with his talon-like fingers. The number of students asked to the front exceeded double digits. The best however was saved to last as the rare sight of a grin began to permeate itself on the face of the orchestrator as the final two students were summoned.

"Masters Blackstone and Willows, will you join me at the front?" he asked in a devious manner.

All eyes were fixed on them as they walked towards the front of the hall.

"Take a look at that corner, gentlemen. What do you and those children have in common?".

"We broke school rules," mumbled Conor.

"Precisely, you broke the school rules but you did not just break them. You were the catalyst that made the other children think it was okay to imitate you," he sneered.

Marvin and Simon looked on with added interest. They still harboured resentment towards Conor and Ryan for what transpired after their detention as Gravethorpe continued bombarding Conor with questions. But Simon had devised a plan to ensure Conor would regret ever setting foot in Ravensborough High. He informed Marvin of his plan and as he went into detail Marvin began laughing softly before showing his understanding of what was required of him.

Humiliated, Conor and Ryan skulked over to the corner as Mr Gravethorpe had finished his public ousting of them. As there was barely any space left in the corner they were forced to stand by the doors. As they were bypassing the other students Simon nodded to Marvin who began following Conor and Ryan. Marvin then positioned himself behind Conor and Ryan before pushing Ryan to one side placing himself in between the two friends

"What are you doing? We don't want any trouble," said Ryan.

"Pipe down, Willows! I'm here to talk to Conor," snarled Marvin.

"Why do you want to speak me? Like Ryan said I don't want any trouble."

"What trouble? Oh forget what happened after detention, that's water under the bridge," replied Marvin.

"Really, so why do you want to speak to me?".

"I just wanted to let you know even though we don't always see eye to eye that I thought the way Gravethorpe treated you was wrong."

"Tell me about it. I'm sure that he has a problem with me. I just don't get it,".

"I hear you but don't you wish that he could feel the humiliation that he made you feel?" asked Marvin.

"Yes, but I'd rather show him by getting stuck in and proving him wrong," said Conor defiantly.

Mr Gravethorpe had reached the final part of his assembly where he announced that he was going to be enforcing new school rules with immediate effect. He then ordered a microphone to be brought as he wanted to ensure that every student and teacher was able to hear him. With the microphone in his hand he began to speak. His voice powerful as reverberated throughout the hall.

He cleared his throat but as he began to speak the microphone began to act strangely. His voice began to change going from one extreme to another as it turned demonically deep before turning ear-piercingly high. Hushed and then growing laughter emerged from the children. Mr Gravethorpe began snarling at them and threw the microphone to the ground bringing silence momentarily to the hall.

The silence did not remain long as the pupils began talking at what had just transpired. Seeing this, Mr Gravethorpe improvised asking Professor Marigold to provide him with a projector as he wanted to project the new rules. The projector was set up and the rules were beamed across the wall as Mr Gravethorpe ordered the children to recite the rules before taking a seat and rejoicing as the pupils spoke in unison. Laughter filled the hall which caught Mr Gravethorpe off guard. He rose from his seat and looked on in disbelief as the words on the wall were not the ones he had written but instead had been an unflattering picture from his youth. Incensed, he rushed over to the projector to remove the photo but as he went to grab it, it began to fly around the room.

The room became frantic as both teachers and Gravethorpe chased the photo around the hall. As this was happening Marvin began moving back towards the corner where Simon had been. The two boys then began to laugh as Simon expertly manipulated the paper around the hall. He began to toy with the teachers as he had made the photo reach the highest point of the hall before handing the wand to Marvin to complete the final part of the plan. As the photo gently floated down to the ground Mr Gravethorpe snatched it before stuffing it in his pocket.

"SILENCE AT ONCE," he ordered.

The room fell silent as the pupils returned to their seats while Marvin returned to standing beside Conor quietly slipping Simon's wand into the opening of Conor's bag.

"I DEMAND TO KNOW WHO IS RESPONSIBLE FOR THIS?" The hall remained silent. "Fine, if no one wants to claim responsibility for this but from today every student at Ravensborough High School will serve a detention after school for the remainder of the term."

This was met with disapproving murmurs and sighs.

Conor looked backwards towards Ryan asking him whether he had any idea of who could have been responsible but Ryan shrugged his shoulders. Mr Gravethorpe began walking back and forth at the front. He undid his tie as he rethought his approach because his normal demeanour was not bringing him any luck in finding the perpetrator.

"Students of Ravensborough High School I implore you to reveal the identity of the student who has allowed this assembly to descend into utter chaos. You remaining silent would only be doing them a disservice," he exclaimed .

As he continued to ramble Marvin proceeded to move closer to Conor. Feeling uneasy Conor placed his hand by his side intimating to Marvin to move. He felt his space but Marvin was persistently moving Conor's hand aside. Defeated, Conor allowed Marvin to prop himself beside him. Gravethorpe had finished speaking and as the final words passed through his lips Marvin leaned into Conor.

"I told you I'm the king," he whispered.

Unsure of what he had meant by that statement, Conor pushed Marvin away from him but the commotion had caught the eye of Gravethorpe who began walking towards them.

"Do you have some information that you would like to divulge with the rest of us?" he asked.

"No, Mr Gravethorpe," replied Conor.

Marvin who had retreated when Mr Gravethorpe arrived stood slightly in front of Conor before placing a hand on his shoulder.

"I'm sorry, Conor but I cannot remain silent anymore," muttered Marvin.

Marvin then spoke. He was eloquent and remained calm. He spoke slowly making sure not to mince his words. Conor looked on in horror as every lie that came from Marvin's mouth.

"LIES" growled Conor "he's lying it was him"

"ME" whimpered Marvin. "Weren't you the one who said some should teach Headmaster Gravethorpe a lesson".

Mr Gravethorpe asked whether he had uttered those words. Conor sighed and admitted he had but remained defiant that he had not sabotaged the assembly. Conor looked around the hall. Every face portrayed puzzlement and disbelief. Ryan stepped forward and dismissed the notion that Conor could have been guilty revealing to Mr Gravethorpe that Conor had broken his wand over the weekend. But again Marvin was quick to refute Ryan's claims claiming that Conor had given him this wand to keep for him but he had refused much to Conor's annoyance before panicking and stashing the wand in his bag.

Conor was seething by this point imploring Mr Gravethorpe to inspect his bag as he would just be wasting his time. Conor handed over his bag. His smirk was that of confidence. The sound of his bag hitting the floor caused him to turn around. The smirk had melted away as Mr Gravethorpe stood there with a wand in his hand. But this was not any wand, it was the wand that was an exact replica of his destroyed wand. Conor began frantically speaking pleading his innocence but it fell on deaf ears as both teachers and students began to look at Conor in shock and disbelief. Marvin began to chuckle softly which caught Conor's attention as it dawned on him that he had been set up by Marvin. Overwhelmed with rage, Conor launched himself at Marvin tackling him to the ground.

"Why? What have I ever done to you?" he shouted whilst throttling Marvin.

"I'm sorry, Conor. I know I promised I wouldn't tell but it wouldn't be fair on the other students to suffer for your actions," quivered Marvin.

"Stop lying, you know I didn't do it."

Before Conor could garner a response from Marvin the two boys were separated by Mr Gravethorpe and Ryan who did not want his friend to get into any further trouble.

Conor was ushered to the side with Gravethorpe instructing the teachers to take their students to class for registration. The hall began to empty quickly again. Professor Marigold's class was last to leave. Conor looked on disapprovingly while his classmates walked out of the room. How could they think that he was capable of such a thing? The last two students to leave the hall were Marvin and Simon and as they walked past Conor, Simon told Marvin to bow before placing an imaginary crown over his head.

Professor Marigold's class remained silent as they walked back to the classroom but the silence was broken as Marvin and Simon re-joined the line in triumphant mood. They began laughing and congratulating each other on executing their plan. The laughing began to annoy Ryan

"I know it was you two" he then snarled. "I'm telling, sir"

"I don't think so Willows. You've seen what we're capable of so you'd be wise to get back in line and keep your mouth shut otherwise your year will become a lot worse," hissed Simon.

Although the thought of his friend being unfairly excused sickened him Ryan realised that ultimately it would just be his word against that of Simon and Marvin's before he begrudgingly got back in line.

Conor was surprised by the response that Gravethorpe had afforded him as there was no change in attitude nor was there any shouting directed at him.

"Master Blackstone, you shall help me clear up the hall before we head to my office to discuss your punishment.".

They finished their tasks before heading to Mr Gravethorpe's office.

"Master Blackstone, do you remember what you promised the council when you stood before us all those months ago?" he asked.

"I do. I said that I would hold the school's motto in the highest regard and respect my fellow peers," replied Conor.

"Do you feel that you have lived by those promises because since you have been attending Ravensborough High School you have been nothing but disruptive?"

"While I'd admit that I have not had the easiest start, I did not disrupt that assembly today. It was Marvin. He framed me," barked Conor.

"Master Blackstone, I've had enough of these outlandish accusations. What reason would Marvin have to frame you and why you remain so defiant astounds me especially when there is irrefutable evidence pointing to you being the culprit; you have to take responsibility for your actions. I want you to issue an apology to your peers for wasting their time with preposterous allegations," demanded Mr Gravethorpe.

"No, I refuse to apologise and I refuse to take responsibility for something I did not do but I'm not going to waste my breath arguing. It's clear, you do not like me."

"For the millionth time Master Blackstone I harbour no resentment towards you. I am an educator who only has my students' best interests at heart," he stressed.

"I don't believe you. From the moment we met at the town hall I've felt the way you have been around me tentative, uneasy and miserable is because I'm a witch. That's why you sabotaged my assessment," sneered Conor.

"ENOUGH... how dare you! Before I became headmaster Ravensborough High School was only available to the elite wizards of our community, something that I fought tirelessly to abolish. So, before you accuse me of having a hatred towards witches, I suggest you do your research."

"I'm sorry, I had no idea," said Conor.

"I have nothing more to say, just head to class."

Conor slowly left the office. The remainder of the school day seemed to pass quickly as everyone remained on edge waiting for Mr Gravethorpe to respond. Two hours had passed since the school day had ended. Gravethorpe had remained in his office mulling over what had just transpired. Conor's word had struck a nerve with him causing him to call an emergency meeting with the teachers as a drastic change was in order.

The teachers waited outside his office. They were highly anxious as they were unsure of what to expect but before any of them were able to talk they had been summoned into the office. Various chairs had been positioned across the room and a giant whiteboard had been placed in the middle of the room with the words CONOR BLACKSTONE written in block capitals.

"While still in its infancy, this term at Ravensborough High School has been highly eventful and one of the most stressful I've encountered in my twenty years as headmaster and this can be attributed to one factor," he said pointing towards the board.

"Conor?" asked Miss Joyce.

"With all due respect, Mortimer while I understand that there have been some teething problems integrating Conor into school life, I find it a tad harsh to blame this entirely on him," said Professor Marigold.

"While I respect your opinion Cornelius, I have a duty to every pupil that attends my school so I have decided to place Master Blackstone on the witches' timetable as I feel that he would benefit being with people that he can relate to."

"I think this is ridiculous. How is relocating Conor going to help his transition to full time schooling and removing him from his friends?" questioned Miss Joyce.

"Are you sure that you are making the right decision? While I haven't taught him yet he seems to be a nice chap," added Mr Allister.

"Mortimer, listen to us. I know you have the best interests of the pupils in mind but removing Conor from the wizard timetable will be detrimental to the others as they won't fully have the chance to make a new friend and learn that our differences are insignificant," pleaded Professor Marigold.

"I know it seems that I'm being the villain but he has got into a fight and seems unwilling to make multiple friends not to mention what he did today. I am not going to change my mind on this. Starting tomorrow Master Blackstone will no longer be on the wizards' timetable."

His statement had been the final one of the meeting but as the teachers left the office they could not help but feel there was an ulterior motive behind his decision. However, the teachers respected him because of his longevity and stewardship of the school.

The following day Conor arrived at Ravensborough High unusually early as he was determined to make amends as the magnitude of what Mr Gravethorpe had endured; the ridicule and threats that had been levelled his way all to ensure that witches would no longer be discriminated against and denied the right to attend school. This had been explained to Conor in great detail by his grandmother. Gravethorpe was in his office as he began to recite to himself the way he was going to inform Conor of his decision to remove him from the wizard timetable but his train of thought was interrupted by a knock on the door.

He ordered the person who had knocked to go away but his voice was muffled and Conor couldn't hear what had been said. He waited a few moments before entering. Mr Gravethorpe sat in his chair facing his window. Hearing footsteps in his office, he turned sharply and was about to unleash a tirade on the person who had defied his wishes of leaving him alone but quickly refrained a he realised it was Conor.

"Master Blackstone. What do I owe thee for gracing me with your presence at this rather peculiar time?"

"I came to say sorry and thank you as I took your advice and asked my Gran about what you did and she told me about some of the things you had to endure and well, I was wrong to call into question your professionalism," replied Conor.

Mr Gravethorpe looked on as Conor's apology seemed sincere and was articulated beautifully. This had caused him to reconsider whether he had made the right decision but as Conor finished speaking Mr Gravethorpe had been brought back to reality and reassured himself that he was doing the right thing for better cohesion at Ravensborough High. but more importantly it was the best thing for Conor. Conor began to question whether he had accepted his apology as he did his best to avoid eye contact.

"No thanks are required. I merely did what had to be done on a pressing matter. After yesterday's events the teachers and I have decided that effective immediately you shall be placed on the witches' timetable," he explained.

"Why? I've already explained that I was not responsible for what happened yesterday," bemoaned Conor.

"I understand your frustration but you cannot argue Master Blackstone that since you began attending Ravensborough High the other wizards haven't taken to you and I have to think about their education as much as yours," the headmaster replied.

Angered by the decision that had been made, Conor politely asked to be excused before grabbing his new timetable. The corridor perfectly portrayed how Conor was feeling: emptiness. He began sobbing. He knew that what Gravethorpe had said was true but he could not understand why the wizards had not been welcoming. Perhaps if he had been quieter and not challenged those who had the power to influence other wizards, maybe he would have fitted in better.

Professor Marigold bolted through the main building front door. He was in an urgent rush but as he reached Gravethorpe's office he spotted Conor sat beside the door. Professor Marigold's heart sank as he knew that Conor had been informed of the decision.

"Conor, Conor are you all right?"

Startled by Professor Marigold's presence, Conor began furiously to wipe the tears from his face before composing himself. But he was still upset and refused to look at the professor.

"I'm fine," mumbled Conor.

"Conor, look at me. I will not allow headmaster

Gravethorpe to do this. Okay?" grunted Professor Marigold.

"What are you going to do? He is the headmaster, his words are final."

"He cannot do this. I have a letter signed by the grand council stating that he cannot change a student's timetable without just cause."

Conor sat up. He was unsure if he had heard correctly but he saw the note in Professor Marigold's hand and asked if he could read it. As he read on Professor Marigold began to smile but that smile soon faded as Conor began ripping up the note. Professor Marigold looked on in disbelief before snatching the remainder of the note from Conor and scrambling around the hall retrieving the rest of it.

"Conor, why did you do such a thing?"

"I'm tired of people bending over backwards for me. I just want to come to school and learn and I'm not fussed where it is," he replied.

Conor's decision had stunned Professor Marigold who was understandably annoyed as he had worked tirelessly to convince the grand council to delay Gravethorpe's decision but the feeling of annoyance soon faded and was replaced with respect and admiration. Conor got to his feet and headed outside.

The sound of his fellow peers became louder and louder as Conor began walking aimlessly through the school's compound. By chance he bumped into Ryan who began to question where Conor had been all morning but his words had completely bypassed Conor who asked for quiet before explaining.

"He can't do" hissed Ryan "I'll talk to my dad he'll tell the council they've stopped him before we'll do it again"

"I appreciate it but I got my dream I'm here, besides how bad can it be".

Ryan's chuckle was only halted by the bell. The compound

quickly emptied as Conor and Ryan walked to class with Conor's new class being located on the third floor. It meant he was soon alone Professor Scarletwound stood outside her classroom waiting anxiously for her new student to arrive but as the second bell sounded she headed back inside to begin teaching.

Conor had become lost as the third floor was complex and hard to navigate. Just as he took another look at his timetable to check what room he had to go to the second bell rang. He began to panic as he began entering classrooms none of which was his intended destination. Sure that he had gone to the wrong floor he went to headmaster Gravethorpe's office to ask where his classroom was located.

Ten minutes had passed since the second bell and with Conor nowhere to be seen Professor Scarletwound informed her class that she would be stepping out momentarily. As she left her classroom she began knocking on other classroom doors asking both teachers and students alike whether they had seen Conor but each classroom brought negative responses. Assuming that Conor had eventually found the correct way, Miss Scarletwound retreated to her classroom. Conor returned from headmaster Gravethorpe's office. His facial expression was one of embarrassment as he had been reading his old timetable. He spotted a teacher walking in front of him.

"Excuse me, Miss. I was wondering if you could help me?" asked Conor.

"Why of course. Oh, it's you, I have been looking everywhere for you. Where have you been?"

"I'm sorry, but what reason would you have to be looking for me?" queried Conor.

Professor Scarletwound then introduced before pointing to a small white door where Conor was to report every morning for registration. Conor then began asking questions as he wanted to know if there were any differences between the witches and wizards' timetables. Professor Scarletwound reassured Conor that his transition would be seamless as the two curriculums were virtually identical. Conor still had many questions on his mind but before he could project them to his they had reached the door.

Conor had been invited to open the door by Professor Scarletwound. As he entered the classroom the incessant chatting that could be heard from the outside prior to Conor's entrance desisted and none of the students glared or looked at Conor for a prolonged period of time. This surprised Conor. It was not what he had expected but it was welcomed. As he looked for somewhere to sit, he noticed the strange arrangement of the chairs which had been patterned to resemble an inverted U. The only seat vacant was at the very end of the classroom.

"Morning Class" beamed Professor Scarletwound. "I know we did introductions last week but we have a new student joining us so why don't we all introduce ourselves who'd like to go first".

The words that Conor had uttered to Professor Marigold immediately sprang to mind as Professor Scarletwound continued to talk.

"I'd like to go first Professor" squeaked Conor. "If that's ok"?

He was greeted with a nod and a smile. Conor took his place in the middle before introducing himself and inviting his classmates to ask him some questions. The witches looked up at Conor before returning to their various activities. A familiar feeling came over the young witch again. Unwilling to prolong his embarrassment any further, he went to sit down but was halted by Professor Scarletwound who told Conor to remain at the front.

"Excuse me Class" she then said. "I know it's going to be change for all of us to adjust too but we are witches and we stick together no matter, Master Blackstone… I mean Conor has asked if anyone had any questions for him".

The room then fell silent again a look of intense fury became sprawled across the professor's face but just as she launched into a tirade a chair shuffled and someone stood. There was no need for an introduction or niceties as Conor knew exactly who stood before him it was Saffron Wolfmoon, a proud witch who was strong minded and wise beyond her years.

"Fine, if you want me to partake in this tedious activity I will. Okay Conor, why did you feel it necessary to intrude into our class?" she then retorted venomously .

"Well, I didn't really intrude I was placed in your class. After all I am a witch," replied Conor.

Unimpressed with the response that Conor had given Saffron became more remorseless with her questioning.

"You may be a witch by design but you will never be a real witch in my eyes," she barked.

The tension in the room was palpable as Conor and Saffron traded verbal insults and the other witches looked on entranced by what they were witnessing.

"ENOUGH" howled Professor Scarletwound "Both of you apologise now before I give you a detention".

But even the threat of another afternoon in that torrid shack was going to stop either young witch but just as they looked to continue their verbal match the bell sounded. Conor headed to the library for some peace and solace after his heated exchange. The sight of books flying through the air made him reconsider whether it would be a quiet enough place for him to collect his thoughts but the librarian Mrs Autumn reassured him that no one else was present in the library but the books were merely returning themselves to their rightful section before letting Conor know that she would be briefly stepping out. With his mind at ease, he continued to venture through the library.

Despite it being an amiable place for relaxation Conor could not help but wonder why it was so desolate. Just then a book that interested him flew past. He began to chase it but the book had returned to the highest shelf in the library and without a functioning wand there was no way for it to be retrieved. Disappointed, Conor left that section of the library to find a seat. Once seated, he noticed an unattended book.

He thought nothing of it and placed his head on the table. Just then a presence above him caught his attention and as he looked up, he was stunned to see the book that had eluded him float into his hands. Confused, he stood up and began looking and asking around to see who had given him the book but nobody claimed responsibility. Unsure of what to do next, he headed back to his seat to see out the final few minutes of his free time. A crunching noise caused him to look down as he picked up the object. It had been a pencil case with the initials AW written on it.

A strange feeling inside him was telling him to keep the pencil case rather than hand it in to Mrs Autumn. It may have belonged to the person who had given him the book. He put the pencil case into his bag before cutting his free time short and heading back to class wanting to avoid a similar situation that had occurred in the morning.

The second floor was filled with noise as the witches murmured with excitement as Enchantment class was about to start. This had presented Conor with a problem as he did not have a functioning wand. The pupils flooded into the classroom and as each witch passed the front desk they paused as they noticed it had been covered causing the excitement in the room to rise. Miss Scarletwound kept her instructions brief instructing her pupils to retrieve their potions whilst getting into their partnerships as this week's session would be a continuation of last week. The witches' movements were frantic as they scrambled to be seated amongst the commotion.

"Erm Miss.... Sorry Professor could I work alone". "I don't think there's anyone left"

"I don't think that's true Conor" smiled Professor Scarletwound gesturing behind her.

The witch in question was Angelica Wolfmoon, the youngest in the class. She was highly intellectual and well-spoken but remained aloof which hadn't endeared her to her fellow classmates who harboured resentment towards her.

Angelica remained motionless as Conor sat beside her. The first part of the lesson had failed to live up to expectations and as Miss Scarletwound insisted on recapping on her previous lessons for Conor's benefit, the boredom began to become more and more evident by the lack of engagement. Sensing this, Miss Scarletwound momentarily halted the lesson and began preparation for the next part of it. During this brief period of inactivity Conor found himself thinking about the pencil case he had found. Just as he was about to hand it over to Professor Scarletwound the sound of ruffling behind him caught his attention. It was Angelica who had been rifling through her bag. A worried look of desperation was etched on her face as her searching became more frantic. A book belonging to her fell off the desk. Seeing this, Conor went to retrieve it and as he held it in his hand he noticed that he had seen it before. It was the same book that had been left unattended beside him. It then became apparent to Conor that he had in his possession the item that Angelica had been searching for. Conor swiftly returned to his seat and placed the pencil case and book on the desk. Angelica looked on in disbelief.

"Where did you find it" she beamed.

but before Conor could answer Miss Scarletwound asked for quiet as she explained to the witches that they would be transforming snakes into various different objects. Conor began panicking as he knew that he would be able to participate without a wand. He began asking the other witches what he should do and much to his annoyance, each witch suggested he should ask Saffron. Conor approached Saffron tentatively.

"Hey Saffron". "Erm I was just wondering if you could help, I don't have a wand at the moment"

"Why should I help you" scoffed Saffron.

"I won't beg" replied Conor sharply. Knowing it was a waste of his time the young witch headed back to his seat.

"Wait.... Fine I keep a spare wand with Miss ask her and she'll give it to you"

"Really thanks Saffron"

"We're witches right gotta stick together".

Perhaps this wasn't going to be bad after all as he headed to the front a notable skip in his step but as he reached the front of the class to ask Professor Scarletwound for a temporary wand, light chuckling could be heard behind him. Thinking nothing of it, Conor continued but his voice was drowned out by hysterical laughter.

Visibly annoyed, Professor Scarletwound ordered that everyone remained silent as she asked Conor to repeat what he had asked as she had been unable to hear what he had said. "I came to ask fo..... BAAAAAAA"

"Excuse me Conor"

"Sorry Miss I...... BAAAAAA"

The Class shuddered such was the sound and ferocity of the laughter. to save himself further embarrassment Conor quickly returned to his seat and the lesson resumed. The forlorn expression on Conor's face troubled Angelica as she knew what it felt like to be deemed an outcast by others.

"Why would you need a wand, Conor?" she asked.

"What do you mean? I was going to ask you where all of your wands were."

112

"We are witches, we don't use wands," explained Angelica.

"Give over haha, how do you do spells then"

Angelica smiled, Conor then looked on in amazement as his new friend began to transform the snake into various different objects., he was witnessing pure artistry.

"You're amazing" he swooned. "You have to teach me how to do that".

This had bought another smile from angelica feeling more comfortable she then quizzed Conor on why he had wanted a book of comical spells.

"I wanted to get back at Saffron for this morning... but I know I should be the bigger person"

Conor continued with his backtracking but to his surprise Angelica began to giggle . Unbeknown to Conor, Angelica was the younger cousin of Saffron. The positive interactions between Conor and Angelica began to irk Saffron who was determined to bring an immediate halt by summoning Angelica. As she approached Saffron, Angelica felt uneasy as Scarlett's scowl intimated an unpleasant conversation was about to start. The other witches quickly surrounded the table.

"What are you doing" growled Saffron through gritted teeth

"we're just talking, he's nice" bemoaned Angelica,

Conor looked on as the crowd began to engulf Angelica, he had half wondered whether he should say something but not wanting anymore trouble he remained seated. Saffron then asked for hush as their mini cascade had bought a few glances from Professor Scarletwound she then issued her cousin with the wickedest of ultimatum: either she ceased her interaction with Conor or Saffron would report her to her mother who resented the Blackstone family as she had missed out on becoming head witch to Amelia.

"That's not fair," bemoaned Angelica.

"I'm sorry for putting you in this predicament Angie

but you leave me no choice."

Angelica pushed through the other witches and returned to her seat.

"What was all that about?" enquired Conor, but his question remained unanswered. "So, I was wondering what days you'd be free to teach me".

Again, silence reigned supreme, unsure of what to do Conor stared towards the front, but he felt uneasy he couldn't spurn another opportunity to make new friends but as he turned to speak again the desk reverberated as Angelica stood and left. The remainder of the school day seemed a blur, his mind was still with Angelica. Conor waited by the school gates for Ryan to leave the building.

"You haven't half been missed mate" chuckled Ryan. this had bought a smile to Conor at least he was wanted somewhere, "But how was your first day with those lot".

Conor paused before he spoke would it do him any good to telling Ryan he loved his friend but he often thought with his heart rather than his head. "Boring, I promise…. wanna grab something from Harrowood's my treat"

"Now were talking "chuckled Ryan

That evening Amelia asked Conor if Professor Marigold had shown him the note and whether he had remained on the wizard timetable. Conor informed his grandmother that he had seen the note but he had not remained on the wizard timetable and had moved it.

Amelia was incensed and began cursing Mr Gravethorpe. Conor ordered his grandmother to stop and explained that it had been his own decision to move timetable as he did not feel accepted by the wizards. He then asked for his grandmother to respect his decision to which Amelia agreed before heading upstairs. Conor's school schedule was peculiar at best as while he had left the wizard timetable he still remained in the wizard

English class, a fact that had pleased Conor as it meant avoiding Saffron for the day.

Saffron's absence from school presented Angelica with the opportunity to explain to Conor why she had ignored him but as she reached the classroom, she was reminded by Saffron's best friend Hilda Devonshire that if she went back on her promise that she would inform Saffron. Angelica was unfocused for the duration of the English class as the thought of losing her new friend saddened her. She decided, despite Hilda's warning, that she was going to speak to Conor at lunch.

The wizards' dining room was vastly different to the witches' lunchroom Angelica noticed as she ventured through looking for Conor who she had spotted at the back sitting beside Ryan. But before she was able to get to him a group of female wizards surrounded her taking offence to a witch daring to intrude in their space. The dining room became incredibly frantic as wizards and witches swarmed to see what was happening. Ryan pleaded with Conor to allow them to see what was going on but Conor refused until he heard Angelica's voice which had become strained because of her distress.

Conor raced out of the lunchroom to get both Professors Marigold and Scarletwound. They followed Conor back causing the crowd to disperse and return to their appropriate dining room. A visibly shaken Angelica was escorted to the main office by Professor Scarletwound. Conor followed closely behind..

"I knew you could hold your own against them wizards," chuckled Conor.

"I'm a witch, we have to stand up for ourselves."

"So, you are talking to me now?"

Conor then asked Angelica if he had offended her as he could not understand why she had just been ignoring him. Angelica decided that she was going to defy Saffron's wishes and quickly scrambled for a piece of paper and began scribbling furiously. She then folded up the note and handed it to Conor and instructed him not to open it until the end of the day. She then told Conor that he had not offended her and ushered him away as Professor Scarletwound approached again.

CHAPTER SIX

TEMPTATION OF TIME

Potions class had become an afterthought for Conor as the temptation to read the note that Angelica had given him was tightly gripping him. It had begun to overwhelm him he found himself continually glancing over to his bag. Such was his lack of focus he began to blindly mix potions resulting in a foul odour. Deciding he could not trust himself he handed his bag to Ryan who was bemused by his request but not wanting to intrude in his friend's affairs he merely took the bag and placed it beside his own.

The clock had become Conor's enemy as every minute seemed to take an eternity to pass and still unfocused, he asked to be excused. The bathroom briefly provided solace but it was fleeting as thoughts of the note resurfaced. He began pacing in the toilet as he contemplated feigning an illness such was his desire to read the note but that idea soon faded. He stood before a mirror glaring at his reflection and began questioning himself. His eagerness to read the note was beginning to interfere with his focus. He chuckled to himself as the thought of him feigning illness sounded preposterous on reflection. The trip to the bathroom had done the trick. Conor was ready to learn but as he was leaving the door from a cubicle creaked open and Marvin emerged.

"Marvin, what are you doing here?"

"French is not my cup of tea so I thought I'd give it a miss," replied Marvin looking at Conor smugly. "What's the rush, Blackpepple? Where do you need to go so suddenly?"

Conor looked on bemused. What was Marvin harping on about, he thought. It then dawned on him that he may have been mumbling loud enough to where Marvin had heard his plan. He then tried to steer the conversation back to what had occurred during the assembly but Marvin bypassed his frantic and distorted questions before reaffirming his position of dominance in the conversation by asking his own questions about Conor's sudden need to leave Ravensborough High.

"I mean it was good plan pulling a sickie but you can do better why don't you just......

"Why don't I just what" parroted Conor

"Time manipulation".

Conor briefly entertained Marvin's suggestion before denouncing the idea. He, as well as Marvin, knew he did not possess the magical capabilities to execute time manipulation flawlessly.

"Besides, that could get you expelled but I'd bet you'd like that," remarked Conor.

But despite Conor's refusal Marvin remained relentless. He wasn't convinced by Conor's staunch refusal and became more cunning and devious in his approach reminding Conor that he could not be expelled as he did not have a functioning wand so the spell could not be traced back to him. Marvin's prodding had worked as Conor began to re-evaluate the situation but before he had made his decision the bathroom door opened. It was Ryan.

"What are you doing?"

Ryan then ushered Conor to one side. "Why are you talking to him? Don't you remember what he's done to us or do witches have short memories?"

"Marvin was just apologising for the whole assembly

thing, weren't you?" replied Conor.

"Yh, again I'm sorry pal, Simon is too"

An awkward silence ensued as both Conor and Marvin waited with bated breath hoping Ryan had bought their lies. The silence was broken as Ryan implored that they should hurry back to class as they were missing an important part of the lesson. Agreeing, Conor and Ryan left the bathroom. As they walked through the corridor Conor glanced back to where Marvin was standing in the doorway.

All eyes became fixed towards the front of the classroom as Professor Marigold began furiously mixing potions to combat the boredom that had begun to set in which had been evident up to this point. Since returning to the classroom Ryan began to notice Conor's strange behaviour.

"Conor, why do you keep staring at the clock?"

"It's just been a long day," replied Conor.

"Are you sure? It's just with you giving me your bag and constantly looking at the clock. You're acting rather oddly," mentioned Ryan. "It's that twit Marvin, isn't it? He threatened you in the toilet. That's why you're looking at the clock. I told Gravethorpe that he should exclude him."

"It's not Marvin. Like I said, it's been a long day."

"If you're scared, we can go to Gravethorpe. He won't let Marvin bother you anymore."

"You're not listening. There's nothing wrong," grunted Conor.

"Fine. We can go to Professor Marigold or Miss Scarletwound if you don't trust headmaster Gravethorpe to deal with it."

"RYAN, LEAVE IT!"

Professor Marigold ceased talking and the classroom fell silent.

"Lads, is there a problem back there?" asked

Professor Marigold.

"No, sir. We were just having a disagreement about what happens when you mix certain potions," replied Ryan.

"It that true, Conor?"

"Yes, sir."

"If that's the case why don't you come to the front and show us what this disagreement was about Ryan?"

"No, it's all right, sir. We've sorted it out."

"Nonsense, Ryan. You're one of my top students and I'm sure Conor would benefit from you demonstrating."

"I couldn't agree more, sir. I think a demonstration wouldn't only benefit me but the entire class," grinned Conor.

"That's the attitude I like to see Conor. So Master Willows, could you join me at the front, please?"

Ryan begrudgingly stood up and skulked towards the front. As he did so he looked back at Conor and began scowling. He had mentioned to Conor that he was definitely afraid of performing magic in front of large groups of people.

Conor's infatuation with the note began to resurface. Another look at the clock had not been kind to Conor as there was still a significant part of the lesson to go. Professor Marigold invited the remainder of the class to come to the front to get a better look as Ryan was ready to begin. Conor who had been sitting towards the back had not been offered the best view. He would have to be content with a spot beside the door. Ryan then begun explaining.

Ryan's explanation was in its infancy as Conor looked on gleefully. A light knock of the door had stolen his attention. He glanced towards the door. It was Marvin asking why the time had not been manipulated. Going against his better judgement, Conor responded by pointing towards Professor Marigold. But Marvin became increasingly frustrated by Conor's excuses and decided to take matters into his own hands.

SMASH!

Giggles and murmurs began to reach a crescendo as Conor turned around sharply. Ryan began frantically to dive towards the floor trying to catch the remaining bottles. The giggles had turned into uncontrollable laughter.

"Shut it the lot of you!" demanded Ryan.

Becoming red in the face, he stormed out of the room with Professor Marigold closely following behind. As the door began to close it halted as Marvin then slipped into the room.

"Come on, Blackstone. I've bought you some time so now get on with it," grumbled Marvin.

"How could you do that to Ryan? He's distraught. He was right, you are a twit," snarled Conor "besides why are you so desperate for me to manipulate the time. How does it benefit you?"

"I was just trying to be a friend," remarked Marvin with a sinister laugh. "No, but seriously what's stopping you from ending the school day now? You get to where you want and Willows is saved from any further embarrassment."

Marvin's words had some semblance of truth. After all his actions had caused Ryan's unpleasant predicament. Deciding he had no other choice, Conor agreed to manipulate the time but without a wand he would be unable to perform the spell again. Marvin provided the solution offering his own wand.

"You won't regret it," winked Marvin.

Conor was initially hesitant unsure about whether he could trust a person who had gone to incredible lengths to cause him the utmost distress but with little other options he took Marvin's wand before reading himself to perform the spell. He took a sharp intake of breath and raised the wand but before the spell could be cast Conor had remembered what Marvin had mentioned to him earlier. Realising he had once again been set up, Conor looked down at the wand in his hand which began to swell as it doubled in size. Unsure of what was going to occur he quickly threw the wand towards the front of the room and as it landed a large cloud of smoke began pouring from it. Conor dove behind a desk.

The sound of flapping and screaming caused Conor to peer over his table, a look of shock on his face. Marvin's wand had turned the other pupils into pigeons. Unwilling to suffer a similar fate as the remainder of his classmates, Conor quickly left the room. The final bell rang out. Unsure of what to do Conor went to retrieve his bag but a flock of pigeons had surrounded him. A tectonic struggle commenced as he began flailing his arms around causing his classmates to fly to one corner of the room. Seeing that his bag had finally been left unattended he headed towards the door but as he entered the sound of footsteps began to fill the corridor. The footsteps were an afterthought as Conor had realised he had forgotten the note Angelica had given him in Ryan's bag.

The sound of bottles smashing greeted Conor as he quickly re-entered the classroom and headed for Ryan's bag to retrieve the note. This was surprisingly easy as he half expected to be swarmed by his classmates. With the note in his possession Conor prepared to leave the classroom again. A pigeon flew beside him and began staring. The pigeon's intent stare troubled Conor but he knew he could not leave his classmates in their current predicament so he placed his bag to one side. He then began looking for a solution but none was forthcoming.

With not many other options Conor decided to read the note that Angelica had written but before he could unfold it a large thud in the middle of the room had startled him. The contents of Ryan's bag were scattered across the middle of the room. Conor then began placing Ryan's things back into his bag. He noticed Ryan's wand underneath the desk and as he grabbed the wand the same pigeon that had been staring at him earlier had resumed its intense gazing. Ryan's wand was the answer to his and his classmates predicament.

Now in a boisterous mood Conor gathered all his classmates and brought them towards the front before lining them up. He drew the wand back to perform the transformation spell. He paused as self-doubt began to creep into his mind unsure of what effect a witch using a wizard wand would have on the spell. Conor refocused himself and once again drew the wand back. As he shut his eyes and began to recite the words, the classroom door opened.

"WHAT HAVE YOU DONE?"

Professor Marigold's boisterous voice had startled the pigeons and they fled from the line they had been placed in. A firm grab of his wrist had stopped Conor's recital of the spell. Sure it had been Marvin who had grabbed his wrist but Conor quickly regained control of his hand and pointed the wand in the direction of his classmate before casting the spell. Conor opened his eyes and was stunned not see his classmates standing before him. Instead it was Professor Marigold with a look of bemusement etched on his face. The situation worsened for Conor as Ryan had re-entered.

Ryan began interrogating Conor on why he had been using his wand but before he could answer Professor Marigold began his own interrogation asking why there were birds in the classroom and why the students' belongings were there..

Conor spoke ensuring he was meticulous in his explaining. He briefly paused to regain his breath before hastily continuing. Ryan and Professor Marigold began looked at each other in disbelief as they tried to come to terms with what they had been told. Professor Marigold stood up and asked both boys to retrieve the pigeons so he could begin the arduous transformation process. They struggled to contain their classmates. Professor Marigold sat at his desk mulling through what Conor had said and could not decide whether he could trust what Conor had told him. While Marvin was a devious troublemaker there was no evidence pointing to him being in the classroom. The ringing of Ryan's phone intruded Professor Marigold's train of thought. He then stood up and collected the pigeons from Conor before informing the boys they were free to leave.

The corridor seemed like hallowed turf to Conor who was glad to be out of the classroom. But his relief soon vanished as Ryan began tentatively asking if he'd explain what had happened again but again the ringing of Ryan's phone halted the conversation. Ryan walked further along the corridor as his conversation prolonged his facial and body expression and rapidly began to change... Seeing this, Conor contemplated whether he should approach Ryan as he bolted through the doors.

For the first time Conor's urgency to read Angelica's note was a second thought as his concern for Ryan took centre stage. Deciding that he needed some time to decompress Conor headed to the library. Its vastness became apparent to Conor as without the books flying throughout the room the simplicity in its design and the artistry displayed was something to behold. Conor took his seat and retrieved the note from his bag. He spotted the book that he had been reading earlier and began to smile.

The opening of the note brought a pleasant surprise as Angelica's voice rang out throughout the library it began to recite the note word for word. As he listened Angelica went into great detail explaining why she had shunned him earlier on and why they would have to keep their friendship secret. The deluge of information that Conor had to take in began to overwhelm him as Angelica's reasoning and ideas began to confuse him. He quickly closed the note allowing himself time to digest the information he had just received.

He reopened the note and began listening more intently as Angelica divulged to him that she expected him to struggle with the quantity of information that she given him. The end of the note had instructed him to retrieve a book from the library when they returned to school the following day. Conor thought his luck was beginning to change as he would able to get the book today.

The ticking of the library clock seemed to be increasing in sound as a quick glance up indicated the passing of ten minutes. Since Conor began to look for the book his frustration and annoyance increased. It was more and more apparent as Angelica's note had not provided the location of the book and its elusiveness seemed to becoming greater each passing minute. The search had become increasingly tedious. Conor headed to the second floor hoping his search would prove more fruitful. But once there he was instantly halted by Mrs Autumn.

"The correction process begins in five minutes, Master Blackstone."

The search for the book became more sporadic and frantic as Conor knew he could not leave it to chance to find the book tomorrow. The constant sound of books dropping began to irk Mrs Autumn who politely asked Conor to cease his disruptive noise. Conor who was becoming more desperate in his search seemed to see the librarian's request as a hindrance and became noisier. With no seeming end to the noise the librarian decided to confront Conor and threaten him hoping that this would do the trick. But as she approached him the noise of books falling had stopped and been replaced with the sound of rapid footsteps as Conor descended from the second floor with the book he had yearned for: *The History of the Town of Ravensborough.*

He was in no need of a history lesson but was perplexed as to how this book would provide the answers as to why the two young witches could not be friends. Sure, that he had been the butt of some sort of joke concocted by the other witches, he hurled the book onto the table. Furious at allowing himself to be tricked, he banged his fist on the table before reaching for the note Angelica had written. As he looked at the writing his anger intensified but he relented as an extra fold of the note had not been unfurled. At first he refused to entertain the idea of reading the remainder of it sure it would only cement the humiliation he already felt. He tossed it aside before standing up to return the book to its shelf.

Angelica's kindness towards him began to replay in his mind as he reached the second floor. He wondered if he had jumped to an unfair conclusion with regards to the intentions of her letter deciding that he owed her the benefit of the doubt. He rushed downstairs to retrieve the note but to his shock it had vanished. He panicked and began searching for it.

Mrs Autumn wandered through the library ensuring that everything was in pristine condition before the reshelving began. A stray book on the floor caught her attention. Visibly annoyed, she skulked over to collect it but as she bent down to retrieve it, Conor emerged from underneath the table.

"Oh, Master Blackstone, you gave me a right fright."

"Sorry, Miss. You haven't seen a scrunched-up piece of paper by any chance? It's crucial that I find it."

"Why yes, I have Master Blackstone but I'm afraid I've thrown it away. You know the school has a zero tolerance for littering."

"What bin did you put it in? Was it that one beside the front door?"

Conor leapt from underneath the table and began

rummaging through the library bin. Seeing the frenzied and panicked look on his face Mrs Autumn implored him to desist from searching through the bin as it was unsanitary before asking him to follow her to her office so she could retrieve the note from her filing room.

She offered him a seat before informing him that finding the note could take some time. The boredom became unbearable as after being seated for several minutes peculiar and fascinating items garnered his attention. One item in particular was of interest to him. It was a chest that had been heavily chained with an unusual lock his interest getting the better of him Conor began creeping through the office. The movement from behind the filing room door caused him to become swifter in his movements but his swiftness soon turned to recklessness as he had disturbed Mrs Autumn's book shelf causing the books to fall on the floor. Sure, that the falling books would alert Mrs Autumn Conor began picking them up and returning them back on the shelf when a tiny shimmer caught his eye. It was a key.

The abnormal shape of the key resembled that of the lock on the chest. Conor picked it up and began to inspect it. As he examined it he noticed an inscription that was in the same writing as that which had been etched onto Mr Harrowood's wand. The turning sound of the filing room door lock startled Conor who quickly pocketed the key as he began placing the books back onto the shelf before quickly rushing to his seat. Mrs Autumn emerged from the filing room with the note.

Conor quickly exited Mrs Autumn's office and returned to his book. Once seated he began to straighten out the note and start to read through it again but remained guarded still sure that he was a part of a practical joke. As he reached the end of the note, he slowly unbent the final part of it which revealed to him what chapter he should read to uncover the truth.

Relieved, Conor opened the book and went to the chapter that Angelica had instructed but as he began to read, he could not understand why he had been asked to read it but with every new page he read it had become abundantly clear that Conor knew nothing about the town of Ravensborough. It's jovial and perfect image began to unravel its dark history was being described before his very eyes. He struggled to turn each page as the sweat from his fingers made the page near impossible to grip. His heart began pounding as the chapter was drawing to a close. Conor yearned for more knowledge of his town's history and continued reading unsure of what the following chapter held. He slowly turned the page but to his horror the next chapter had been torn out of the book.

The revelations and missing pages from the book had both confused and stunned him. Desperate for more information he approached Mrs Autumn as he was sure that she would be able to help.

"Excuse me, Mrs Autumn I have some questions about this book that I am reading."

"Of course, Master Blackstone. What is the name of the book in question if you don't mind me asking?"

Conor then placed the book on the table. Mrs Autumn's seemingly permanent smile disappeared as did the twinkle in her eye. She picked up the book and headed to her office slamming the door behind her. A stunned Conor quickly followed sure he had uncovered something big.

"Master Blackstone, leave my office immediately!" ordered Mrs Autumn. "who told you about this book? How did it come into your possession? It was in my drawer. Did go through my drawer? I could have you expelled for this," she added.

"I did no such thing. I found the book on the second floor. It was underneath a shelf and that it is the honest truth," implored Conor. "But you saw the book on the floor beside me. Did you not see the title of the book?"

"Preposterous, the book I saw beside you was the encyclopaedia of wands," thundered Mrs Autumn. "That book was in my desk less than an hour ago and if you do not reveal to me the true nature of how you came to have it you will leave me no choice, but to inform headmaster Gravethorpe, Master Blackstone."

"What's the point? You clearly don't believe me."

Conor then slumped into Mrs Autumn's chair. Mrs Autumn looked at him and her hardened stance began to soften as Conor's demeanour was not that of someone who had just taken something unjustly. She then began to comfort him.

"Are we going to headmaster Gravethorpe's now?" mumbled Conor.

"No, Master Blackstone. While all the signs point to you taking the book from my office, I could not allow a fellow witch to be subjected to punishment without irrefutable evidence."

"Thank you."

The buzzing of an alarm caught the attention of Mrs Autumn who began to panic. She had not got the library ready for the reshelving process. Seeing Mrs Autumn's desperation Conor decided to offer his services hoping that his kindness and hard work would be rewarded with Mrs Autumn revealing what she knew about the missing chapter. Conor's hard work had increased Mrs Autumn's trust in him. Seeing this, Conor began trying to shift the conversation to the contents of the book and the missing pages.

"What were on those missing pages of the book?" asked Conor. "Are they in the locked chest in your office?"

"That is none of your concern, Master Blackstone. Besides, I have told you that I am under strict instructions not to discuss that information with you."

"Why are adults always so secretive?" bemoaned

Conor.

Both Mrs Autumn's and Conor's work production began to slow as Conor's questioning became more intense and strategic. Time began to tick by and with the library still not ready for the reshelving, Mrs Autumn wilted and relented to Conor's request but stipulated that if he did not resume aiding her in readying the library she would not reveal what she knew.

"I have finished doing what you have asked. Could you now tell me about the missing pages?"

"The person who swore me to secrecy was your grandmother."

"What? Why would my gran not want me to know about this book?" asked Conor.

"Master Blackstone, what I'm about to say will be unpleasant. Are you sure want me to continue?" murmured Mrs Autumn.

"Yes," said Conor hesitantly.

The warning in Angelica's note had done nothing to prepare Conor for what he had to endure as he instantly regretted his decision. The severity of the atrocities that his grandmother had committed rendered Conor speechless. He began to press Mrs Autumn for more information as surely she had been misinformed. How could his grandmother be capable of such horror?

"You're mistaken, Miss. My gran wouldn't do any of those things," retorted Conor.

"Master Blackstone, I warned you that what I was about to tell you would be unpleasant, I have seen the pages myself and I assure you there would be no reason for me to lie."

"NO, I'm not going to sit here and allow my family to be dragged through the mud. You're just like the rest of the witches, you old trollop."

Expecting an instant response Conor was surprised by the lack of reaction he received. Still angered, he then

130

snatched the book from in front of Mrs Autumn and headed for the door but as he walked towards it Mrs Autumn stood in front of him.

"Master Blackstone, your grandmother has been burdened by this secret for years but she has been able to deflect away from it but I implore you to ask her about the book as she won't be able to lie to you," uttered Mrs Autumn before calmly walking into her office.

The afternoon breeze had been replaced with a frosty evening chill. Conor left Ravensborough High, the magnitude of the information that he had received dawned on the young witch who needed some closure on the matter. He raced towards the bus stop. A three-minute waiting time for the bus only heightened his anxiety as thousands of different scenarios began going through his mind of how he was going to approach his gran.

The bus ride seemed fleeting as he reached his stop. Surprised by the quickness of the journey Conor reluctantly got off the bus. The street became illuminated as the lights began to be switched on. The Blackstone driveway could be seen in the distance but it seemed an eternity away for Conor who began pacing along the street still aghast at what he had learned but the disapproving looks of a few neighbours from their windows soon put an end to the frenetic pacing.

The creak of the gate seemed to last longer than usual. Conor began to feel a sharp stinging sensation as he had nicked his finger on the gate. This was symbolic of his day, he thought. He wiped the blood quickly from his finger onto his collar and approached his front door. Faint voices and laughter could be heard from the living room and for a brief moment he wondered whether he should refrain from confronting his grandmother as maintaining her image was vastly important to her role as head witch. But the thought quickly passed as the despicable acts carried out by her began replaying in his mind.

The incessant laughter from the living room was abruptly halted as the forceful opening of the door had startled Amelia. To Conor's surprise the individual having a conversation with his grandmother was Professor Marigold

"STICKY" wailed Amelia suddenly, "what happened it was that Marvin boy wasn't it where are you bleeding"

"I'm fine… it's just my finger" grunted Conor

"So why do you look so upset…. is it because your professor is here you aren't in any trouble, he was just explaining what happened at school today"

"I don't care" mumbled Conor

"What was that sticky you know I hate when you mumble"

"I DON'T CARE" roared Conor slamming his bag to the floor.

The jovial laughter that had filled the room earlier was long gone every eye darted around the room, five minutes seemed to flitter by before another word was uttered it had been Amelia thanking Professor Marigold for the productive meeting they'd had before walking him to the front door. He'd had wished Conor a good evening but that was met with a cold silence. Inside, the tension throughout the room was palpable as Amelia sat across from her grandson unsure of what to say .

"What happened to you Conor this is not how Blackstone's act."

"STOP!"

Conor rifled through his bag and retrieved the book which he slammed on the table. Amelia's anger ebbed away and she stumbled over her words.

"What do Blackstone's act like, Gran? Because if we're going by the book I've acted accordingly,"

"Where did you get this book from?" murmured Amelia. "You have to understand Conor that what I did was for the betterment of all witches."

"Save it, you're despicable."

"Please Conor, allow me to explain why I did what I did," she pleaded. "Belinda Wolfmoon was a selfish leader who did nothing for the witch community so me and the other witches decided that drastic action had to be taken to remove her from her position."

"You don't get it. CURSED A CHILD, A FELLOW WITCH, her life ruined all because you were upset at not being in charge any more. How can you say your only goal was to help witches?"

"I care about my community and if there was any other way, we could have gone about it differently we would. I'm not that person any more. I've changed."

"How can I believe you've changed?"

"Sticky, you've known me your entire life. Please don't forget what we've been through together and I have dedicated my life to ensure that we wouldn't be discriminated against by the wizards. I promise you that from this moment on there will be no secrets between us."

"Okay, why was there a chapter removed from the book?"

"No good will come of you digging in the past. I don't want to hear any more on this matter. Understood?"

"You just said there would be no more secrets between us."

"CONOR BLACKSTONE, I SAID I WANT TO HEAR NOTHING MORE ON THE MATTER," howled Amelia.

Before he could reply Amelia took the book from the table and thundered her way up the stairs but Conor remained undeterred. His desire to uncover the truth had only increased. A mixture of stubbornness and pride had sentenced the Blackstone household to silence for the remainder of the night.

Conor found himself in an all too familiar position seated at his desk unable to sleep. Thankfully, the weekend was the next day, he thought. He then reached for his bag pulling out a piece of paper and began to write to his mother again but halfway through he began to ponder whether his mother was aware of what his grandmother had done. He hoped that his mother had taken the same stance as he did. He hadn't given it a second thought, of course she would have. He placed the key he had taken on his desk and headed to bed.

CHAPTER SEVEN

FIRST FLIGHT

A small gap in the curtains allowed the autumn sunlight to intrude on 84 Durfold Street. Betrayed, Conor turned trying to find solace on the other side of his bedroom, but this was to be a mistake as a quick look to his bedside table revealed the youthfulness of the new day. Still tired, he tried to drift back into slumber.

THUD!

"UP! GET UP THIS INSTANT!"

Conor's eyes flashed open. Amelia began berating her grandson about the state of his bedroom which had been in a right state in all fairness. He had been up all night thinking of theories of why a chapter had gone missing and how Gravethorpe was surely involved but he now regretted that as the sound of scrunched up papers being picked up off the floor rattled around his head. Becoming increasingly annoyed by the brashness of his grandmother the young witch pulled the covers over himself and closed his eyes. Silence filled the room. Had it worked? Had his grandmother finally taken the hint and allowed him to rest. "AHHH!" Conor wailed suddenly, fully removing himself from the covers. "Let me down!" he spluttered and shuffled towards the end of his bed where his grandmother began looking at him and laughing sinisterly.

"I see you are awake now."

"Please let me down," pleaded an increasingly frightened Conor. "You know I'm afraid of heights."

"Oh, all right," chuckled Amelia as she stopped performing the levitation spell. With her grandson in an almost mummified state she began firing off plans for the weekend like a seasoned army general. "Understood," she said finishing off her tirade. This had brought a feeble nod from the younger Blackstone who was still too shaken to muster any words. He peered through his curtains and began to scowl. As his grandmother sat in her car waiting for him it had finally dawned on him that his weekend plans which had only consisted of him heading to Ryan's house to share theories, were now ruined. Three loud honks then sounded. Amelia had begun to become impatient so not wanting to anger her any further he bolted for the door.

BANG!

He let out an ear deafening screech after colliding with his desk and sat on his bed rubbing his knee. He noticed the key on the floor and began sprawling off his bed. He picked it up and put it in his pocket. He was at first thankful his grandmother hadn't found it but just as he inched towards his bedroom door a smile had begun to form. He wasn't about to have his weekend ruined being stuck at the town hall. He was going to sneak away and meet up with Ryan. After all, if he had been right with Gravethorpe taking the chapter then surely no good would come of it. Another honk sounded and he began limping downstairs. The drive to the town hall was tiresome for Conor as his grandmother spent the duration going into great detail about her duties as head witch but he remained uninterested merely looking out of the window as he concocted a plan to escape her clutches.

"Conor, are you listening?" asked Amelia. "You can ignore me if you want but the day will only go slower as you will not be going to meet up with Ryan."

Conor knew his grandmother was right as his disinterested demeanour was doing him no favours. If he were to escape, he would have to regain his grandmother's trust so he decided to change his approach. "You're right, Gran. Could you go over what you were saying earlier? I didn't quite catch it all," he said forcing a smile. "Not every witch is lucky enough to have their grandmother be head witch you know," remarked Amelia proudly.

This had seemed to do the trick Conor thought as the drive seemed to speed up and whilst most of his interest was feigned the young witch had found a higher level of respect for his grandmother seeing and hearing all she did. But the time for games was over. The town hall's vastness had surprised Conor as Amelia, seeing her grandson's new-found eagerness and enthusiasm, had decided to take him through every district. With the afternoon quickly approaching Conor knew if he were to escape, he had to do it now and the filing floor provided the perfect opportunity due to its share size. Thousands of files zoomed through the air. Conor's eyes darted around the room his mind ablaze with thoughts of what secrets and stories were in those files, but the sound of a small pitter-patter of feet soon caught the young witch's focus.

"Gran, what are those things?" he asked pointing towards three short hatted men.

"Never let people tell you that normals don't have their uses. Those are called gnomes, very hardworking individuals perfect for organisation and to think normals used to just put them in their gardens. What a waste of productivity," she said.

The filing floor was highly animated as the gnomes who ran the floor began ordering around the ogres who had become frenzied as some files had been misplaced. Two large filing cabinets that stood side by side had caught Conor's eyes. Seeing his grandmother preoccupied by frantic gnomes, Conor slithered towards them and began leaning on the drawers.

"Silly child, come away from those drawers. They are sensitive and cannot be mishandled," exclaimed Quentin, head guard of the town hall.

"Sorry, what are in them?"

"These drawers contain the personal information for every witch and wizard in Ravensborough. It has stood in that place for hundreds of years and if opened incorrectly the effects would be catastrophic."

Conor again apologised before walking away. As he did, he began to smile deviously and then waited for the gnome to move. Five minutes had passed but Quentin was becoming increasingly impatient. Conor grabbed an empty file and began filling it with blank pieces of paper. He then slid it towards Quentin's feet who assumed it to be the missing file. He left his post and went to hand it to the head gnome.

With the files finally unattended Conor snuck over and tried to open the drawer but it was stubborn. As it was slightly ajar, his second attempt was successful as the drawer opened but with the force used Conor had knocked over both filing cabinets. Paper filled the filing room. Panic then ensued as the gnomes and ogres began running uncontrollably around the room plucking papers from the air trying to salvage their hard work.

Amelia, overwhelmed by the pleas of dozens of angered gnomes and ogres, had not realised that her grandson had left the room. Sirens began to sound throughout the town hall as an emergency shutdown had been called. Conor looked on from afar as he began to ponder whether the actions, he had taken exceeded what was necessary and whether he should return but remembering how his grandmother had treated him he dismissed the idea and headed for home. Once there, he contacted Ryan with the two boys agreeing to meet at

Ryan's house. at Christwood Meadows. Conor collapsed onto his bed and began staring at the ceiling.

A knock on the door jolted him from falling asleep. He was visibly annoyed and stomped to his window. The knocking became louder and more frequent as Conor pulled his curtains aside his anger turned to nervousness as it had been Angelica who had been at the door. Quickly closing the curtains, he tiptoed towards his bed hoping his previous brashness had not alerted Angelica to him being at home. The knocking ceased but Angelica's persistence had been detrimental to Conor's plans as the bus would soon be arriving and he was not ready. He sped out but it was to no avail as the bus drove past him. The sound of the bus driving away had begun to be drowned out as Conor's name rang out throughout Durfold Street. It was Angelica who began approaching him. Both Conor and Angelica traded awkward glances at one another unsure of what to say.

"Hi, Angelica, how did you know I was at home?" stuttered Conor avoiding eye contact.

"I saw your curtains moving," replied Angelica. "You read the book, didn't you?"

"What makes you say that?"

"A lack of eye contact can tell you a lot about someone's mindset."

Angelica's demeanour had surprised Conor as he wondered why she wasn't angrier or even upset. His admiration for her increased and an overwhelming sense of shame came over him. He fell to his knees and began imploring Angelica to forgive him. The wind had begun to pick up as it blew past Conor who remained on the floor. Angelica began to chuckle before also falling to her knees.

"Conor, why are you apologising?" said Angelica. "You have nothing to apologise for."

"Yes, I do. My family is responsible for despicable things and your sister could have died!"

"Your family, not you have done despicable things," replied Angelica before lifting Conor's head.

"Why are you being so nice?"

"Because me shouting at you wouldn't make me feel better." "Do you mind if we stand up? My knees are killing me."

A smile appeared on Conor's face and then he began softly laughing before getting to his feet and inviting Angelica in. Once inside, Conor asked Angelica if she wanted something to eat or drink. Not wanting to be seen as rude or ungrateful she asked for a bottle of water. As she walked around the living room, her eyes became fixed on the pictures displayed by the stairs and one picture in particular caught her eye.

Quietly, Conor sneaked behind Angelica before giving her a fright as the sound of shattering glass reverberated through the room. Stunned by what had just happened, Angelica slowly began to back away from the table revealing the shattered remains of the picture frame. The very smile that Angelica had brought to Conor's face began to dissolve as he looked down at the photo frame that had been broken. He then turned to Angelica, his face void of any emotion and handed her a bottle of water before slowly shuffling and sitting beside the photo frame.

"Conor, I'm so sorry. I'll fix it. I promise."

The room fell silent.

Her words had no effect on Conor who looked up in Angelica's direction before climbing the stairs. Angelica carefully began brushing the remaining shattered glass off the photo. She was frustrated because she had been unable to restore the photo frame to its exact likeness. She took deep breaths and refocused herself before placing her hand over the photo.

Relief and satisfaction were felt by Angelica as she gleefully skipped upstairs clutching the restored picture frame ever so tightly as she went looking for Conor. She needed not look for any significant period of time as Conor's feet could be seen at the top of the stairway. Angelica placed the photo frame behind her as she approached Conor. Once at the top she proudly held out the picture frame and handing it to Conor but again he remained unmoved.

"Conor, again I'm sorry for breaking the picture frame but I've fixed it. Is all this fuss necessary? After all it's just a picture frame."

Conor instantly rose from his mummy like state.

"It's not just a picture frame, it was the last thing that me and my mother made together before she died so I'm sorry I'm not hailing you as a saviour."

Angelica's mood and tone instantly changed as she placed the picture frame beside Conor before asking him if he was comfortable with talking about his mother. It was a request that Conor politely declined before asking her if he could be left alone. .Conor turned around to see if Angelica had gone back downstairs. and seeing that she had he took the picture frame, placed it on his chest and began reminiscing about his mother. The sound of running water had calmed him further as it had brought on another memory of himself and his mother. Angelica began clearing her throat vigorously hoping to garner Conor's attention but he remained in his mesmerised state.

SPLASH!

Conor's picturesque memories had been abruptly halted as Angelica had drenched him in water and he began to shudder.

"Have you lost the plot?" barked Conor. "Why would you do that?"

"Now that I have your attention would you mind following me?"

"Why in the world would I follow you now I'm soaked?"

Angelica was at an impasse with her plan to coerce Conor out of his slump seemingly backfiring. She resorted to drastic action launching herself at Conor and tackling him to the ground before snatching the picture frame and then sprinting out of the house. Conor lay on the floor stunned by what had just transpired. He then leapt up and headed to the front door. He reached for the door handle but was unable to turn it. A knock at the window had caught his attention. It had been Angelica who informed him that if he wished to leave his home that he would have to change his mood and become more cheerful as she had placed a laughter charm spell on all the doors and windows.

Conor's first attempts to unlock the door had failed miserably as several more locks had been placed on the door. His mood only worsened realising that if he did not become more cheerful and relaxed his prized photo frame could be lost forever. The persistent vibrating noise from the kitchen did nothing to relax the young witch. He began looking for where the sound had been coming from. A quick rummage through the drawer revealed it to be his phone and angrily, he answered. Ryan's voice had been drowned out by unintelligible ranting from Conor who demanded to know who had been calling him so frequently.

"Who is this?" asked Conor aggressively.

"It's me, Ryan. Who else would it be?" "Where are you? I thought you said you were coming over. What happened, did you get lost?"

"If I told you what has happened to me today you wouldn't believe a word I said," said Conor shaking his head. "Actually, Ryan could you do me a favour?"

"Sure, what is it?"

"I've been feeling down lately. Do you mind telling me some jokes?"

Ryan, slightly taken aback by Conor's request,

agreed. Confident that Ryan would be key in helping him unlock his front door, Conor strode confidently through the living room and asked Ryan to start his joke telling. The confidence shown by Conor had not been misplaced as Ryan's unorthodox and quirky nature had been perfect. The locks began to vanish and the door flew open producing a gust of wind that pinched Conor's already cold skin.

He then set off still dripping, he stood at Angelica's door contemplating what he should do as the thought of encountering Angelica's mother terrified him. She reminded him of Saffron, only larger and more dominating, but he could not allow his most treasured possession to become lost. Conor had made up his mind. His heart began pounding as he took long slow breaths to calm himself. He knocked but there was no answer. He knocked again, more forcefully than before but again there was no answer. Conor remained knocking on the Wolfmoons' door for a further five minutes before trudging slowly towards the gate. The sudden rustling of grass behind had unnerved him and he turned around to see a large black cat charging towards him. Even more surprising was Angelica still with Conor's picture frame in her hand chasing after the cat which had leapt into Conor's hands.

"Swap," said Conor gleefully smiling.

Angelica's back garden was a sight to behold as Conor gently placed the cat onto the freshly cut grass before asking her to enchant his clothes dry.

"You've had your fun, Angelica. I want my picture back," he demanded.

"I will on one condition," replied Angelica.

"Fine," said Conor begrudgingly.

"I want you to follow me to this."

Angelica handed Conor a small colourful leaflet.

"No chance, people will stare and point at me."

143

"I won't let them."

The forlorn look on Angelica's face unsettled Conor who began thinking to himself that maybe it would be fun for him to go to Ravensborough Fair being held in Christwood Meadows. Besides Angelica did say she would not allow people to ridicule him.

"Fine, I'll come but the buses to Christwood Meadows will be packed. How will we get there?" asked Conor.

"No problem. It was never my intention to take the bus," giggled Angelica.

She then began skipping through the back garden before crashing into the back door. She struggled with the door, such was her excitement before finally opening it and disappearing into the house. It seemed an eternity since Angelica had left and such was Conor's boredom he found himself talking to her cat. Then, a thunderous bang came from the house followed by an eerily long silence. Conor began walking towards the back door which was still slightly opened and as he entered the door began creaking which annoyed Conor and he quickly closed it.

The Wolfmoon household was a sight to behold as everything was neatly ordered and in pristine condition almost as if nothing had been touched in years. Another bang reverberated throughout the house again. Conor ran upstairs calling out for Angelica and heard a muffled response from the attic. Conor began climbing the metallic stairs. Once in the attic he again called out for her. With his heart racing and palms sweating Conor began to knock over boxes leaving a trail of shattered potion bottles. He found Angelica sprawled on the floor and quickly helped her up. But what had laid beside her bewitched Conor. It had been a broom but not an ordinary broom. It was slimmer and a distinctive shade of light blue with a small gold star gently carved on the edge.

"Is th---hat yours?" stuttered Conor.

"Yes, I made it myself," said Angelica proudly.

"Is that how we are getting to Christwood Meadows?"

Angelica nodded before inviting Conor to touch the broom. At first, he was hesitant. He had never handled a broom before. What if it was heavy, he thought. He began shaking his head before carefully picking up the broom and following Angelica out of the attic. Once outside Angelica asked Conor for the broom before divulging to him her pristine expertise in broom flying. She then hopped onto the broom before inviting Conor to also hop aboard. The quickness in which Angelica wanted to go had startled Conor.

"Are you ready?" asked Angelica.

"No," squeaked Conor.

Feeling a mixture of both excitement and nerves Conor tightly held Angelica by the waist as he readied himself for his first broom ride. Angelica then instructed the broom to lift off. Slowly, those words had calmed Conor's earlier fears but that soon changed as they shot up in the air tilting back and forth.

"I thought you said you were an experienced flyer."

"I am well more experienced than you."

"That's it. Let me down this instant. You clearly have no idea what you're doing," demanded Conor.

"I don't know how to let you down. Hold on, it's going to be a long ride."

Angelica then tilted forward and the broom sped off. It had been ten minutes since her latest near miss. Conor who had previously kept his eyes shut for the duration of the flight started to become more relaxed and slowly began to open his eyes. The sight that greeted him was wondrous as the sun pierced the clouds which seemed whiter and fluffier than usual. The air felt and smelled differently and he allowed it to move his hand. Becoming more and more comfortable, Conor decided to ask Angelica a question that had been on his mind for a while.

"Angelica, if you don't mind me asking, Mrs Autumn said that the history of Ravensborough book was in her office but I found it on the second floor of the library?"

"Do you want the honest truth?" replied Angelica.

"Of course,.."

"The day I gave you the note I snuck back into school and cast an invisible spell on myself to retrieve the book from Mrs Autumn's office but by the time I had got it you were in the library so I waited for you to go to the second floor before placing it beside you."

"So, it was you who placed the book beside me?" said Conor.

"Yes."

"So, I assume when Mrs Autumn looked at the book the first time it was you who changed the title and you were the one that had been reading the note out loud?"

"Guilty," murmured Angelica. "Brace yourself, we'll be there soon."

As they neared Christwood Meadows Angelica tilted downwards causing the broom to descend. She then bragged about her flying skill whilst narrowly avoiding oncoming chimneys which had brought faint, angry shouts in their direction. They landed with minimal fuss, something that Angelica was again quick to mention. The streets were packed as hundreds of witches and wizards, both young and old, walked towards the fair but as they neared its Angelica noticed a girl in the distance who had been staring at them intently.

"Conor, do you know that girl over there?" asked Angelica.

Her question went unanswered as Conor had moved from beside her and had raced towards the entrance. Angelica quickly set off trying to catch up with Conor who had disappeared into the crowd. At the front of the fair Mr Basil had set up a small stand and on seeing Conor he began waving to invite him over.

"Good afternoon, Mr Basil, why are you not at Witchhaven Valley?"

"The Ravensborough Fair is the day I get the most orders for wands. I could miss out on a lot of business."

"Speaking of business were you able to fix my wand?"

"I was able to mend it but it has no magical essence left in it rendering it useless," said Mr Basil handing it over to Conor.

"Will you make me a new wand then, Mr Basil?" asked Conor.

"No need. I've been working on something for years. It's a unisex wand I call Rose which is capable of being used by both witches and wizards.," he added.

"No offence but that's an awful name for a wand," chuckled Conor.

Mr Basil then placed a wooden box on the table. Conor slowly opened it. It was beautiful much thicker than any wand he had seen before. It was as straight as an arrow and the wood shone almost as if it had been glossed with unicorn tears. Conor then began running his finger along his new wand which then began glowing as it etched CB on itself. Mr Basil quickly shut the box and issued Conor with a warning.

"Don't show this to anyone and do not use it unless it is absolutely necessary," demanded Mr Basil.

"Why?"

"Technically, what I have done is illegal and if your grandmother or anyone else from the grand council found out I would be threatened with banishment."

"Banishment, what's that?" asked Conor.

"Magical banishment is when you become ostracised from the magical society and are forced to leave your town. It has only happened once before."

"To whom?"

"I've said too much. Leave, take the wand and go,"

ordered Mr Basil.

Seeing that Mr Basil had been shaken up by their conversation Conor quickly collected his wand and left but before he did so Mr Basil again warned him that he must remain quiet about it. Angelica had just found her way into the fair and spotted Conor wandering aimlessly.

"Where did you go?" she asked.

"I got a tad excited and stormed in. I then saw Mr Basil's stall and went to get my wand back," said Conor. "Were you worried?"

"Yes, of course. It's your first festival and you could have got lost," replied Angelica. "That's a pretty special box for a standard wand repair. Did you get a new wand?"

"No, it's just a protective case," said Conor.

Angelica saw through Conor's lie instantly but before she could challenge him the girl, she had seen earlier began approaching them accompanied by two large girls. The three girls then surrounded Conor and Angelica.

"Hi, my name is Margret Wiggumworth. I work for the *Christwood Chronicle* at Christwood Academy. Are you Conor Blackstone?"

"Hi, Margret. I am Conor," he said hesitantly.

"Great! I have a few questions for you."

Margret then clicked her fingers. The two large girls stood in front of Angelica as Margret began walking with Conor. Seeing his friend being put in an awkward position Conor asked why Angelica had not been with them. Margret instantly responded asking if Angelica not being close by was affecting him. Conor shook his head. Margret again clicked her fingers and the two large girls instantly separated. Angelica then stumbled through and joined Conor and Margret.

"Can the questioning begin please?" said Margret becoming increasingly impatient.

"Okay, what is your first question?"

"What does it feel like to be the only male witch in the

entire country?"

"Well," said Conor.

"Have you ever been called a freak? Do you wish that you could be a wizard?"

Margret's questioning became more and more vile and personal.

"I don't want to answer any more questions. Leave me alone," hissed Conor as he began to walking away.

Margret again clicked her fingers and the two girls instantly moved in front of Conor. Angelica became incensed and ordered Margret to leave them alone but her threats fell on deaf ears. Left with no choice, Angelica began reciting a spell and fired it in the direction of the three girls who then flew up in the air. They then began screaming and began pleading to be let down but Angelica was having fun and began making the girls spin and turn upside down. Shocked by Angelica's actions Conor demanded that she let the girls down. Angelica was annoyed by Conor's request but didn't want to upset him further and ceased casting the spell.

"I am so sorry," said Conor helping Margret up.

Once on her feet again Margret clicked her fingers and ordered the girls to grab Conor and Angelica but they remained seated. Stunned, Margret clicked again. The girls then stood up and began towering over Margret before chasing her out of the fair.

"What happened? Why did they chase their friend like that?" asked a bemused Conor.

"She was using a mind control spell on them. That's why I had to break it," replied Angelica.

"I'm glad you freed those girls but you could have gone about it differently."

"You sound like my mother. All that spell casting has made me hungry. Do you want something to eat?"

"Yes, but I haven't brought any money," said Conor.

"No worries. I invited you. It's my treat. I'll be back

in a few minutes. Could you hold my broom?"

It had been no fewer than two minutes since Angelica had left Conor to purchase the food then she had returned more frantic than ever. She panicked to talk then grabbed Conor before bundling him into the bathroom.

"What happened? Why have you brought me into the girls' bathroom?" asked an embarrassed Conor.

"My Mum is here," replied Angelica still breathing heavily.

"What? I've got to leave. If she sees us together you'll get into so much trouble."

"I know, but this was your first fair."

"I'll go next year but I need to go now."

"Wait, I have an idea."

Angelica then entered a bathroom stall and began mumbling. She seemed to be arguing with herself. This went on for about two minutes before she re-emerged with a grin on her face that made Conor feel uneasy.

"So, what is this plan?"

"I'll transform you into a female witch temporarily so you get to stay and enjoy your first festival," said Angelica.

"Transform? I'm not a bloody toy. Have you ever done something like this before?" questioned Conor.

"Yes, loads of time."

"Like the countless times you've flown your broom." "Fair point but were running out of time". Angelica instructed Conor to stand by the bathroom door as she readied herself to perform the transformation spell but unbeknown to Conor was that Angelica was incredibly nervous. She he had never performed the transformation spell on a person before. The nervousness began transmitting through the room as millions of thoughts began going through his mind: What if it hurt? How long would it take to transform and how long did the spell last? But before he could express any of his concerns Angelica began performing the spell.

One of Conor's questions had been answered as the transformation had lasted no longer than a minute. Anxious to see who Angelica had transformed him into, he then walked over to the mirror. A look of shock became etched on his face as he began touching it still unable to fathom what had happened. His short curly and frizzy chestnut brown hair had been replaced by long curly jet-black hair and his light eyes were now an intense dark hazel. Angelica had turned Conor into Saffron.

"Of all the witches in Ravensborough, you chose Saffron."

"I'm sorry. I panicked," said Angelica apologetically. "Besides she is ill so there is no chance of you running into her."

"I guess that's so," slurred Conor still not used to his new mouth.

Angelica's poor attempt to conceal her laughter had not gone unnoticed as Conor, still in a delirious state, became furious with her lack of sensitivity to his situation.

"Can we just go?" he roared.

The fair had taken on new life for Conor as the sneaky but blatant stares and mumbled murmuring had stopped but something else had taken its place, something that had surprised him as wherever he and Angelica went throughout the fair they were greeted and treated with the utmost respect by the other witches. It was something that Conor was not accustomed to. Such was the attention that both he and Angelica was receiving meant that they were unable to enjoy everything the fair had to offer. The fanfare surrounding himself and Angelica had subsidised allowing the two to re-emerge into the fair but to Conor and Angelica's surprise the stalls and stands were locked and deserted.

"Where is everyone?"

"I'm not sure. The fair isn't over yet," replied

Angelica who was equally confused by what was going on.

"Wait, look over there! That small building is still open. Maybe we can ask the owner where everyone has gone," uttered Conor.

"That's odd. Who brings an entire building to the fair?"

Such was his urgency to get to the building that Angelica's question had completely bypassed him. And she hurriedly followed him. The building was dimly lit as Conor peered through the window so he headed to the back to inspect it further. Angelica, becoming impatient at Conor's cautiousness, headed towards the door but as she reached for the handle it flew open. Slightly taken aback, Angelica hastily stepped away. Hearing the door opening Conor headed towards the front where he met a slightly frightened Angelica. The two young witches then headed into the building. Once inside the overwhelming sweet aroma of unicorns filled the room. It had been the candles laminating the room. Tentatively, they manoeuvred themselves around the room as the contents on offer both surprised and intrigued them.

"Scented candles," said Angelica. "Dragon Mucus. Who wants that as a scent? That's grotesque."

"Dragon Mucus is not that bad. Trust me, I've drunk it," said Conor smirking.

"Why did you drink dragon M ..."
CRASH!

The sound of dropping boxes reverberated throughout the room stopping Angelica in her tracks. The room then fell silent as both Conor and Angelica began looking at each other. The stares were intense almost as if they were talking through their eyes. A slight yelp could be heard from where the initial crashing sound had come. Quickly recognising the voice, Conor sped to the back where he was met with the sight of dented boxes and broken candles. Another yelp sounded but unlike the first this one was louder. Conor quickly navigated his way through the boxes but his worry soon turned to humour as a shuddering Ryan lay there with his eyes firmly shut.

"Are you all right, Ryan?" said Conor trying his best to conceal his laughter before helping Ryan to his feet.

"Yeah, I am. Whoa, it's you," replied Ryan. "You'd be the last person I'd expect to help me."

"Why would I not help you? You're my frie...." Conor paused as he realised that he was not talking to Ryan as himself but as Saffron.

"What are you doing in here? "Asked Conor.

"I was helping Miss Scarletwound move some boxes so she would take me to your aunt's big announcement," responded Ryan. "Speaking of which, the announcement is due to take place at any moment. Do you want to come?"

"I'm not sure. I've actually been quite ill so I think it would be best for me to head home," said Conor who began coughing aggressively in an attempt to convince Ryan.

"Nonsense! I think this is exactly what you need to get over that nasty cough; some fresh air surrounded by friends."

Ryan then charged towards Conor before grabbing him by the hand. A stunned Conor followed Ryan who ushered them out of the room. Angelica looked on as both Conor and Ryan sped past them and hastily left the shop not sure of what was going on. Angelica quickly followed suit also leaving the store. But once outside Ryan suddenly stopped.

"I'm sorry...for dragging you out like this. It's just I was meant to be meeting my friend here but I guess he's still mad at me for not believing him. You don't have to come if you don't want to." Ryan then began to skulk away.

"Wait!" shouted Conor. "I'll come."

Ryan responded with a smile and began pointing in

the direction of where the announcement was due to take place but before either of them had taken a step towards the announcement Ryan shot up into the air. "What are you doing? Put him down."

"No, he cannot be trusted. I saw the way he forced his way out of the shop," replied Angelica snarling at Ryan.

"I'm fine. Ryan was just taking me to your mum's big announcement."

"Announcement?" said Angelica bewildered. "What is she announcing?" But still visibly shaken and petrified, Ryan remained speechless. "Let's just go. I'm sure Ryan will fill us in along the way," Conor said nervously. But a walk Conor had hoped would have been littered with conversation and excitement had been a disappointment as Ryan remained silent still too frightened to talk fearing that any attempt to communicate with Saffron would lead to another unwanted trip off the ground. Angelica, still angry at Conor, also remained silent.

It would not remain for much longer as deafening chatting and music could be heard over the horizon. Ryan, still too afraid to talk, pointed forward informing both Conor and Angelica that they had arrived. A large stage had been erected in the middle of Christwood Fields. It had been surrounded by hundreds of highly excitable young witches and wizards.

"I'm going to find my mother and see what this announcement is all about. Wait here!" ordered Angelica before pushing her way through the restless crowd.

"I'm glad she's gone," sighed Ryan. "I don't know why everyone says you're the wickedest witch. Angelica is really nasty."

"No, she is really not that bad. She's a nice person. She's just protective," replied Conor.

"Maybe you're ri... What's the matter?"

"I wish we were closer to the front," murmured Conor. "Can't see anything from here." Ryan then began to grin again. "I can fix this," he said before disappearing into the crowd. "Wait! Where are you going?" But Conor would not have to wait long for his answer as Ryan returned. "That was quick. Where'd you go?" Again Ryan simply smiled before gesturing for his friend to follow him which Conor reluctantly did. But to his surprise the new spot Ryan had chosen was perfect. The surprises didn't end there as the boys were soon joined by Miss Scarletwound.

"Hi, Professor," said Conor.

"Why this is a pleasant surprise, Saffron. I heard you were sick and weren't going to be able to attend. Also, I'd like to thank you Ryan for all your help this afternoon."

"No problem, Miss," beamed Ryan.

"What is going on, Professor? What is the announcement about?" asked Conor.

"You know what Saffron, I'm not sure."

The music resumed causing the disgruntled murmurs to be replaced with hopeful anticipation. Conor was in awe as half of the stage had been taken up by a large box. His mind was racing with endless thoughts of what the box was concealing. A hand on his shoulder had taken him out of his joyous mood. It had been Angelica but she was in a state that he had never seen in her before. .She was panicked and frantic imploring him to follow her as they needed to leave immediately but Conor for the first time in the day was enjoying himself and had no plans to leave especially since the announcement was moments away. Footsteps could be heard ascending the stage. The curtains had been drawn back but as they fully opened Conor's excitement drained from his body as Angelica's mother, Belinda Wolfmoon stepped onto the stage.

"Good afternoon, young sorcerers and sorceresses. Today marks a monumental day in Ravensborough's history as I'm pleased to announce that Draco Iudiciis shall be returning to the school curriculum," she announced.

She then paused. Saffron's name then rang out throughout the field. Conor's heart sank as he was then invited onto the stage. The walk to the stage seemed endless and he and Angelica exchanged uneasy glances once there. Belinda began heaping praise on her niece highlighting her excellent magical skills as the primary reason for her being on stage but what Belinda said next both shocked and excited the crowd. Saffron was to tame a dragon. A slow glance towards the box on the stage had brought about ferocious movement from it. Conor knew that he did not process the same magical skill as Saffron. He would not be able to tame a full-sized dragon and knew he needed to concoct a plan to get out of this perilous situation.

THUD!

"Saffron, Saffron are you all, right?"

Slowly, Conor began to open his eyes. He had been surrounded by Belinda, Angelica and Professor Scarletwound after he had fainted. Angelica then suggested to her mother that Conor was in no fit state to perform his duties and that it would be best if she took him home. Reluctantly, Belinda Wolfmoon agreed. Conor and Angelica then gingerly walked back towards the bathroom where Angelica collected her broom. Angelica's flying was more fluent and focused Conor had noticed once a fair distance away from the festival. Conor confessed to Angelica that he had faked fainting in order for them to leave but there was no response. Angelica merely turned to look at him before refocusing on flying. Despite her frosty response Conor knew deep down that Angelica was grateful for what he had done.

Nightfall had arrived by the time Angelica and Conor had returned. Once on the ground Angelica changed Conor back and an awkward silence then ensued. Angelica broke it by asking Conor to wait. She then quickly rushed into her home. Ten minutes had passed since Angelica had headed inside and the cool wind had turned to a blistering breeze. She re-emerged, her hands full. She then handed back Conor's treasured possession, his picture frame as well as a book. A quick look at the title had brought a small smile and light chuckle: *Wandless Magic: Beginners edition.* Conor thanked Angelica for giving him one of the best days he'd had in a long time before heading home for supper.

CHAPTER EIGHT

DRACO IUDICIIS

It had been a month since an assembly had taken place at Ravensborough High School so it had come as a surprise to Conor to see his classmates being lined up outside waiting to be let into the building. A feeling of nervousness began flowing throughout the playground as Conor walked towards his year group. The disastrous events that had transpired during the previous assembly had caused headmaster Gravethorpe to cancel all future assemblies for the remainder of the school year. Conor himself began feeling nervous as he had not seen Marvin and Simon in the line and his heart began racing. The constant noise of unzipping behind him had caused him to place his bag on the floor in front of himself knowing that he could not allow a repeat of what had happened during the previous assembly and he began scanning the playground looking for his tormentors.

"Mate, are you all right?" asked Ryan.

"You haven't seen Marvin or Simon lurking around, have you?"

"No. Actually, I did see them talking to each other earlier on. I think they're planning to do something much worse to us," stuttered Ryan as he began quivering. "I think we should skip the assembly as I don't want to get blamed for anything that might go wrong."

Conor's eyes widened. Agreeing with Ryan, he began to slowly creep towards the exit but as they reached it, Ryan burst out laughing.

"What's so funny? Come on, let's get a move on," said Conor with a puzzled look on his face.

"I'm sorry, mate that I was having a laugh at your expense," stuttered Ryan with tears streaming down his face. "We don't have to go anywhere. Marvin and Simon are already inside."

"Inside?"

"Yeah, I saw them helping Mr Allister with a few boxes."

"Are you sure?"

"Yes," laughed Ryan.

The serious look etched on Ryan's face had caused Conor to relax as headed back towards the line. The wait to be allowed into the building seemed endless as only one class had gone through in twenty minutes.

"What's the hold up?" sighed Conor

"It's Gravethorpe" replied Ryan. "He's checking every bag now for wands we gotta hand em in before now"

That had made sense Conor thought. "At least you don't have to worry about him getting his grubby mitts on your bag" then snorted Ryan. The two then began laughing but Conor's laughter was short lived as he remembered he had just got a new wand, a wand that could not be seen by anyone especially by headmaster Gravethorpe, a member of the grand council. Conor knew that he had to hide his wand but was wary of placing it anywhere as, if Mr Basil was to be believed, this wand was special. He could not afford for it to fall into the hands of Simon and Marvin or even worse headmaster Gravethorpe. Just then the perfect hiding spot presented itself but before he was able to do anything he was interrupted by Ryan who had come to inform him of the strange events that occurred at the fair. Conor tried his best to feign interest but getting his wand from potentially prying eyes was his first thought, he needed a distraction. This was the perfect time to try some of the spells from the spell book that Angelica had given him. A shrieking plant would be perfect, he thought, as its rarity at this time of year would surely draw attention. Putting one hand behind his back Conor closed his eyes and focused but his first attempt was unsuccessful. Getting angered, Conor tried several more times but each time he failed miserably. Knowing that Mr Basil's citizenship in Ravensborough rested on him, Conor took a deep breath and relaxed. He attempted the spell one final time and a clanking sound was music to his ears as it meant that his spell had worked.

"What's that?" asked Conor pointing forward.

"I'm not sure, it looks like a plant," replied Ryan.

"Are you sure, because it looks like a shrieking plant from here?"

"Impossible. Do you know how rare these are at this time of year?" laughed Ryan.

Conor's words had put doubt into Ryan's mind and he began walking towards the plant. "EEEEEEEEEEEEEEEE" wailed Ryan pointing frantically. A large crowd then began to gather, there chatter and panic became music to Conor's ears as he slipped away and headed towards the old classroom where he had served his detention. But as he reached the door, he encountered a problem it was locked.

A subtle rattling noise had drawn Conor's attention. It had been his wand and the rattling had become more ferocious. He then decided to try something, slowly stepping back he raised his wand making sure to hold his hand steady. He then pointed it towards the lock. Two blue flashes flew out of his wand, the lock opened. Conor then looked down at his wand.

The faint sound of running and screaming coupled with a wretched stench engulfing the playground had brought a smirk from Conor. The shrieking plant had exploded. He then hurriedly walked towards the classroom. It had been just as he remembered, a whiff of dust narrowly missing his blazer as he opened the door. He then headed for the desk where he placed his wand. Conor noticed a few new additions to the room: a bunch of books had been placed on a cupboard.

The majority of them had been about potions and elixir making but one book had caught his eye. It was different from the others, or so he assumed. As with most things in the room, it had collected its fair share of dust He handled it carefully as it was worn out but as he brushed the dust off his excitement turned to frustration as the writing had been in the same language that was etched into both Mr Harrowood's wand and the key to Mrs Autumn's chest. Still annoyed, Conor hit the cupboard before placing the book back. He then headed towards the door.

THUD!

The noise came from the cupboard. Conor thought nothing of it, probably some books falling against the door because he had hit the cupboard. He continued towards the door. THUD, THUD! This time the noise was louder and synchronised with every step he took almost as if someone had been trying to gain his attention.

Conor was in two minds. The lack of noise coming from the outside had suggested that things had cleared up meaning that if he stayed, he would surely miss the assembly but if something dangerous was in there he couldn't allow it to get out and create havoc throughout the school. He had made up his mind. He had talked himself into staying. It also helped that he would no longer have to be searched by headmaster Gravethorpe. He quickly retrieved his wand and began slowly to approach the cupboard. He then stopped and readied his wand.

"Claro," he whispered.

The cupboard's contents slowly became visible through the door Conor held his wand steady ready to bewitch whatever was inside but to his surprise the only objects that had shown up was more books and the statue of a head. Not content with what the spell had shown up. Conor crept forward and began slowly opening the door.

"Hello!"

Conor quickly slammed the door shut. Had his ears deceived him? Had the statue spoken to him? Muffled noises continued to come from the cupboard so he hadn't gone crazy. The statue had spoken. Still stunned, Conor began pacing in front of the cupboard before slowly opening the door and snatching the statue and placing it on the desk.

"Can you understand me?" asked Conor.

"Well of course I can," replied the statue.

"Sorry for snatching you back there. My name is…"

"I'm aware of who you are Master Blackstone. No introduction is needed. Are you aware of who I am?"

"Sorry, no."

The statue then went on a miniature tirade hurling various insults about both headmaster Gravethorpe and Mr Marto, the caretaker. This had brought a smile to Conor's face. He thought he should interject but decided against it as the statue's anger seemed to have been born out of frustration. Besides the Gravethorpe bashing was going down a treat.

"Sorry to interrupt but I still have no idea who you are."

"It's quite all right. I am Philip Ulius."

"You're Philip Ulius the youngest wizard ever to graduate from Ravensborough High not to mention the greatest headmaster this school has ever seen. But you look nothing like your pictures," replied Conor in awe.

"I decided to go for a youthful look. This is what I looked like when I was twenty. And thank you for the compliment."

"If you don't mind me asking, how do you know who

162

I am and why are you locked in a cupboard? You should be displayed proudly in the main building."

"You're quite kind, Master Blackstone. I know because I love this school.,. I am aware of every student that passed through those hallowed gates. I've seen them all. I used to be in the main building but I suppose headmaster Gravethorpe got a tad jealous of my presence and ordered that I be removed. I don't blame him his authority. He must have been undermined," confessed Philip.

"Well, that's still a rotten reason to get rid of you. I'm sure we the students would love for you to impart some of your wisdom."

"I am content with my situation but there is one thing that I do find to be unbearable."

"What's that?" asked Conor.

"That caretaker Carl. I've never met I man with such a peculiar fascination with winged bugs in all my days. He has spent hours informing me of the difference between a Peruvian and Argentinian three-winged beetle."

The next few minutes were some of the best Conor had spent at Ravensborough High as he and Philip discussed the changing landscape of magic as well as all the students at Ravensborough. But a nagging thought still remained. It was about the book he had selected. He wondered if Philip knew about the mysterious writing that he seemed to be encountering everywhere. He then excused himself and grabbed the book and placed it before Philip.

"Excuse me, Philip. I was wondering if you knew what this book says as I've seen this writing everywhere?"

The statue's eyes glanced down but as he read the front cover his facial expression changed. It was something Conor had noticed and only increased his eagerness to gain more information. Philip then looked at Conor for a moment but there was an awkward silence.

"Well, do you understand it? What does it say?" asked Conor impatiently.

"Indeed, I do Master Blackstone. I'd hoped that I'd never have to encounter such a language or book again as it has brought so much pain and torment," he said, the distress in his voice apparent.

"Is it really that bad?"

"This is a dark magic spell book. It is capable of unspeakable evil and has had many owners. But the last owner was someone I knew dearly and their story saddens me as the lure of the book changed him."

"I'm sorry to hear that. Do I know him?"

"No."

"What language is it written it in?" said Conor softly.

Before Philip could respond a shout from the outside pierced through the glass. Conor tiptoed towards the door and again drew for his wand. "Claro," he whispered. Conor's worst fears were confirmed. It had been Mr Marto.

"I know you're in there Blackstone. Come out before I find headmaster Gravethorpe to get you," said Mr Marto, his voice devoid of any emotion.

Conor slowly backed away.

"It's Mr Marto. I'm sorry, Philip, I have to go or I'll get into trouble."

"It's fine. I understand the upholding of rules It's something I'd hope all students of Ravensborough High follow."

Conor then pointed his wand at Philip. "*Novis*," he uttered and the statue then began to float and returned to the cupboard. He did the same with the book and placed his wand back into the desk. The door suddenly burst open.

"Sorry, sir. I was just looking for my pen that I'd lost when we had detention in here," said Conor holding up the pen.

"No excuses, you've held up the assembly for ten

164

minutes. Now hurry up and head to the main building. Headmaster Gravethorpe is waiting for you,".

Conor hurriedly got up off the floor and followed Mr Marto out of the room. The stench of the shrieking plant tickled Conor's nose as he walked away from the room. "Just wait till I tell the headmaster what you've done" . But that was the least of his worries. He thought that what headmaster Gravethorpe had in store for him was much scarier. Mr Marto had not been wrong. By the doors of the assembly hall stood Gravethorpe, the annoyance and disdain etched on his face.

"Finally, the great Master Blackstone has arrived," said Gravethorpe.

"Sorry, sir."

"I'm sure you are aware due to your little stunt I am personally checking every student for their wands."

Still annoyed at the fact that Gravethorpe had not believed that he had not sabotaged the previous assembly Conor removed his blazer and dropped it to the ground. Gravethorpe remained unmoved looking at the blazer sprawled on the floor before glancing up at Conor and smiling before pulling out his wand.

"*Rectus*," he bellowed.

The blazer flew up and stood up right beside its owner. Gravethorpe then began rifling through Conor's blazer pockets but much to his annoyance found nothing. Conor then grabbed his blazer before smiling at Gravethorpe as he began walking past him. He then entered the assembly hall. The true odour of the shrieking plant had revealed itself to Conor so the sight of the side entrance to the assembly hall which rarely was ever opened being opened, uplifted the young witch. Mr Allister walked to the front of the hall and then faced the third-year students who began talking in hushed whispers as they waited for the assembly to begin.

"Good morning, third years," said Mr Allister walking

though the assembly hall. "This assembly will be brief as many of you will probably be aware of what I am going to say. As it was announced at the fair over the weekend there will be a change in the sporting curriculum as *Drago Iudiciis* or (Dragon Trails) will be reintroduced."

A tremendous roar of cheers erupted from the wizard side of the hall. This was in stark contrast from the witches' side where boos and jeers seemed to be just as loud if not louder. Conor looked on as the game seemed intriguing but he had his reservations. Mr Allister then asked for quiet.

"Miss Joyce, if you will," beamed Mr Allister.

The room lights darkened and all across the walls the rules of *Drago Iudiciis* were sprawled for all to see.

DRACO IUDCIIS RULES

- EACH TEAM IS COMPRISED OF FIVE PARTICIPANTS.
- THE MATCH WILL CONSIST OF THREE SEPARATE MINI MATCHES.
- THE WINNER IS THE TEAM WITH THE QUICKEST OVERALL TIME.
- TWENTY MINUTE TIME LIMIT.
- THE TIME WILL STOP WHEN THE DRAGON REMAINS GROUNDED FOR 15 SECONDS
- IN CASE OF A TIE ANOTHER ROUND WITH EACH PARTCIPANT TAKING PART WILL TAKE PLACE.

"I would like to invite the joint team captains to join me at the front," said Mr Allister.

The doors of the hall flew open as Simon and Marvin walked in. The two boys and Conor exchanged glances with each other. This seemed endless for Conor as the glance Simon had given him had extinguished the hope in his eyes. He knew any chance of him being able to participate had disappeared. Once at the front Marvin and Simon announced that tomorrow's PE lesson would be trials for the team as they had a match against Christwood Academy scheduled for the following week. Mr Allister interjected stating that he would have the final say on who joined the team. This restored some faith in Conor. Mr Allister then brought the assembly to a close. The room quickly emptied. Conor had caught up with Ryan whose optimism seemed to be waning.

"Aren't you excited?" asked Conor.

"Not really."

"Why not? Did you not hear what Mr Allister said? He has the final decision on who joins so Marvin and Simon can't stop us."

"It's not that. It's just that I was talking to Jay Swarbrick and he said that this game would be replacing football for the remainder of the term," sighed Ryan. "This is going to ruin my plans to become the first wizard to play for Manchester United I could just imagine it Willows 1-0 and Old Trafford chanting Willows."

"I guess that's lucky for them. I've seen you play and no amount of magical ability will make you any better," chuckled Conor.

"Ha, ha! Very funny."

"So, are you going to try-out?"

"I'm not sure, maybe."

The tannoy sounded. Conor panicked leaving Ryan behind. He was late for registration, the third time this month. He knew that meant detention and he wouldn't be able to participate in PE tomorrow. He began speeding through the school ignoring several warnings from teachers to slow down. The tannoy sounded for a second time just as Conor reached the hallway. He rushed over to the door hoping that he would be able to reason and talk Professor Scarletwound round into not giving him a detention but he paused before opening the door and listened as the sound of voices talking over each other got louder and louder. Seeing an opportunity to sneak in Conor slowly opened the door before taking a seat beside Angelica.

"Where were you? Miss was about to send me out to look for you," said Angelica.

"I was with Ryan and lost track of time. What's going on in here? I could hear you from outside."

"They're debating about Draco. Half the class including Miss are putting together a petition to have it re-banned while the other half, mainly Saffron's friends, are saying there is nothing wrong with the game. It's actually quite funny."

Angelica had not been wrong. The conversation was fascinating as both he and Angelica looked on as everyone had something to say. Even Eva Featherowe, a witch even quieter than Angelica, had something to add to the conversation suggesting that dragons' rights were being violated. But her argument was quickly shot down by Saffron's best friend Layla Morris who questioned why Eva was even commenting, something that Professor Scarletwound quickly frowned on ordering Layla to apologise which reluctantly she did. Amongst the commotion Conor noticed something rather strange as lack of engagement from Saffron was unexpected as she seemed to be at the forefront of any discussion involving witches but she merely sat at her desk reading a book taking occasional breaks to look at the front door. Professor Scarletwound then called for hush before asking whether Conor or Angelica had anything to say.

KNOCK!

The knock at the door had caused Saffron to leap out of her seat. It was Mr Allister who firstly apologised for disturbing registration. Saffron remained next to Mr Allister who entered the classroom and stood at the front.

"Good morning, witches. I noticed from assembly that the idea of Draco Iudiciis being reintroduced into curriculum did not go down so well so I thought I would come here and dispel any rumours they may be floating around. If you have any questions don't hesitate to ask."

Eva immediately raised her hand. "Will any dragons be harmed during the game as I've read that former renditions of this game required you kill the dragon at the end?"

"No, I assure you that no dragons will be harmed. The spells being used will merely tire and slow the dragon down," replied Mr Allister.

Layla's hand shot straight up. "Will witches be allowed to participate?"

Mr Allister began smiling before thanking Layla for her question. "As you are aware historically witches were not allowed to participate." A worried Conor sat up. He hadn't known that witches weren't allowed to compete and continued to listen hoping Mr Allister would provide him with some good news.

"But in answer to your question Miss Morris yes for the first time a single witch will be allowed to join the team and I'm delighted to announce that the witch to be given the prestigious honour will be Saffron Wolfmoon."

The classroom erupted with cheers and clapping as Saffron stood proudly at the front but for Conor it was a devastating blow because he would not be able to participate. The noise suddenly halted as Saffron had vacated her spot from the front and had made her way to the desk being occupied by Conor and Angelica.

"Is there a problem, Conor? You were the only one that didn't seem happy. What was is it? Are you jealous?" scoffed Saffron.

For the first time that day the sound of the tannoy had been welcomed by Conor who immediately got up as he did not want to admit to Saffron that he was indeed jealous

169

of her accomplishment. The good news for Conor was still forthcoming as his timetable revealed that he had English, Maths and Science, three lessons universally hated by the students of Ravensborough High due to the strictness of the teachers. This was just what he needed, he thought, as any talk of Drago Iudiciis would surely be shut down. Or so he thought.

Conor could not believe his eyes or fathom what he was hearing as English with sorceress Elro had seemed to be personal torture for him as the creative writing had seemed to spawn endless stories of Drago Iudiciis. Such was the craze even Ryan who no longer than an hour earlier had seemed bored by the idea of reintroduced sport, had been swept up with the hype.

Conor's forlorn expression had been noticed by both Ryan and sorceress Elro who both queried about his state but each question was met with a smile and "I'm fine" as he did not want to dampen the mood for the other excited students. But he was glad the lesson had come to an end. Lunch had brought its own challenges as an attempt to retrieve his wand would be tough as he was sure that Mr Marto would be patrolling the room. His suspicions were proven to be true as Mr Marto had been in the vicinity of the room.

"What are you doing?"

Conor swiftly turned around, it had been Angelica. Unsure on whether her words had alerted Mr Marto, he quickly ushered her to one side before explaining his predicament. Angelica provided some suggestions but each was shot down by Conor as they were too intricate and time consuming.

"Actually, I have an idea," whispered Conor. "I could distract Mr Marto while you sneak in and get my wand. There's also a book that's in there I could use."

"How would I sneak in there. Sir would surely see me."

"You can cast invisibility on yourself."

Angelica's demeanour changed. She wanted to aid her friend but if caught this would lead to serious trouble and potentially tarnish her spotless record. But going against her better judgement she then rifled through her bag before retrieving her wand and handing it to Conor who followed Angelica's instructions. "*Espectral*," he said, and Angelica vanished before Conor's eyes. The two young witches then plodded towards the room with Conor leading.

KNOCK!

Conor waited anxiously as he could hear footsteps approaching the door.

"What do you want, Blackstone?" snarled Mr Marto.

Conor began talking at a frantic pace explaining to Mr Marto that there had been a massive spillage of potions at the entrance to the main building and his assistance was needed urgently. As Conor led Mr Marto away, Angelica set off. As she entered the room, she was careful to open the door slowly seeing that opening it too firmly would lead to dust flying onto her and potentially exposing her. Angelica quickly gathered the wand and then set about looking for the book Conor had described but despite her best efforts no book she encountered matched the description. With no sign of Conor or Mr Marto, Angelica decided to indulge herself as the deluge of books at her disposal proved too tempting to ignore.

Several minutes passed as she became engrossed in the book she had selected for reading entitled *The Art of Human Transfiguration* but just as she started the second chapter the sound of discussion from the outside jolted her.,

"You little rat" howled Marto. "Waste my time like that again and this place will become your holiday home that's how much detention you'll have". Mr Marto's threats fell on deaf ears as the sight of the door remaining closed was more of a concern as it meant Angelica was still inside. Knowing that he had to stall Mr Marto once again Conor then engaged the caretaker by asking about winged beetles.

Mr Marto's anger seemed to melt away as he began speaking passionately about the different variations of beetle and what countries you would find them in. Conor merely nodded slightly shifting his body to glare at the door which remained unopened. The bell rang signalling the end of the lunch period. Mr Marto encouraged Conor to come and find him if he had any more questions about beetles.

The courtyard quickly emptied but Conor remained hoping for Angelica to resurface. Unable to wait any longer, Conor headed to science but to his surprise Angelica had already been in the lesson. Conor waited for the lesson to start before pulling Angelica to one side.

"What happened?". "I waited outside for you. How did you become visible again?"

Angelica left to return to her desk and explained to Conor that she had been in the old classroom but she didn't want to disturb his riveting conversation with Mr Marto. She then giggled. Lost for words, Conor responded with a slow clap. Saffron walked past the two of them clearing her throat causing Angelica to return to her seat.

The following day was in complete contrast as Conor tried his best to convince his grandmother that he was unwell and couldn't go to school. But his grandmother was not buying it insisting that she would take him there. When Conor arrived the entirety of the third-year boys plus Saffron were by the front gates. Two minibuses suddenly arrived.

"What's going on? Isn't today the trials?" asked Conor.

"Yeah, it is but the field here is too small so we're

going over to Christwood Academy as their field is bigger," replied Ryan.

The bus ride to Christwood Academy was no different to a regular ride to school. Conor still felt like an outsider as the bus was filled with chatter which changed to genuine excitement. It had even affected Ryan who seemed more determined than ever to make the team. This surprised Conor who had hoped he would have had Ryan's company for the duration of the lesson. Ryan then went into great detail explaining the deep history that his family had with Draco Iudiciis stating that his father and grandfather both played it; they were even captains. Family honour was something Conor understood better than anyone and he harboured no resentment towards his friend.

The bus came to an abrupt halt. They had arrived.

"Masters Blackstone and Norwood, follow me," said Mr Allister.

The winter sun had emerged from the clouds as Conor and Logan got off the bus. Mr Allister led the two boys across the field. The grass was freshly cut and seemed to be dancing with the wind. Three differently sized boxes stood perfectly still in the centre of the field with various targets and cones sprawled around. A table with two chairs had been placed at the edge of the field. Once seated, Mr Allister explained to the two boys their task for the day. They were to be timekeepers. He then went on to explain the importance of the task they had be given. Both boys knew this was Mr Allister's way of trying to involve them.

The field erupted with noise as Marvin, Simon and Saffron were given the lead for the session. Conor and Logan looked on at the spectacle unfolding before their eyes as arrant spells missed every target set up and flew around the field. Mr Allister looked on partly covering his eyes. then leapt up off his chair and headed inside the building. This brought both boys to the brink of laughter.

173

A large clanking sound on the table jolted Conor back into an upright position; it had been a book.

"What book is that?" asked Conor.

"It's a book about dragons."

"Whoa! I've never heard you speak before. Your accent's weird, you're not from here, are you?"

"No, I'm not, I'm American. My family moved to Ravensborough two years ago. "My dad is Ryan's dad's assistant."

"If you don't mind me asking, why aren't you taking part?"

"My Mom said I wasn't allowed," sighed Logan. "Do you know what dragons are in the box?"

"No."

Logan moved the book between him and Conor and pointed to the page. "The dragon in the small box is a silver tipped Whifflesnout. It's incredibly fast with an incredible range to breathe fire but it is susceptible to gaseous spells with its widened nostrils as well as light spells due to its poor eyesight. The most skilled wizard or witch should usually take it on."

Logan's attention to detail resonated with Conor who had become engrossed by the information being fed to him. Such was his intrigue he asked for more details about the other dragons, something Logan was delighted to do. He then pointed to the middle box, by far the largest.

"That one contains the two-headed Hagglemuff."

"Two-headed" murmured Conor.

"Yep, but don't be fooled by its large frame. It's deceptively quick with huge wings making it harder to hit with any spell and is by far the best dragon at defending itself. But its major weakness is the lack of cohesion between the heads. If you can target one the other tends to get jealous leaving it open to be hit," said Logan taking a short break to regain his breath.

"What about that one?" said Conor pointing at the

final box
"That's a N----

Logan's answer had been interrupted as Marvin had snapped. He began berating all of his classmates highlighting their inability to hit the targets as shameful. He then shifted his attention to Mr Allister questioning why they had not been allowed to train with the real dragons before heading over to the boxes and hitting them furiously.

"He shouldn't do that," uttered Logan, shaking his head.

"Yeah, I know. He's such a brute."

"No, you don't understand. If not correctly coursed out of their boxes they become wild and unstable and will kill whoever disturbed them," stuttered Logan.

Conor sighed. As much as he despised and hated Marvin and his brother, he could not allow Marvin to get himself killed especially since everyone else was too paralysed by fear to confront him. Conor then poured the contents of his bag onto the table before grabbing his wand and heading onto the field.

"Marvin! Stop, you're going to get us all killed," thundered Conor.

"Pipe down, Blackpepple. I've trained for years. I know what I'm doing. Go back to your seat,"

Marvin banged on the box again. It rattled before bursting and a large yellow and green scaled creature towered over Marvin. Its red pupils were becoming ever wider. It was the two-headed Hagglemuff. Shouts of "move" fell on deaf ears as Marvin remained still petrified in a trans-like state. The right head of the dragon lowered until it had reached a point where it and Marvin were eye to eye.

"LATERALIS," screeched Conor moving Marvin out of the way.

The patch of grass that had been occupied by Marvin was ablaze. The two-headed Hagglemuff let out a tremendous roar before moving. Each footstep was shuddering. It had been heading in the direction of Marvin who still lay sprawled across the ground motionless. The yells of the other wizards did nothing to change him from his zombified state. Saffron had headed inside to inform Mr Allister but Conor knew that time was of the essence as he then began running alongside the dragon trying to gather its attention. This yielded no response from the two-headed beast who continued to trudge towards Marvin.

The feeling of hopelessness was evident in Conor as he began looking around the field in the hope of guidance. A shout had gained his attention. It had been Logan who began pointing furiously at his book. Conor understood what he had to do and stood before the dragon. He then fired a sneezing curse at the right head. This infuriated the left head which began snarling at its counterpart. *"Mentis imperium,"* yelped Conor. He had control of the dragon and led it away from Marvin. He had then charmed the tannoy system and the soft strum of a lute blared out. This had coursed the dragon back into a slumber. Conor fell to his knees exhausted but his rest was momentary as he had been hoisted up back onto his feet by Ryan. Applause filled the field.

"ENOUGH," screeched Simon who was knelt beside his brother. "How can you applaud? It was probably Blackstone who charmed the dragon to attack Marvin."

"Conor would never do that," said Ryan.

"Pipe down, Willows," barked Simon.

Still insistent on Conor's guilt, Simon left his brother's side and began approaching Conor who started to back away but he was not quick enough as Simon leapt onto him snatching the wand out of his hand. Simon held it aloft then pointed it at Conor before uttering "*mentis imperium"* but nothing happened. Simon reperformed the spell again but again, nothing happened. The wand began rattling, something Conor had been used to but this had been different. Suddenly, it let out a yellow flash that had thrown Simon back and the wand nestled in the grass. Mr Allister and Saffron emerged and Mr Allister ordered everyone inside.

The reception of the main building had presented a weird vibe for Conor who had been swamped by wizards who were all scrambling to congratulate him on his performance but something else had drawn his attention as Mr Allister, Saffron, Marvin who had finally moved again and Simon were nowhere to be found.

"Master Blackstone, could I have a word with you?" said Mr Allister.

Conor pushed through his newfound support and wondered what Mr Allister wanted to discuss. His thoughts soon turned negative. He was sure that Marvin and Simon had probably convinced Mr Allister that it had been him that had bewitched the Hagglemuff. His fears weren't allayed as in the room with him had been Saffron as well as Simon and Marvin.

"Please take a seat," said Mr Allister. "I'm sure you're wondering why I asked you in here, Master Blackstone. Don't worry, you're not in any trouble."

"If I'm not in trouble then why am I here?" asked Conor.

"Miss Wolfmoon has informed me that she feels that you would be a valuable asset in retaining the Raven's shield so I want to formally invite you to join the team."

Conor was stunned. Had he heard correctly? Saffron had something pleasant to say about him. He turned to face Saffron and began smiling. She responded with a lengthy scowl.

"Wipe that smirk off your face, Blackstone. All I'm interested in is winning and you could contribute to that. This does not mean I like you," barked Saffron.

"But sir I'm a witch. I thought there was only one witch allowed per team," said Conor.

"Don't worry about that Master Blackstone. The rarity of your case means you would be allowed to participate"

"Is everyone happy with your decision, sir"? asked Conor.

"While I have the final decision, Simon has agreed to you joining the team while Marvin still has not spoken. I need your decision Master Blackstone."

Conor was brimming with excitement. Did Mr Allister really need to ask whether he was going to join the team? Of course, he was. Conor went to speak but just then a splendid idea popped into his mind.

"I will join but I have two small requests," he said. "I want Ryan to be the final member of the team and my partner and finally I think Logan should help us as he really knows about dragons."

Mr Allister looked at Conor strangely. "While your requests are peculiar, I don't have any immediate problems with them. You have a deal."

"No," screeched Marvin; he had found his voice. "Willows was the worst one out on the field today. He was even worse than Nigel Woodburn and his wand was bent."

"He was a tad nervous, I've seen his skills and he's really good," fibbed Conor.

"Do you have a better suggestion of who the final place on the team should go to Master Davies?" queried Mr Allister.

Marvin remained silent.

"Master Blackstone should get the final say on who he'd like to partner him."

Mr Allister then ushered the newly formed team out of the room. Ryan found it hard to control him when Conor informed him of what had gone on. Logan, on the other hand, proved stubborn initially informing both Conor and Mr Allister that he would be unable to help them. For the duration of the bus ride back to Ravensborough High Conor was on the charm offensive showering Logan with praise stating that the school was dependent on his knowledge to defeat Christwood Academy. Thankfully for Conor, his efforts were not in vain as Logan reluctantly accepted the role.

Conor never fully understood the first piece of advice his gran had given him until now. When he returned to Ravensborough High word of news of his supposed heroics had made the rounds with the fifth years and students who'd never normally speak to anyone below the fourth year greeting him. As he had got off the bus even headmaster Gravethorpe had been nice to him privately commending his behaviour. But sweetest of all was the look of absolute fury that had become permanent fixtures on both Simon and Marvin's faces. He could get used to this, he thought, on the journey home.

Conor had been greeted at the front door by his grandmother who gripped him tightly before checking him over thoroughly. Conor had guessed by his grandmother's friendly welcome that she too had heard about the day's events. Conor had hoped this would spare him from helping with the gardening but he was sadly mistaken. The remainder of the school week had been largely boring although potions class had proved rather eventful as Jay Swarbrick had managed to cause the closure of the entire fourth floor with his reckless potion mixing.

Excitement at Ravensborough High had reached uncontrollable levels so much so that due to several complaints from teachers about lack of engagement in lessons headmaster Gravethorpe issued a school wide ban of any mention of Draco Iudiciis. He had also done something unprecedented as he had allowed Mr Allister to take Conor and the others out of lessons to prepare for the game.

"Come on Willows, you're slowing the time down,"

bemoaned Marvin.

"Your shouting won't help his trying," replied Conor.

"What was the overall time, sir?" asked Simon.

"One hour and forty-five seconds."

"It's still not good enough. I heard Christwood was down at fifty-eight minutes," added Saffron.

"If we lose on Friday, it's on you Blackstone," snarled Marvin as he barged past Conor.

Seeing that the tension amongst the team was at breaking point Logan suggested to Mr Allister that perhaps a day off from training would do everyone good. Mr Allister agreed. The following day Mr Allister informed the group that instead of training they would be going to collect their uniforms from Uniforme de Magie, a shop owned by Madame Lacroix located at Witchhaven Valley. It had been Conor's second time there and it seemed different. But he was unsure as to whether it had really changed or whether his excitement of collecting his school uniform had caused him to miss the intricate details that made the store unique.

"Morning, Madame Lacroix," said Mr Allister.

Madame Lacroix merely nodded. She had a piece of cloth in her hands and pins in her mouth.

"We are here to collect the uniforms for the match on Friday."

Unable to control her excitement Madame Lacroix dropped everything before heading into the back. She quickly re-emerged requesting Saffron to follow her. Simon and Marvin began questioning Logan intently about anything other than dragons while Conor and Ryan began enchanting spools as they waited for Madame Lacroix to return.

"It is ready," proclaimed Madame Lacroix proudly.

Saffron stepped out from behind Madame Lacroix. The uniform was a pink jumper with the crest of a raven neatly stitched into it.

"PINK! That's a girl colour," scoffed Marvin.

"Is that a problem, Monsieur Davies?"

"It's pink because it's made from a fighting worm from Malta. It's the only thing that dragon fire can't burn," said Logan.

"Zip it, Norwood!" snarled Simon.

Madame Lacroix then summoned the boys one by one to take their measurements. Conor had been chosen last so he quickly decided to step outside. As he left the shop the sight of Mr Basil entering had provided him with the perfect opportunity to speak to him as he had some questions about the wand he had been given.

"Good morning," said Conor.

"I'd been expecting you, |Conor."

"Why?" asked Conor.

"The wand's power has stunned you."

"How did you know?" whispered Conor.

"I told you that wand had the capability of special things. It is not made of your typical unicorn hair and firewood," scoffed Mr Basil.

"So, what is it made of?"

Mr Basil paused as Mr Willows had entered the shop.

"Morning, Basil. I've come to collect the Mrs's wand," .

"Ah yes, it's in the back. I'll go and get it."

"Good thing I saw you when I did Conor. Your dragon is ready to be picked up."

"Really, when should I come and get him?" said Conor excitedly.

"Friday after school."

A furious tapping on the glass had attracted the attention of both Conor and Mr Willows. It had been Simon who began gesturing wildly. Conor then hastily left Basil's wand shop and re-entered Uniforme de Magie. The sight that greeted him had brought him near to tears. Marvin snarled at him before becoming rabid in his attempt to remove the uniform and the smile towards Conor was quickly quashed as Mr Allister handed him his jumper. It was slightly big for his frame but Conor had not minded as the weather forecast for Friday was awful.

The Thursday morning provided one final opportunity for Mr Allister and his team to iron out any teething problems they had. Logan's confidence had grown so that he had taken lead of the final training session. His book was seen as a secret weapon and he spent most of his time with Ryan. Surprisingly, this seemed to have had an effect as Conor and Ryan's improved time had been brought down by two minutes as the Christwood Academy team looked on.

The day had arrived, Conor's breakfast remained untouched. He began tapping the table furiously as any nails he had, had been bitten off. and his breaths seemed endless. In an attempt to relieve any pressure her grandson may have been feeling Amelia tried and failed miserably at reciting some jokes but undeterred she then insisted on driving him to school. In a few hours Conor would be taking on a fully-grown dragon in front of hundreds of his peers. He was nervous but also excited as these were the days he had longed for when stuck at home. Few words were spoken on the drive as Amelia was wary of unnerving her grandson further. They arrived at Ravensborough High where Amelia wished her grandson luck before confirming the time the event started.

Conor focused himself as he walked through the front gates. Such was his focus Ryan's appearance and story of how had been training tirelessly throughout the night had gone completely unnoticed but Ryan had managed to briefly disturb his friend's focus by reminding him about collecting his dragon from his father. This halted him in his tracks. How could he have forgotten his plans immediately changed as there would be no time for any last-minute practice? He thought this could potentially be a good thing as any additional training would probably worsen his nerves. Professor Higginbotham's history lesson seemed to take an eternity to end but then again it always did as it was her last year of teaching. As she would be turning seventy-one, every lesson seemed to finish with endless stories of her many years at Ravensborough High. This would soon turn into her bursting into tears. Such was the regularity of this occurring everyone had brought tissues with them.

Lunch had really hammered home the reality of what Conor and the others were about to embark on as banners began being unfurled. The beauty and care resonated with him as he turned to fully appreciate the artistry but as he turned back he had been greeted by a note from Simon and Marvin who had asked Conor to meet them at the end of the school day. Usually, Conor would have torn up the note but with the game starting in a couple of hours Conor was sure that there would be no problems. The end of the school day duly arrived.

"Blackstone!" shouted Marvin.

Conor turned to see who had called him and the sight of Simon standing behind him had reminded him of the note. He told Simon that he could not stay for too long before following him. The ringing of a bell could be heard and it began to get louder as the two approached.

"My bike," said Conor running towards it. Marvin stepped in front of the bike.

"What's going on?" asked Conor.

"My brother Marvin told me about how he was looking for an opportunity to give you this back so why not today I said," replied Simon pacing around Conor.

"Thank you."

"There's just one thing before we give it you back," sniggered Simon.

"What, anything?"

"Drop Willows as your partner," shouted Marvin "We've even got you a new partner, Swarbrick."

Conor was stunned. Did Simon and Marvin really think that little of him, that he was that shallow? He turned and faced Simon; it must have been his idea. Marvin was a lot of things but he was not so cunning.

"No," bellowed Conor.

"URO," shouted Marvin. The bike burst into flames; Simon glared at Marvin before chasing after Conor.

"I'm sorry about him," said Marvin blocking Conor's path.

"Can you move? I have somewhere to go."

Simon remained still before grabbing hold of Conor's shoulders.

"I understand Willows is your friend. But you know how much this means to the school and do you want to be the one that everyone blames when Willows eventually mucks everything up cause you know he will?" said Simon.

Conor wrestled Simon off him but his shoulders still felt heavy. For as much as he had hated what Simon said he had not been entirely wrong as Ryan was the weakest member of the team. Conor was deep in thought. Maybe it would be best for everyone if he did take Jay to be his new partner as it would save Ryan from the ridicule of others if they lost something Conor was all too familiar with. Mr Allister emerged from the building.

"Come on lads, we have a shield to win," he said.

"Sir, I have to go somewhere," said Conor.

Mr Allister looked at Conor before pointing towards the bus. Conor regrettably got on. Mr Allister and Logan spent most of the journey explaining how Conor, Simon and Marvin should approach their matches but Conor was uninterested as the Willows family was on his mind. He was sure Mr Willows would be furious with him for not coming to collect his dragon. What about Ryan? How would he tell him that he no longer wanted him to be his partner? The bus had arrived. Eyes were fixed on the boys as they made their way to the field, but these soon turned to whispers and slight giggling. The field looked nothing like the one they had trained on. The grass seemed greener. As it glistened, the Christwood Academy crest had been mowed into it. The stands filled quickly as it seemed that the entirety of Christwood Academy had come to watch. Marvin began prodding Conor who jolted his neck to see that Ryan had arrived.

"Have you seen my dad," said Ryan looking nervous.

"No, why?" replied Conor.

"Didn't you come with him? I thought you were supposed to pick up your dragon. Actually, never mind I see him, he's next to your gran."

Ryan began waving frantically. Conor slowly turned around fully expecting a scowl to greet him but to his surprise smiles and waves were forthcoming from both his gran and Mr Willows. In that moment he knew he could not betray his friend. Conor then pushed past Ryan, and the smiles on Simon and Marvin's faces disappeared as Conor informed him of his decision. But before they could say anything their names sounded. It had been the headmistress of Christwood Academy, Belinda Wolfmoon. The game was about to begin.

It had been a rare sight to see someone tower over Simon and Marvin but Phoenix Flinthook, a final year student of Christwood Academy did just that and he began glaring at the two boys during the coin toss. Simon raised his fist in triumph; they had won it. Simon, Marvin, Conor and Ryan took their seats as boos began raining down from the crowd as Saffron stepped onto the field. Her face was stern but she was ready. The dragon was then released and it was the Whifflesnout who let out a tremendous roar.

As the match started the only sounds that could be

185

heard were from the Ravensborough bench as Marvin and Simon began cheering. Saffron was masterful in her craft; her wand movement resembled that of a conductor leading an orchestra. Such was the level of skill the grass remained unscorched. Conor and Ryan were in awe as they hadn't even heard of some of the spells Saffron had performed. The Whifflesnout was no match for her and finally the ground shuddered as the Whifflesnout fell. Saffron bowed to the crowd. She had clocked up a time of ten minutes.

The crowd did not remain silent for long as Aaron Shadowstorm, formerly of Ravensborough High, made his way onto the field. He was not as graceful or elegant as Saffron. Well, that's what Conor thought at least but he had managed to post a respectable time of thirteen minutes. Another coin toss had gone in favour of Ravensborough; Simon and Marvin seemed more interested in annoying the crowd than actually participating, their antics bringing a stern warning from the referee.

Mr Allister held his head in his hands as Marvin and Simon's performance had been nothing short of an embarrassment. They had been unable to ground the two-headed Hagglemuff reaching the thirty five minute limit, a first in Draco Iudiciis history, bemoaned Mr Allister, and their bickering had been drowned by thunderous cheers.

The Hagglemuff proved rather tricky as even an experienced wizard, Phoenix Flintscaw and his partner Delilah Gloompelt, a final year witch, also struggled but their teamwork proved vital as the Hagglemuff had defeated itself. The time had been logged at twenty seven minutes. Conor and Ryan readied themselves sure that they would be next but they would be made to wait as they had lost the coin toss. As the final box was wheeled onto the field two burly figures then made their way onto the grass; they had been the girls that Conor had met at the fair. The dragon then stepped onto the field. It was tremendous much more majestic than the others. It was as white as a sheet of paper and its eyes a mesmeric yellow.

"Tremendous stuff from the Trunchbull Twins posting a quite ridiculous time of twenty five minutes. Surely the Raven's shield will be staying at Christwood Academy," exclaimed Monty Marrowmonth who up to this point had remained silent.

Faint boos could be heard but they were soon drowned by cheers from both the Christwood bench and the crowd. Conor looked on more determined than ever to bring the shield back to Ravensborough High. He rushed to Logan hoping for any last-minute advice but the hush of the crowd had meant the final game was about to begin.

"Ravensborough High will need to ground the dragon within nineteen minutes to win outright with twenty minutes taking it to another round," said Monty smiling into the microphone

Conor and Ryan stood side by side only looking at each other briefly as they waited for the dragon. Ryan began fiddling with his helmet. The dragon now stood before them, its eyes widening as the whistle sounded. The first five minutes were uneventful as two light spells performed by Conor had hardly troubled the dragon. The only spell Ryan had managed to hit the dragon with was a fireball jinx which would have been catastrophic if Saffron had not enchanted the grass. Seeing the time passing, Conor became more aggressive. *"Mentis imperium"* he cried as the dragon halted in the middle of the field, almost statuesque.

The boos and jeers turned to deafening silence.

Conor then began rotating his wand and the dragon began moving at his beck and call. The cheers grew from the Ravensborough bench but it was quickly hushed as the dragon began chasing Ryan. Something had gone wrong. Conor flicked his wand again but the dragon did not respond. He could not understand why the spell had stopped working and glanced towards the bench. Logan's eyes met Conor's as he gestured towards the crowd. Conor spotted the reporter from the fair. It had been Margret who stood at the back smirking devilishly. She had been performing a counter spell. Knowing that Ryan's life was in potential danger Conor ran across the field before leaping into the crowd.

"*LATUS,*" screeched Conor.

The spell had narrowly missed Margret but it had caused her to stumble temporarily ending her counter spell.

"*FLUCTUM IGNIS,*" thundered Margret regaining her balance.

Flames began arrowing towards Conor as he stumbled backwards onto the field. The whistle sounded. Only a few minutes remained. Conor stumbled to his feet and a massive shadow shrouded him in darkness. It was the dragon who stood above him looking menacing.

"*ALLIGES DUPLICIA,*" roared Ryan.

A blue rope-like bolt whizzed through the air as Ryan began pulling the dragon towards him. The ground shuddered as it crashed into the ground. The whistled sounded again.

RAVENSBOROUGH HIGH HAD WON.

Mr Allister rushed onto the field quickly followed by Saffron, Logan and Conor. They were eventually joined by Simon and Marvin who skulked over and looked like they would explode. It had been all worth it, Conor thought after seeing Simon and Marvin's expression.

"How did you do that?" asked a stunned Conor.

"I told you; I'd been practising."

The conversation went no further as the ceremony was about to begin. Belinda Wolfmoon congratulated each member of the team individually. When she reached Conor, she began scowling before begrudgingly holding out her hand. Conor did the same and the two then shook each other's hand. It was brief and cold.

"May the captain join me at the front?" asked Miss Wolfmoon. Her bitterness was apparent.

Simon and Marvin began squabbling to see who would go first. Mr Allister stepped in front of them and ushered them to one side. Conor looked on as Simon and Marvin became more and more animated. Ryan was then called over by Mr Allister. Their conversation was brief before Ryan rushed back over to Conor.

"What did Sir want?" whispered Conor.

"He said he wants me to lift the shield," mumbled Ryan. "Do you want to do it with me?"

Conor wanted to scream yes but remained quiet.

"No, you deserve to do it," said Ryan.

Ryan seemed to be disappointed by Conor's decision. Miss Wolfmoon again asked for the captain to join her. Conor ushered Ryan towards the stage and he thanked Miss Wolfmoon before collecting the shield.

Ryan held the shield aloft proudly. Marvin then charged towards him. Unsure of his intentions, Conor readied his wand but it was quickly lowered as Marvin had hoisted Ryan onto his shoulders. The lack of celebration or cheering had not come as a surprise as only a few students from Ravensborough High had been allowed in. It was eerily silent; they had at least expected some heckling even some booing but nothing. Conor noticed a large crowd gathering by the spectators' stand. He began to worry because his grandmother had been sitting there. He quickly rushed over followed by Ryan. They waded through the crowd and the looks on the many faces indicated this was serious. Conor had still not spotted his grandmother nor had Ryan seen his father. Each took a breath as they made their way past the last few people and abruptly stopped when they saw somebody on the ground.

"Dad!" cried Ryan rushing to his side. "What happened?" he screeched.

The crowd remained silent, visibly lost; Conor then looked to his grandmother.

"Gran, what happened?" said a shaken Conor.

"I—I don't know. We were clapping and he just fell," stuttered Amelia.

"Ryan, is that you?" whispered Mr Willows, his eye now barely open.

Ryan responded holding his father tightly. His hands became white. "What is this?" he demanded. Saffron informed him that it was nymph dust which had the ability to conceal fatal wounds. Ryan then wiped the remainder of his father's neck which had three scratches on it. The air left Conor's body as he sunk to his knees. He knew who had inflicted those wounds. It had been his dragon. He looked at the ground unable to look at his friend.

"C—Conor," mumbled Mr Willows.

Conor crawled towards him not once raising his head.

"I'm sorry. This is all my fault," whispered Conor.

Mr Willows slowly raised his arm before laying a finger on Conor's mouth.

"I need you to look after Ryan. I know you won't let me down, you're a good boy." Conor held Mr Willows' hand tightly as he mustered a smile. Their eyes met and Conor saw no hate, only gratitude.

"I promise," he uttered as Conor left to be beside his grandmother.

Ryan lay beside his father placing his head on his chest. Mr Willows began running his fingers through his son's hair. "I'm proud of you," mumbled Mr Willows which brought a smile from Ryan.

Mr Willows pressed his chest closer to Ryan's head. Its warmth soothed his son who began to shut his eyes. Few words were spoken after that as the two just enjoyed each other's company. Ryan slowly got to his feet. He stared blankly; his eyes soulless. His father's chest had gone cold.

CHAPTER NINE

A FAMILIAR TOUCH

"The train from London to Dover will be departing in ten minutes," said a voice over the tannoy.

Conor sat beside his grandmother as they waited at St Pancras Station for their train. It had been the first time he had been to London. He had always wanted to leave Ravensborough but just wished it had been to visit somewhere nicer or rather somebody nicer. They had been going to visit his great aunt Celia and her two daughters, Connie and Clara who were both older than Conor. Unfortunately for him they were all terrible in their own ways. his great aunt Celia wasn't all that bad but rather suffocating as she insisted on being in the know about everything whenever she'd visited Ravensborough. He dreaded to think what she'd be like with home comforts but her daughters were much worse. Connie, the eldest, was her mother's daughter and rather snooty as she always dismissed Conor when he attempted to speak to her. He was sure it had been at least five years since he last heard her speak.

But the ultimate scourge was, and had always been, Clara. She made his life a misery. It was almost as if she was playing a game toying with him and seeing how many times a day she could get him into trouble The thought of her made Conor question whether he disliked her more than Simon and Marvin. It was something he'd never thought would be possible.

"Why are we going to great aunt Celia's?" asked Conor sulkily.

"I thought you deserved a treat. Your Aunt Celia has said Connie and Clara can't wait for you to visit," beamed Amelia.

What a rotten treat, he thought, but he wasn't buying it. He knew this was an attempt to take his mind off what had happened to Mr Willows. It had been two weeks since Conor had last seen or spoken to Ryan and he often thought of visiting but was unsure of what to say or do so decided against it. Guilt still swept through him. It often kept him awake, something he confided in with Mr Harrowood who suggested that he should speak to his grandmother and explain what he was going through. Mr Harrowood's advice had never steered Conor in the wrong direction. Perhaps telling his grandmother would ease some of his guilt.

The screech of the tannoy sounded again telling them their train had arrived.

As they waited for it to come to a halt Conor quickly checked the journey time. Perfect, he thought. He would have plenty of time to tell his gran how he was feeling. He then quickly boarded the train as the guard began scowling at him. Conor looked on in astonishment as he reached his seat for his grandmother had fallen asleep. This wasn't going to deter Conor as he saw this as a chance to do something he had always wanted: talk to a normal. The train seemed to be moving at a frantic pace as Conor felt he was performing an obstacle course and as he made his way through the walkway the train sped up again throwing the young witch backwards.

"Get off me, you little runt!" hissed a man.

Conor leapt off him.

"Are you not going to apologise? Look at me, I'm soaked."

Conor remained still, He felt as if was drowning as the man continued with his relentless interrogation.

"My apologies. He gets restless on long journeys," said a voice.

Stunned, Conor turned to see who had come to his aid. A short, old, scruffy looking man stood before him but before he could say anything the man instructed him to follow him. Normally Conor would have refused but anywhere else was better than where he currently found himself. Eyes began following Conor and the old man as they continued through the train. For the first time the stares were the least of his worries as the man had not said a thing since asking him to follow him.

The man then suddenly halted stepping aside allowing Conor to reach a seat. The next ten minutes seemed endless as the man refused to say anything merely grunting as he struggled with a crossword. Fog appeared on the carriage window allowing Conor to combat his boredom by playing noughts and crosses. After three tightly contested games in which he somehow managed to draw each one, Conor decided that he could wait no longer. He had to know why the man had asked him to follow him.

"MAGIC!" howled the man.

"Sorry?"

"I've finally cracked it; a five-letter word. What do people most desire? It has to be magic. Right, well that's what I would want anyway."

"I don't think it's magic, more likely to be money," replied Conor.

"Yes, I suppose money would be better," said the man looking disappointed.

Conor began to smirk but quickly restrained himself as he still had pressing questions to ask the man. "Why did you ask me to follow you?" he said softly.

"I needed someone to keep that side warm for me just in case I wanted to change seat," he giggled.

Conor was tired of constantly being the butt of people's jokes and stood up to return to his seat. His first encounter with a normal had been a disappointment.

"Wait, I see you're not a fan of jokes but in all seriousness, I just wanted some company. It's my first trip without my Lucy."

Conor stood there. As much as he wanted to leave he couldn't. The man seemed genuinely upset and alone and he more than anyone knew what it was like to feel that way. Besides, he still hadn't thanked the man for helping him."

"If you don't mind me asking who's Lucy? Was she your wife?"

"No, she's me dog. Bloody cousin's allergic to 'em so I couldn't bring her," replied the man.

"Oh, I'm sorry to hear that."

"It's all right, I'll be fine. You have a name? No wait, don't tell me, I'll guess it. I have a gift for that sort of thing. I'm a fortune teller, you see."

"Do you have name?" asked Conor.

"The name's Ryan but that's name's too posh for me so everyone calls me General Would you like me to tell you your fortune?" he added.

Conor began giggling to himself. He wondered if all people named Ryan were this colourful and eccentric. General then began tapping the table waiting for Conor's response.

"Go on then, tell me my fortune."

Excited, General swooped underneath the table before placing a large rucksack on it. He then began rummaging through it for a while before placing three crystals on the table.

"Stones? How are stones going to tell me my fortune?" scoffed Conor.

"Crystals, not stones. They speak to me; they tell me the secrets of the soul."

Before Conor could say anything in response General shut his eyes and began mumbling. This went on for what seemed forever. He then suddenly opened his eyes and began shuddering, his skin now resembling that of a porcelain doll.

"What is it? What did the crystals say?" asked Conor jokingly still not taking the old man seriously.

"I saw murky water, I saw hands and I heard hissing," mumbled General.

"Seriously, I think you should get your crystals checked. I can hardly swim so I wouldn't go near water and there are no snakes in Dover," chuckled Conor.

"Perhaps you're right. These things do have their moments of madness," replied General.

He then spent the next few minutes telling Conor about his life and travels. Conor was in awe as he listened. The stories that had floated around the playground about normals hadn't been true; they weren't boring, unexcitable people. Far from it because if General was to be believed he had done things much more exciting than anyone who had ever come from Ravensborough.

"Wow! You've been to all those countries," said Conor.

"It's been fun," replied General.

The tannoy screeched again announcing they would be arriving in Dover shortly. This had brought a forlorn expression from General who then asked Conor if he had any exciting stories. Of course, he did but for obvious reasons Conor could not tell his new friend about the hectic change in his life as what had happened to him in the last six months alone could fill a book. As Conor began formulating a made-up story his ears began burning. Sticky began ringing through the train and he began sinking further and further into his seat.

"What's the matter? ."

"That's my Gran shouting. She can be so

195

embarrassing sometimes."

"I'm sure she's not that bad I'm looking forward to meeting her," remarked General.

The carriage door flew open. Conor's heart began racing as the carriage seemed to be shrinking. As the footsteps approaching his seat grew louder and more ferocious, he heard a yelp.. His grandmother had arrived.

"Thank gosh! Where have you been Sticky? I've been looking everywhere for you," said Amelia.

"Gran," bemoaned Conor.

"Sorry, it's my fault. He was just keeping me company," said General.

Amelia began looking at him intently almost as if she was inspecting him. This had not gone unnoticed by General who began looking back at Amelia trying to match her intent stare. But he couldn't maintain it. It was not in his nature and he began to smirk. This quickly turned into laughter.

"Who's your friend, Sticky?"

Conor who was virtually under the table at this point remained silent. He was lost for words or rather too embarrassed to say anything.

"The name is Ryan but everyone calls me General. Pleasured to meet your acquaintance," he said in a serious manner.

"Well, General, I hope you don't mind me taking my grandson off your hands," Amelia laughed forcefully.

Conor slithered out from underneath the table before gathering his belongings. He then asked if he could say goodbye to the man. His grandmother reluctantly agreed as she stood by the carriage door.

"I never got to thank you for helping me earlier so thank you," said Conor.

"No problem. I think you should be getting a move on before your gran explodes over there," joked General.

Conor then headed towards the carriage door.

"Oh, Conor, thank you for giving me one of the best days I've had in a long time."

"I guess them crystals are not that bad. You got my name right," said Conor.

"They still need a polishing. Your name is stitched onto your bag," chuckled General.

Gradually the train began to slow down as Conor and his grandmother passed through the carriages. As they reached their original seats the train had fully halted. They had arrived. . Conor's mood had changed for the first time. He hadn't minded visiting his great aunt as if his encounter with General was anything to go by, the week would be fun.

Dover Priory Station was suddenly filled with screams and commotion as great aunt Celia had arrived with Clara much to Conor's annoyance. It had come as a surprise when great aunt Celia announced that she had a surprise planned. Clara quickly interrupted reminding her mother to inform Conor of her number one rule.

"Thank you, sweetie. There is one rule that I must insist you follow Conor. No magic around the normals. Is that understood?" said great aunt Celia.

Her rule wasn't a problem as Conor hadn't planned to use magic. So much so that he hadn't bothered to bring his wand but he soon began to feel uneasy as Clara began smirking at him. He was sure she was planning something big. Amelia then asked where they were going. Clara blurted out the location. They were heading for Dover Castle. Amelia and Celia then began recounting the many times that they'd in the castle.

The excitement of the castle quickly faded as Conor focused all of his energy on watching Clara as he was sure she was planning something big but as of yet she posed a threat.

The tour had reached the final room. Conor became ever more relaxed and began to take in his surroundings.

They were in a medieval dining room. The shields on the wall in particular caught his attention but for the wrong reasons as they began to rattle. They were becoming detached from the wall. There was no need to turn around Conor knew who was tampering with the shield. "Clara," he grunted before charging towards her.

"What are you doing? Your mum said no magic in front of the normals," said an exasperated Conor.

"We've been traipsing around this castle all day. Now I want to have some fun."

Luckily for Conor the tour guide had kept the attention of the normals as well as his gran and great aunt. He knew he had to stop Clara as the blame would surely be put on him. To his surprise Clara had left the shield as she was unable to get it off the wall but Conor knew his cousin well. She had something else in her sight. The walls of the dining became a false gold as the sky was filled with chalices.

"Stop, please," squeaked Conor.

His words fell on deaf ears as Clara began sending the chalices around the room floating them delicately above the oblivious crowd. Time stood still for Conor as without his wand his wandless magic skill was far less of Clara's. Seeing no other viable options he quietly crept behind her before leaping on her. Gasps rang out throughout the room as Conor struggled to contain Clara who had become irate. The chalices then began to rain down.

"IMÓVEL!" exploded great aunt Celia.

The frantic moving around the room stopped. Great aunt Celia and Amelia glided across the room. Conor and Clara wrestled each other both trying to get to their feet first. Clara had won. Conor listened disbelievingly as Clara's demeanour had changed and she had spun a convincing lie. Knowing how this would end Conor quickly intervened and it quickly changed into a shouting match between the two.

"QUIET" shouted Amelia. "You both know the rules, no magic in front of the normals. What were you thinking?"

"Sorry, Aunt Amelia," sobbed Clara.

Clara and Conor spoke at the same time. They asked the same thing: what was going to happen to the normals? Amelia was unsure and tried explaining but great aunt Celia quickly intervened as Amelia began stumbling over her words.

"We're going to have to erase their memories," said great aunt Celia.

"Is that necessary Celia? Can't we just reverse time instead?" asked Amelia.

"We cannot risk it. I'll only erase the last hour."

"We can erase memories," said a stunned Conor.

"Of course, we can but it takes a delicate touch and extreme focus."

Conor and Clara were then ushered out of the room by Amelia. Both he and Clara began peering past the wall they were both quietly excited. As his great aunt positioned herself in the centre of the normals a cry of *REPEL MEMORI* filled the room. Celia then unfroze the normals before hastily walking out of the room. The fun, the excitable mood had vanished and been replaced by an uneasy awkwardness as even Clara remained silent for the remainder of the journey home. A chuckle from Conor had broken the silence. He could not believe his eyes as the house eerily resembled that of his own. The smile was firmly wiped off Conor's face as great aunt Celia announced the sleeping arrangements.

"No way," bellowed Conor.

"This is not fair, Mum. Can't he sleep on the sofa?" argued Clara.

"Enough, both of you. This is not up for discussion so get over it."

Clara stormed upstairs. Once settled in Conor was

invited by his grandmother to join her and his great aunt for a game of Scrabble. Conor was reluctant at first knowing his grandmother's competitive side but he accepted as he hoped this time would be different. It hadn't as day soon turned to night and the game became highly competitive. Conor soon found himself constantly flicking through a dictionary trying to find words that would keep him in the game. His eyes soon began to wander.

"Gran, can I go to bed? I'm tired."

"Quitting already! What are you teaching them at Ravensborough, Amelia," teased great aunt Celia.

"Pay no attention to her. She's only teasing, we'll finish the game."

Loud chatter reverberated through the house and even to the top of the stairs waking Conor in the process. The conversation made for interesting listening. As Conor walked to the kitchen accusations of cheating were being thrown back and forth. The chatter and accusations suddenly stopped as he entered the room. All eyes were directed towards him.

"What's wrong, did I do something?"

Connie and Clara began sniggering.

"What are you laughing about?" barked Conor.

Clara, still laughing, handed Conor a spoon. A thundering scream filled the house as Conor began frantically running around the house. Five minutes passed before he made his way back to the kitchen. He was inconsolable.

"Don't worry, Conor, it's not that bad," lied his grandmother.

"Don't worry, I'm blooming blue," shrilled Conor. "It was you, wasn't it? Change me back," he barked in the direction of Clara.

Apologetic, great aunt Celia then ordered Clara to undo whatever she had done. Clara was furious that she was being accused but her pleas were ignored and she slithered up the stairs. Once downstairs Clara ushered Conor to one side before performing the counter spell but to her horror Conor remained blue.

"What are we going to do? We're leaving tomorrow. I can't go back to Ravensborough looking like this," bemoaned Conor.

"We'll fix this, I promise," said great aunt Celia.
The remainder of the day was spent in the kitchen as both his grandmother and great aunt began making a range of potions trying to reverse the spell. Conor began to worry that he would sprout a third eye such was the prominence of eye of newt in every potion. He hated the taste. What was even worse was that it had all been in vain as no potion had managed to change Conor back. Disappointment was the overriding emotion in the house as everyone headed to bed.

The house was up early as Amelia, Celia and Connie headed to London to gather more ingredients. Conor too was up early. He couldn't sleep as the thought of what would be awaiting him if he returned to Ravensborough. Blue began to play on his mind. Clara then strode into the room.

"How is my favourite cousin doing this morning?"

"Go away," barked Conor.

"You only have yourself to blame for still being blue."

"What are you banging on about?"

Clara began smirking. "It's a mood spell. It shows how you're feeling. To be honest I half expected you to be red by now. What do you have to be sad about?" she said.

"Some got hurt because of me," murmured Conor. Clara stopped smirking before sitting beside Conor who was visibly upset.

"What happened?" asked Clara.

Conor then began explaining what had transpired. Clara remained silent gripped by what she was being told. For the first time there was no animosity between the two as Clara began comforting her younger cousin. A weight had been lifted off Conor; while he still felt slight guilt. Having someone to talk to had helped. Clara quickly headed to the kitchen. She then handed Conor a spoon. He began smiling as his skin started to return to its natural brownish honey tone.

"Thanks for listening," said Conor.

"We're Blackstones, that's what we do," replied Clara.

As much as Conor hated to admit it, he was going to miss Dover. His grandmother's inclination had been right. The trip had helped although he was never going to admit that to her. The train back into London hadn't lived up to the first journey but Conor hadn't minded as it was unlikely that any normal would have matched General. It had been two hours since they had arrived back in Ravensborough but Conor found himself in an all too familiar position, as he stared blankly at his bedroom ceiling unable to sleep. A sleeping charm helped although it had been a struggle to take effect as thoughts and emotions were still swirling around his head.

The sound of creaking filled the upstairs hallway. It had been coming from Conor's room. His duvet was sprawled across the floor as he began tossing and turning furiously. He was having a nightmare and his pillow, normally a heavenly white, had become stained with sweat. A shout of *sorry* filled his room. He jolted upwards and began panting. He then clutched his chest trying to control his breathing. His nightmare had been about Mr Willows. This had to end, Conor thought, but he was unsure about how to stop the guilt, the torment. Suddenly the perfect solution became apparent. He floated off his bed before grabbing a pen off his desk and headed downstairs.

The living room floor became blanketed with scrunched up pieces of paper as heavy sighing would have to replace the furious banging on the table Conor would normally do to vent his frustration as he did not want to alert his grandmother. "Why is this so hard?" Conor mumbled to himself. He had done this hundreds of times before and had been trying to write a letter to Mr Willows hoping that this would bring the closure that he desperately wanted. He began shuffling across the dining room table hoping a new seat would unlock his thoughts but again the page remained empty. As he reached the final seat the sound of scurrying could be heard. It had been coming from his grandmother's bearded dragon tank.

To his surprise the bearded dragon was nowhere to be found. The scurrying resumed. It had been coming from inside the wall Conor began following it and it had led him back upstairs. As he began tiptoeing around the upstairs landing the scurrying became more and more feint. Conor sighed as he knew this had meant the bearded dragon was in the attic.

Slowly, he crept out of his room after retrieving his wand then positioned himself underneath the attic door before summoning the steps down. The cold metal stairs kissed the soles of Conor's bare feet it tickled. A sharp gust of wind brushed his face as he got to his feet. He had remembered why the attic was rarely visited as the window was broken but Conor pressed ahead as the scurrying noise was louder than ever. He was sure he could pass for an acrobat such was the amount of shuffling and bending he was made to do to avoid the mounds of boxes that were piled up.

The scurrying was now being accompanied by hissing but rather strangely the sounds were beginning to echo., Conor had known it had been coming from the Blackstone family birthing cauldron.

"What are you doing up here?" he whispered.

He then picked up the reptile and began running his fingers along its back. Hisses of approval sounded out.

BANG!

Conor mustered a faint yelp before stumbling backwards. He began scanning the floor looking for what he had crashed into. It had been a chest. Odd, he thought, he had never seen it before. Intrigued, he slowly lifted the lid. It was a uniform, a Ravensborough High uniform. Further rummaging through the chest soon revealed the owner. It had been his mother. Night soon turned to day as Conor found himself learning new information about her. It was a pleasant surprise. His mother had been quite troublesome as the chest had been filled with letters from Philip, one item, a photo, had really attracted Conor's attention.

The creak of the floorboard had drawn Conor's attention.

"Conor, what are you doing up here? It's freezing."

"It was Queenie. I heard her in the walls and followed her up here," said Conor.

"Really, she's never done that before. What have you got there?" said Amelia pointing at the photo.

"Gran, who's this?" he asked handing his grandmother the photo.

"It's your Mum and Mrs Autumn. They were quite inseparable, sort of like you and Ryan."

"I know that's Miss. You can't mistake those green glasses; I meant the boy in the background. Who is he?"

Amelia inspected the photo. She was hesitant almost as if she had been shocked at what she had seen. This hadn't gone unnoticed as Conor then questioned whether his grandmother was okay. Quickly snapping out of her trans-like state, Amelia spoke.

"Ah, this was one of your mum's friends, a wizard. His name escapes me but he has since left town. Speaking of wizards, don't you think it's time that you paid one a visit?"

Conor initially had a look of bewilderment on his face but it quickly faded as he realised who his grandmother had been talking about. The two then exited the attic. The sound of Conor's heavy breathing was all that could be heard in her car. His uneasiness was apparent and he felt as if his heart was going to jump out of his chest.

"Gran, please can we go back home? I can't do this," pleaded Conor.

"Conor, you can't avoid Ryan forever. He is going to need all his friends around him now more than ever," replied Amelia.

"It's my fault. If I'd just forgotten about the stupid bike maybe I could have saved him, and maybe Mr Willows would still be here."

"You mustn't blame yourself, Conor. I'm glad you didn't make it to meet Mr Willows. I couldn't bear the thought of losing you as well. Besides I saw the way Mr Willows looked at you. He didn't blame you for what happened, it was just an unfortunate accident."

Conor knew that not for the first time his grandmother was right and he began thinking of all the times Ryan had come to his aid. Without even giving it a second thought, it was time to return the favour. He owed Ryan that much. The car came to a premature stop because of roadworks. Conor stepped out and clutched his shirt as his nerves returned more rampant than ever. He then shuffled across thinking the longer he waited the more likely he would be to back out.

It had been the first time Conor had ever been to Ryan's house. It resembled his own but then so did every house in Ravensborough. Conor began folding the sleeve of his jumper over his hand as the sweatiness of his palms had not allowed him to grip the door knocker. He knocked and his heart began racing. He was glad there was no immediate answer as he didn't even know what he was going to say to whoever answered. Flowers, he thought, how could he have forgotten about flowers? Slowly, he began to leave but the creak of the front door had drawn him back but as he turned around the person that stood before him was a surprise. It had not been Ryan or his mum but a small boy.

Surely his grandmother had driven him to the wrong house. Ryan never mentioned that he had a younger brother. The boy's stare was intense as he began inspecting Conor with his eyes.

"Did you knock on my door? What do you want?" he squeaked.

"Sorry, does Ryan live here?"

"He's not in," said the boy.

The sound of ruffling from inside the house caused Conor to glance upwards. It had been coming from an upstairs bedroom. Conor knew Ryan was home but not wanting to damage further their relationship he asked the boy to pass on a message.

"When he does come back can you tell him Conor said sorry?"

"Wait! Don't go! You're Conor Blackstone, that's so cool," marvelled the boy.

Before Conor could say anything, the boy vanished back into the house. He was flattered if not a little surprised. How had the little boy known about him? Was he really that well known? The boy re-emerged.

"Do you have a name?" asked Conor.

"The name's Duncan Willows. I'm Ryan's cousin." You're a witch aren't you? Does that mean you can control cats? Imagine, your very own army of cats. That would be so wicked," beamed Duncan.

Conor could believe that Duncan was Ryan's cousin. Duncan's mood and presence had instantly cheered up the young witch who was originally going to tell Duncan that he couldn't control cats but decided against it. He didn't want to extinguish the excitement Duncan was feeling. It

206

wasn't technically untrue as he had never tried it before.

"Can I show you something?" Duncan asked before quickly shuffling behind the front door. He then returned holding in his hand a bearded dragon similar to the one his grandmother owned.

"Oh, my gran has one of those. Can I hold it?" asked Conor.

Duncan at first was hesitant but he didn't want to seem uncool especially in front of Conor. Slowly, he handed it over to Conor who in turn was careful when handling it. He then began stroking it.

"Does he have name?"

"His name's Angus. We go everywhere together. Can I have him back now? He gets easily frightened around new people."

Conor was rather disappointed as he was enjoying the reptile's company. He went to hand Angus back to Duncan when suddenly the reptile jumped out of his hand before scuttling into the road. It had been heading for the open drain hole. Conor panicked and pulled out his wand and fired at the drain cover. But it was in vain as Angus had fallen into the sewer. Duncan pushed past Conor before peering down the hole, but he couldn't see anything.

"I am so sorry. I'll get you a new one. I promise."

"You don't understand. Angus is not mine, he's me sisters. She'll know if we replace him. We have to get him back otherwise she'll turn me into haggis," bemoaned Duncan.

A hissing sound echoed from the hole.

"I'm coming Angus, hold on tight," shouted Duncan who then began lowering himself into the black hole.

"Wait, what are you doing? It's too dangerous, you don't know what's down there. I won't let you. I'll talk to your sister, say it's my fault."

Duncan ignored Conor's pleas as he dropped into the sewer and then began bemoaning the stench of the water.

Conor, riddled with guilt, knew he couldn't allow Duncan to enter the unknown by himself especially since it was his fault that Angus had escaped. He then prepared himself to enter the drain hole.

SPLOSH!

Conor grunted as the water had soaked his clothes. The repugnant stench from the water had caught him off guard but he continued to push through. Duncan's name rang out but the echo of Conor's voice was all that could be heard. Again, a quick flick and shake of his wand had illuminated the path. The sudden sounds of footsteps were a welcome relief as Conor followed them to locate Duncan. The two then began walking but neither saying anything. In an attempt to break the awkward silence Conor began asking Duncan a few questions hoping to learn more about him.

"Is there a reason why you called him Angus?"

"It's where my Granny lives. She was the one that brought him," replied Duncan.

"So, you're from Scotland?"

Duncan did not answer. Conor tried to speak again but Duncan began gesturing for quiet. "Can you not hear that?" he said. Conor listened. It was a faint hissing sound and both boys beamed with excitement. Duncan ran towards him. Conor had been no slouch but he struggled to keep up. Suddenly the heavy sploshing sound of water stopped.

"Have you found him?" panted Conor trying to regain his breath.

At first Duncan remained silent before letting out a faint yelp. He pointed towards the water. Not being able to see what Duncan had been pointing at Conor re-illuminated his wand before shining it onto the water. Two bright yellow eyes stared back at him. It had been a snake but it was unlike anything he had seen before. Its skin blended in with the murky water; the water then began trembling as a monstrous hiss echoed throughout the sewer. The snake began approaching slowly. It had Angus in its sights.

"Come on Duncan, we have to go," whispered Conor.

"What about Angus? We can't just leave him here, it's not right," replied Duncan refusing to move from where he was standing.

"We have to. The snake will kill us if we try to take him."

Duncan turned to face Conor. Slowly, he smiled before turning back to face the snake and then leapt into the water quickly grabbing Angus. The sploshing of the water had riled the snake who began picking up tremendous speed and it reached Duncan in mere seconds. Stricken by fear, Duncan stumbled over as he tried to evade the snake it stopped revealing its fangs. It was preparing to pounce.

"MEA GRAVITAS."

Duncan began to float narrowly avoiding the snake which leapt into the air. There was an even louder hiss from the snake which had turned its attention to Conor, its eyes bigger than ever.

SPLOSH!

Conor had fallen over but kept his hand steady still performing the levitation spell, Duncan looked on clutching Angus tightly. Conor then began kicking out hoping the water would put off the snake but it hadn't as it glided through the waves. It again stopped before revealing its fangs then charged at Conor who had shut his eyes accepting his fate.

"Ahhh!" he wailed.

The once boisterous hissing became fainter and fainter as Duncan had fired a lighting spell at the snake. Conor slowly opened his eyes and as he did a sharp pain coursed through his body. He looked down. The water had turned red; the snake had bitten his leg. Duncan gasped. "Your leg," he whimpered.

"Don't worry about it, I'll be fine," grimaced Conor.

"That was so cool," purred Duncan as he helped Conor to his feet.

As they made their way back through the sewer the initial burning sensation Conor had felt returned but this was unlike the first time as it began spreading throughout his entire body. He decided against telling Duncan or at least right away as it would only have slowed them down, something that he wasn't willing to do with the snake was still on the loose. They had finally made it back as Conor pulled himself out of the hole. He began to feel slightly better as he took a prolonged sharp breath.

"Is Angus okay?" he asked.

Duncan replied or at least Conor thought he did. He was sure he saw Duncan's mouth moving but he couldn't hear anything. Odd, he thought. In all the books he had read over the years none mentioned this as a potential side effect to a snake bite but then again, he had never encountered a snake like that before. Its piercing yellow eyes became permanently etched into his mind. Conor then found himself having to blink furiously to keep his eyes open and began clutching his chest as it felt as if the air had been knocked out of him.

CRASH!

"Conor, Conor are you all right?" said Duncan fretfully.

Duncan seemed to be fading away. Conor couldn't hold out any longer. His eyes were shutting rapidly and then stretched his hand out but was unsure if Duncan had got hold of it as Conor was now shrouded in darkness. The sound of whispering was a welcome surprise for Conor as it meant he hadn't died but he was still unable to open his eyes. His thoughts soon turned to the bashing he was going to receive when he was awake as he was sure his gran wouldn't leave his side for the remainder of the year.

Conor's thoughts were disrupted as his name began sounding out but it was not his grandmother's voice. It was similar but softer, almost angelic. He had heard it before, he was sure of it. A presence then placed itself beside him. He felt it a hand then run alongside his face. It was a touch that was all too familiar, a touch he hadn't felt in many a year. Slowly, he opened his eyes.

"Mum is that— I thought—"

She giggled before running her hand along her son's face again.

"I'd never thought I'd see the day my Sticky was lost for words."

Conor then leapt out of his covers, then wrapped himself around his mother. The perfume she had been wearing tickled his nostrils.

"What was that for?"

Conor remained silent, too elated to talk. He went to hug his mother again but she evaded his grip before sliding off the bed.

"I see what you're trying to do Conor Blackstone. You can try and butter me up all you want but I'm not telling you where we're going. It's a surprise."

She left the room with Conor quickly following her. The washing of dishes never seemed so interesting, Conor thought. He had never found himself focusing on anything so intently as he followed his mother's every moment so much so that his breakfast remained untouched. This had brought a frown from his mum and he then began shuffling pieces of soggy toast into his mouth.

"Where is gran? said Conor still chewing. "She's gone down to London for the day. Look at you, such a messy eater," she giggled. "Now go upstairs and clean yourself up. Your surprise won't wait forever."

Once upstairs Conor's rational side came out as he began questioning where he was. He knew that he was at home but it still didn't explain why his mother was here. He then swooped underneath his bed hoping his snake textbook would provide some much-needed answers. It made for an interesting read. Conor now knew what he was experiencing. It had been a hallucination meaning it wasn't real but Conor hadn't minded as one more day with his mother was worth anything that was awaiting him when he returned to reality.

Finally, out of the house Conor's mother partly revealed the surprise; they would be going to Witchhaven Valley. The bus ride had revealed something Conor couldn't quite fathom. As he gazed through the window he saw his reflection. He wasn't in his normal body but that of his four-year-old self but he thought nothing thinking that it came as part and parcel of the hallucination as that was the last time, he had seen his mother. Conor tightly gripped his mother's hand as they entered the valley. It had been vastly different from what was there in reality. Conor wasn't really the imaging type but he had been quietly impressed with how his mind had managed to reinvent the valley in such a way.

"Mum, can you tell me what the surprise is?" pleaded Conor.

"No, I'll show you."

She then stepped aside. Conor's excitement disappeared as it had been Mr Basil's shop or at least this was where it normally was, they then entered the store. Hundreds of photographs were sprawled across the walls; it definitely wasn't Mr Basil's shop any more, Conor thought as he and his mother arrived at the front desk.

A man then emerged from the back. To Conor's astonishment it had been Mr Basil but he looked different. His hair was fuller; he seemed taller and most noticeable of all he hadn't been wearing his glasses.

"Cora, Master Blackstone, how are you doing this fine morning?" he beamed.

"Not too bad," replied Cora.

As his mother and Mr Basil continued with their conversation, Conor began wandering around the shop hoping to find Mr Basil's wand workshop. But before he could do any proper sleuthing his name rang out through the shop. Conor then rejoined his mother who began rummaging through her bag and handed him a photo. It had been one of him and his mother. Conor gazed at the photo which had seen before.

"Conor, follow Mr Basil. He'll take you to your surprise."

Mr Basil stepped aside before gesturing to the back office. Conor began smiling gleefully. Finally, he thought he was going to see how a wand was made. He bolted towards the curtain that separated himself and the wand making room, took a deep breath and stepped through the curtains.

It hadn't been a wand making room rather it had been something much more wondrous as hundreds of picture frames floated in the air. They danced around the room.

"Splendid, isn't it?" said Mr Basil. "I understand its beauty often leaves many unable to speak."

"What am I supposed to do?" Conor asked.

"Choose one."

Conor looked up. He knew which one he was going to pick and pointed at his choice. Mr Basil smiled as he summoned the frame towards him before heading to his desk. As Mr Basil went to work fixing the picture frame Conor couldn't escape his own thoughts. He decided he should ask Mr Basil where his wand station was.

BANG!

The entire shop seemed to shake.

"What on earth was that?" said Mr Basil. "Wait here,"

he said forcefully.

Conor nodded.

It had been five minutes since Mr Basil had left his office. Conor began to become restless. What was taking him so long, he thought, as he began to walk to the curtains. Suddenly, he stopped as he heard panicked whispers but as he began to peer through the curtains the whispering stopped.

"Mum, what's going on?"

His mother rushed towards him. She gripped his hand tightly and their eyes met. Conor knew something was wrong as the life and happiness that usually filled her eyes had been extinguished and had been replaced with worry and fear.

"Sticky, I need you to do a special job for me. I need you to follow Mr Basil," she trembled.

"Why? Where are you going?"

"There is somewhere I need to go."

"Will I see you again?" asked Conor looking lost.

"I'm not sure but you know that I love you and I will always be with you in here," she said placing her hand on Conor's chest.

"No, I'm not leaving you. Please don't make me go," blubbered Conor.

Cora hugged her son and began stroking his face in an all too familiar manner then whispered in his ear before standing up and waving. Conor took Mr Basil's hand as they headed out of the shop. The sight that greeted Conor outside was horrifying as Witchhaven Valley was ablaze and the screams of frantic people running pierced Conor's ears. He felt sick.

"Come on, we have to go," said Mr Basil.

"Where are we going?"

"I don't know."

The smoke that filled the air began to overwhelm Mr Basil who slowed down then fell to his knees, Conor who had sped out of the valley quickly returned to help Mr Basil to his feet but as he did a large grey hooded figure appeared. Slowly, it began raising its arm before pointing at Conor and then began walking towards them.

"GO! LEAVE NOW!" screamed Mr Basil as he began firing at the hooded figure.

"No, I won't leave you. I'll stay and fight."

"GO!"

Conor knew his was fighting a losing battle and sped off. He glanced back at Mr Basil who had fully engaged the hooded figure, but was unsure about where he should go as he was certain that something bad would be awaiting him if chose to go home. No, he needed somewhere he would be able to hide. "Yes," he cried, he knew exactly where he could go. He just hoped it would be there.

Conor collapsed onto the leaves that were scattered across the ground at Kenbury Forest as he had been running for what seemed like twenty minutes but his rest was brief as he continued onwards. He reached his destination; the cave would provide the perfect hiding spot he thought as who would think to check the forest? It would mean in a few hours he would be able to go home untroubled. As the time passed Conor began to wonder why he hadn't awoken yet. Why had the hallucination taken him to his mother? Or maybe it hadn't been a hallucination at all. Maybe this was something much darker and dangerous. He let out an uneasy laugh as the thought of this being anything else than a hallucination was preposterous.

BANG!

Another bang reverberated through the cave jolting Conor out of his slumber.

"Hello, who's there?" he shouted.

Conor then began advancing through the cave again calling out but again no one responded. A groan then sounded. Conor turned. His heart sank as it had not been his mother or Mr Basil. It had been the grey hooded figure but unlike their previous encounter there had been more than one.

"What do you want?"

But the figures remained silent as they began approaching him. Stunned, Conor stumbled backwards but he was cornered. Frantic, he drew for his wand but it was in his hand only for a few seconds before the hooded figure had summoned it away from him. The figures had finally reached Conor. One figure emerged from the pack and began clutching its fist. Conor began grabbing his neck. He could not breathe. He was being choked and his eyes were shutting. He began breathing his last breaths.

"*LEPOREM LUMINS*" cried a voice.

The cave became heavenly white. Conor quickly shut his eyes. This time he had been glad that all he could see was darkness. He had a sense of *déjà vu* as again he tried to open his eyes but he couldn't and again the sound of voices was all that could be heard.

"Sticky!" screeched Amelia.

"Gran, where am I?"

"You're in the hospital. you gave me quite a fright."

Before Conor could say anything else the doors burst open and a large, shrieking, smiling woman entered. She then rushed to Conor's bedside before pouncing on him. He hadn't felt a hug so strong in a long time, in fact, ever.

"Thank you for saving me wee boy and Angus too," wailed the woman.

"No problem."

The next few hours seemed to fly by as Duncan's mother began heaping praise on Conor. "You're a hero," she said repeatedly. He hadn't felt like one but who was he to say no to being called a hero. The day got better still as Ryan had arrived. He and Conor never actually spoke but this hadn't bothered Conor as Ryan being there was enough.

"Visiting hours are almost done," announced the nurse.

By now it had only been Conor and his grandmother as Duncan, his mother and Ryan had left a while ago but not before Duncan's mother had given Conor several more hugs. A lingering thought still remained as Conor wondered whether he should tell his grandmother about the hallucination. He needed not to think any longer as his grandmother spoke.

"Conor, when you were sleeping you were saying some things, things that frightened me. What was happening in your dream?"

"I don't know. It was weird. I was back with mum and we went to Witchhaven Valley. But it was different. Everything was going well then I lost her again. She told me to follow Mr Basil but I lost him too and then I went to---

"A cave," uttered his grandmother.

"Yes, but how did you know?"

"I've been dreading this day, but you must understand I did this for your own good."

"Did what? What did you do for my own good?"

The door opened

"Excuse me, Miss Blackstone, it's time," said the nurse.

"Wait, tell me what you meant please, Gran."

Amelia stood up from the bed and walked towards the door not once turning to look at her grandson.

CHAPTER TEN

A LETTER FOR A DEAR FRIEND

Conor had wanted to go home. After his first night at the hospital, he had felt fine. It was nothing more than a scratch but his grandmother being her normal overprotective self was having none of it as she told her grandson in no uncertain terms that he would be remaining in hospital until his leg had fully healed. This had brought a feeble sigh from Conor for as much as he hated the hospital, he knew his grandmother was probably right. As the day progressed he began warming to the idea of remaining in hospital as Ryan who had recently arrived from school began angrily rambling Sorceress Elro's English lesson.

"Look at it, how am I supposed do all this by Friday?" bemoaned Ryan pointing towards a large stack of papers.

"I've never seen Miss give out this much homework. What did you do?"

"Used magic in class and before you say why would you do that I had to. Swarbrick was talking saying you were faking it but I put him in his place."

"What did you do to him?"

"Let's just say he left the class in stitches and I didn't tell him any jokes," smirked Ryan.

"You're a numpty, you know. What does Miss always say about using magic in class?"

They grinned at one another before reciting in tandem

what their teacher had always said *"There is no place for magic in English as the words of many a people can give you the same excitement as waving a bit of wood."* They then began laughing.

BUZZ

The laughter stopped as the buzzing continued. It had been Ryan's phone. Ryan then quickly gathered his things before rushing out of the door slightly surprised by what had just happened. Conor decided to use the short free time he would get from his grandmother to get some rest but this was brief as the door suddenly swung open. It had been his grandmother who took a moment to regain her breath before announcing that she had got him moved to a bigger room.

Conor quickly thanked her as he didn't want to come across as ungrateful but, in all honesty, he hadn't minded his cosy room he was in or his roommate, a boy who seemed to have a new story every day about why he had flowers growing from his ears. Conor had hoped moving to a new room without a roommate would finally allow him and his grandmother to talk about his dream as he had felt uneasy talking about it with someone else in the room. But his hope soon turned to frustration as any attempt to talk would be met with a umming and ahhing before an eventual change in subject. This persisted for the remainder of the week until his grandmother, becoming increasingly tired of the relentless questioning, snapped.

"That's enough, Conor. I told you before I just guessed what you were going to say. I know nothing else about this dream you had,".

It had been a week since the dream and Conor felt he was no closer to uncovering the truth. He knew there was more to it. There had to be but the only person that could help him seemed hell bent on doing the opposite. He couldn't understand it. He and his grandmother had always been able to talk but ever since he began attending Ravensborough High that understanding had seemed to disappear. It was as if he didn't really know his gran any more.

KNOCK!

This had caught both Conor and his grandmother off guard as they hadn't been expecting any visitors. The door slowly creaked opened and the anger that had been etched all over Conor's face disappeared. It was Angelica.

"I'm not disturbing anything, am I? If so, I can come back later," said Angelica in an apologetic tone.

"No, of course not. Come in, I was just leaving," said Amelia who quickly exited the room.

A brief silence then ensued. Both were unsure of what to say to one another they then traded brief glances this quickly turned to smiles and the silence was broken with Angelica finally mustering the courage to speak.

"I'm sorry. I would have come earlier." She then began rifling through her bag before placing a small piece of card on Conor's lap and then lightly tapped the card with her wand. The card began to unfold itself. It was massive with the words GET WELL SOON sprawled across it. "I got everyone to sign it even Saffron," said Angelica.

Conor was lost for words. He loved the card. It was majestic and just what he needed to take his mind off the dream but his facial expression painted another picture. It was one of sadness this hadn't gone unnoticed either.

"You hate it, don't you? I knew it was a dumb idea. Why would he need a card?"

"No, it's nice. Thank you, it's just …"

"What is it?" whispered Angelica.

Conor explained everything that had transpired over the last week. Angelica listened intently. Her mind was racing with questions but she held off as it seemed her friend just needed someone to listen to. The room then went quiet and Conor lent in towards her.

"Do you think I'm overacting, that I should just let it go?" asked Conor.

"Maybe your gran is just trying to protect you. Sometimes it's better to leave the past where it belongs," replied Angelica.

Conor had been slightly disappointed as it hadn't been the answer he had hoped for but he understood Angelica's opinion. His gran was probably trying to protect him. Maybe he was putting too much stock into his dream as there must have been a reason why he had forgotten about what had happened.

KNOCK!

The room then became filled with noise as Ryan entered. He was in an excitable mood and threw his tie to the floor triumphantly.

"I've finally finished, I thought my head was gonna explode," he cried.

"Have you handed it in to Miss yet?" asked Conor

"No---

Ryan stopped abruptly as he and Angelica traded glances. It had been the first time they had been in each other's presence since the fair and Conor could feel the tension. He was unsure about what to do as he didn't want to be seen taking sides but his window to find a resolution was closing fast as Ryan headed towards the door.

"Wait, this is childish," said Conor.

"You weren't there. She threw me up in the air" snarled Ryan

"I'm sure she's sorry. Right, Angelica?"

"Of course, I'll do anything to put this right," said Angelica in a sarcastic manner.

Ryan stepped away from the door. The grin on his face was mischievous. He was going to have some fun he had decided but how would Angelica make it up to him? "I want you to teach me that spell."

Angelica laughed. Surely Ryan hadn't been serious but as she glanced in his direction her laughter stopped. He had been serious so she quickly looked to Conor hoping he would intervene but his wondering eyes said it all. "Fine," she grunted. Satisfied with himself, Ryan then sat down, his grin now larger than ever.

"I heard what you guys were talking about and I hope you're not going to listen to her" said Ryan.

"And why wouldn't he listen to me?" hissed Angelica.

"Conor, you have to find out what happened. You don't forget something like that. Don't you want to find out the truth?"

"What truth? Nothing happened. Wouldn't we remember if the valley was attacked," scoffed Angelica.

"Come on, Angelica. Do you think Conor would really imagine the valley being attacked in such detail? I'm telling you there is more to this. You owe it to yourself to find out what happened."

Not for the first time the opening of the Conor's room door had put an end to a conversation. It had been his grandmother. Now was the perfect opportunity, Conor thought, as with both Angelica and Ryan being here, there was no way his grandmother would be able to avoid his questioning.

"Gran, I need to …

"Sorry to interrupt but I have some good news, Sticky I've been speaking with the nurse and she said that you are going to be able to come home today. Sorry, what did you want to say?"

Conor went to speak but paused. He began having second thoughts as he knew this would likely be his last chance to engage his grandmother about the subject. He decided he would wait until a better moment presented itself. It wasn't important, he fibbed.

A strong scent of lemon drifted through the air. His grandmother had been cleaning again as every piece of furniture seemed to glisten in the light. As much as he wanted to admire her work he was tired and his bed he began to head upstairs to his bed but he was quickly halted his grandmother who ordered him onto the sofa. "I'm making us dinner, you need to get your strength up because you've got school tomorrow," she said.

Conor found himself counting the number of spots on the living room wallpaper to combat the immense boredom he was feeling; 1,321 spots in case you were wondering. The next several minutes the kitchen resembled a revolving door as the dining room table vanished underneath all the plates of food. Conor quickly took his seat at the table and rubbed his hands together vigorously. He had been spoilt for choice how could this get any better he thought, the kitchen door opened for a final time Conor was mesmerised as the sight of a giant chocolate cake on the table had brought him to near tears.

Amelia's attempt to start a conversation failed miserably as her grandson had become a blur. Such was the speed he had been eating at the sound of metal clanking on the table was music to her ears.

"Thanks Gran, this was just what I needed," said Conor gleefully. "I see I wasn't the only one who's been spoilt, you got Queenie a new tank."

"There won't be any more daring escapes."

Conor then looked around the room to see if he could spot any more changes but thankfully for him he hadn't so far which had been a good sign because if had his gran probably would have made changes upstairs, too, especially in his room but as his gaze took him to the desk by the stairs he noticed something different, something saddening. A picture had gone missing but not any old picture, it had been the one of him and his mother.

"Gran, where's the picture of me and Mum?" he

asked.

"There was an accident when I was cleaning. It was damaged but I kept it. It's upstairs. Do you want me to get it?"

"Where's the frame? Did you keep it?"

"No, why?"

"I can fix it. Well, Angelica can fix it. I just need the pieces. Are they in the kitchen?" said Conor as he got up from his seat.

"No," screeched Amelia. "It's just a bit of glass isn't it? If the picture is the most important thing I'll get you a new frame," she added.

Conor slumped back into his seat. He couldn't believe what he was hearing, it wasn't just a piece of glass, it was the last thing that he had of his mother. "Can I be excused?" Conor said. He had lost his appetite.

CLICK!

The sound of the bathroom light being turned off had sparked Conor into action.. As he waited for his grandmother to head to bed he slowly crept out of his bedroom. He hadn't cared what she had said. He was going to get his frame back. He headed to the kitchen. The dripping of the tap began to unnerve him as he began rifling through the bin.

"Ahhh!" he whispered, quickly inspecting his finger before slowly placing his hand back into the bin. He then pulled out a large piece of the frame before leaving it on the counter. The remaining pieces were retrieved with minimal fuss. The lamp beside the stairs would have to provide the light Conor needed. It was dim but sufficient enough for him to put the shattered pieces back together. But he hadn't put more than two pieces together before stopping for what was unfolding before him was astonishing. The frame had changed colour; it was no longer red but rather a crystal blue.

The flick of a switch bathed the living room in light. Conor stumbled backwards. He couldn't believe his eyes. It had been the picture frame from his dream, the one he had picked so it hadn't been a dream but rather a memory.

Pacing would become Conor's best friend when he faced conflict and now was no different as he glided throughout the living room thinking what he should do next. His grandmother had lied to him again but why? It didn't make sense. Why was she being so secretive? Conor now found himself questioning everything his gran had told him. Could he even trust her anymore? he thought as he trudged back upstairs towards his room.

He suddenly stopped for you see there had been a third bedroom in the Blackstone household his mother's room. it was rarely spoken of he wasn't banned from going in there but there was an understanding between himself and his grandmother that it would be best that the room was left untroubled as the memories that would come with entering would be too hard to cope with.

Conor began to wonder whether his grandmother had just been using that as a ruse. What if the room hid something more sinister? Something that would shed more light on what truly happened at the Valley. He had to know. He paused as he moved his hand on the door handle but was having second thoughts as he knew that everything was about to change. He then began chuckling to himself and slowly opened the door. His grandmother had been right. Memories had begun flooding back but he hadn't felt sad, he was filled with joy as the sight of ordinary objects placed across the room could tell a story but he only allowed his nostalgic mood to be present briefly as there were more pressing matters ahead. The dresser was the first item Conor searched. He was thorough but careful not wanting to disturb anything but he was to be disappointed as nothing unusual had presented itself. The bedside drawer was next to be checked but again disappointment.

What was he doing? Conor thought as he lay on his mother's bed but something didn't feel right as he moved his head onto the pillow. It was rather lumpy and a closer look had shown the outline of something. It was a letter and written on it was the name Cecil.

"Mr Basil?" he whispered.

His eyes lit up. Was this what he had been looking for? He certainly hoped so. His mind began moving quickly as he wondered what other reason would his mother write to Mr Basil. Surely it had to do with the valley. Sure that he wouldn't find anything of use Conor quickly left the room. He had managed to muster a brief smile as reached his room but he was quickly hit with the realisation that he had to be sure that this letter contained information about the Valley. He reached for his wand before pressing the tip onto the back of the letter.

"Claro," he said. The writing then began revealing itself. He did not have to read long as the reasoning behind the letter quickly became apparent. He then placed the note onto his desk for as much as he wanted to tear it open and read it in full he couldn't bring himself to do so as it wouldn't have been fair to Mr Basil or his mum. There was the small matter of him having to wake up in a few hours for school.

He didn't know how he had managed to get to sleep. He had half hoped it had all been a dream but the sight of the letter on his desk had brought back the same questions that he had yesterday. He didn't have time to mull things over as he was already running late.

The wind seemed more boisterous than usual as it reddened Conor's cheeks. Granted, it had been late November but it almost seemed like the wind had been punishing him for not taking the bus. But he was glad he had braved the elements as the walk had allowed him to think of what he was going to do with the letter.

Miss Scarletwound's normal morning registration

which was normally fun and inciteful seemed to flitter by as Conor spent the majority of the time with his head on his desk. History with Professor Higginbottom was the perfect opportunity for him to catch up on some much-needed rest but as he made his way out of the classroom the tannoy began whining. He found this rather odd as the announcements usually took place before the start of registration and he listened on with added interest.

"Good morning, this is a message to Miss Joyce's Third Year students. There has been a change in the timetable. You now have history with Professor Higginbottom."

Conor had a sickening feeling in the pit of his stomach. He knew this day was bound to come but he just hoped it hadn't been in a lesson with Simon and Marvin. He was dreading it as trouble was sure to follow. Murmurs and grunts filled the corridor as both sets of students waited before being allowed to enter.

"What happened? Did you talk to your gran?" asked Ryan excitedly

This had caught Conor off guard. He wasn't sure whether he wanted to tell Ryan about what had happened. Thankfully for the young witch, he wouldn't have to disappoint his friend as the door to the class opened. Conor took his seat with Ryan quickly following still determined to get an answer to his question. The day had thrown another curveball the young witch's way as the desk behind him shuddered. It had been Simon and Marvin.

"This is going to fun," smirked Simon.

As much as Conor enjoyed history, the history of unicorn hair and its importance wasn't something that had captivated him and he wasn't alone as the classroom was filled with whispered conversation. With the lesson coming to an end Conor found himself in an all too familiar position staring at the clock.

"Well?" said Ryan in a hushed tone.

"Well what?"

"Did you find out what happened? Did it really happen?"

"I'll tell you later."

"Miss!" screeched Marvin.

The classroom fell silent as everyone turned to face Marvin. "Yes, Master Davies. Is there problem?"

"Yes, there is, professor. Conor and Ryan are constantly talking and it's really distracting," bemoaned Marvin struggling to contain his devious smile.

"Is this true?" asked Professor Higginbottom.

"No, of course not, professor," snapped Ryan.

"He's lying, Miss. We can hear them from over here," hissed Saffron.

"I think they should share it with the class, Miss," said Simon.

"I couldn't agree more. Master Blackstone, stand and tell the class about your conversation that's so important it couldn't wait till after class."

Time seemed to stand still as Conor slowly got to his feet. He quickly turned to look at Simon and Marvin who were beaming, proud of what they had done. But Conor simply smiled back at them for little did they know he was prepared. He knew exactly what he was going to say.

"Me and Ryan were just talking about how history next year won't be the same without you professor. We're going to miss you," he said soulfully.

"Really, you're too kind," sniffled Professor Higginbottom as she made her way back towards her desk.

A large clap then sounded as the classroom became shrouded in darkness. Professor Higginbottom began fiddling with her wand and a collective sigh performed in unison rang out as the white board became filled with pictures. The final ten minutes of the lesson was stop, start as Professor Higginbottom would show ten pictures before bursting into tears. Conor again turned to look at Simon and Marvin but unlike before they had not been smiling no rather their faces were burrowed into their arms. Saffron hadn't escaped Conor's attention's either as when he glanced over to her she could hardly be seen. Such was the level she had slumped too and this had brought a devious chuckle from Conor.

"You're a wicked witch, Conor Blackstone," chuckled Ryan.

"I have no idea what you mean," smiled Conor.

The corridor resembled a stampede as the tannoy sounded bringing an end to Professor Higginbottom's lesson. Conor and Ryan were the last to leave as they made their way out of the building. Ryan began coughing loudly almost as if he was trying to gain his friend's attention.

"Is there something you want to ask me?" said Conor shaking his head.

"Sorry, I just want to know what happened yesterday."

Conor glanced all around himself before ushering Ryan back inside. They soon found themselves at the back of the library away from prying ears and eyes. Ryan sat upright. His knees were twitching as he waited for Conor to tell him everything and he was not disappointed. The remainder of break seemed to evaporate as Conor told Ryan everything that had happened yesterday.

"Bloody hell, I thought my life was crazy. What are you going to do?" said Ryan taking a breath.

"I dunno. I guess I'm gonna have to talk to Mr Basil."

"Can I come?" asked Ryan excitedly.

"I'm not sure. I think it would be better if I went alone."

The tannoy sounded as a disappointed but understanding Ryan stood up and headed towards the door but before he left he turned to face his friend before raising his hand. Conor did the same before the two boys went their separate ways.

KNOCK!

A startled Ryan sprang out of bed still half asleep. He stumbled towards his window where the knocking had been coming from. Now more aware of his surroundings, Ryan slowly began to draw back the curtains.

"Conor," he whispered.

He quickly opened his window sure that he was dreaming.

"What are you doing here?" he asked.

"You said you wanted to follow me to the Valley to see Mr Basil."

Ryan let out a forceful laugh and then began rambling. He was confused still sure he was dreaming. Conor too was confused unable to understand anything his friend was saying.

"Wait!" said Ryan. "Are you flying a broom? Where did you get that? I thought they were outlawed. Is that how we're getting to the Valley?"

Conor smiled and nodded. "It's not mine. Angelica let me borrow it. Now hurry up. You coming or what?"

Ryan's face dropped. "Do you really expect me to get on that knowing it's hers? She hates me. What if it crashes as soon as I get on it?" he remarked, slowly edging away from the window.

"Maybe you're right now you mention it. It was leaning off to the right a lot when I was getting here," said Conor.

"Really!" gulped Ryan.

"No, you numpty. Now can we get going?"

"Ha, very funny but how do I get on that thing?"

"You just hop on."

Ryan took a deep breath before opening his window as far as it would go. He was so excited. He had always wanted to fly on a broom but also nervous about falling off. He closed his eyes and began climbing out of his window but suddenly felt a tug at his pyjama bottoms. It was Duncan.

"What are you doing? Can I come?" he asked excitedly

"No, go away."

"Please I'll be quieter than a wee mouse," pleaded Duncan hardly tugging at Ryan

"Oooh, none of this is real. It's all a dream. Go back to bed or I'll get you."

Conor began smirking shaking his head disapprovingly as did Duncan who was straight faced. He was stunned that his cousin wouldn't even try such a thing. "If you don't let me come I'll tell your mum you're sneaking out."

Cornered and still half dangling out of his window, Ryan turned to his friend "Is it all right if Duncan comes along?" he asked begrudgingly

"That's fine. I like Duncan but I don't think the broom is gonna fit all of us so I guess we're walking," said Conor.

The moon was out in force as the trio made their way to Witchhaven Valley. Ryan refused to speak. He was still upset that he had been robbed of the chance of his first broom flight but Conor hadn't noticed. He was having fun as Duncan began telling jokes.

"Why do witches like honey?" asked Duncan.

"Why?" replied Conor waiting excitedly for a response.

"Because it's bewitching," cackled Duncan.

This had been the best joke yet as Conor stumbled forward because he had been laughing so hard. It had even brought a smile from Ryan but as they neared the valley the tone changed as the jokes stopped Duncan wanted to know why they had been going to the valley at the dead of night but as Conor was about to explain they were interrupted by Ryan.

"Shhhh, do you hear that? I think someone's coming,"

he whispered.

Conor hadn't heard anything. Duncan hadn't either but Ryan was taking no chances as he grabbed his cousin and friend, bundling them into a hedge. He then began peering out of the hedge he was quickly proven right as the sound of footsteps and chatter filled the street, Ryan then began chuckling.

"What, what's so funny? Who's out there?" asked Conor.

"You're not gonna believe this. It's sir and Mr Marto coming out of the valley," Ryan said softly.

"Really!" Conor then peered through the hedge and watched intriguingly as the voices became louder as Mr Marto began moaning about Mr Basil "t-that o-ld b-bat still owes me a wand," he said slurring his words. Professor Marigold began consoling him and this brought hushed laughter from the young witch for whatever happened after this point would be a bonus. A gentle rustle from behind them had been enough for both Conor and Ryan to retreat into the hedge. A worrying sight greeted them as Duncan's face was scrunched up with his eyes resembling a leaking tap.

"What's wrong with him?" asked Ryan.

"How am I supposed to know he's your cousin?"

"I-I T-T-think I'm allergic to this bush," sniffled Duncan holding his nose.

Conor and Ryan began looking at each other. What were they going to do? They couldn't have Duncan blowing their cover as any moment from now their teachers would be walking past them. With no time to waste Ryan quickly took charge drawing for his wand and pointing it at Duncan "Etrar," he said. Three large stitches then appeared over Duncan's mouth.

"I've been dying to do that spell again," said Ryan.

Professor Marigold and Mr Marto passed the hedge totally unaware that two of their students were kneeling perfectly still on the other side. The sound of fading voices in the distance had brought sighs from both Conor and Ryan and a mumble from Duncan. The three then continued on their journey.

"Aren't you going to reverse the spell?" asked Conor as Duncan's mumbling became louder and louder.

"Nah, I like him better this way."

They had arrived. The Valley had looked vastly different as a combination of the night sky and dimly lit street lights had brought a new shine to the shops. Conor could not contain how he was feeling any longer as he began speeding through the valley with Ryan and Duncan trailing behind. The smell of burning wax was a guide, he thought, as he neared Mr Basil's wand shop. Conor halted and began staring blankly. "What was he waiting for?" he whispered. Only a door had separated him from the truth. He slowly began to push it and it creaked.

"Hello, Mr Basil. Are you here?" he said.

There was no response. Mr Basil should have been there. Again, Conor asked, "Is anyone here?" but again there was no reply. Conor began traipsing through the shop towards the office but again nobody was there. The creaking door had .brought him rushing back through the curtains but to his disappointment it had been only been Ryan and Duncan.

"Come on, let's go," he mumbled.

Ryan hadn't bothered asking what had happened as Conor's face had said it all. The three then trudged out of the store defeated. Ryan became uneasy as they walked back towards the entrance of the valley. He had wanted to comfort his friend but he was unsure how. He came to a halt as somebody had been standing at the entrance. It had been a troll no taller than Duncan. It remained silent before smiling welcomingly almost as if they had been waiting for them

"Ted?" said Ryan, shocked.

"Who's Ted?" asked Conor.

"That's two-faced Ted. He works with Simon and Marvin's dad. They own Bill and Ted's Artefacts near Uniforme de Magic."

Conor began wondering why the troll had been called two faced but he soon wondered no more as the troll stepped into the moonlight and began twisting its head. It was eerily beautiful and the process was finished as another face was revealed.

"Oh, it's the Willows' boy. Ghastly business what happened to your dad." "Get to the rose," snarled the other face. "Ah yes, a little birdie told me one of you has a rose."

Rose? The three boys began looking at each other. They didn't have a rose and weren't even sure that roses grew in Ravensborough. Suddenly Conor's pocket began to rattle. his wand which had been named Rose. But how had they known? He had never seen Ted before but then again, he hadn't exactly followed Mr Basil's instructions of only using it when necessary.

"Come on lads, I'm in trouble with the missus and she really loves roses. I'll even give you two kippers and few squid for it," said Ted winking.

"Sorry, we don't have any roses," said Conor as he slowly began backing away.

Ted then spoke in hushed whispers. He would briefly stop before glancing in the boys' direction and seemed to be taking a particular interest in Duncan.

"All right but I do like look of that broom I'm a bit of a clean freak and I think that broom there would really help when cleaning the shop," said Ted smiling.

Conor grabbed the broom out of Duncan's hand before backing away at a faster rate but as he took a few more steps he stopped, or rather something had stopped him, and he quickly turned to see who it was. His eyes immediately lit up. It was Mr Basil.

"Is there a problem here, Ted?"

"No, Basil me old chum. We were just leaving," replied Ted who slowly began to back out of the valley, cursing as he did so.

Conor went to speak but he was interrupted by Mr Basil. He was irate reminding the boys about how dangerous the valley was at night especially for unescorted children. He then ordered them to follow him as he would be sending them home via a wizard transportation note but Conor refused still determined to find out the truth. Mr Basil was having none of it as he began walking towards his shop.

"I KNOW ABOUT THE PICTURE SHOP," yelled Conor

Conor quickly held his hand over his mouth not wanting anything else to spew out. Mr Basil then turned, a look of astonishment sketched across his face. He didn't say a word only throwing his hand over his shoulder before continuing walking. The boys had taken this a sign to follow. They were worryingly surprised as they passed the wand shop where had they been heading. They trudged on a few more feet before coming to an abrupt halt. It had been the shop Conor had first noticed on his first trip to the valley. They entered the shop which was in a terrible state as hundreds of tiny boxes were stacked in one corner. Mr Basil then went into the back and the sound of whistle then sounded..

"Tea anyone?" asked Mr Basil avoiding eye contact.

"No, thank you," replied Conor.

"We don't want any tea. We just want to know what happened to the valley and don't try and deny it. You know what we're talking about," said Ryan becoming increasingly impatient.

"Ryan!" shouted an angered Conor.

"No, his right. I've had this bottled up for eight years but I must ask Conor if you want to know what happened?"

Conor nodded.

Mr Basil sighed before beginning to speak. "On that day eight years ago it was an ambush Ravensborough wasn't ready for. They laid siege on the valley destroying everything or anyone that stood in their way and they weren't going to leave until they had got what they came for."

"Who came?" asked Conor.

"It was normals," whispered Mr Basil almost as if he had been ashamed to say it.

"Normals! Come on, Conor, let's go. He hasn't got a clue what happened. He's having us on," shouted Ryan as he stood up.

"But how? There aren't any normals in Ravensborough."

"That's true but haven't you boys ever wondered why a wall randomly stands in Kenbury Forest as if it's separating us from something or someone?"

Conor and Ryan had the same look across their faces. They had always wondered if there had been a wall.

"A-are there normals on the other side of that wall?" gulped Conor. "But why would they attack the valley? What did they want?" he asked.

"It is believed that they were after you," said Mr Basil.

"Me, why would they want me?" chocked Conor

"Nobody knows, but I believe they were acting on behalf of someone. Dark magic has great power. It can control people, offer them things beyond their wildest dreams, right mistakes of the past. Even the strongest minded wizard or witch would be foolish to resist the allure of magic if it presented itself. So naturally a Normal wouldn't stand a chance if such power was offered to them especially the leader of the normals who is a particularly nasty man."

"But why didn't Conor remember this happening?" asked Ryan who was now beginning to believe Mr Basil, "and why is he remembering all of this now?"

"The council used a memory charm on him," said Mr Basil grimacing as he relived the memory. "I too am wondering how Conor had come to remember the attack."

Duncan who had been silent up to this point then began moaning and grunting. It seemed like he knew why Conor had remembered the valley attack and quickly reached for his wand undoing Ryan's stitching spell.

"It was a Sythenix," said Duncan.

"Sythenix?" asked Conor slightly confused.

"The snake that bit you in the sewer had to be a Sythenix. Its venom is the only know thing that can reverse a mind charm," added Duncan.

"They're coming for me again, aren't they? Is that why you gave me this wand? You said it yourself. It isn't a normal," said Conor as he looked at his wand.

"You are right. Your wand isn't like any other. It contains something special, something that offers its owner great protection."

"But you must be worried about another attack. Is that why you made this wand and gave it to me?"

The question had gone unanswered as Mr Basil stood and slowly began retreating to the office. Conor followed wanting to make sure that he hadn't upset the wandmaker. The office was dark for a brief moment before becoming dimly lit a large picture was revealed it stood above the desk it had commanded the attention of the room Conor too looked on with added intrigue

"Who's that?" he asked

"That's Rose, the maker of your wand and the owner of this shop. She was the original wandmaker in Ravensborough," shuddered Mr Basil.

"What happened to her?"

"The reason that you and I are alive today is down to her. She gave up the most precious a person can give her life so I could find you in that cave-now you see why I must make wands. Her legacy her passion must live on."

"I'm sorry. I'm sure she was a great person," said Conor looking in awe at the photo.

"She was."

Conor was interested in knowing more about Rose. After all she had saved his life and Mr Basil was more than happy to talk to her. The two then spoke for several minutes but as they were finishing up one question still lingered in the mind of the young witch.

"Can you tell me about my wand? What makes it so special? Why can it do things without me asking?"

"As you know normal, a wand usual contains one strand of hair from a magical creature but yours contains two, the first being from a Calygreyhound, a creature so swift and agile and so majestic it is rarely ever caught. The second strand is where the true greatness of the wand lies as it's from Kenbury Ravensborough, our town founder. That wand in your hand is the most powerful in all of Ravensborough."

"But why give it to me?" asked Conor reluctantly not wanting to seem ungrateful.

Mr Basil smirked as he looked at Conor. "I have given that wand to many a witch and wizard over the years, both young and old, hoping to find it a home. But it has always found its way back to me. Often people crave great power but when presented with it there is a lack of understanding about how to control it. I'd almost given up hope of finding Rose a home but when I couldn't fix your mother's wand I knew Rose had found her home for you see sometimes the greatest need trumps the greatest want."

Conor took a step back unsure of what to say. Had Mr Basil really entrusted him with such power and why? A flurry of questions flooded his mind but as he went to speak he quickly stopped as Mr Basil had beaten him to the punch.

"I'd imagine you have quite a few questions but I think they should wait for another time as it seems your friends are rather tired you'd best be off," said the wandmaker as the sound of snoring grew louder and louder.

"But I have so many questions about the wand and the normal," bemoaned Conor as he began walking out of the office.

"Wait!" cried Mr Basil as he began rummaging through the drawer before pulling out a large book. "This book should answer any questions you have about the normal. Page 256 should have what you're looking for," he added.

"Thanks."

"Best not to tell your gran about this. You wouldn't want to get bitten by a snake again," winked Mr Basil.

"Actually, I have something for you," said Conor.

"What is it?"

"It's a letter from my mum. I think you know what it's about."

"Your mother was a good person," said Mr Basil.

"I know, "smiled Conor.

The sound of a large hushed sigh filled the room. Conor had arrived home. His bed shook as he collapsed onto it but his rest was brief as he reached for the book. Two hours, maybe more, had passed since Conor had begun reading and he hadn't gone to page 256. He couldn't, the book was far too interesting with every page explaining the history between normals and witches and wizards.

Conor had duly arrived at page 256 at 2.56 am. This had made him chuckle. Fate, he thought. But the chuckles quickly stopped as to his surprise the page had just been a map of Ravensborough or so he thought. On closer inspection the map had revealed something. Murlayfield, he said to himself. It had been another town. He couldn't believe it. The normals that attacked the valley had only lived a forest away from them. He read on as page after page revealed the connection between the two towns. It was gripping.

THUD!

The floor creaked as Conor trembled. His face was as white as a sheet. He had seen what he thought he saw but he hoped not. Maybe his mind had been playing tricks on him because of the lateness of the hour. He bent down to pick up the book and began pouring over the page. It had been dedicated to the leaders of Murlayfield showing photos of each one. Conor's face grimaced as he stared at a particular photo. It was of the current mayor of Murlayfield, the person who had most likely sanctioned the attack on Ravensborough. His mind hadn't been playing tricks on him. He had seen this person before or rather the person had been shown to him. It had been Emily's dad.

CHAPTER ELEVEN

MURLAYFIELD

"3...2...1"

Emily grunted in frustration quickly throwing a pillow over her face. The constant stop and starting of counting had woken her up. It had been coming from outside her door by her two older brothers' Oliver and Leo. It soon stopped but it was brief as the two began speaking in hushed whispers. They had been talking about her. Emily's ears were burning as she listened in. Whenever they tended to talk about her they were usually planning to play a prank on her.

"I don't think this is good idea. You know she's been acting weird ever since she found out about those things on the other side of the forest. What if she tries to bite us if we do it?" whispered Leo, the fear in his voice obvious.

She hadn't been acting weird. Emily felt her behaviour was pretty normal. How was she supposed to act after finding out that only forest separated her town from witches and wizards but not only that; her father, the town mayor, had made the whole town fear their neighbours. Her thoughts soon took a back seat as her brothers had resumed their conversation.

"That exactly why we should do it. I know how I felt when mum told me about those things," said Oliver.

Emily was stunned. This had been the first time she had ever seen or heard her brothers take into account her emotions. Maybe they weren't planning a prank after all.

"Besides, we do this every year. It's a Grey family tradition," said Oliver defiantly. "Well, it's our tradition. Now let's do this before she wakes up," he quickly added.

Traditions? What were her brothers talking about? Emily's previous thought was quickly rescinded as she was now sure her brothers were planning something but what? Her face quickly whitened as she had realised the date: December 1st. She quietly threw the covers off hers not wanting to alert her brothers she then began frantically tiptoeing around her room gathering a bunch of her clothes before throwing them onto her bed making sure to cover them.

Emily was now in her cupboard and quickly put her hand over her mouth. Her breathing was frantic as the sound of footsteps grew closer and closer. Her door creaked, it seemed to take an eternity to open. The whispering voices had returned. Emily listened as her two brothers began laughing. She too joined in chuckling to herself as she waited to pounce.

SPLASH!

The room went silent. "What where is she?" asked Oliver looking furiously at Leo.

The cupboard door flew open.

"What is that? W-w-what are you going to do with t-those?" stuttered Leo.

Emily laughed. "What's the matter? it's the 1st of December. Like you always say it's time to embrace the season and cool off," she said slowly before spraying her brothers with water. The stairs barely had time to shudder such was the speed Emily was travelling as she made her way to the kitchen.

"Oooh!" said Emily's mother as Emily hugged her tightly from behind.

"M-morning M-mum," said Emily panting.

The Grey household smelled wondrous as the breakfast table was filled with an assortment of delights. Emily sat down gazing at the feast before deciding what to eat first. She thought she already knew the answer. Sausages were her favourite. She then waltzed over to the cupboard but as she reached for the handle the ceiling above her shook. She ran back to the table as her brothers were coming downstairs.

"What on earth are you two playing at? What's with all the noise?" asked their mother frantically.

Her question had gone unanswered as both Oliver and Leo too had been lured to the table by the sight and aroma of the feast. Emily sighed as she made her way back to the cupboard. There would be no backlash for her actions, well not any time soon, as her brothers were still starry eyed at all the food on offer but as Emily had finally got the ketchup her attention was drawn to her mother speaking.

"Ah, not those. They are for your father when he gets home," she said pointing at the plate of sausages.

Emily rolled her eyes and began shaking her head. She had wanted the sausages but that was not the reason for her change in demeanour. It had been the mention of her father. He had recently created the night society, a group of townspeople who would patrol the forest every night to ensure that no unwanted visitors would try to intrude. The table shuddered as Emily took her seat; a plate bore the brunt of her frustration. She had lost her appetite. A scream rang out throughout the house. It had come from upstairs. The stairs then shook as Emily's younger brother Matthew bundled downstairs rambling.

"This is not good. Why did you let me sleep so long? We're going to be late," he said fiddling with his school tie.

"Relax, darling. We'll make it."

"My appointment is at nine thirty," replied Matthew becoming increasingly flustered at the thought of being late.

"It's only 9.01, metal mouth," sniggered Leo.

"I'm aware of the time but the dentist is twenty-five minutes away, thirty-three with traffic which is going to be the most likely scenario as it is a Monday. Did you know you're ten times more likely to get stuck in traffic on a Monday?"

"Oh really," said their Mother. "We'd best get a move on then, wouldn't want to be late," she added playfully.

"Wait!" said Emily "How are me and Leo going to get school?"

"Oh, your father will take you. He shouldn't be any longer. Speaking of school, shouldn't you get dressed?"

"But Mum..." moaned Emily.

"Sorry, darling. We'll talk later."

And with that Emily trudged upstairs to get ready for school.

BEEP!

"Come on, Emily," shouted Leo honking the horn again.

Emily had hoped if she laboured long enough her father and Leo would simply become bored waiting and leave without her. But unfortunately that hadn't been the case as the honking only intensified. Finally admitting defeat, Emily traipsed downstairs and got into her father's car. Matthew's fact about traffic had rung true as Emily and her father had found themselves in that exact predicament. But sadly for Emily the torment wouldn't stop there as the conversation between her father and Leo took a sinister turn.

"Stop!" said Emily forcefully.

"Why?" scoffed Leo. "I can't wait to see what dad's gonna do when he catches one of those freaks on our side," he said looking proudly at his father.

"Now, son, we educate those who do not know the

truth not berate them. Apologise to your sister," said Mr Grey.

"Sorry," murmured Leo.

The traffic had finally moved briefly halting the conversation but neither Emily nor her father had finished speaking their minds. "You're a smart girl Emily but I suggest you do your research if you feel anything other than contempt for those disgusting creatures on the other side of the forest," hissed her father.

"Maybe they're not that bad," replied Emily. "Have you ever tried talking to them?" she suggested.

"Typical girl, eh Leo, always about reasoning. You can't talk to those things that show weakness. You have to take action," roared Mr Grey.

"STOP THE CAR!" shouted Emily.

The car came to a screeching halt, "What's the matter? Is everything okay?" asked Mr Grey, but it wasn't. Emily, now more furious than ever. angrily unbuckled her seatbelt before quickly exiting the car. Stunned, Mr Grey pulled up alongside his daughter before winding down his window but Emily spurned any attempt of a reconciliation. The car quickly sped off.

As Emily continued on her now prolonged journey to school she couldn't stop thinking about what her father had said to her. How dare he, she mumbled. She wasn't in any need of education when it came to witches and wizards as unlike her father she had actually spoken to them. She was sure that they were no threat and she couldn't understand why her father and the rest of Murlayfield harboured so much resentment to their neighbours across the forest. But as she began to wonder just why that was the case, the sound of running snatched her focus. It had been her best friend, Kelly Milkton.

"Happy anniversary, Tee," said Kelly excitedly.

Emily, initially bemused by Kelly's outburst, quickly realised what her friend had been talking about. How could she have forgotten that today marked a year since her mother, herself and her brothers had moved back to Murlayfield? "Thank you," she said.

"I got you a present," said Kelly wiping her glasses as it had begun to rain.

"Ah really, you didn't have to.."

The light rain had quickly turned into a heavy shower and they found themselves running for Murlayfield Tech. A car horn had attracted the attention of both girls who had paused to catch their breath.

"Lovely weather, isn't it girls?" laughed Mr Grey.

Emily sighed as she watched her father drive off but as she about to shout her voice was drowned out by the sound of the Murlayfield tech bell. The two girls ran the short distance to their school hoping they would not have to face headmistress Upton who made it her mission to personally greet every late student before issuing them with a detention. The word peculiar had become synonymous with Emily as it would best describe her life at the moment and today was no different as the emptiness of the playground shocked both her and Kelly.

"Where's Upton? She's always waiting," said Emily.

"She probably inside waiting at the front desk. You know she'd never risk her clown face running with all this rain," joked Kelly.

This had brought a smile to Emily's face. The two girls then walked towards the main building side by side. "Ah, I almost forgot," said Kelly halting abruptly. She began rummaging through her bag before pulling out a small silver box. It was beautiful, thought Emily, as she held the box in her hand. Her smile widened as Emily was sure she knew what the box contained but to her surprise it hadn't been what she had thought. It was a piece of paper neatly folded "What is it?" she then asked.

"Open it and see."

Emily smirked as it hadn't been a mere piece of paper

but rather a photo of Kelly herself. "You're really something, you know," said Emily, her smirk wider than ever.

"I know but you'd have to admit it's been a hell of a year."

Kelly hadn't been wrong. Emily dreaded to think about how her time at Murlayfield Tech would have differed if she hadn't met her bespectacled friend. As for her all her faults and there were many, Kelly had been just what Emily needed most in the world during this time: a friend. Emily glanced at her gift one final time as they neared the classroom. Again she smiled but this smile was different to all others before it was genuine. She had received a great gift. Suddenly the classroom door flew open the two girls became statuesque slowly turning to face each other as the figure blocking their passage moved forward.

"M-m-mrs Up-pton!" blurted Kelly.

Mrs Upton's face remained unmoved. It was still as uninviting as ever.

"We're so sorry we're late. It was all my fault," said Kelly.

The hallway was filled with the laughter of Mrs Upton which seemed to go on for an eternity. She suddenly stopped before composing herself.. "It's quite all right, Miss Milkton. Now why don't you head on inside. Registration it about to end."

"Are you feeling all right, Miss?" joked Kelly as she headed inside.

"Never better, Miss Milkton," replied Mrs Upton. "Actually, before I forget, could I borrow you Miss Grey? I need to have a word with you."

"Me," squeaked Emily.

Emily was taken aback by her classmate's expression as she backed out of the classroom to follow Mrs Upton. It had been the same as hers, that of astonishment as it was well known around the school that herself and Mrs Upton hadn't always seen eye to eye during her first year at Murlayfield Tech and the relationship had only soured since the incident. "Come on, Miss Grey, I haven't got all day," said Mrs Upton.

Emily hurriedly exited the classroom. As they walked through the corridor Emily became increasingly nervous as Mrs Upton's earlier warm behaviour had vanished and she hadn't looked at Emily once. She was sure that this meeting was not going to end well.

"Wait!" said Emily.

Mrs Upton stopped abruptly she quickly turned scowling at Emily. "Is something the matter, Miss Grey?"

"No, Miss. It's just I heard your office had some unwanted visitors," said Emily. Her voice was getting fainter and fainter with each word.

"You mustn't always believe playground rumours, Emily," replied Mrs Upton. "Now if there are any more problems please save them until we get to my office."

Emily remained silent as they climbed the stairs to reach the office, but once inside her eye suddenly lit up. By the sight that greeted her. The walls were filled with picture frames but they weren't of achievements but rather that of the headmistress's son, Edward who was in Emily's year.

"It's glorious, isn't it?" swooned Mrs Upton strutting around her office.

"It's something," murmured Emily.

"Please take a seat. You're probably wondering why you're even here but don't worry you're not in any trouble. A rather exciting opportunity has come up," said Mrs Upton, her smile returning.

"Opportunity?" said Emily intrigued.

"Yes, as you know every year we have assembly where all students of Murlayfield Tech come together. and one student from each year volunteers to speak about a group of people that we should have in our thoughts over the holiday period. Isn't Edward speaking for my year?"

"Unfortunately, my Eddiekins has got the flu and won't be able to do it and he has chosen you to replace him."

"ME!" choked Emily.

"I too had I similar reaction, but it's seems my Eddiekins is of the forgiving nature. He gets that from his father, you know."

"I'm not sure that I can do this, Miss."

"Miss Grey, you will be making a speech this Friday. I've already had a word with your father who said you'd be more than happy to do it."

"But Miss…"

"Ah, Miss Grey," said Mrs Upton pointing at the clock. "There is learning to be had. I'll be looking forward to hearing your speech next Friday," she added whilst ushering Emily towards the door.

Emily sighed as she collapsed onto the seat outside Mrs Upton's office. There was still a few minutes until the bell went for first lessons. Had today really happened? Emily began chuckling to herself. Of course it had. That's just the way her life had been going. She didn't know how she was going to write a speech in six days or whether it was even possible. She didn't even know what she could talk about, but just as ideas were moving in her mind, the bell rang.

BANG! The corridor doors flew open. Startled, Emily leapt behind her chair before peering over to see, to her relief, Kelly.

"Well, what did Upton want?" she asked.

"You're looking at Year Nines new speech maker" said Emily whilst getting to her feet.

"What? I thought her precious Eddiekins was doing it."

"He's got the flu."

"The flu? Really," questioned Kelly.

"Oh, it gets better. He was the one that chose me to replace him."

"You don't think this is his way of getting back at you for not coming to his birthday party?"

"I don't, maybe?"

"I guess you could say he's one upped you," said Kelly as she burst out laughing.

"Come on, let's go before we get a detention for being late," said Emily as she headed towards the doors.

"What you didn't like the joke?" shouted Kelly quickly following her friend.

Between English, Latin and Science, all subjects Emily despised, as well as having to contend with Kelly's continuous attempts to atone for her earlier terrible joke Emily wondered how she had made it through the school day but as she walked towards the front entrance of Murlayfield Tech she was in a more upbeat mood. It was Friday meaning she wouldn't have to think about Mrs Upton or the speech for two whole days but keeping to the theme of the day Emily's name rang out. It was Mrs Upton who slowly trudged over.

"Ah, Emily. I know I'm cutting into your weekend so I'll keep this brief. The assembly has been brought forward to Wednesday," she said.

"What? Why?" asked Emily.

"Ah, ah, ah, Miss Grey," said Mrs Upton gesturing to her wrist. "I don't want to keep you any longer. Besides, you have someone waiting for you."

Emily didn't need to turn around to know it had been Kelly waiting for her. She was also sure that she would face a barrage of questions and sure enough as the two walked through the gates the questioning started. But it ended before it ever truly begun as understandably Emily had only one thing on her mind: her speech. She was terrified how was she going to prepare it for Wednesday but trying to remain positive she remembered that it would be just her and her mother at home as Oliver had headed back to London to university, whilst Leo and Matthew had sleepovers.

Mrs Grey began huffing and puffing as the ceiling above her shook. As the clock struck six Emily let out a blood-curdling shriek before leaping out of her desk chair. She began pacing around her room stomping her feet hoping it would help with her idea process as up to this point her notepad had been empty. The pacing quickly stopped as Emily's door thudded. Another hour passed. Again, Emily's notepad was empty. Sensing that nothing was going to happen Emily closed her notepad and got dressed for bed hoping an early night would help her formulate new ideas.

"Up, wake up!" shouted Mrs Grey.

Emily leapt out of bed to find her mother zooming around her room stuffing her clothes into a bag. "Mum, what are you doing? What's going on?" she asked concerned by her mother's behaviour.

"No time to explain," huffed her mother, "get dressed. You're going to Miss Little's."

"Do I have to? She's weird not to mention Jake and her cat Jingles," bemoaned Emily.

"I don't want to hear it. NOW GO AND WAIT DOWNSTAIRS," barked Mrs Grey.

Emily was still stunned as they drove to Miss Little's house. Seeing this, her mother apologised before informing her that her father he been in hospital. But Emily was still more worried about Miss Little's house as her father had a tendency to exaggerate his injuries. The moon was partly big as Emily waited outside for somebody to answer the door.

"Oh, it's you. Miss Little, she's here" shouted a voice.

"Nice seeing you too, Matthew," said Emily as she entered.

The smell of cabbage was distinct as Emily walked towards the living room. She paused briefly as Jingles strutted across her path in a dismissive manner.

"Emily!" shrilled Miss Little grabbing hold of her guest. "Sorry, please take a seat. Dinner's almost ready."

"What, on that?" asked Emily pointing towards a bean bag.

"We don't do sofas here unfortunately," smiled Miss Little.

Emily sunk lower and lower into her beanbag hoping it would swallow her whole as the hours torturously went by. She began to trudge towards the stairs such was her boredom. But Miss Little, ever the optimist, tried her best to get her new guest involved by suggesting a game of Monopoly. Emily was glad she had been talked out of going to bed as she would have never forgiven herself if she had missed out on the spectacle that was unfolding before her eyes.

"You always do this. I wanted Mayfair," bemoaned Jake.

Jingles screeched as she scuttled towards the door. Emily too found herself diving behind the beanbags for cover as miniature red houses began whizzing through the air.

"What on earth is going on? Both of you, BED NOW!" snapped Miss Little stroking Jingles softly.

"What about dinner?" squeaked Jake.

Miss Little's scowl had both Matthew and Jake scrambling for the staircase. Emily was slightly disappointed as that had signalled the end of her entertainment for the evening and worse still dinner was finally ready. The thought of actual chairs was the only thing that was appealing to Emily as she trudged towards the kitchen. The table resembled that of an allotment garden as its content was disappointingly green. Emily ponderously moved a large piece of broccoli around her plate. She wasn't really in the mood for eating.

"Is something the matter, Emily? Don't worry about those two upstairs. I'll bring them a sandwich later," said Miss Little.

"I'm not worried about those two," replied Emily.

"It's about your speech."

"Wait how did you kn..."

"I heard Matthew talking about it earlier... struggling for ideas?" asked Miss Grey

"You could say that. I don't suppose you have any?" smiled Emily.

"Well, often at times when I'm in need of guidance I often look close to home," remarked Miss Grey.

Emily remained at the table after dinner had finished. Her mind was hard at work. She was sure that Miss Little had been trying to tell her something but what? Murlayfield wasn't exactly teeming with problems. Deciding that she needed to know what her host had meant Emily quickly exited the kitchen and headed for the living room.

"Ah, Emily, would you be a dear and hand me that book on the shelf there?" asked Miss Grey moving her knitting to one side.

Emily sighed as it hadn't been a book but rather a picture album. "Could I ask you a question Miss Little?" said Emily.

"Of course, but I'd like to show you something first if you don't mind." The old lady then began flipping through the album before abruptly stopping. "Do you know who this is?" asked Miss Grey.

Emily now sitting beside Miss Grey had recognised the person in the photo. "Of course, that's my grandad but I don't know who that is."

"That was your grandad's best friend, a wizard," announced Miss Grey.

"I think you're mistaken. My grandad hated

253

wizards…witches, too."

"That he did but that wasn't always the case just as the town across the forest wasn't always the enemy but before I continue you had a question."

Emily had completely forgotten her original question but it hadn't mattered as she had thought of a new one.. "What do you mean, the town across the forest wasn't always the enemy?"

Miss Grey took a deep breath before she spoke. "For many years Murlayfield and Ravensborough had a special relationship. We needed each other but that all changed when your grandfather became mayor."

"Why?" asked Emily hesitantly.

"He wanted something precious to the people of Ravensborough… magic," whispered Miss Little.

For the first time tonight Emily had been glad there hadn't been any chairs. If there had been she probably would have fallen off, such was her shock. "Why did he want magic?"

"For money, many people, magical or not, good and bad, would give anything for magic," said Miss Grey.

"What happened, did he get the magic?"

"No, but the damage was already done. Ravensborough wanted nothing more to do with Murlayfield. That's why a wall is now in the forest."

"What wall?" asked Emily.

Miss Little gasped her face instantly lit up "You can't see the wall," she smiled.

"No, is that bad?"

"No, it's wondrous. The wall is only visible to those who fear. To some it would be 100 ft. tall and to others be small as a pebble," said Miss Little. She then began smiling at Emily but it didn't last long. "It's just a shame that you and your peers won't get the chance to fully experience the wonder of Ravensborough."

"Maybe we still can do my speech. I could tell

everyone that Ravensborough is not a place to be feared I've been there you know" said Emily leaping off the beanbag she had finally understood what Miss Little had been hinting at.

"Wait where are you going?" asked Miss Little as Emily began climbing the stairs.

"Bed I have a speech to write" smiled Emily.

Mrs Grey was stunned by her daughter's sudden refusal to return home that Sunday morning but Emily had good reason as she was sure that Miss Little's stories about Ravensborough would prove useful in helping her writing her speech and she hadn't been wrong as Emily found herself unable to put her pen down. For the first time that day Emily's mind hadn't been on her speech but rather on ways to show her gratitude towards Miss Little for all her help.

"Get out!" screamed Emily. The kitchen floor thudded as Jake and Matthew scampered towards the door. Emily had decided that she would make tea for herself and Miss Little but it hadn't been going to plan as the cabbage looked greyer then green. The dinner table was miserable as not a word was spoken well almost as Jingles purred whilst lapping up her saucer of milk.

"What is this?" asked Jake lifting a watery piece of cabbage from his plate.

"Jake, don't be rude. It's lovely Emily."

Emily was no fool. Her meal had been terrible but she appreciated Miss Little's lie. The front door rattled. Mrs Grey had arrived. Emily merely waved as she walked out of the front door unsure that any words would do Miss Little justice. The street lights were particularly bright on the drive home.

"You see, I told you that Miss Little wasn't that bad, Did you have fun?" asked Mrs Grey.

"You could say that," smiled Emily.

Emily's nerves were rampant that Wednesday

morning. The day had finally arrived and in a few hours she would be giving her speech. Emily had half hoped that her mother would make her favourite food but she hadn't.

"It's good for you. It's what your gran gave me whenever I had a big test," said Mrs Grey. Emily looked on as the turgid grey paste splodged off her spoon. This had brought a chuckle from Matthew who peered over his chess magazine. "What about Matthew? Doesn't he have a big chess game today?"

"You're right," said Mrs Grey readying another bowl of slop. "So what time is your speech?"

But as Emily went to answer the front door opened flew open. It had been her father who had returned from another night society patrol. He had a large bandage around his head.

"I do wish you'd would stop wearing that silly thing. Is it really necessary? After all, it's just a little bump," said Mrs Grey.

"Just a BUMP! I want people to see what those things have done to me," boomed Mr Grey.

A knock at the door was welcomed as Emily wasn't looking forward to hear another one of her father's tirades. She quickly gathered her notes before heading out the door. The library had been rarely used by Emily. She wasn't really a book person but she would have to be and as she made the finishing touches to her speech she was soon joined by Kelly.

"I got 'em, it wasn't easy," said Kelly placing three large books on the desk. "Had to tell my mum and dad I was thinking about joining them."

"Thanks. "Oh no, where is it?" Emily said panicking.

"What's the matter?"

"My notepad, you haven't seen it, have you?"

"No …wait I think I do. It's over there by those books. I'll get it."

"You're the best" smiled Emily.

"What's tea without a bit of milk?" said Kelly as she skipped away.

It had taken Emily a few moments to realise what her friend had just said but when she had she couldn't stop laughing. This had brought nasty looks from other student not to mention a scowl from the librarian but she hadn't cared. "Is something wrong?" asked Emily.

"I-I-I tried to tell him you didn't want to see him" stuttered Kelly.

"Who wants to see me?"

"I do," said a voice.

Emily turned. It had been Edward looking on smugly. "What do you want?" she hissed.

"I've just come to tell you something," he replied smiling devilishly.

"What... what do you want to tell me?" snapped Emily.

"I hope you've brought something to read. You'll be going last. It took some work but mummy finally came around," he chuckled.

"You can't do that" shouted Emily.

"I just did."

"Ah, is Eddiekins still upset Emily missed his ikle party? You're a joke," said Kelly.

"I'd mind who you're calling a joke. Isn't your mother a cleaner here? It would be a shame if she'd lose her job." Edward then began cackling before he began gazing at Emily. Something had caught his eye. "Ooh, is that your speech? Let's have a read."

"NO!" whispered Emily leaping over the table. A scuffle then ensued with both Emily and Edward using all their might. It was a miracle the paper hadn't ripped already. BOOM! Edward fell backwards. He quickly got his feet but as he did the hushed laughter stopped. "You'll regret that," he said before sliding away. Emily was sure Edward had meant what he said.

"Thank you," shouted Michael Fudge. The assembly all rose in a tremendous applause, well almost everyone. Emily remained seated, half bored and half terrified. She was up next. Her mind wasn't on her speech but rather what Edward had said. She was sure he was going to do something. She then turned to Kelly who had just retaken her seat. "You haven't seen Edward, have you?"

"Oh, don't worry about him. Violet Arthurworry saw him leaving probably too embarrassed to show his face... You ready?"

"I am now, "sighed Emily.

The microphone boomed as Mrs Upton began tapping it furiously. "That was certainly a treat but don't dose off just yet. We have one more speaker. Would Miss Emily Grey join me on stage?"

Emily hadn't got the same level of applause as those who went before her but she hadn't really cared as all she wanted to do was give her speech. She sped up the steps, her smile becoming wider with each passing step. Mrs Upton then stepped to one side. Emily took a deep breath as she walked up to the microphone.

"Hi everyone… Today I am going to talk about…"

BOOM! The hall doors swung open and Edward strode in. "STOP HER!" he cried. "Don't let her speak, she's going to talk about those freaks on the other side of the forest."

Boos rang out.

"Get her off the stage," yelled a voice. "Didn't she see what they did to her dad?" bellowed another.

"SILENCE!" ordered Mrs Upton. "Is this true Emily?"

"Well…"

"MY OFFICE NOW," yelped Mrs Upton.

The boos restarted and they were deafening, Emily looked to the floor as she walked out of the hall too afraid to meet the gaze of another. It had barely been four days since she last set foot in Mrs Upton's office but it was vastly different. The pictures of Edward still remained but they had changed. They were all of him smiling almost as if he was mocking her. Emily quickly got to her feet as the door handle rattled. Mrs Upton then strode in.

"I would just like to say that…" Mrs Upton's swiftly raised hand halted Emily in her tracks. "No need to explain," said Mrs Upton. "You're free to go. Your father has assured me you'll be severely punished."

Emily didn't waste any time as she hastily left Mrs Upton's office. As she walked through the now deserted hallway she sighed as for the first time that day she wasn't filled with worry as she was sure her father's punishment wouldn't be bad. And she hadn't been wrong. The punishment wasn't bad, it was a nightmare as her father had dragged her along to a night society meeting. The meeting was separated into three sections, the first was so dull Emily found herself talking to Matthew about chess. He, too had come along wanting to parade his trophy.

Emily had often wondered what took place at her father's meetings but having been here for the best part of an hour it was safe to say that if Murlayfield had been under attack by witches and wizards they would be doomed as the second section was just them watching TV.

"I don't understand all the fuss about this *EastEnders* rubbish, a show that's been on for 25 years. Sure sign of witchcraft, don't you think?" moaned Miss Fletcher. Emily politely nodded although she wasn't sure what this had to do with Murlayfield or even Ravensborough. But worse still, the third section was about to start. The furniture was quickly rearranged in a circle as Mr Grey rose to speak. "I've got some exciting news, I was going to announce it at the next town meeting… but I can't wait. I'm very close to dealing with those freaks on the other side."

The room erupted in applause and cheers. "Your

father would've been proud," blubbered Miss Fletcher.

"Not a moment too soon if you ask me," said Mrs Fooupe. "I'm sure those creatures have messing with my pluming again," she added, flicking her hair to one side.

"You think you've got problems," moaned Mr Hooper scratching his beard. "I've had a bloody rat following me. I'm sure it's one of those things you can turn into.."

Emily remained seated in the corner her facing become more and more scrunched by the minute. She couldn't believe what she was hearing. This was unbearable. She quickly got to her feet. "ENOUGH!" she bellowed. The room fell silent.

"Is something the matter, deary?" said Miss Fletcher.

"You're all mad," snapped Emily. "Can you hear yourselves, pluming and rats... they are people just like me and they have their own lives and problems and they are certainly not freaks." Miss Fooupe sprang up, her face screwed as if it had been kissed by a lemon. "Are you going to let her speak to us like that, William?" she howled.

"Emily, apologise," said a disinterested Mr Grey.

"No," said Emily bolting for the door. Her heart began to race. The voices from inside suggested she wouldn't be welcomed back in but she hadn't really minded. Her mind suddenly began to rattle. Where could she go? She then answered her own question by walking towards the gate as leaving this place would be a start.

Matthew sat at the top of the stairs as Mr and Mrs Grey continued arguing. It was ten p.m. and Emily still hadn't returned home.

"I've told you Helena," said Mr Grey firmly. "She just ran out and I have no idea where she went."

Matthew had known where his sister was. Well at least he thought he knew. He then quickly and quietly headed back upstairs; he was going to bring Emily back home. He had decided to go alone as bringing either one or both of his parents would have been more trouble than it was worth. The moon was beautifully big that Wednesday night as Matthew made his way through the forest. Suddenly he stopped as he reached a massive log and just as he suspected sat upon that log was Emily.

"Emily," said Matthew softly.

Stunned, Emily quickly turned round. "Matthew, what are you doing here... how did you find me?"

"A diary can tell you a lot about a person," chuckled Matthew but his attempt at a joke had failed miserably. Emily remained unmoved "You really care about them, don't you?"

"I do but nobody else does. What's the point?" sighed Emily.

"Oh, stop feeling sorry for yourself," tutted Matthew. "Look, I don't know if dad is right about those things. To be fair, he's wrong about a lot of things but the one thing he is right about is that you have to be passionate about the things you care about as how do you expect anyone else to care if you don't."

Matthew's words had given Emily food for thought. As much as she hated to admit it her brother, and to a lesser extent her father, had been right. She couldn't just give up. She had to make her town see sense especially after what her father had said that evening. "When did you get so smart?" smiled Emily getting to her feet.

Caught out by his sister's compliment Matthew looked on unsure of what to say before finally squeaking out a "thank you." "Come on, let's go," said Emily. "I know you've dying to show off your trophy."

"Just a little," grinned Matthew.

SWOOSH!

The forest fell silent. Emily and Matthew had barely taken two steps before coming to halt as a large black bird with a shimmering beak sat before them. But even more strange a piece of paper as white as the moon was affixed to the bird's mouth. The bird then swiftly began to inch towards the children who were transfixed to the ground. "What does it want?" whispered Matthew. But before Emily could say a word the raven let out a tremendous screech before spitting the piece onto the ground and flying away. Emily's feet then took on a mind of its own as she began inching towards the note. "What does it say? Is it for you?" asked Matthew..

Emily remained quiet as she stared at the paper. The note had been from Conor.

CHAPTER TWELVE

A BURNING EAR

The sight of Professor Marigold struggling to carry the Christmas tree through the lunch hall meant one thing: the famous Ravensborough winter had arrived and snow was sure to follow. It was the first time Conor hadn't minded the weather as it gave him the perfect excuse to remain indoors or rather remain in the library as he was determined to learn more about Murlayfield and many burning questions still lingered. Due to the regularity and frequency that Conor visited the library Mrs Autumn had granted him special access to a restricted part which was only open to teachers and fourth and fifth year students.. The fifth of December had almost folklore-like status at Ravensborough High as it was when Professor Higginbottom would be handing out pieces of her famous Christmas cake to the first fifty students that arrived. Ryan seemed to be frothing at the mouth as he began whingeing at Conor as they made their way to school.

"I'm sorry, I didn't mean to snap, it's just I've never managed to get a piece but this year is going to be different," said Ryan smirking.

"How is it going to be different?" asked Conor.

"You'll see, now come on."

"I'm coming. I hope it's worth all this fuss."

But there would be no need for Ryan to answer his friend's question as the smell of cinnamon ensnared the young witch. Conor's legs seemed non-existent as he floated around the corner, the aroma proving more and more alluring.

THUD! "Oi, wait your turn" snarled a boy. "Sorry," replied Conor hastily taking a step back. Maybe Ryan hadn't been exaggerating as a line had formed leading from the front gate to the end of the street.

"See, I told ya, everyone wants a piece," Ryan swooned.

"Do you see the line? We'll never get one," cursed Conor.

"Don't worry, my friend. I prepared for this. Swarbrick is at the front for us."

"How'd you managed that," blurted the young witch. "He's Simon's personal lap dog. He hates us."

"It was easy. I said I'd get you to make him a love potion."

Conor was stunned for as much as he wanted Ryan to have the cake he couldn't do it at price of making a love potion. It would be too weird not to mention all the questions that would follow from Professor Marigold and the rest of the class. There was no other choice. He'd have to tell Ryan he couldn't do it but he'd have to wait as Swarbrick had summoned Ryan to the front. Conor wouldn't have long to wait as the sound of grunting and angry mumbling was all that could be heard on Ravensborough Road.

"That little weasel," frothed Ryan. "I knew I couldn't trust him." "Why, what happened?" asked Conor, sure he already knew the answer.

"Can you imagine the weasel had the cheek to look down his nose at me. I would have turned him into a rat if Duncan hadn't lost my wand."

Conor was sort of half glad that they had been shunned as it meant he didn't have to make a love potion but not wanting to look too happy, he said, "Why did he change his mind?"

"Apparently he got a better offer from Saffron."

"Can't we outbid her? Does he want another potion?"

"We can but I don't think you gonna like it. He wants you to tell Angelica that he wants to take her on a date," murmured Ryan.

"WHAT! No chance," chuckled Conor. "I mean she would never do it anyway. She hates him more than us. Forget him. Anyway, we'll still get a piece, we'll just have to wait."

Ryan sighed before retaking his place behind Conor. Conor thought that the countless time spent waiting in line over the last few months would stand him in good stead but he was mistaken as the wait seemed longer than ever. Professor Higginbottom thanked everyone who took a slice, but unlike the other times spent waiting in line this one had been worth it as Conor and Ryan finally reached the gate. Ryan's eyes lit up and he began panting as he pushed past Conor mentally counting how many steps it would take to reach Professor Higginbottom.

CRASH!

Ryan trudged over to help his friend after seeing that Conor had fallen or rather the mass of books he had been carrying. He had waited all this time a few more seconds wouldn't be disastrous. After gathering all the books and handing them back to Conor, Ryan seemed to float towards the front door. Conor quickly followed.

"Could I—I have a slice, professor," stuttered Ryan.

"Me, too," added Conor.

"I'm so sorry boys, headmaster Gravethorpe has taken the last two pieces. No worries, there's always next year," apologised Professor Higginbottom.

"Aren't you retiring this year, Miss?"

"Ah. Yes. Sorry about that."

Ryan had vanished guilt-ridden. Conor chased after

his friend but Ryan was great at not being seen when he wanted too but Conor too was stubborn and waded his way through the fifth years clutching his books tightly in the process. Battered and bruised, Conor finally caught up with Ryan.

"You and your blooming books. Why do you have so many anyway?" huffed Ryan.

"You know why."

"Don't tell me you're still going on about what Mr Basil told us. No one is after you. Trust me, if someone was still after you why would they wait nine years to try again? Besides, we don't even know why they were after you. Maybe they got what they wanted," he added.

"I thought about that but then it hit me. Ever since the town meeting weird things have been happening."

"How'd you mean?" asked Ryan.

"Think about it. During my assessment the doll tries to attack me and then Sticky goes crazy when we go to visit him for the first time. when before that he hadn't caused any problems. And finally what happened to your dad? What if it was the dragon that was meant to kill me?"

Ryan stopped and began looking at Conor but it was not with a look of assurance or understanding, but of bemusement. He then set about trying to disprove Conor's theory stating that everything that happened could be chalked up to mere circumstance.

"Trust me, forget about all of this normals stuff you'll feel— ahhh!"

"What happened? Are you all right?"

"Yeah, just stepped on this bloody key," moaned Ryan.

He held the key afloat and it gleamed in the light. Conor gasped. He could not believe his eyes. It had been the key to Mrs Autumn's chest. Impossible, he thought. The key was under his bed just this morning. It then dawned on him: who had the key belonged to? Why had

266

there been another key and just how many were there. A figure then appeared behind him.

"Ah, Master Willows, you have found my key?" said headmaster Gravethorpe.

"Morning, sir. This belongs to you."

"Yes, now hand it over and head to class," snarled headmaster Gravethorpe before snatching the key and swooping back around the corner.

"You'd think he'd be more grateful. I could have easily kept that" remarked Ryan as he made his way to the staircase.

Conor remained glued to the spot..

"Mate, are you all right? We have to go. You know Sorceress Elro won't go easy on us this time if we're late."

Conor finally moved grabbing Ryan before racing outside.

"It's him, of course it was. I'm so stupid. How could I not see it? He is behind all of this. He is working with the normal. He helped them attack the valley," said Conor breathing heavily.

"What are you talking about?"

Conor began scanning his surroundings before ushering Ryan towards the abandoned classroom. Ryan again looked at Conor. His worry was evident. He could not believe what he being told; his intrigue got the better of him as he began interrupting before quickly apologising. But Conor was not mad as he too would probably would have a lot of questions.

"I was going to do this by myself but I need your help. We have to get that chest before Gravethorpe, it probably contains the missing chapter about the valley attack and more incriminating things," babbled Conor. "Better, yet we'll come back tonight as we can't risk him getting there before us," he added.

"There's just one problem."

"If you're worried about getting into trouble I'll take

the blame and say I used *Mentis imperium* on you," reassured Conor.

"It's not that. Aren't you supposed to be meeting Emily tonight?" said Ryan

Conor held his head in hands. How could he have forgotten about the meeting with Emily. What was he going to do? He couldn't just cancel as it wouldn't be fair to Emily not to mention it. He had to know whether she knew that her townspeople were after him and the rest of Ravensborough.

As Conor remained deep in thought the sight of Mr Marto approaching had been enough to scare Ryan who quickly grabbed Conor before heading inside. The time had finally arrived as potions class had taken on a new focus. Professor Marigold looked on intriguingly at Conor and Ryan's desk as it was littered with chamomile and other herbs they had been brewing for a sleeping potion to use on their family members.

Ryan held the potion in his hand as he and Conor waited at the bus stop. His heart was racing. He was having second thoughts because he had never done anything like this before. What if Conor had been wrong about headmaster Gravethorpe? Conor, seeing his friend in distress, reassured Ryan that what they were about to do was necessary as the safety of the entire town was at stake.

"You know, we have to do this right, It's bigger than you and me," said Conor.

"I know."

The bus then arrived.

Harrowood's café had always been a place of safety and security for Conor so he could think of no better place to wait as he had arranged to meet Emily at Kenbury Forest that night as his need for answers was too great to ignore. The door to the café slowly opened. Ryans face was devoid of any colour; he was in a zombified state. Duncan quickly followed. His face was that of complete contrast to his cousin as unlike Ryan, Duncan was radiant as he couldn't stop smiling. They sat down beside Conor.

"How was it? Were you able to do it?" asked Conor.

"He couldn't so I had to," replied Duncan.

"They were all just talking, laughing and Duncan handed them the tea. Then boom, out like a light," remarked Ryan staring blankly.

"Good thing you were there Duncan. Has Ryan told you what we're going to do tonight?"

Duncan's smile widened even more before he spoke. "We're going to break into Ravensborough High. You guys are awesome," he added.

"We are but there's been a slight change. We're going to meet a girl called Emily first."

"WHAT!" belted out Ryan. "Why are we meeting her? She lied to us by not mentioning her dad tried to destroy Ravensborough and kill you."

"I need to know why she came to Ravensborough in the first place. She didn't lie, we both just assumed she was magical."

"Fine, but I won't face a normal on an empty stomach. Where's Harrowood to take my order?" said Ryan.

"He's not here. Apparently he's ill," said Conor.

"Really, I never thought I'd see the day Harrowood sick. You know Swarbrick swears blind that he saw him brewing an anti-sickness potion once."

BUZZ!

The buzzing noise sounded again. It was Conor's phone. Emily had arrived.

The nerves Ryan had initially been feeling had transmitted to Conor as the three boys began walking towards Kenbury Forest in silence unsure what would be there to greet them. The wind seemed unusually strong as it pinched Conor's ears. It was almost as if it had been trying to gain his attention. Ryan then broke the silence asking what Conor planned to when they arrived at their destination. The question had flustered the young witch. He didn't know what he was going to do but he would soon have to make up his mind as the forest was before them.

The leaves squelched underneath their feet as they made their way to the meeting pointing. The constant questioning from Ryan ceased. even Duncan who could normally pluck a joke from seemingly nowhere was hushed as they reached the pond where it had all begun. The moonlight beamed onto the water and a gentle rustle of leaves left them guarded. Emily then emerged. Conor was in awe as the beauty of the pond seemed repugnant compared to Emily. Her piercing blue eyes danced with the moonlight while her hair glistened similarly to his own wand.

"Hi!" squeaked Emily.

"Hi!"

The forest became shrouded in silence as the two children stood across from each other. Their eyes didn't move an inch. Both moved forward as if they wanted to speak but no words were spoken this seemed to gone for an eternity. Ryan, increasingly annoyed, stepped forward and jolted his friend in the back.

"Emily, I…"

"Yes," she interrupted. "Sorry."

"I need to ask you something and I need you to be honest with me."

"Hurry up! I want to get to school," said Duncan

"You're going to your school, could I come, please?"

Conor went to answer but before the words could pass his lips he was dragged away by Ryan. Bemused, Conor demanded to know why he had been so roughly removed, Ryan remained silent merely smirking. His eyebrows too were raised and he spoke.

"I've got an idea," he beamed.

"What is it? Emily will be getting suspicious," frothed Conor.

"Don't worry about her. Duncan's keeping her busy. Hear me out, let's take her to the school."

"I thought I couldn't trust her because she was a normal. What if she tries to steal something?" whispered Conor still glancing in Emily's direction.

"Exactly. If she's innocent and knows nothing about her father's doing she'll come to no harm but if she does try something we can stop her and we'll be heroes," giggled Ryan.

Conor stared intently at Ryan his face remained still almost stone like as if it had been bewitched. Feeling his plan had been rejected Ryan began to walk away he had taken no more than two steps before the sound of shrilled laughter summoned him back..

"Have I told you you're brilliant?" said Conor smiling.

"Maybe once."

"Oi, Duncan, cut that out!" cried Conor.

The two boys then hurriedly returned to the pond as Emily's facial expression said many words Duncan's antics began to scare her. "Sorry about that, he gets a bit excited around new people," remarked Ryan.

"It's all right so can I come with you guys?" said Emily.

Ryan, not for the first time, nudged his friend forward which brought a scowl from Conor who took a short breath before he spoke. "Of course, but I warn there will be many dangers we'll face," he said. Emily's expression changed. She wanted to go as the thought of seeing a school solely dedicated to magic was wonderful but she wasn't a witch or wizard so how would she defend herself against the dangers Conor spoke about?

"Emily, it was a joke. No one is going to be there," chuckled Conor.

271

SNAP!

"What was that?" questioned Duncan.

Conor and Ryan drew for their wands as the snapping of twigs grew louder and louder. Somebody else was in the forest with them. A silhouette then appeared through the darkness. It was of similar build to theirs. Shouts of "who are you?" went ignored as the figure continued approaching the forest then became silent as it reached the now infamous puddle.

"Edward!" gasped Emily.

After the initial shock of who stood before her had passed Emily similarly to Ryan grabbed Edward and ushered him away. Conor and Ryan looked on with intrigue as Emily and Edward began arguing in hushed whispers. It was brief but intense and the two then trudged over.

"Who's your friend, Emily?" asked Conor.

"I can speak for myself," scoffed the boy "The name is Edward Percival Upton and I'm pleasured to meet your acquaintance," he added whilst sloppily holding out a hand. "PERCY!" cried Duncan before bursting into laughter. He was quickly joined by Ryan who became bright red. "How dare you!" growled Edward. "My name is not Percy, it's Percival."

But Edward's scowls had done nothing as the laughter only grew louder. Conor's lip began to tremble as he fought the urge to laugh but it was tough. He would have given anything to join in but alas he couldn't as it would have brought more trouble than it was worth. The young witch then sighed before reluctantly grunting in the direction of the laughter as the forest then fell silent. The birds serenading of the moon was all that could be heard as the five children made their way to Ravensborough High but whilst only a few feet apart Conor felt a million miles away from his guests as hardly a word was uttered

272

and this was despite Duncan's best efforts. But the silence was soon broken.

"Is this it?" sniffed Edward.

They had arrived. "Yes, is there a problem?" snarled Ryan.

"I just thought a place with so much magic would look a little nicer. It's rather shabby."

"Edward," snapped Emily. "Pay no attention to him, I think it's amazing," she smiled.

"Have you learnt nothing from my mother, Emily?" said Edward "You mustn't fib. This place is awful."

"I can show you real magic if you want," smiled Ryan devilishly.

But as Edward went to respond he was interrupted by a panicked Duncan. "Shhhh, you shouldn't be so loud," he whispered.

"Why?" asked Conor.

Duncan, lost for words. slowly pointed towards the main building doors which slowly began to creak open.

"What are they doing here?" huffed Ryan peering over a bush.

"You believe me now. Gravethorpe's probably got them patrolling looking for us," murmured Conor.

"Sorry, but who are these people and why would they be looking for you?" asked Emily hesitantly.

"Trust me, you don't want to know."

"So, what are we going to do?" asked Ryan.

"We only have one option," replied Conor.

"And what's tha..."

But before Edward could finish his sentence a strange tingling sensation coursed through his body. A feigned yelp rang out as Edward could no longer see his hand or any other part of his body. "What have you done? Where am I?" he barked.

"Oh relax, you'll live," chuckled Ryan. "Come on, keep up,"

The silence returned as Conor and the others made the short distance from the bushes back to the front gates which were navigated with minimal fuss but the greater task was still to come. The journey to get to the front doors had become chess like as Simon and Marvin had become dog like quickly turning at the slightest movement. Conor looked on with bated breath as Edward's impatience was sure to undo their work. But not for the first time Duncan took control and somehow managed to lure both Simon and Marvin away with just the tip of his wand. This led Conor to question, not for the first time, how he and they were the same age.

"Come, let's go," Conor whispered.

The warmth of the main building was welcomed as again the heavens were unforgiving with their tears. But it had been nothing compared to the anger and frustration that had been festering inside Ryan as every laboured expression and groan from Edward had inched Ryan's hand ever closer to his pocket. "Is this it? The famed Ravensborough High?" huffed Edward.

"It's a school. What did you expect? Flying dragons? snarled Ryan.

"Pay no attention to him, I'm sure it's great," said Emily. "Conor, what are we waiting for?" added Emily.

"We're waiti…, just then the main building doors crept open and the floor began squelching as Duncan joined the others. "Urgh, I'm soaked."

"Don't worry, I'll sort you out," said Conor as he whipped out his wand. And with a slight flick of his wrist Duncan was dry. "Where are those two?" he then asked pointing towards the door.

"Oh, don't worry about them. They won't be bothering us anytime soon," giggled Duncan. "I don't know why you're always banging on about them when you're sleeping Ryan. They aren't that scary."

For the first time that evening everyone seemed to be

on the same page as whished giggles echoed throughout the hallways. "All right, you've had your laugh. What's the next part of the plan?" said Ryan.

"Right, me and Duncan are gonna go upstairs to the libra…"

"Really!" said Duncan unable to contain his smile. "Yeah, really," groaned Ryan.

"Really besides don't you remember Ryan that thing we talked about I need you to show these two the potions class"

"Finally," cried Edward "Are we going to get to see some real magic now?"

This had brought the first smile of the night from Ryan. "I'll show you some real magic," smirked the young wizard.

"Play nice, Ryan," said Conor as Ryan shuttled towards the door. "I will; come on, follow me."

With the corridor once again shrouded in darkness Conor and an excitable Duncan made their way towards the first floor of the main building. Each door was opened with the softest touch but as much as Conor had trusted Duncan he couldn't escape the feeling that Marvin and Simon could return at any moment. With the library fast approaching the young witch finally allowed himself some rest as his nerves ebbed away and in his relaxed state Conor was able to fully admire the serenity of Ravensborough High as each classroom seemed to shimmer in the moonlight. Its beauty was only bettered by the wand of our young witch.

But this soon became an afterthought. As the final corridor approached each footstep thudded the ground, its noise only triumphed by the beating of Conor's heart. They had arrived and only the wooden double doors separated Conor from the truth. His nerves that had long dispersed suddenly came streaming back but some long sharp intakes of breath steadied the young witch he then grasped the cold metal handle but as he went to swing the door open he stopped. "Wait!" whispered Duncan. "Can't you hear that I think someone's in there?."

He could hear something but that was impossible. Why would Mrs Autumn be in the library at this time? She was supposed going to London that evening. "Maybe we should come back later," said Duncan in a suggestive tone. Conor had been a rational person but there was no way he could come back later. He couldn't afford headmaster Gravethorpe a chance to get the chest. Another deep breath was taken and without thinking Conor bolted through the doors. but what greeted him was not Mrs Autumn no but rather the sound of classical music of course how could he have forgotten and again without hesitation the young witch summoned Duncan in. "Are you sure it safe?" asked Duncan perhaps showing his age for the first time that evening.

"It is. It was just music playing," smirked Conor.

"Music."

"Yep. Miss is always banging on about music and books being spiritual brothers so she always plays some whenever she leaves."

"Oh, you guys in Ravensborough are really weird."

This had brought a smile and chuckle from Conor who refocused himself on the task in hand. "All right, Duncan I need you to wait by the door and tap it if you see anyone coming. I just have to get something from the office quickly."

Duncan nodded before turning to face the door. This was it. Conor took a moment before moving. He couldn't believe it had been this easy. Just then the music restarted and for the first time in a confident mood the young witch waltzed towards the office door which was pushed open effortlessly. As Conor strode into the office he couldn't help but notice how pristine it looked almost as if it hadn't been touched since he was in there all those months ago.

He made his way past the desk towards the shelf. He was careful memorising every book's position and not wanting to leave any trace of himself. There it was, the chest without a speck of dust on it. It was carefully lifted from its position and placed ever so softly on the desk. A quick rummage through his pocket had unearthed the key but as Conor went to guide it into the lock he paused and began glaring at the chest. He couldn't understand how something so alluring could harbour something so sinister.

CLICK!

The sound of the chain hitting the desk was wondrous. A single bead of sweat stained the top of the chest as Conor placed his hand on it. But just as he was about to lift the lid, BANG, BANG!. No, he had been so close. That knock had meant only one thing broken. Conor trudged towards the door, suddenly it flashed open and in hurtled Duncan who had been in a mood never witnessed by Conor before as questions such as what happened and who's out there? went unanswered as Duncan remained silent. But this had only been for a moment as barge of rambles pelted the young witch. Such was the speed that Duncan was talking Conor was sure that even the use of magic would prove useless in his attempts to understand what was being said.

"WAIT!" roared Conor finally. "Slow down! What's happened? Is someone coming?"

Duncan shook his head. "I don't know and I know you said I should watch the door but I couldn't. It was boring so I went to look out of the window and I saw something." Not sure whether to be furious or concerned Conor merely asked another question, "What did you see?" Seeming to lose his voice again, Duncan remained silent only pointing in the direction of the window. The moonlight welcomed Conor as he stepped out of the office. The same stride he had taken earlier had gone as the young witch was slow and lethargic as he headed towards the window but his bristly demeanour soon vanished as his gaze met that of what was outside. Fury began pulsating through Conor's body as what he had seen outside had threatened to ruin everything for what he had seen outside was Ryan and Edward arguing.

Conor, now back inside the office, grabbed the chest before a bark of "come on" in Duncan's direction had awoken him from a transfixed state. The stairs barely had time to shriek such was the speed of Duncan and Conor. The squelching of the grass pierced through the silence as Ryan and his adversary were nowhere to be found. "They might have gone back inside," squeaked Duncan. The soft touch applied when previously opening doors had been abandoned as Conor burst through the Canterbury building main doors where the sound of arguing could be heard.

"Relax it isn't that bad," said a muffled voice

"It really isn't."

Creak!

"What on earth is going on in here," said Conor as the potions room resembled that of a crime scene as a stream of anti-sickness potion trickled past his feet. "Oooh, what happened to your face?" interjected Duncan.

"You see, you've scared me," wailed Edward.

"Shut it, Duncan. Trust me, Percy. It isn't that bad, just a little bump."

"It's PERCIVAL."

"Why hasn't anyone answered me? What happened?" asked Conor.

"It was an accident. I was doing what you asked and things got out of hand. You've got to a believe me, mate," pleaded Ryan.

"Out of hand?" questioned Conor.

"He's telling the truth," murmured Emily. "He was showing us how to make a potion when Edward tried taking another bottle from the cabinet and Ryan tried to stop him and that's how he got that bump. The door hit him. It was an accident." Conor looked away disgusted with himself for doubting his friend .He then stepped into the classroom and placed the chest on the table. "It really isn't that bad, Edward. I'd still put some ice on it though". But Edward wasn't interested at all rather using a discarded potion bottle to check his reflection. "We should probably clean up otherwise Professor Marigold will go spare," mentioned Conor.

"We'll have time to do that later," blurted Ryan. "Where the pages in there? Was it Gravethorpe?"

"I'm not sure. I haven't checked yet."

"What are you waiting for?"

Conor had no answer to Ryan's question. What had he been waiting for? He hadn't been nervous and the chest hadn't been locked. The young witch stroked the lid before carefully lifting it but optimism that had built up quickly dissipated as another lock had revealed itself. Fortunately, it had matched the one that had come before it.

CLANK, CRUNCH!

The floor rattled as the battered and bruised key hit the ground but worse still the chest began to rattle before spitting out a piece of scarlet paper with emerald writing sprawled on it. "What does it say?" asked a slightly stunned Ryan.

Conor, holding the paper tightly, began reading aloud, his voice quivering. *"The wrong key will not work on me if you wish to see what's inside of me then provide me with the name of the person I most wish to see."*

"What on earth does that mean?" said Ryan more befuddled than ever.

"It means you lot are stuffed," sniggered Edward still glancing into a potion bottle

Conor collapsed onto the seat and began smirking. He hadn't known why he had been kidding himself for if that last four months was anything to go by this was bound to happen. "I'm sorry, mate. It's not like Gravethorpe is going to tell you what's inside," murmured Ryan in a sombre tone.

"THAT'S IT."

"What's it?"

"What would I do without you? Come on!" swooned Conor grabbing the chest and bolting for the door. Ryan and the others were no slouches but even they struggled to keep up with Conor who was moving at a frantic pace. The young witch had led them to the abandoned classroom but again Edward was left unimpressed.

"Why have you brought us here? You're looking to finish me off, aren't you?" howled Edward.

"Oh, shut it Edward, it isn't always about you," barked Emily. "Conor, if you don't mind me asking, why have you brought us here?"

"You'll see," smiled Conor.

Conor still tightly clutching the chest crept over to the cupboard before giving it a gentle knock. The room then fell silent. "Have you lost your marbles?" chuckled Edward, his face radiant with a smile. But his smile soon vanished as he heard a knock. "Who's there?" whispered a voice.

"It's me," replied Conor opening the cupboard.

"Master Blackstone, how lovely to see you and you've brought guests which is even better although I do wish you would have come during school hours," smiled Philip.

"Sorry!"

"It's all right but I know you didn't come here for a chat. What is it that that you'd like to know? I know that exams are right around the corner."

"They are," chuckled Conor. "But that's not why I'm here. You used to be in headmaster Gravethorpe's office. Did he ever mention a chest?"

"Me and he spoke about a lot of things, too many to remember. We might have talked about it. What did the chest look like?"

Conor held the chest out "Have you seen it before? Did Gravethorpe talk about it?"

"No" said Philip hurriedly "I don't think he did. Sorry."

"He's lying," said Edward.

"I beg your pardon," growled Philip.

"Edward," hissed Emily. "Apologise."

"What for? He trusted me. I know a thing or two about lying."

Conor turned to Philip unsure of what to say as for some strange reason he believed Edward. "Philip, is it true?"

"No, I promise." But the lack of eye contact was telling Philip he had been lying. But why? Conor knew he had to be honest if he was to get the truth. "Headmaster Gravethorpe isn't who you think he is. He's evil."

Philip began to laugh; he hadn't heard anything so preposterous. "Mortimer is a lot of things but evil? No. I'm a man of my word and the contents of the chest will remain between him and me."

"It's true," thundered Ryan. "Mr Basil told us all about it and not to mention it. The chapter about it in the Ravensborough book has gone missing."

The smile on the former headmaster's face diminishing his face became almost lifelike as for the first time in his life he was lost for words. "No, it can't be. How could he do that to his town?"

"We can stop him but we need to know what's in the chest. Will you help us open it?" said Conor softly.

"All right, what do I have to do?" asked Philip, still shaken. Conor then read the message aloud.

"Oh, Mortimer, you soft touch."

"You know it?" asked Conor excitedly.

"I do. The answer to his riddle is...

BANG, BANG. "BLACKSTONE, WILLOWS I

KNOW YOU'RE IN THERE. COME OUT NOW."

"Oi, Duncan. Go check who's out there," whispered Ryan. Everybody waited with bated breath as Duncan slowly crept over to the window "Well who's out there?" asked Ryan nervously.

"It's a man, a really short man and he doesn't look happy," giggled Duncan amused at the man's appearance. Ryan too had begun creeping over towards the window. He raised his head for no more than two seconds before shuttling back. "No, it's Marto with Simon and Marvin."

"Oh no, not him. I can't bear another chat about winged beetles," bemoaned Philip.

"What are we going to do?" murmured Ryan. Conor knew what he had to do and as much as it pained his very mind to even think about it he couldn't risk Mr Marto telling Gravethorpe about what they were up to. "Emily, put Philip back into the cupboard." Emily nodded as he slithered away.

"I'M GIVING YOU BOYS ONE MINUTE TO GET OUT HERE OR I'M COMING IN," barked Mr Marto as he hammered away at the door.

With Philip safely away, Conor readied his next instruction. "Ryan, I need you to turn yourself and them invisible and get them back to the forest and over the wall. I'll stay and face Marto."

"No chance, I'm not going anywhere."

Conor didn't bother arguing as Ryan wouldn't have listened anyway but as he thought of what to do next the young witch felt a slight tap on his shoulder. "You knew," said Emily as Conor turned to face her. Conor nodded. "We'll talk later," he said quickly before turning to Duncan. "You'll have to do it Duncan. Take Ryan's wand and make sure you get them to the forest."

Duncan nodded as he readied himself to perform the spell. Meanwhile both Conor and Ryan got to their feet and approached the door. They turned back as the sight of nothing had left them only one thing to do. The creak of the door seemed everlasting but worse still the brightness of Mr Marto's wand had half blinded them.

"Well, well, what do we have here?" sniggered Mr Marto.

"Lovely evening don't you think, sir?" laughed Ryan forcefully.

"Shut it! Willows, inside now, you too Blackstone," growled Mr Marto.

The sound of strutting had returned as Marvin and Simon strode into the building pleased with themselves but this soon vanished as an all too familiar sight greeted them. "Are you having us on?" bellowed Marvin. "We told you Gravethorpe asked us here tonight," hissed Simon.

"The headmaster asking you two jokers back? Give it a rest and take a seat. I've got some calls to make."

Mr Marto had remained beside the boys for a moment making even eye contact an impossibility but as the corridor doors closed and with Mr Marto gone Marvin took centre stage. "If you think the last four months have been rough just wait till Monday."

"Oh, shut up Marvin! We aren't afraid of what you're gonna do," said Ryan almost falling off his stool as he did so.

"I weren't talking to you Willows. I was talking to him."

But Conor remained unmoved totally unconcerned by Marvin's threat as something else had drawn his attention. He was sure he could hear something and the young witch got off his stool and walked down the corridor. "Oi, I'm talking to you Blackpepple," barked Marvin again. "Back off, Marvin!" said Ryan venomously.

Again, Conor continued, his ears burning as what had received his attention seemed to be getting louder and louder. His wondering had led to a metal door. "Gravethorpe," grumbled Conor. Reaching for his wand

Conor uttered, "Claro" and as the room began to reveal itself the distinguishable gangly figure of headmaster Gravethorpe was there for all to see. But just as the young witch stopped casting the spell the muttering ceased. Conor was sure a conversation was taking place and without thinking about it his mouth began to move.

"Ears hear me now widen your mind
Render the world motionless
Allow me to hear the information I Seek
make the speaker's words echo for me."

And with that Conor could hear everything. The floor screeched as Conor fell backwards, his hands shaking, his ears ringing, his stomach churning. Had he heard correctly. A shout of "OI, GET AWAY FROM THERE" had snapped the young witch out of his trance. "ON YOUR FEET, BLACKSTONE" barked Mr Marto. "I've just spoken to your grandmother and she can't wait to see you," cackled the old caretaker. The wind was unforgiving as Mr Marto and the boys made their way to the front gates but again this hadn't seemed to matter to Conor.

"Oi, oh it's you," said Ryan as Conor tugged away at his hoodie. "Mate, are you all right. It looks like you've seen a ghost."

"He did it," spewed Conor.

"Who did it? Did what?"

"We're not safe, it was Gravethorpe. He admitted it."

CHAPTER THIRTEEN

The Trail of Gravethorpe

It had been an hour since Emily had returned to Murlayfield. Her heart was still pounding. That had been the most fun she'd had in a while, certainly more fun than anything she had done with anyone here but behind her smile laid a deep resentment towards her town as again she struggled to understand how they could hate their neighbours across the forest. But remembering what Matthew had said Emily's smile soon returned as tonight had only made her desire for reconciliation stronger.

BANG!

Emily's eyes flicked open as the banging from downstairs grew louder and louder. Had she been dreaming? She was sure her clock read ten p.m. which was far too late for any visitors. But just as Emily had dragged herself out of bed the banging stopped and was replaced with the grizzly voice of her eldest brother taking its place. Eyes still droopy, Emily climbed back into bed hoping to salvage a good night's sleep. But her hopes were soon shattered as a cry of UNACCEPTABLE reverberated through the house and worse still, the voice had belonged to none other than Mrs Upton. Still a little dazed and confused, Emily sluggishly made her way to the top of the stairs eager to find out why her headmistress had been at her home at this unusual time.

"What do you expect me to do?" begged Mr Grey.

"Something, anything. Look at what they've done to

my Eddiekins," wailed Mrs Upton angrily.

"It was awful, mummy. They kept calling me names," sobbed Edward

The stairs creaked violently as Emily fought to restrain herself. "The rat," she whispered as Edward's crocodile tears threatened to put even more distance between the two towns but as Emily got to her feet to charge downstairs. Edward's cries stopped and the domineering voice of his mother resumed.

"WELL," boomed Mrs Upton. "What are you going to do, MAYOR Grey?"

"I'd like to say something if you don't mind," interjected Mrs Grey suddenly as she turned towards Edward. "Are you sure it was those people from over the wall that did this to you?"

"Edward, get your coat. We're leaving. HOW DARE YOU ACCUSE MY SON OF LIEING," hissed Mrs Upton.

"I wasn't."

"I didn't want to have to do this, William but you've left me no choice. I'm going to have to tell the town about this. They deserve to know what type of mayor they have especially with an election next year."

The door had barely shut before Emily came hurtling down the stairs. But the sight that would have normally made her smile had left her in despair as her father lay on the couch broken. "Come on, get up Dad! You have to stop her." Mr Grey leapt to his feet. "You're right. I'll stop her. Calm her down, use some of that Grey charm. We won't let her ruin this election," said Mr Grey triumphantly as he sped towards the door.

"WAIT!" cried Emily. "This isn't about your stupid election. You have to stop her because Edward is lying about how he got that bump."

"How did you know he had a bump?" asked Mrs Grey softly.

"I know because I was there when it happened."

"What happened then?" said Mr Grey.

It was almost as if a volcano had erupted as Emily explained to her parents about everything that had happened over the last four months. The words came out of her mouth like a locomotive train and few pauses were taken if any. "Please say something," murmured Emily. "Anything."

"You've been bewitched," mumbled Mr Grey.

"What?" said Mrs Grey.

"I HAVE NOT," thundered Emily.

"That's it, they've crossed the line. It's time to get rid of those FREAKS once and for all," bellowed Mr Grey as he stormed out of the house.

"What's he going to do, mum?" asked Emily stunned.

"I'm not sure," replied Mrs Grey with worry in her voice for the first time that evening.

TAP, TAP!

"Come on, move!" growled Mr Marto, his breath staining Queenie's tank. "You call this a Dragon. Thing's useless."

"It's a bearded Dragon," said Conor.

"You've got a nice place here Blackstone."

"Thanks."

"No need to be ashamed. It's a good thing. Means you won't get bored when headmaster Gravethorpe suspends you for trespassing," cackled Mr Marto.

But the caretaker's cackling was brief as Amelia entered the room. But surprisingly to all, she bore a smile. Conor, Ryan and even Mr Marto all traded bemused looks as all had expected a barrage of thunderous questions. "I'll take it from here, Mark. You have a good evening," said Amelia finally, her smile not retracting an inch, "Yes, Miss Blackstone, you have a good evening, too," replied Mr Marto as he moved towards the door. "I'll see you soon, boys," said the caretaker, his face hidden behind a menacing smile. The act was over as Amelia's warming smile vanished with a scowl.

"I only have one question for you, boys. Why?" asked Ameila as towered over them, her scowl as piercing as ever.

"We'll explain later Miss Blackstone but Conor has something to tell you," said Ryan turning to his friend.

"Is this true, Conor?"

"No, nothing springs to mind," replied Conor, his eyes shifting in every direction except his grandmother's.

"He's lying," pleaded Ryan. "Tell her," he grunted. He, too, was now scowling.

"Okay, fine. The real reason we were at the school tonight was to duel with Simon and Mar...

"I CAN'T DO THIS ANY MORE," bellowed Ryan. "We know about the attack at the valley and we know that there are normals on the other side of the wall."

Ryan's words had moved Amelia from her domineering position over the boys as she began pacing around the room. "Ha, ha, you boys are pranking me aren't you? It's a good try but I won't be fooled this time," said Amelia smiling. But unlike before, her smile was brief and weak.

"Were not joking. We know who was behind it, too. It was headmaster Gravethorpe. Conor heard him admit it, didn't you, mate?" replied Ryan. He, too, had begun to walk around the room.

"You know I think I'd best get you home Ryan. Your mum is probably worried sick. Come on, let's go!" said Amelia hurriedly.

"Gran, wait!" said Conor speeding for the door "Ryan's telling the truth. It was headmaster Gravethorpe."

Amelia came to a screeching halt and slowly turned to face her grandson. "Are you sure, Sticky?"

"I'm sure of it. I used mum's spell," said Conor softly. "Wait Gran! Where are you going?" But for the first time in what seemed an eternity Conor's pleas to his grandmother went unanswered as she calmly walked back towards the house. "GRAN," howled Conor. Silence reigned over Durfold Street as Amelia stopped. "What are you going to do?" asked Conor as he inched slowly towards his grandmother.

"Just wait here," said Amelia, her voice as cold as the wind. Ten minutes slowly dripped by as Conor's worries intensified as stop, start conversations flooded from the house. "Is your gran gonna be all right? I'm freezing out here," said Ryan. "Yeah, she'll be fine, probably coming up with a plan to get Gravethorpe," waffled Conor. But the truth was Conor didn't know whether his grandmother was all right. He had never seen her act this way like this before. Her calm, confident demeanour had gone. Another two minutes passed but Conor and Ryan remained in the cold. "That's it," shrieked Ryan as he stormed towards the front door. But the young wizard's new found confidence melted away as the front door flew open.

"Is everything all right, Ryan? Have you forgotten something?" asked Amelia, her voice as soft as cotton.

"I...I j-j-j," said Ryan.

"We just wanted to know if you were all right, Gran," said Conor hesitantly.

"I've never felt better," smiled Amelia. "Come on, boys."

"Where are we going?" asked Conor.

But again, Conor's question went unanswered but to be fair to his grandmother, it had been a silly question as where else could they be going other than Ryan's house? But as the journey went on the question seemed less and less silly as they were nowhere near Christwood Meadows. The young witch's eyes darted all around the car but he didn't ask his grandmother where they were going. His eyes soon met those of Ryan. Again, their faces were doing all the talking. The boys wouldn't have to wait long for their answer though as in the distance the unmistakable town hall roof peered at them but even more was what greeted them.

The normally dimly lit street opposite was no more as a warm, orange glow had taken its place and even more scorching were the chants of "BANISHMENT". As a crowd threatened to stampede a row of ogres stood as tall as the very building they had been guarding. They were rigid in their formation only separating once as Conor, his grandmother and Ryan entered the building. The shriek of the town raven was tremendous as a monstrous symphony of noise whirled throughout the town hall. But amongst all the noise one voice stood out.

"THIS IS ABSURD" cried headmaster Gravethorpe as he struggled to loosen the grip of the two ogres escorting him. But as they were turning the corner and through the crowd's disapproving looks, their eyes met. It was brief but powerful as time seemed to stand still.

"CONOR!" roared headmaster Gravethorpe, his voice seeming to grow louder and louder. Conor seemed to magnetise to his grandmother as Gravethorpe's voice coursed through his body. "Don't worry, Sticky. If he wants you he'll have to kill me," said Amelia defiantly. Conor smiled as they continued on towards the main room but his grandmother's words had made him more anxious than ever. The young witch found himself repeatedly rubbing his eyes as they entered the main room. He was sure that it had least doubled in size since his meeting. Waves of benches and chairs had been placed all along the room and it had seemed as if half of Ravensborough had attended. The scowling faces of Simon and Marvin were at the front as well as the disinterred murmurs of Saffron towards the back but amongst the rabid eyes there had been no calming, effervescent gaze of Angelica which Conor had needed desperately.

A lonely wooden stool had been paraded in the middle

of the room and on that chained to the floor was headmaster Gravethorpe whose aura of invincibility laid in ruins. Amelia, now donning a silvery black gown, rose to speak. "I'm sure you are all well aware that new evidence has come to light in our hunt for the perpetrator behind the attack on our beloved town. I will know all once Professor Marigold has begun the interrogation." Professor Marigold shot up, his face stern. "Would the accused please state their full name?" he said, his face stoic.

"Mortimer Aloysius Gravethorpe," he smirked. "Cornelius is this really necc---"

"SILENCE!" boomed Professor Marigold, his voice reverberating throughout the hall. "As Amelia stated new evidence has come to light. Could you tell us about your whereabouts this evening?"

"Well, as you'd know Cornelius. I was at the school for several hours going through the fifth years projects and after that I went home."

"Really," smirked Professor Marigold. "Would Simon and Marvin please stand?" Professor Marigolds smirk turning into a grin. But Professor Marigold smirk would soon vanish as the opportunity to show up their teacher proved too good to miss. "Why were you at the school this evening?" screeched Professor Marigold.

"Oi, Marvin, I thought school took place during the day?" said Simon.

"It does," giggled Marvin. Headmaster Gravethorpe's head rattled as he gazed all around the room his smile widening with each disgruntled look. He was loving this but the best was yet to come as he finally reached the face of Conor which had been etched with worry. But Conor's face soon rose as the flitter of headmaster Gravethorpe's left eye had enraged him. He then looked to his grandmother hoping she'd have an idea. Thankfully for the young witch she had as she rose to her feet.

"Mr Davies," Amelia said before retaking her seat.

The floor shrieked as a big burly man got to his feet. "All right, boys you've had your fun. Answer your professor's question." Professor Marigold quickly got to his feet before asking his question again. "Well," he said.

"Headmaster Gravethorpe asked us to. He came over to our house and promised us that if we did what we asked we wouldn't have to do any homework again," added Simon.

"LIES," roared headmaster Gravethorpe, his smile once again disappearing. "Are you really going to believe these scoundrels, Cornelius?" But before Professor Marigold could utter a word the floor shook again. "DON'T YOU DARE CALL MY BOYS LIARS," growled Mr Davies "I knew you'd try something like this. That's why I brought this," said Mr Davies holding a piece of paper aloft. He then pulled out his wand before lightly tapping on the paper. Within seconds the small piece of paper was no more as it had grown into a lofty sheet. Mr Gravethorpe's eyes widened as the paper had been a note from him. "I did not write that," he squeaked. Murmurs filled the room as Mr Davies walked around the room parading the paper proudly. Headmaster Gravethorpe's aura again disappeared as he sat back on the stool. This hadn't gone unnoticed as Professor Marigold asked for hush as he stepped into the middle.

"Thank you, Simon and Marvin," said Professor Marigold as he gestured to Mr Davies to retake his seat. "With Mr Gravethorpe's lies still fresh in your mind I'd like to call my next witness, Conor Blackstone.. Will you stand, please?" Time seemed to stand still as all eyes in the room turned towards Conor. This was it; a chance to put an end to all of this, a chance to get all the questions that lingered answered. So why couldn't he do it? Why couldn't he stand? Conor's name rang out again but again he remained seated.

"Come on, Sticky. You can do it," said a smiling Amelia. This had brought devious sniggers from Simon and Marvin but Conor hadn't cared as he simply smiled back at his grandmother before getting to his feet. "Is everything all right Conor. Will you be able to answer my questions?" asked a slightly concerned Professor Marigold. "I will."

"Could you tell me where you where this evening?"

"I was at the school with Ryan," replied Conor.

"Was there a particular reason why you and Master Willows were at the school this evening?" asked the professor as he began walking around the room.

"We were looking for the lost pages of the Ravensborough book but we didn't find it."

"Your grandmother says you heard something while you were at the school. Is this correct?" asked Professor Marigold as he stopped right in front of headmaster Gravethorpe.

"Yes."

"Who did you hear?"

"It was headmaster Gravethorpe. He was talking about the attack. He was gloating and said he hated Ravensborough."

"BANISH HIM NOW!" roared Mr Davies. The boisterous roars returned as the noise shot off the walls. "Order, Order," boomed Amelia. The noise slowly began to fade as she got to her feet. "Well, Mortimer, do you have anything to say for yourself?"

A slow clap echoed throughout the room quickly followed by a cold grizzly laugh. "You ought to keep an eye on what your grandson is watching Amelia. That Normal TV has got him spewing lies."

"I'm not lying," growled Conor. "I heard you." Headmaster Gravethorpe swooped to his feet. "Sit down, Mortimer and answer Amelia's question," squeaked a timid Professor Marigold. "Oh, be quiet, Cornelius. I'm asking the questions now."

"Master Davies, do you remember what Master Blackstone told you with regards to me all those months ago?"

"Yeah, he said he hated you," replied Marvin. Murmurs began bubbling around the room. Conor could feel the eyes slowly turning on him. "Is Master Davies's statement untrue, Master Blackstone?" purred headmaster Gravethorpe as he glided around the room.

"No," murmured Conor. "But I heard—"

"Yes, you heard me apparently say something." "Master Willows, you were present at the school this evening. Correct?" asked Gravethorpe.

"Yes, sir," replied Ryan nervously.

"Master Willows, could you attest to Master Blackstone's statement being true?"

"No, sir, I can't but I do believe him."

The murmurs resumed as every word said rattled around Conor's head. "SILENCE!" shrieked headmaster Gravethorpe. The floor creaked slowly as he approached Ryan. "And why wouldn't you believe him? From what I can see you two have become good friends," he said calmly, but skulking away. "But that doesn't mean we should always believe what they tell us." For the first time that evening Conor felt something that he hadn't felt in a long-time: loneliness. For a while Ryan hadn't said anything. His face, not for the first time, said everything. "I'm not lying," said Conor weakly as he began to question what he'd heard. A cold callous laugh filled the room.

"I admire you Master Blackstone. Your commitment cannot be questioned. It's just a shame that it's on unactual statements. I think you owe the people of Ravensborough an apology, don't you?" Conor looked around the room, the scowling eyes had returned more ferocious than ever. Maybe he had misheard. Whatever the case Conor's worst nightmare was about to come true. He would have to apologise to headmaster Gravethorpe.

"Well," said Gravethorpe.

"I want to say sorry," whispered Conor.

"You're sorry for what?"

Conor huffed. His throat was dry. "For lying."

BANG!

The main room door burst open. All heads turned as the short grizzly figure of Mr Marto strode in. "He's not the liar, you are Mortimer."

"What's the meaning of this, Martin. Are you feeling all right?"

Mr Marto remained silent as he continued on into the middle of the room before turning back to his friend. "I heard what happened, sir. I couldn't believe it. I knew you could never do something like that. You just needed to prove it."

"What are you banging on about, Martin? You been playing cards with Mr Basil again. Someone get him out of here," growled Professor Marigold.

"Wait, let's hear what he has to say," interjected Amelia.

"I couldn't believe it, not Mortimer, so I went back to school to his office. His seat was cold so he couldn't have been there. But then I found this," said Mr Marto as he took a letter out of his pocket and began to read. All was quiet. Each line was more damning than the other. Once again, headmaster Gravethorpe's confidence lay in ruins but unlike before there was no chance of it returning. Mr Marto suddenly stopped as he reached the final line. He then took a breath before continuing. "I hope you get your wish and this wretched town is burned to the ground".

"Why?" asked Mr Marto finally.

"Martin, my friend, I didn't write that."

"No more lies. You must have done. It's on the paper I gave you for your birthday, the paper only you can write on."

"I don't know how that's—"

"Just save it, Mortimer. It's over," hissed Professor Marigold. "Amelia."

Amelia rose like an eagle, her face stone like. "Mortimer Gravethorpe, with the evidence presented I have no choice but to relieve you of your duties as headmaster of Ravensborough High. You are also hereby banished from the town Ravensborough." The town hall exploded with cheers and Conor's smile had returned. Finally it was over, he thought, as he waded through the joyous onlookers to greet his grandmother.

"Take him away!" roared Amelia.

"You'll regret this, Blackstone," screeched Mr Gravethorpe as he was dragged towards the doors.

BANG!

The frantic pitter-patter of footsteps echoed throughout the room as the head gnome Quintain ran in. "Quintain, join us it's a wondrous evening. The dark cloud over Ravensborough has finally been lifted," cheered Professor Marigold.

"No time," snapped the agitated gnome. "Ma'am, the wall has been breached. The NORMALS ARE ATTACKING AGAIN." The collective smile of the room disappeared. "Quintain, are you sure?" asked Amelia timidly. The gnome gulped. "Yes, ma'am." Frenzied chatter swept through the room as everyone waited for an instruction.

"It's happening again, isn't it?" remarked Mrs Willows.

"We'll be ready for them this time," said Mr Davies in a reassuring tone.

"People of Ravensborough, the time has come to defend our town," said Amelia confidently. "As you are aware we have been planning for this. Mrs Willows, you and a group of wizards will head over to the forest."

"Okay. You stay here, Ryan and please be safe," said Mrs Willows as she prepared her group.

"Belinda," said Amelia hesitantly. "I know we haven't always seen eye to e—"

"Now is not the time, Amelia" blurted Belinda. "All that matters is Ravensborough. What do you need me to do?" she added.

"You and a group of witches shall head to Christwood Meadows."

"Oh, Auntie Belinda, please I want to fight," wailed Saffron as she stood in front of the doors.

"As much as I'd love another Wolfmoon out there your mother would never forgive me if something happened to you."

Saffron begrudgingly stepped aside but as the people of Ravensborough readied themselves Amelia rose to speak one final time. "Remember, no deadly spells unless it's absolutely necessary. After all, they're just Normals." This had brought a few chuckles but as the door opened Conor tugged at his grandmother. "What should I do?"

"Stay here and be safe," whispered Amelia before she too headed towards the door. "Quintain, do not let any of them out under any circumstances."

"Yes, ma'am."

A horrible orange glow had replaced the alluring night sky as Conor, propped up by a stool, remained glued to the window. "Master Blackstone, for the last time please get down. You might hurt yourself," wailed Quintain. "Fine," hissed Conor as he jumped down onto a cold wooden bench. Another two minutes passed by as Conor, more nervous than ever, began pacing. How were they doing it? How were they not panicking, thought the young witch as Marvin and Simon began hitting each other whilst Ryan sat upright almost as if he had been waiting for a lesson to begin. "Pssst!" Conor turned to see the long fingers of

297

Saffron beckoning him. Creeping over, Conor waited for Saffron's messages. "I don't know about you but I'm not just going to sit here while my town is burned to the ground."

"I want to help too but what can I do?" asked Conor.

"Well, for a start you can get those three ready because we're getting out of here."

"Look at 'em, how am I supposed to get them ready?"

"You're a witch, you'll figure something."

"Even if I were to talk them round we'd still have the problem of him," whispered Conor pointing at suspicious Quintain.

"Don't you worry about him, just follow my lead," smirked Saffron. Quintain's hardened face seemed to wither away as the two young witches towered over him. "Door, open it now!" barked Saffron.

"I can't do that Miss Wolfmoon," said Quintain cowering. "Ma'am said I mustn't let you out under any circumstances."

"If you don't open that door now Conor will tell his Gran that you and the other gnomes have been racing the ogres again"

The floor thudded as Quintain fell to his knees. "Master Blackstone, I beg of you. Don't tell ma'am, I'll be put on file sorting again."

Conor gulped. "Fine, then do what Saffron said and open the door."

"Fine, but allow me to come with you. I promised ma'am no harm would come to any of you," pleaded Quintain.

"Deal," said Saffron skipping past the hapless gnome. "Your turn, Blackstone."

Conor took a deep breath as he timidly approached the other corner of the room. "Is everything all right, mate? What's going on?" asked Ryan still perfectly upright.

"We're leaving, we're gonna go and fight."

"Ha, little Blackpepple going to fight, I'd love to see that if it were true. Nope, I'm fine right where I am. It's only Normals," scoffed Marvin.

"SHUT IT!" bellowed Conor. "It's true. What's going on? Is it bigger than you and me right now? People we care about are outside fighting for our town so if you don't have anything productive to say, BE QUIET!" Not uttering another word, Conor, quickly followed by Ryan, headed towards the door.

"WAIT!" roared Simon. "We're coming too but if you talk to me like that again you'll regret it," said Marvin. Once in the corridor Saffron retook charge as she led them upstairs. The stairs seemed endless as even Quintain had become perplexed as to where Saffron had been leading them but just as Conor readied himself to speak Saffron stopped. "We're here," she said.

"I assure you Miss Wolfmoon, there is nothing behind that door. Ma'am told me so."

"Well my auntie Belinda would never lie to me," replied Saffron as she slowly opened the door. The silence was deafening as the room was empty. "I tried to warn you Miss Wolfmoon," said Quintain smugly. "What now?" asked Ryan. But again, silence reigned over the room as Saffron trudged towards the door. "Hold on!" said Conor suddenly. Even through the ominous orange glow the beauty of the moonlight presented itself. But even more stunning was what it revealed. "Yes," wailed Saffron as she sprinted towards the corner of the room. "Has anyone flown one of these before?" asked the young witch cradling the broom.

"Conor has, haven't you?" blurted Ryan.

"Maybe you are a real witch after all Blackstone," remarked Saffron, still unable to take her eyes off the broom.

"Oi, Wolfmoon, we've got a problem," boomed Simon.

"And what's that?" hissed Saffron annoyed at being disturbed.

"There's only four brooms and there's six of us."

"No problem," smiled Saffron "Since me and Blackstone are the only ones to have flown before we'll get our own and you lot will just have to share."

Marvin began chuckling menacingly. "I'm sharing with Willows."

Saffron then handed out the brooms. But as Conor took the final broom his mind was uneasy as Ryan had been wrong. He hadn't flown a broom before so what was he supposed to do, he thought, as he didn't want to let Ravensborough down not to mention the respect he felt from Simon, Marvin and Saffron. But as Conor continued to battle with his mind Saffron's voice rang out and with that Conor slithered towards the door. The stairs seemed to vanish as in no time at all they had reached the roof. An unwelcome frosty kiss greeted Conor as he stepped onto the roof.

"All right, this is it," shouted Saffron. "Is everyone ready?"

"Course," huffed Marvin. Everyone then looked on as Marvin effortlessly floated off the ground before returning for Ryan. Not about to be upstaged, Simon quickly joined his brother in the air. "Ha, four seconds a second quicker than you," yelped Simon grinning. Looking on unimpressed Saffron quickly floated above both boys almost too embarrassed to be seen with them.

"Come on Blackstone, we haven't got all day," hissed Saffron. Conor took a deep breath, shut his eyes and began running. Alone with his thoughts he tried desperately to remember what Angelica had told him as he still felt the ground beneath him. "CONOR, LOOK OUT!" screamed Ryan suddenly. Stunned, Conor's eyes flashed open but he soon wished they hadn't as he was hurtling towards the edge. Every attempt to slow down seemed only to do the opposite. Conor shut his eyes once again as the hard ledge kissed his feet. Silence filled Conor's ears. He had been petrified to scream but something then happened as Conor slowly opened his eyes. He was floating but still shaken and tightly gripped the edge of his broom before floating upwards.

"Show off!" scoffed Simon. "You all right, mate?" asked Ryan. "I'm fine," squeaked a fragile Conor. "All right, let's get a move on," thundered Saffron. Simon was first to move, the wind whistling violently as he headed towards the forest again. Not wanting to be upstaged, Marvin eagerly and somewhat uncontrollably followed much to Ryan's annoyance. "Okay, it's our turn," said Saffron. "Okay."

"My auntie Belinda said she was heading to the valley so that's where we're going. Understood?" said a stone faced Saffron. Conor, still clutching his broom as tightly as ever, nodded. "Steady on," yelped Saffron as a gust of wind jolted her, but her pleas fell on deaf ears as Conor's nerves were a distant memory. Only now did the young witch fully understand his grandmother's grumblings as he twirled through the air, but the twirls soon stopped with Saffron finally catching up.

"Sorry," murmured Conor.

Saffron merely giggled. "Impressive," she said. Taken aback by Saffron's second compliment of the night Conor began stumbling over his words before finally being able to muster a "Thank... LOOK OUT!" Conor then roared pushing himself off to one side. A bolt of sparkling blue light arrowed past the two witches. "WE'RE GONNA GET RID OF YOU FREAKS ONE BY ONE," yelled a voice. Not wanting to give their attacker a second chance, both Conor and Saffron sped off. With the valley fast approaching Conor thought it best to say something as Saffron had not uttered a word since the attack.

"Are you okay?" asked Conor subtlety.

"You were right." replied Saffron sombrely. "He's given them wands. What are we going to do?"

"We fight," smiled Conor. This had brought a smile from Saffron but it was unlike her usual confident smirk. No, this had been a smile brought about by fear. The ominous vibrant glow had returned as the young witches flew above the valley. The black smoke stained the tip of Conor's broom as he waded through.

"Miss Wolfmoon…Mr Basil."

The lack of a response made Conor's stomach churn; his thoughts quickly became dark. Had they been too late? "What's going on down there? Is everything okay?" shouted Saffron timidly. For the first time that evening Conor hadn't been lost for words as fake optimism would do anyone no favours. But just as he went to respond a screech pierced through the smoke. Conor's eyes lit up. A smile then came on his face as he had recognised the voice, but the young witch soon found his flying skills being called into question as he moved frantically to avoid the stampede of people hurtling towards him.

"We were ready for you Norms this time," growled two-faced Ted as he chased the last of the attackers out of the valley. "Conor, what are you doing here? It isn't safe," bemoaned Mr Basil wiping the smoke off his face.

"We came to fight."

Mr Basil grinned. "It's over, right?" Conor then asked. "You've scared them off." Mr Basil's grin quickly disappeared. "I'm afraid not. They've gone back to the forest for reinforcements." Conor remained still, almost statuesque. "Gran," he whispered. "Conor is everything all right". But Mr Basil's word fell on deaf ears as Conor sped off on his broom.

"Emily, get back in here now," whispered Mrs Grey tiptoeing towards the entrance of the cave. But Emily remained where she stood only her eyes moving as spells flew through the air. "This is all my fault, isn't it?"

murmured Emily as she traipsed towards her mother. "Should've have just kept my mouth shut." A warm arm around the shoulder was gladly welcomed by Emily. "Listen to me, none of this is your fault... your father can be so stubborn sometimes". I just hope his stubbornness doesn't get anyone seriously hurt." "I hope so too," sighed Mrs Grey.

SNAP!

"What was that?" whispered Emily.

"Where's that wand your father gave me?" whimpered Mrs Grey as she patted the ground furiously. But the sound of her frantic pattering was soon drowned out by the sound of laughter. "I don't think you're going to need the wand," mumbled Emily who was still giggling. A large squeal reverberated around the cave. "It's just a pig, mum." Mrs Grey's facial expression remained unchanged as she searched for the wand. "Yes," whispered a frenetic Mrs Grey." Get behind me, Emily."

"But Mum."

"I'm not going to ask you again. That thing could turn into anything. Behind me, NOW!" Emily begrudgingly began to shuffle her feet towards her mother. With her daughter behind her she timidly approached the squealing pig but as she went to raise her wand... "Mum stop look... its tail." Entangled in the pig's tail was a tattered piece of clothing that Emily was sure she had recognised. "Matthew, is that you?" The pig let out a tremendous squeal; stunned silence filled the cave. Mrs Grey fell to her knees "My baby, what have they done to you?" The floor shuddered as she stomped towards the entrance of the cave.

"Mum," said Emily despairingly.

"Watch your brother. I'm going to put a stop to all this madness."

Emily's eyes remained transfixed to the cave's

entrance as she anxiously waited for her mother to return. Where had she gone? How was she going to stop the fighting? These were just a few of the questions that had been swirling through Emily's mind as she contemplated about leaving the cave. But just as she got to her feet the welcome shadow of her mother filled the cave.

"Where have you been?" asked Emily angrily as she tightly clutched her mother.

"I went to get this." Mrs Grey held out a small black book. Emily was initially hesitant as she struggled to see how an ordinary book would stop the fighting but trusting her mother she held out her hand. The cave fell silent as what Emily had received hadn't been a book at all but rather a journal and even more shocking was who it had belonged to.

"It's Dad's journal." "But how is this going to help st..."

"Page fifteen."

Not needing a second invitation Emily carefully opened her father's journal. Instantly the first line of the diary beckoned for Emily's attention but remaining focused, she soldiered on. Page after page was reluctantly flipped as Emily trudged towards page fifteen. Time seemed to stand still as Emily finally flipped onto page fifteen. Only a few words needed to be read for Emily to fully understand why her mother had given it to her. The sound of manic breathing filled the cave as Emily reread the page. "I CANNOT BELIEVE HIM." She then roared and stomped towards the exit.

"Emily, wait!" pleaded Mrs Grey.

But blinded by fury Emily ignored her mother's pleas. But she soon wished she hadn't as the two sets of townspeople marched towards one another.

CHAPTER FOURTEEN

JUST THE BEGINNING

"Wait!" screeched Emily.

The marching halted. Everyone looked on as Emily moved in between the two battling communities. She then opened the journal and began to reveal its contents.

Dear Journal,

My father was right which burns my very soul to write as I absolutely loathe him but he was right. Those creatures over the wall are evil and uncivilised. My dreams have been shattered. Those things denied me entry into their magical school. Imagine the cheek, they should be grateful that I wanted to even grace their pitiful school. On this day, the 14th of December, I vow to get my vengeance on those wretched creatures. I will make it my life's mission to make them feel the same pain that is pulsing through my body now.

For the first time that evening the forest was shrouded in silence but this had only been for a brief moment as stunned and confused murmurs began to fill the air. "BEWITCHED!" erupted Mr Grey suddenly. "I have not." But just like her mother before her Emily's words went unnoticed as her father began circling her menacingly. "Of course, you have. For what other reason would you be spewing such rubbish?" chuckled Mr Grey.

"I've not been bewitched," gritted Emily "And it's not rubbish, it's the truth."

"Pay her no attention, people. She has been bewitched. I'll prove it. Give me the journal, Emily," ordered Mr Grey. "No," replied Emily as she backpedalled towards the cave clutching the journal tightly. "I SAID, GIVE IT TO ME!" roared Mr Grey firing his wand. The sound of the journal nestling amongst some leaves reverberated through the forest. Mr Grey, not affording his daughter a glance, headed towards the journal but to his sheer disbelief it suddenly flashed over his head before exploding. An enraged Mr Grey turned sharply.

"Who did that?" he bellowed. "Show yourself."

"It was me," said Conor glaring at Mr Grey. "What type of monster harms their own child?"

Still enraged, Mr Grey drew for his wand and began firing but his attempts were weak and feeble. Sure that Emily wouldn't want any serious harm to come to her father, Conor merely fired a stunning spell that sent Mr Grey hurtling backwards. As he lay on the ground the noise around him seemed to intensify but one noise towered over the others. It had been Emily still on the ground riddled with shame and guilt. Mr Grey slowly crawled towards his daughter.

"Emily, I'm so sorry. Are you all right?"

"I'm fine," she squeaked mustering a weak smile.

Mr Grey wiped the tears from his face and helped his daughter to her feet. Emily, still slightly hurt, limped towards her mother. Both the townspeople of Ravensborough and Murlayfield waited with bated breath for Mr Grey's next action but what he did surprised everyone as he asked to speak to Conor.

Conor gingerly began walking towards him. His mind was full of questions such as why Mr Grey wanted to speak to him. Should he even listen to what he had to say especially since he had just tried to destroy his town? But as he was about to reach Mr Grey, the domineering figure of his grandmother towered over him. Amelia then pointed

306

her wand at Mr Grey.

"Gran, what are you doing?" asked Conor forcefully.

"I'm not letting you anywhere near that evil man," replied Amelia still pointing her wand at Mr Grey.

"That's not your choice. Ravensborough's very existence is at stake." "Trust me, I know what I'm doing."

Amelia reluctantly lowered her wand before stepping aside. Conor now stood face to face with Mr Grey who stuck out his hand but Conor uninterested in exchanging niceties quickly asked Mr Grey what he wanted. Mr Grey then spoke. "Thank you for calling off your grandmother," he murmured.

Conor remained silent merely glaring at Mr Grey as he readied himself to speak.

"People of Murlayfield, for too long the needs of the Grey family have been put before your own and for that I'm sorry. As our neighbours should not be feared but rather cherished and celebrated so I implore you to put down your wands and embrace our new friends."

"What was that?" asked Ryan.

"I don't know but it looks like it came from the school."

Headmaster Gravethorpe's words suddenly began replaying in Conor's mind. The threat that he made at the town hall did not seem so empty now but it then dawned on him that his love for the school coupled with headmaster Gravethorpe's hatred for him and his grandmother had made him realise that the only way Gravethorpe would be able to fulfil his promise would be by destroying something Conor loved. With his mind made up Conor then began sneaking away from the crowd but he did not get far.

"Where are you going?" asked Ryan.

"To save our school," replied Conor.

"Have you lost your marbles?" whispered Ryan. "No offence, mate but you have no chance against headmaster

Gravethorpe."

"Thanks."

"You know what I mean. He is a heavily skilled wizard and you're just Conor who can't really fight."

"It won't come to that because you're coming with me."

"No chance, he'll kill us," laughed Ryan.

"He won't. I will try to speak to him and calm him down."

"I don't think he'll be in the mood to talk."

"Are you coming or not?" demanded Conor.

"All right I'll come but I have to tell my mum."

"No, she'll tell my gran and you know they'll never let us do it. We have to go now," bemoaned Conor.

In the commotion Conor and Ryan snuck away. The two boys began walking towards the unknown. "So, what's the plan?" asked Ryan anxiously.

They had reached the front gates of Ravensborough High but their only route of entry had been blocked as the gate had been enchanted shut with the same lock that had been on the chest in Mrs Autumn's office. Conor then drew for his wand and fired at the lock but the spell merely bounced off the lock. Stunned, he fired again but he soon found himself ducking as the spell came hurtling back towards him.

"*Duro reserare*," said Ryan.

His unlocking spell bounced off the lock. Becoming increasingly agitated he then began performing various spells but still the lock remained as it was. "What's happening? What kind of lock is that?" clucked Ryan.

"Don't you remember? It's the same lock on the chest we were trying to get into tonight."

"Oh yeah, that's a good thing and means you have the key to open it," beamed Ryan. "Go on, get a move on."

"Can't my gran take the key at the town hall? Why don't you go and check round the back see if we can get in that way," suggested Conor.

Ryan's brief absence had given Conor some much needed time to think. As much as he hated to admit it Ryan was right. This would not be a matter that would be resolved by talking. After all it had been him who had ruined headmaster Gravethorpe's reputation and led to his banishment. A better plan had to be thought out but the sight of Ryan returning had put this on the backburner; the look on Ryan face said it all, the back door had proved useless.

"What do we do now?"

Ryan shrugged. His eyes suddenly lit up and he smiled before gesturing behind him. Confused, Conor turned, his hopes rising but this hope soon turned to despair. It had been a drain cover.

"No, absolutely not," said an exasperated Conor.

"Do you have a better idea?"

Ryan then enchanted the drain cover before lowering himself in. Conor slithered over still unhappy at having to be made to go in the sewer again. The splash of the water had brought back unsavoury memories. It had been wetter and slimier than he remembered. Hissing sounds filled the sewer as Ryan began teasing Conor. Thankfully for him the walk had not been long.

"*Moveri Sursum*" said Ryan. The drain cover popped off and they slowly made their way up.

The sewer had led them to the dining hall kitchen. The dining room was bathed in an ominous green glow; it was blinding. Conor paused and began breathing heavily. A nudge in the back from Ryan had got him moving. They hastily left the dining room. The corridor was filled with green smoke which had been coming from the assembly hall. The two boys moved in unison. Treading cautiously, the thickness of the smoke soon overwhelmed Ryan who fell to his knees.

"Ryan, are you okay?" yelped Conor.

"Quiet, do you want Gravethorpe to hear us?" coughed Ryan as he got to his feet slowly.

"Are you sure you're all right?" asked Conor again.

"I'm fine. You're worse than my mum," laughed Ryan.

Conor smiled. They continued on towards the doors which were almost unrecognisable and the paint had been completely stripped off. Conor stopped. He put his ear to the door to listen but heard nothing.

"Come on, aren't we going in?" said Ryan.

Conor turned silently.

"Conor, what's going on? Let's do this."

"I will, you won't."

"What?" said Ryan confused

"I promised your dad I'd look out for you and Gravethorpe wants me, not you."

"I'm not a baby. I'm older than you. We're doing this together," whispered Ryan angrily.

"Please," said Conor turning away from his friend for the final time.

"Fine," grumbled Ryan as he stormed off mumbling angrily about Conor. This had upset Conor but he would take the insults if it meant his friend remained safe. The young witch retrieved his wand from his back pocket. He looked at it. Even through the smoke it glistened. He was ready. He entered the hall as darkness again greeted him.

CLICK!

The room slowly began to light up and only one corner remained shrouded in darkness as the final light flickered on. Conor raised his wand ready for whatever greeted him but it was quickly lowered. The green smoke had been coming from a cauldron. Conor's eyes widened. It had been the Blackstone family birthing cauldron that had been in his attic only a few days ago but even more shocking was who was standing behind it.

"Mr Harrowood," stuttered Conor.

Mr Harrowood remained silent as he continued mixing.

"What's going on?" Conor asked.

Again, silence greeted the young witch; there had to be an explanation for this, Conor thought. Maybe headmaster Gravethorpe had bewitched his friend. That had to be it. He then began walking tentatively towards Mr Harrowood and the cauldron but he had not taken more than two steps before the room filled with noise.

"Irony is quite a funny thing, isn't it?" said Mr Harrowood calmly.

"I suppose. What's going on? Where's headmaster Gravethorpe?" asked Conor.

"People often question Cat's loyalty but people, magical or not, are the most deceitful and disgusting creatures as they will do and say anything for their own betterment. Wouldn't you agree?" spewed Mr Harrowood as he left his position from behind the cauldron and began walking towards Conor.

Conor remained silent.

"Would you not agree?" thundered Mr Harrowood as he glided past Conor into the darkness.

"I don't know. Where is headmaster Gravethorpe?" murmured Conor becoming increasingly concerned.

Mr Harrowood re-emerged from the darkness. He clicked his fingers; the corner shrouded in darkness was no more. Mr Harrowood began laughing as he walked past Conor. What had been hiding in the corner stunned him. It had not been what he was expecting. He then saw the figure of headmaster Gravethorpe. Conor rushed over to him. He was in an awful state, his face a sickening blue, his arms tied and his mouth gagged. Laughter then filled the hall again but it was slower and more callous. "I told you people were disgusting."

Conor turned and pointed his wand at Mr Harrowood

but the sight that greeted him had turned him numb. His wand fell out of his hand and the sound echoed throughout the room. It had been Mr Harrowood's voice. He had heard it but it had been headmaster Gravethorpe who stared back at him.

"It was you," he yelped.

"Yes," whispered Mr Harrowood.

Conor turned to the real headmaster Gravethorpe. His eyes apologetic, he touched Gravethorpe's face. It was warm but heavily bruised. "Why?" he asked.

"All will be revealed," chuckled Mr Harrowood walking back towards the cauldron.

"So, it was you that gave Mr Grey the anti- wands."

"You're a clever one." Hopelessness overwhelmed Conor. He felt stuck unable to do anything. A flash had caught his eye. It was his wand. He grasped it. He knew what he must do. "*Impetum Erum*" he bellowed. Bats began quickly filling the assembly hall. They swooped by Mr Harrowood who seemed unaffected by it and merely laughed. His eyes were fixed on Conor the entire time.

"*LEPOREM LUMINS,*" he then thundered.

The hall turned a heavenly white. The bats' squeaks faded as the light had vaporised them. Conor barely had time to shield his eyes such was the ferocity and speed of the light.

"You have learned a lot since your training, Conor. The school has taught you well. It's a pity that future generations won't be afforded the same luxury once I destroy it," cackled Mr Harrowood.

"I won't let you," growled Conor.

"Confidence, too. This truly is a school of magic." An awkward silence ensued almost as both were waiting for the other to strike first.

"*Mentis Imperium,*" shouted Conor.

"*Novis,*" replied Mr Harrowood.

The two spells collided in the centre of the room; it

was eerily beautiful. Conor began being pushed back as Mr Harrowood stepped forward. His eyes were rabid; he was enjoying himself. The flow of magic stopped as Conor fell to the ground. Mr Harrowood stood above him.

"You humour me, Blackstone. I admire your efforts but you're foolish if you thought a mind control spell would work on me. I'm quite insulted actually."

A bubbling sound had attracted Mr Harrowood's attention and he rushed over to the cauldron. He pushed his face to the edge inhaling the fumes.

"It's almost ready," said Mr Harrowood gleefully. "Are you not going to ask what I'm brewing? It's quite special !"

"I don't care."

"How rude! Didn't your mother teach manners?"

"DON'T SPEAK ABOUT MY MUM," hissed Conor.

"Touchy, touchy, Blackstone. You ought to move on. No point in sulking over the dead," giggled Mr Harrowood. Conor, blinded by rage, got to his feet and readied his wand.

"*CONFUSIS*" bellowed Mr Harrowood.

Conor was thrown against a wall. His body tingled as he lay slumped on the floor. He glanced to his left. His wand lay there. He reached for it but immediately stopped as Mr Harrowood again stood over him.

"Ahhh, Rose's final wand a thing of beauty," said Mr Harrowood picking up the wand. "I bet Basil told you it would protect you."

SNAP!

"Oops!" laughed Mr Harrowood.

Conor's heart sank as his wand lay on the ground in tatters; its unmistakable shine had vanished. "Why are you doing this? What have I ever done to you?" muttered Conor.

"What's with the questions, Conor? Who said you've

done something to me? Maybe I'm just bad," replied Mr Harrowood laughing. "This look is getting rather boring don't you think". And with that Mr Harrowood changed back from headmaster Gravethorpe.

Conor looked at Gravethorpe who looked away. Both were feeling the same thing: defeated. Conor then shut his eyes. He was alone with his thoughts. Why had he shunned Ryan's help? His thoughts soon turned to his grandmother. Was he ever going to see her again as Mr Harrowood had said it would only be a matter of time before he killed him and headmaster Gravethorpe?

THUD, THUD!

Conor's eyes flew open. The banging which had been coming from the cupboard grew louder.

"Ah, I see our guest has got a tad lonely," said Mr Harrowood. "BLACKSTONE, COME HERE!" Conor begrudgingly got up. He hadn't wanted to but with somebody else's life at stake he didn't want to risk it.

"Hurry! Don't you want to let our guest out? I'm sure you'll be pleasantly surprised," cackled Mr Harrowood.

Conor walked over to the cupboard and as he opened the door a muffled scream sounded. He gasped. It had been Angelica and he instantly rushed to her. Her hands were also bound together but unlike Gravethorpe her binds were the shrieking plant vines which were virtually indestructible without magic.

"Let her go!" shrieked Conor.

Mr Harrowood glared at Conor momentarily before turning back to the cauldron.

The hall door swung open and Amelia strode in.

"Gran," cried Conor.

"What's going on in here? Ben," gasped Amelia.

"At last our final guest has arrived," sniggered Mr Harrowood. "Let's play a game, shall we? Who am I?"

Are you feeling quite all right, Ben?" asked Amelia.

"I've never felt better," he said. He then began walking towards her. She tried moving backwards but her legs betrayed her.

"Who are you?" asked Mr Harrowood.

"I'm Amelia Blackstone."

"Good, who am I?"

"What's with the silly questions?"

"JUST ANSWER THE QUESTION," growled Mr Harrowood.

"Ben... Ben Harrowood."

"No," he whispered.

Mr Harrowood began laughing again as he crept backwards slowly not breaking his eye contact with Amelia. Conor looked on fully expecting him to transform into Mr Gravethorpe but he had not. A tall gangly man had taken Mr Harrowood's place. His hair and eyes were brown similar to Conor and a long blue gown covered him.

"G-e-t-t behind me, children."

"Why...who's he?" asked Conor.

"JUST DO IT."

Conor had never seen his grandmother like this. He gave it no second thought. He did what he was told and got behind his grandmother.

"What's the matter? You look like you've seen a ghost, Mother," said Mr Harrowood.

"MOTHER!" blurted Conor.

Mr Harrowood shuffled forward. He began stroking Amelia's face. He leant in and whispered before returning to the cauldron. Conor stepped out from his grandmother. "LIAR!" he shouted.

The cauldron erupted as the green colour vanished and the mixture became yellow. He then poured it into an empty bottle. Gravethorpe was frantic as Mr Harrowood approached him. Mr Harrowood stroked his face. He untied him before moving towards Conor. "Who are you?" mumbled Conor.

"I'm a man of my word and all shall be revealed. I am Elijah Blackstone, my mother and father stand behind you."

"No, that's not possible. Witches and wizards are forbidden to be together in Ravensborough."

Conor turned to look at his Grandmother and Gravethorpe. No words were uttered but their eyes spoke volumes. It had been true. The picture had not been one of his mother's friends but in fact Elijah with his mother and Mrs Autumn.

"Mother, I'm appalled. Have you not told him about me? Although I'm not surprised I was always the black sheep of the family. Never good enough, too weird, too quiet, not strong enough unlike mummy and daddy's golden girl Cora," Elijah exploded.

"That's not true. We loved both of you very much," said Amelia.

"SILENCE, YOU BANISHED ME. Can you imagine being the first person to be banished from your home by your own mother?" he said directing his question to Conor.

"I'm sure she had her reasons" squeaked Conor.

"I did."

"You've got him trained well," mocked Elijah.

"You put the entire town of Ravensborough in danger. What could we have done? You left us no choice, you were performing dark magic."

"YOU HAD A CHOICE. You could have defended me like father did but I thank you as I would have never met my true calling without it. I would have never realised my potential," Elijah said calmly.

"Elijah, enough. You brought this upon yourself. You must take responsibility for your actions and stop acting so childishly. Your sister was never like this," said headmaster Gravethorpe.

"Childish? I was a child when you and this town turned its back on me all for a mistake. You never cared about me only about your careers and my wretched sister."

The room became silent as Conor glanced at Angelica who was still fiddling with the shrieking plant vines. The fiddling stopped as Elijah's pacing had drawn their attention. He would momentarily stop almost as if he wanted to speak before turning and pacing again. The pacing abruptly stopped. Amelia had separated herself from Conor and began walking towards Elijah.

"No, Gran, don't. He was the one working with Normals not headmaster Gravethorpe."

Amelia turned and smiled at her grandson before turning back and continuing to walk towards Elijah. "What do you want, Elijah? Why have you come back? Haven't you caused enough damage? Ravensborough lies in ruins. Are you not satisfied?"

"You make it sound as if I'm the bad guy mother. We all know your past is far from spotless. How is the Wolfmoon's daughter?"

"What happened to you, Elijah? Where did it go so wrong?"

"Why don't you ask Cora?…oops I forgot, you can't. Who do you think gave me the spell book that started it all?" he glared.

"NO, you're lying," cried Amelia falling to her knees.

"Oh, Mother do you recall what father said about me at my banishment hearing".

Ameila remained silent. "SPEAK NOW."

"He said you were a bumbling half-witted oaf unable to conquer such a complex language." Elijah then moved besides Amelia and began running his fingers through her hair. He knelt beside her and began whispering.

"So how would I be able to do all of this on my own? Your precious daughter was right there by my side. What type of mother does that make you, that you were so oblivious you didn't even realise your children were performing forbidden magic?"

Amelia began wailing. Conor looked on. What had Elijah been talking about? Then it hit him. It must have been the spell book he found in the abandoned classroom. Elijah was the student Philip had been talking about. Conor felt a pain in his stomach for if Elijah was to be believed it had been his mother that had introduced him to the dark magic. He had to know more.

"STOP! Leave her alone." Conor quickly rushed beside his grandmother. His heart felt as if it was going to jump out of his body as he stared at Elijah.

"I know gran has made mistakes in the past but you're worse. Innocent people have died because of you," Conor grimaced.

"Ah, Mr Willows and Rose. Both honourable people but they were in the way."

"You're sick. There is no way you're a Blackstone. No one could harbour so much darkness inside themselves so whatever you've come back for just take it and go," snarled Conor.

"I fully intended to and what makes you so sure that you and I are so different? We are more similar than you think."

"Elijah, that's enough," said Amelia.

"Why so secretive, Mother? Doesn't the boy deserve to know?"

"Elijah, listen to your mother. No good will come of this I beg of you," said headmaster Gravethorpe.

Not for the first time Elijah began laughing before again walking towards the cauldron which had stopped bubbling.

"Conor, do you remember what I told you about people being disgusting and deceitful? The person you cared most about, your mother, is no different for she has sentenced you to a life of constant struggle and for what?"

"What are you talking about?"

"Elijah please. Don't," begged Amelia.

318

"Gran. what is going on? What is he talking about?"

Amelia looked at her grandson. Tears were streaming down her face. She tried to speak but she couldn't. She slowly lowered her head, but she was stopped as Conor raised his grandmother's head and began smiling.

"Please, don't shut me out again," he said.

A slow clap filled the hall. "How touching, but if you are not going to tell him I will," thundered Elijah.

"TELL ME WHAT?"

"As you know Conor, witches are meant to be girls by design but then there's you, a most peculiar case. Haven't you ever wondered how in all the centuries that Ravensborough has existed that only one male witch has ever been produced? Doesn't that seem strange to you, almost as if it shouldn't be, almost as if it would have taken something extraordinary to allow this to occur?" said Elijah

"I know how I was made. Gran told me my mum added a special ingredient during my birthing process."

"Indeed she did, but do you know what she used?"

Conor couldn't respond. He wanted to but he would have been lying for he didn't know what his mother had used. "I would take that as a no. Would you like to know? I sense your mind is intrigued but I also sense fear in you but don't allow it to stop your pursuit of truth. So would you like to know?"

"Yes."

"It was Warlock essence my boy" whispered Elijah

"What?"

"WARLOCK ESSENCE!"

The room fell silent. Conor was lost but still quizzical. He had got the answer he had wanted but it was not what he had expected. He didn't know what a warlock was or whether it was a good or bad thing. He began looking around the room in the hope of answers. . As the eyes of the room spoke it had been a bad thing but rather an earth shatteringly bad thing.

"Conor, you must understand that---

"SILENCE, the boy seems as if he wants to say something."

"Who am I?" asked Conor.

"My dear boy, you are who you have always been. You know only now of the great power that lies within you; you have power that most witches and wizards would only dream of. You have nothing to fear."

"He's lying. Don't listen to him, Conor," said Angelica. "Warlocks were an evil race of witches. They were only ever interested in themselves and thought they were better than every other species, be that normals or wizards and even regular witches. The day they were destroyed was the day Ravensborough emerged from its dark cloud."

"You've got yourself a keeper there, Blackstone but your girlfriend is misinformed. If warlocks were truly that despicable then why would your mother give you the essence of one?"

"Gran," said Conor looking for guidance.

"Sticky, look at me. Everything Angelica said is true but you must understand that what your mum did was to protect you as the essence that lies inside you belonged to the leader of the warlocks."

"So, I'm stuck with this thing inside me forever," sighed Conor. "Is there no why I can get rid of it?"

"I'm afraid not," replied Amelia softly.

"I might be able to help," remarked Elijah as he calmly walked towards the cauldron. Instantly intrigued, Conor got to his feet and quickly followed. "Earlier on you mentioned what you were making. Could this help me get rid of this thing?" Elijah nodded as he poured the bubbling liquid into a bottle before handing it to Conor. "Drink it and you'll be free." "Why are you doing this?" asked Conor.

"I want to help. What are families for?" Still cautious, Conor opened the bottle slowly. The aroma was alluring but just as the young witch raised the bottle to drink... "Don't do it" squealed Angelica. "Don't trust him that could do anything."

"She's right," added Amelia. Conor began having second thoughts, after all he hadn't ever felt evil. "Don't listen to them, Conor," interrupted Elijah. "Don't you remember what you told me all those months ago about how you wanted to be normal? This is your chance, don't throw it away." Conor began pacing as he did whenever he was confused as for a brief moment he felt that his friend Mr Harrowood returned but a glance towards Angelica and his grandmother had been enough. Conor had made up his mind.

"I'm sorry, Elijah but I'm happy... besides being normal is boring." Conor then handed the bottle back and headed back towards his grandmother. "No," growled Elijah. "This wasn't a CHOICE." The floor then thudded as the screeching plant vines on Angelica grew larger and tighter.

"Let her go," hissed Conor.

"Give me the essence and I'll let her go," replied Elijah, his menacing smile returning.

"Don't do it," mumbled Angelica as she became completely shrouded in vines.

"Take another step and I'll crush her," growled Elijah in the direction of his mother.

"I'll do it." Conor then began slowly walking towards Elijah. "Attaboy, knew you'd come around to my way of thinking. Drink it quickly, heard it has a nasty aftertaste," cackled Elijah. Conor shut his eyes as he opened the bottle and began to drink. There had been no bitter aftertaste, rather a sickeningly sweet one lingered in the young witch's mouth. The hall was deafeningly quiet as everyone waited anxiously but their wait would be brief as Conor collapsed to his knees.

"STICKY!" wailed Amelia as she quickly rushed to her grandson's side.

"Get away from him! You'll ruin the procedure," barked Elijah.

"Look at him, I'm not going anywhere."

"Still stubborn as ever I see," snarled Elijah as he crept towards his mother. "Wait!" said Conor feebly. "Gran...go. I'll be fine. We can't risk the procedure going wrong".

"Absolutely not," blubbered Amelia.

"I'll be fine, I need you to trust me," smiled Conor. Amelia, through her tears, mustered a smile back as she stroked her grandson's face before reluctantly backing away. Every second that trickled by was agony as Conor tossed and turned furiously on the ground. Surely it was almost over, he thought, as the gangly figure of Elijah appeared above him. "I've done what you wanted now let Angelica go."

"I'm upset ...you still don't trust me," smirked Elijah mockingly. "But I suppose you did keep your end of the deal." And with a snap of his fingers Angelica was free. Another two minutes went by as an increasingly desperate Conor glanced towards Elijah. "Please," he then mumbled. "Hmm," swooned Elijah. "This is bad. I've seen this look before.....but where maybe it was...no, perhaps it was...no, no.. Ah yes, I remember now." The floor shivered as Elijah sat beside Conor.

"It was the same look your mother had before I killed her." Elijah's cackle reverberated through Conor's body as his knees gave way for the first time that evening. But worse still, a sharp-shooting pain pierced his stomach. "Aaahhhh!" he wailed as the pain grew stronger and stronger. This was it, Conor thought, as he shut his eyes. The hall then became bathed in a fiery orange glow. Conor's eyes flashed open. The pain was gone. Was it over? Was he free?

"CONOR," purred Angelica as she ran to her friend's side. "Are you all right?"

"I think so," he replied still a little dazed. "Is it done?"

"No," growled Elijah furiously as he skulked around the hall. "Someone tampered with the potion," he hissed.

"Ha, maybe you aren't as great as you think," mumbled Angelica. Elijah turned sharply, a look of disgust on his face. "It was you, wasn't it ... filthy little witch," grunted Elijah as he charged towards Angelica.

"LEAVE US ALONE!" bellowed Angelica as she fired her wand. All eyes darted towards the centre of the room as Elijah gingerly got to his feet, but to the surprise of everyone he simply began laughing. "FINALLY, a worthy opponent," he chortled as he drew for his wand. Not about to back down, Angelica too raised her wand. "Wait, don't do this," pleaded Conor. "He's too dangerous." But to his dismay, Angelica continued advancing. The hall was soon awash with colour as spell after spell sped through the air. Elijah's confident smirk soon vanished as he was taken aback by Angelica's skill. The floor thudded again as Elijah was sent back by Angelica's spell but unlike the first time no laughter followed as he got to his feet. "ENOUGH!. It's time to rid this town of another Wolfmoon... *LEVI ELECTRICA.*" Elijah's smile returned as Angelica lay on the ground writhing in agony.

The sickly feeling Conor had felt returned as he looked on as Elijah menacingly circled Angelica. What should he do, he thought, as he hadn't been sure what Elijah had been planning next. He just knew that he had to stop him, but the chance for thought quickly faded as Elijah halted. Without a thought in his mind Conor grabbed the wand from his grandmother and sprang into action.

"LEVI ELE..."

"*LEPOREM LUMINS*," thundered Conor.

The hall again became bathed in a white light. Conor's eyes remained shut. Had he done it? Had he stopped Elijah? He didn't dare open his eyes but he would soon be forced to as the noise became too hard to ignore. "FATHER!" screeched Elijah again. Conor remained motionless. He had heard right as it hadn't been Angelica sprawled on the floor any more but headmaster Gravethorpe. "Get away from him!" yelled Conor as he charged towards Elijah. His mind was now a dark cloud of thought, Conor raised his wand. "*LEVI ELECTRICA*" he then cried. His breathing was now frantic, Conor stood above a stunned Elijah ready to strike again.

"Master Blackstone, don't!" pleaded headmaster Gravethorpe feebly. Conor began to tremble as every part of him wanted to ignore Gravethorpe but alas he couldn't. The hall echoed as Conor threw the wand to the ground. "Get up and GO," he scowled following Elijah who limped to the door. "What are you waiting for? GO!"

"Hmm, I told you we were alike," chuckled Elijah.

"I'm nothing like you."

"There's a darkness within you yearning to be free...and as you grow so will it and those closest to you will suffer," scoffed Elijah as he disappeared into the darkness. The focus quickly turned to headmaster Gravethorpe who had remained on the ground. "Thank you, sir," sniffed Angelica. Gravethorpe responded with a smile. "Amelia," he said. "Would you take Miss Wolfmoon back into town. I'm sure her mother will be wondering where she is."

"No, not with you in this state," replied Amelia.

"It's not up for discussion." Amelia remained defiant initially before begrudgingly leaving with Angelica. "Master Blackstone, would you join me?" asked headmaster Gravethorpe.

"Of course," replied Conor as he sat beside Mr

Gravethorpe who still had not moved from the ground. "I just wanted to thank you, sir, for saving Angelica and stopping me."

"I was just doing my job when I became headmaster of Ravensborough High. I vowed that no student would come to any harm and meant every word of it," he said resoundingly.

"Well, thank you again." He managed a laboured smile and noticing this Conor spoke again. "Are you going to be all right, sir or should I get someone?"

"I'm afraid I'm past the point of help," he said , grimacing as he did so.

"I don't understand."

"Elijah was not wrong when he said someone had tampered with the potion he made."

"It was you," gasped Conor. "But why? I wanted to drink it."

"Elijah had no intention of extracting that essence from you. What he gave you was poison... I used a switching spell."

Conor's breaths became deeper and more frantic. "He'll pay for this," growled Conor as he leapt to his feet, but the young witch quickly sat back down as headmaster Gravethorpe's coughing grew louder and louder. "Time is precious. Don't waste it on being angry. Take it from someone who lost everything doing so."

"Sir, are you going to di-di-di...". Headmaster Gravethorpe nodded before running his hand across Conor's sobbing face. It had been a touch Conor had only once felt before. "I remember the day you were born so small, so perfectly imperfect, the best day of my life." Conor smiled but it was brief as something was on his mind.

"Is everything all right, Master Blackstone?" asked headmaster Gravethorpe.

"I'm scared, sir. What if Elijah is right about me?

What if there is a darkness inside me?" murmured Conor.

"I won't hear of it, you didn't harm anyone."

"But I wanted to, I wanted to hurt Elijah... if it hadn't been for you I don't know what I would've done."

"But you didn't hurt him. Life is about our ability to choose between right and wrong, Master Blackstone and while we might get it wrong sometimes the true answer often already lies within us."

"Sir, could I ask you a question?"

"You may," replied Gravethorpe, his voice getting weaker and weaker.

"What was my mum like?"

"She was a lot like you," smiled Gravethorpe. "Smart and stubborn. Gets that from your grandmother but she was also caring and brave and not a day goes by when I don't miss her."

"I miss her, too."

"Master Blackstone, may I ask a favour from you?" Without hesitation Conor nodded as he waited for instructions. "When I give my say-so I want to leave."

"NO," said Conor defiantly. "I'm not going to leave you on your own." Headmaster Gravethorpe began chuckling softly. "I could never be alone here... This school over the years has been my home so I ask again when the time comes to leave."

"If that's what you really want then I will," murmured Conor softly.

The next few minutes were some of the best Conor had as he lay next to headmaster Gravethorpe. No words were spoken nor any looks exchanged as they didn't need to be as in that moment all was well. But Conor soon found himself in a panic as Gravethorpe's coughing worsened.

"Are you all right, sir? Do you need anything?" he asked.

"The time has come Master Blackstone." Conor's heart sank as he quickly wrapped his arms around Mr

Gravethorpe. Mustering all his strength he reciprocated Conor's actions.

"Thank you," whimpered Conor.

"No thank you," whispered Gravethorpe. "I know you'll make me proud." Conor dried his eyes as he slowly got to his feet and headed for the door. As he reached it he looked back one final time. "Bye, Grandad," he said. Headmaster Gravethorpe smiled. "Goodbye, Conor."

Never before had Conor felt so alone as he walked through the hallway which seemed darker than ever. For the first time the thought of what was next terrified him as things couldn't possibly be the same ever again.

THE END